MISPLACED SOULS

Library and Archives Canada
Doidge, Meghan Ciana, 1973—
Misplaced Souls/Meghan Ciana Doidge—
PAPERBACK

Cover design by Gene Mollica Studios

ISBN 978-1-989571-15-6

MISFITS OF THE ADEPT UNIVERSE: BOOK 1

MISPLACED SOULS

MEGHAN CIANA DOIDGE

Published by Old Man in the CrossWalk Productions
Salt Spring Island, BC, Canada

www.madebymeghan.ca

Misplaced Souls is the first book in the Misfits of the Adept Universe series, which is set in the same universe as the Dowser, Oracle, Reconstructionist, and Amplifier series.

The Misfits series directly expands on and incorporates the events and characters first introduced in the Dowser series. Therefore, for the best reading experience, the author recommends reading all nine books in the Dowser series, including Dowser 8.5, before digging into the Misfit tales.

In order to avoid spoilers, the ideal reading order of the full Adept Universe is as follows:

Cupcakes, Trinkets, and Other Deadly Magic (Dowser 1)
Trinkets, Treasures, and Other Bloody Magic (Dowser 2)
Treasures, Demons, and Other Black Magic (Dowser 3)
I See Me (Oracle 1)
Shadows, Maps, and Other Ancient Magic (Dowser 4)
Maps, Artifacts, and Other Arcane Magic (Dowser 5)
I See You (Oracle 2)
Artifacts, Dragons, and Other Lethal Magic (Dowser 6)
I See Us (Oracle 3)
Catching Echoes (Reconstructionist 1)
Tangled Echoes (Reconstructionist 2)
Unleashing Echoes (Reconstructionist 3)
Champagne, Misfits, and Other Shady Magic (Dowser 7)
Misfits, Gemstones, and Other Shattered Magic (Dowser 8)
Graveyards, Visions, and Other Things that Byte (Dowser 8.5)
Gemstones, Elves, and Other Insidious Magic (Dowser 9)
The Amplifier Protocol (Amplifier 0)
Demons and DNA (Amplifier 1)
Bonds and Broken Dreams (Amplifier 2)
Mystics and Mental Blocks (Amplifier 3)
Misplaced Souls (Misfits 1)

Other books in the Amplifier and Misfits series to follow.

More information can be found at
www.madebymeghan.ca/novels

For Michael
As long as I'm with you, I'm always
where I'm meant to be

SIX YEARS, THREE MONTHS, AND TWO DAYS AGO, I WAS KIDNAPPED by a black witch. Then forced to bear witness as she slaughtered witches and sorcerers across Europe, siphoning their magic and corrupting what she could of my own power in order to raise vanquished demons.

Five years, ten months, and twenty days ago, the dowser—Jade Godfrey—backed by a vampire, a werewolf, and a dragon, rescued me in London, England. A lethal quartet, who routinely flung themselves before death in order to save the world. Including me.

One year, nine months, and twenty-eight days ago, I untangled the power that fueled a dimensional portal used by an invading army of elves, helping to thwart a dark destiny while confirming that I wielded far more than basic necromancy.

After all I'd been through, the same powerful Adepts who had rescued me and worked alongside me waited, watching minute by minute. To see if the evil I'd endured was contagious. Because for a witch to go dark was one thing. But for a necromancer, going dark was something far more terrifying.

What with the potential for raising an army of the undead and all.

Six years, three months, two days, and five minutes…

Still not dark yet.

ONE

I STEPPED FROM THE CAB, LINGERING ON THE SIDEWALK WITH MY satchel over my shoulder and a small duffle bag in hand until the taxi had pulled away. Combined, the two bags held every precious possession I owned, not including the magical artifact perpetually slung around my neck and currently hidden under my bulky red poncho.

The cab disappeared around the corner. But instead of traversing the front path leading to the house that corresponded to the address I'd given the cabbie—because I didn't actually live there—I veered left. Jogging across the perpendicular street, I skirted the cul-de-sac that abruptly capped East Thirty-Seventh Avenue for vehicles, even as the road continued east for foot and bike traffic. The beads attached to the multicolored fringe of my hand-knit poncho clacked together, seemingly amplified against the fronts of the closely clustered homes of the residential area.

In another couple of hours, residents would be returning from school or work. But for now, the street was dead quiet.

Practically running—or as close to running as I ever got, at least—I traversed the length of a tall chain-link fence. My heavy boots barely touched down as I crossed through the open metal gates that were all that stood between me and a wide concrete path. A step beyond that entrance, and the magic embedded within every centimeter of the sprawling grounds of Mountain View Cemetery welled up underneath me.

I shuddered, suppressing a groan of contentment. Eyes closed, partially on my tiptoes, I paused to absorb the sensation. It felt intensified, perhaps due to how long I'd been away.

I was home.

I settled back on my heels, content to simply let the magic roiling under my feet just be. For the moment.

Mountain View Cemetery, spreading some ten city blocks north to south and two residential blocks east to west, might have been owned and operated by the City of Vancouver since 1886. But its magic belonged to me, grounded me. Even sustained me. Over 92,000 gravesites and 145,000 interred remains equaled a shit-ton of death magic. And all of it had been tied to me for over three years now, since a few days before my eighteenth birthday.

Ironically, I had claimed the cemetery—at both the witches' and my mother's urging—to keep my path on the side of the light, to balance my burgeoning magic. Everyone had been so worried about me being tainted. Worried about me going dark. And now, upon returning to the city, having completed training the magic that had everyone's panties in a twist, the cemetery was still my first stop. Even before checking in with friends or so-called family, I'd needed to come to Mountain View. The urge had seized me as the wheels of the plane hit the tarmac, then had only intensified in the time it had taken to clear customs and wait in line for a taxi.

Feeling more settled and still hauling my bags, I took a path that cut through to the center of the property. The headstones were a mixture of raised and in-ground through this section, crafted from different types of stone and metal. A few family plots with larger memorials were randomly scattered throughout. My steps were quiet on the wet pavement, though my beaded fringe still clattered with each step.

A few joggers traversed the many paths running parallel and perpendicular to me—not that I needed to worry about being seen. The magic that ebbed and flowed under my feet hid me from casual view. If someone didn't know I was there, wasn't looking for me specifically, my passing presence was absorbed by the energy constantly emanating from the cemetery. That inherent obfuscation would be the same in any graveyard, for any necromancer. But it was more concentrated at Mountain View because I'd claimed the property. Our magic was connected, almost symbiotic.

It wasn't raining, but it had been earlier in the day. The headstones, the paved path, and the bright-green grass were all speckled with tiny droplets that hadn't evaporated yet. Sunlight glinted from the petals of the flowers and the wreaths decorating a number of graves—tokens of grief, celebrations of a life lived, from those who visited their dearly departed.

I stepped onto the damp grass, weaving through a grouping of flush-mounted headstones and passing a three-foot-tall white concrete statue of a woman holding an urn, before I arrived at my favorite gravesite. I stopped there, gaze unfixed, pressing my palm to the top of the tall, light-gray granite headstone. Ignoring the fading name and dates etched into it, I listened. Waiting. Still feeling incomplete, but putting the pieces of myself back together. The pieces that made me the Morana Novak who called Vancouver home, who had claimed Mountain View Cemetery.

The pieces that made me Mory.

The pieces that made me the wielder's necromancer—and everything that went with that title, that position within the so-called misfits who made up the Godfrey coven. The younger subset of that coven, at least.

I wasn't the same Mory who had abruptly left Vancouver in the middle of February over a year and a half ago, less than a week after the offer to take specialized training at the Academy had hit my inbox.

But I could still collect and keep the best pieces of that Mory before I announced my return.

Before everything that had happened almost two years ago, I would never have expected to feel the need to do so. But here I was.

I waited to see if the sweet soul who occasionally haunted her gravesite would visit. I didn't try to summon her or to pull her forth. I was too powerful to play at such things anymore. And if her spirit had finally moved on…well, that was the ultimate goal.

Oh, yes. I was a necromancer. From a long line of necromancers. A soul seer, to be specific. A rare specialty. A frowned-upon branch of magic, because screwing around with souls was as dark as magic could get, even for a necromancer.

Unless that necromancer was trained and certified by the Academy, then gainfully employed by the witches Convocation.

Which I was.

As of just over twelve hours ago.

I wasn't the necromancer of the Godfrey coven, though, which claimed all of Vancouver and beyond as its territory. You know, 'The Necromancer' in capital letters. That was my mother's position.

A slight breeze stirred my hair, tickling my jaw and obscuring my vision. That hair was currently deep purple, shot through with shades of pink and a hint of light blue. It pulled my attention back to the present. No spirit or shade arrived or greeted me. I tried to not feel disappointed.

Instead, I reached into my satchel for Ed, finding my undead turtle tangled up in three strands of yarn. A deep purple, a baby blue, and a multicolored speckle—all merino, silk, and cashmere—were woven around his legs and neck. I'd started a simple knitting project on the plane, and after a fifteen-hour flight from Latvia with a connection through Frankfurt, I was almost at the crown decreases on a marled slouch hat. I was knitting with yarn left over from the shawl I'd completed at the Academy, right before leaving for my final assignment. And yes, it matched my current dye job.

"Ed," I grumbled. "We've talked about you building a nest in my bag."

The red-eared slider blinked his gray-orbed eyes at me as I set about untangling him. His front legs were the worst. He had managed to weave multiple strands through his long nails. Magic glistened from his carapace—power I could see only because it wasn't my own, and because it was particularly intense. That power gave Ed supernatural abilities that went beyond simply being the undead familiar of a necromancer. A soul seer.

I'd actually needed to register Ed with the Academy in order to keep him with me while on the grounds, along with the heavy necklace that I never removed, not even while showering. Such secrets were difficult to keep around dozens of Adepts who could feel the power of both Ed and the artifact without even being in the same room as me. And my magic was rare enough that I didn't need to frighten new acquaintances with my mere presence as well.

Not that officially registering Ed or the necklace had eased that apprehension much. It also didn't help that I was the only soul seer among the specializing necromancers. And that the Academy hadn't trained another soul seer in over twenty-five years.

Ironically, the somewhat obsessive reputation I'd inadvertently built at the Academy with my near-constant knitting, along with my penchant for bestowing hand-knit socks, hats, and arm warmers on my fellow classmates, mitigated that tension far more than anything else had. I knit more than I could justify wearing, and almost everyone preferred to have warm toes, fingers, and heads.

Despite finding myself slightly ostracized for my rare subset of magic at the Academy when I first arrived, I actually couldn't pick up magic as easily as a witch or a sorcerer could. Being on the grounds of a cemetery allowed me to stretch my other senses much farther than usual, though. If an Adept—a person of the magical persuasion—passed me on the sidewalk of a busy street, I wouldn't know it. But I'd know the instant anyone with magic in their blood set one foot over the boundary of a cemetery.

Anywhere else, I could sense other necromancers, of course. And spirits in all forms.

And vampires.

But if an unknown vampire got anywhere near me, I wouldn't be casually brushing shoulders with them. More likely, I'd be running. Screaming down the sidewalk in question. Even with the protections that I wore literally around my neck, tangling with a vampire wasn't something any necromancer sought out. The ingrained rivalry between those magical species went back—as in, all the way back. With the vampires the ultimate victors. On all occasions. Being immortal, supernaturally strong, and able to beguile their victims gave vamps the ultimate advantage when it came to slaughtering those of my ilk.

An unknown vampire wouldn't want to take the chance that I or any other necromancer could control them, bend them to our will.

Ed wiggled in my hands, having spotted the grass. He liked cemeteries as much as I did. He was undead, after all.

Death might be just another beginning—but what it was the beginning of, I couldn't tell you. I could, however, talk to the parts of the soul that remained on this plane of existence. I could also raise the walking dead, human and animal—under very specific circumstances. I'd never tried it with a fish. They'd probably decompose too quickly.

The eighteen months I had just spent at the Academy had been all about proving that I could work with soul magic—not simply death magic—with a level of accuracy needed to get certified. As of completing my last assignment, in Latvia, I officially worked for the witches Convocation as a junior specialist. I was now a resource for the investigative teams tasked with policing a certain subset of the Adept. And also with cleaning up incidents that might draw the attention of the mundanes, aka the nonmagical people who outnumbered the Adept by a massive amount. Like, a million to one or something.

There were two other necromancers who called Vancouver, British Columbia, home. Danica Novak—my mother—and Teresa Garrick. Neither of them had required certification to prove their worth, though. To anyone. My mother had worked with the Vancouver coven since before my father died. Teresa Garrick's presence in Vancouver was still relatively recent, but the Garrick necromancers were well-known badass vampire slayers. Or at least they had been until they'd all been slaughtered by rogue vampires twenty-five years ago. Teresa was the only survivor, and she'd been in hiding with the help of the witches until recently.

The Garrick family's vampire-slaying gig turned out to be seriously ironic. Because one of the only three vampires I wouldn't run from on sight was Teresa's son, Benjamin Garrick.

Benjamin was the reason Teresa wasn't in hiding anymore. He was the reason they lived in Vancouver, under the protection of the Godfrey coven. He was also one of the major reasons I hadn't returned to Vancouver in over a year and a half, selecting work-study assignments and finishing a three-year program in record time, rather than coming home on breaks.

That and the empty house that would have been sure to greet my return.

Necromancers and vampires didn't mix.

And they certainly didn't date.

Or pine for one another.

And certainly not, in this particular instance, when the gorgeous Jasmine also called Vancouver home. Like Benjamin, Jasmine had also been recently remade. With the blood of the executioner of the vampire Conclave reanimating her. And though we'd never spoken of it directly, not in person or by text, Benjamin Garrick was enamored with the golden-haired beauty. And he would likely be so forever. He was epically focused like that.

But unlike Benjamin, I didn't have eternity to wait for a crush to even think about glancing my way. So I'd left Vancouver and that unrequited crush behind, knowing that life changed so quickly that coming home would be sort of a new beginning.

Or at least that was what I was hoping.

Magic shifted, lapping against my toes from the direction of the cemetery's main entrance on Fraser Street. An Adept of some power had just stepped onto the grounds. Facing in that general direction, I perched atop the granite gravestone, pulling my knitting out from my satchel. Ed gamboled around in the damp grass nearby, and I made a mental note that I would need to thoroughly dry him off so he didn't decay. I knew that the power that coated him was more than just mine now, so perhaps that wasn't even a possibility anymore. But it wasn't a risk I would take either way. Ed was part of me. He held a sliver of my soul, so I took care of him. And he grounded me—or more specifically, my power—when I was away from Mountain View.

The latent aspects of necromancy couldn't be turned off or on. My magic was constantly seeking and picking up the dead. The best I could do was mute the intensity, and redirect it. Hence, the creation of Ed. Most necromancers worked with bones or ghosts. Teresa Garrick preferred the corpses of birds. My mother was perpetually tethered to the ghost of her uncle. But being a soul seer, I had Ed, who was continually animated with my own life force.

More magic curled up from the damp ground, slipping up my dangling legs to churn around my hands. I finished straightening my knitting, further untangling the mess Ed had made, and took up my needles.

Sorcerer magic. At best guess.

I'd been away for a while, and though my magic was sharper than it had ever been—focused and full—I didn't know the magic of the Adept traversing the grounds of the cemetery well enough to identify them.

No one knew I was back in Vancouver. I hadn't even texted Benjamin or my witch friend, Burgundy, who was out of town herself at a healers retreat. I'd gotten on the first flight I could, but I'd wanted a soft landing. A gentle reintroduction. One that didn't involve my mother, assuming she was even at home.

It could have been a random Adept approaching. The population of the magically inclined in Vancouver had grown over the last few years. But Benjamin, who made it his business to know such things—like, officially, with a title and everything—would have mentioned if there was a new sorcerer in town. Even though he was one of the reasons I'd left Vancouver, Benjamin and I had texted constantly while I'd been gone. The vampire, aka the chronicler, had maintained that connection, wanting to know every last thing about my training, and about the Academy itself. Vampires were not numbered among the staff or the students.

Thankfully, my weird susceptibility to Benjamin's inadvertent beguilement didn't translate through text message. If the vampire had actually wanted me—me, Mory, rather than the decades of knowledge I'd accumulated while passively living among the Adept—I might never have left Vancouver. And I would have been worse off for it. Untrained and jobless, not just feeling out of place like I presently was.

The sorcerer steadily cutting across the graveyard toward me might not have even been looking for me. But what were the chances of that?

He…him…his magic felt…forceful, insistent. Somehow self-assured. And definitely male. Though sex and gender was one of the first things I could intuit about a corpse, whatever point the person who'd become that corpse had occupied on both those spectrums, that level of sensitivity with the living was new for me. Nice.

I laughed quietly, anticipation welling. Tangling my fingers in the three strands of yarn, I began to knit, slipping the moonstone-skull stitch marker that noted the beginning of the round from my left needle to my right needle. I'd memorized the self-designed pattern so thoroughly that knitting it was practically just muscle memory. I had knit the same hat in different combinations of yarn many times, because it was perfect for using up leftovers from other projects.

I was home.

I was more powerful, more focused than ever.

I was ready to confront the next chapter of my life—perhaps even more ready than I'd thought. So maybe I hadn't needed to gather the pieces of the old Mory at all? Maybe I was still her.

Mory.

Necromancer.

Soul seer.

I could control the dead. I had carved my way through an invading force of mythical beings, using the corpses of the elves the others in my team had killed as an undead shield. Then I'd untangled the soul magic that had powered an other-dimensional portal. A task that only I could have accomplished. Well, without blowing the entire city up, at least.

I had worn the instruments of assassination, the wielder's necklace, at her request, for days—while slowly dying. An artifact that powerful would have killed another at first touch. That was its actual purpose, after all.

I had survived.

With my own soul completely intact.

For years, everyone had watched me, waiting for any sign of darkness born from the trauma of my brother's death and betrayal—yes, in that order.

But I didn't dwell there.

I lived in the light.

So I smiled in the direction of the interloper on my territory, and I waited. Knitting happily, for ever after.

Let the sorcerer come.

I was ready for whatever request I knew he was bringing with him. Because there was no other reason to visit a necromancer in a graveyard. A dealer of death magic. A beguiler of souls.

Though it was unlikely that the sorcerer in question knew that last part. It was, after all, frowned upon. Even when properly trained and certified.

LIAM TALBOT STRODE AROUND A LARGE CHESTNUT TREE THAT hadn't yet lost all its autumn leaves, though its mahogany-colored nuts and the green-spiked split pods that had housed those nuts littered the area around it.

All right, then. Liam was not who I'd anticipated. I had actually thought the visitor might have been his younger brother, Tony, though the tech sorcerer rarely left his basement lair. Or even Liam and Tony's father, Stephan, given the strong tenor of the magic that had preceded the sorcerer.

Liam homed in on me perched on my gravestone with a tilt of his dark-haired head. His pace remained steady even as he shifted course. Despite being only three years older than me, Liam Talbot was self-assured and exceedingly focused. He was wearing a suit, which was typical for most of the sorcerers I'd met. But Liam did so because he was a detective for the Vancouver Police Department. Homicide.

Which meant that seeking out a necromancer made all sorts of sense for this particular sorcerer. Huh. I was annoyed I hadn't put that together more quickly.

I blamed jet lag. I actually wasn't sure what the current time was, at all. Before sunset, which was early evening this far into fall, but not by much.

I was also annoyed because I had no idea how the hell Liam Talbot could possibly have known I was back in Vancouver.

Liam didn't smile, raking his brown-eyed gaze over me as he closed the distance between us. Unlike his typical snotty sorcerer brethren—who usually came from obscene amounts of money accumulated through the practice of black magic—his dark navy suit wasn't tailor-made. He wore a button-down white dress shirt open at the collar, and he'd removed his tie. So he was off duty but hadn't taken the time to go home and change.

Liam's skin was naturally tanned, his shoulders broad. He had what people often referred to as a runner's body. His hair was slightly longer than usual, like he was overdue for his typical cropped cut. A slight shadow of stubble edged his strong jaw. Idiotically, I found that hint of roughness oddly adorable. Despite the fact that, in general, I didn't like Liam Talbot much.

He was controlling, overprotective, and stubborn. Also determined, hardworking, diligent, thorough, and loyal.

But all that was beside the point.

Liam was a sorcerer. And that was enough of a black mark.

All sorcerers were powermongers. It was a natural state of being for them. They literally pulled their power from magical artifacts or written spells. Such items were often inherited, magic passed through generations. And yes, it was possible that I was prejudiced when it came to sorcerers. Anyone would be, after almost being sacrificed by a sorcerer on two separate occasions. The kidnapping that preceded those incidents hadn't helped to soften my judgement either.

"Mory," Liam drawled, pausing a few steps away and offering me a brief smile. Once again, he looked me over as if he'd never seen me before. His accent was American, but with its edge softened by the couple of years he'd spent living in Canada. "Welcome home."

I grinned, liking the sound of him saying my name. Claiming me with his—

Wait…what?

"Sorcerer," I said, covering my weird reaction by mimicking his drawl, "the cemetery is an odd place for a walk."

"Peaceful, though."

"Oh, yes? Come here often, do you?"

His smile widened as if he was…teasing me? "I know you do."

I frowned. "Have you been waiting for me?"

He tilted his head. The smile lingered on his lips as he stuffed his hands in the pockets of his suit pants, a stance that rucked his jacket up at the sides. Sunlight warmed the lighter strands within his dark-brown hair. He should have been wearing an overcoat. Or, at minimum, a scarf. I could knit him one, given a few days and the right yarn. A deep shade of blue or green would bring out his—

I was staring at Liam Talbot.

Like an empty-headed idiot.

I tore my gaze away from the sorcerer. Then, realizing I'd done so, I stared back defiantly.

"Tony's on shift in the map room," Liam finally said. "So yes, he informed me you'd be returning soon. I have been waiting."

My stomach did a weird uncomfortable flutter. Like I'd eaten something that hadn't agreed with me on the plane, but the timing was suspect. Especially because it had been hours since I'd eaten.

All right, then.

For some unknown reason, I was reacting oddly to the sorcerer standing in my cemetery. I would have blamed magic, like a beguiling charm or some such, except such a spell wouldn't be able to get through the dense layer of protection embedded into my necklace. "There are two other necromancers in town."

"Yes. But neither of them are you."

He was teasing again.

I wasn't one of his younger sisters. I readied a snappy comeback, but Liam suddenly crouched, wagging his fingers at Ed before I could formulate it.

"Hey, Ed," the sorcerer said softly. "Welcome home."

My stomach squelched again.

The undead turtle trundled over to Liam, climbing into his outstretched hand. Liam's hands were broad, with strong fingers, neither too long nor too thick. Capable. Just like everything else about the sorcerer. He stroked Ed's carapace, looking as though he was trying to make eye contact with the turtle while he did so.

We had fought about Ed once. Liam had wanted me to use the undead turtle, to walk him through heavy-duty wards the elves had erected around the stadium downtown. Wards that had imprisoned people the sorcerer and I owed allegiance to. People we hadn't been certain were even alive. But I'd been scared of losing Ed, along with the sliver of my soul that animated the undead turtle. At the time, Liam hadn't understood what he'd been asking me to sacrifice. But now he was greeting Ed as though he was important, not just a magical tool. And not just important to me.

Something warmed in my previously unsettled belly.

Something welcoming.

I was seriously jet-lagged.

I so wasn't interested in the sorcerer.

"You were looking for me?" I asked, my voice weirdly stiff.

Liam nodded, still crouched, looking up at me. He raked his gaze from my face to the tips of my still dangling booted feet, lingering on my hands and knitting. For the third time.

And that was just weird.

Shit. Maybe I had something on my face? I stopped myself from checking, or from looking away.

"You look good, Mory. Healthy. You've gained the weight back. That's good."

"Also none of your business, sorcerer."

That wiped the smile from his face.

I was sorry to see it go.

Damn it all.

He straightened, smoothing his suit jacket, and for a moment I saw the bulge of the gun he wore sheathed at his side. Invisibly. He must have had one of the witches spell the sheath. His tone turned crisp. "I have a cold case."

"A dead Adept?"

"No. A mundane."

"Which is why you're coming to me."

"Yes."

I hissed quietly, returning my attention to my knitting. A necromancer could raise any corpse and could speak with nonmagical shades—but both those things were frowned upon. Even in the twenty-first century, the Adept were trying to live alongside the magically lacking in secret. Magic users who violated the rules of conduct put into place to protect Adept anonymity were punished, severely. My mother would have refused Liam outright. Teresa Garrick probably wouldn't even have deigned to meet with a sorcerer, not unless it was arranged through official channels—aka the witches. And even then, not until she'd been wired her hefty consulting fee.

"Mory," Liam said softly. His face was turned away from me, hands back in his pockets. "She was nine. She's interred here. Your territory, yes?"

I didn't answer him, but his hushed tone was doing something painful to my insides. I knew that some sorcerers could bespell their victims with mere words, but that sort of magic didn't work on me. It wouldn't get by the protections of my necklace.

"I don't have a single lead." Liam looked at me then, gaze steady, though there was a layer of frustration and possibly pain underlying his words.

The case was personal somehow.

That made what he was asking even worse. He shouldn't have been that heavily invested in a death that involved a nonmagical. How the hell would he explain any information he got from me? I couldn't sit in a court of law and offer testimony.

I forced myself to meet his brown-eyed gaze, resting my knitting in my lap. I opened my mouth to refuse him.

His expression shifted, as if he'd steeled himself for my rebuff.

And for some stupid reason, I asked a question instead. "She was murdered?"

"I can't prove it. It was deemed natural causes."

"With no underlying health issues."

"Exactly. But she was kidnapped, found away from home."

"Kidnapped? You have proof?"

He stiffened his shoulders, frustration edging his jaw. "No. But she was definitely missing for at least twelve hours."

"She could have died at home," I said, trying to keep my tone steady, professional. As if we weren't discussing the possible murder of a nine-year-old child. "Been moved by a relative."

"To what end? She wasn't hidden. She was left on a park bench, in one of those downtown parks that…" He pulled his hands from his pockets and clenched them into fists, seemingly unable to fully articulate his recounting of the heart-wrenching event.

"I don't need to know that part. That much detail."

"No." His tone was shuttered now. "You don't."

"How involved are you, Liam?" I tried to keep my tone nonconfrontational, but the muscle in his jaw jerked anyway and he didn't answer me. "You said it was a cold case, but I know most of the children interred here." I was especially drawn to the graves of children, including the one I was currently perched over. When I was younger, I used to insist that the shades of children would whisper to me, and I would leave them flowers pilfered from other graves to appease their requests. Naturally, my mother always maintained that such shades hadn't actually manifested at all. So I used to think those ghostly whispers had been my version of imaginary friends.

Then I learned I was a soul seer. Within the presence of the dead, I could see and hear and manipulate what my mother couldn't.

"The case isn't that cold," Liam finally said. "She died almost three years ago, but wasn't…buried until after you'd left town."

"But it's not officially a murder investigation."

"No. Her parents tried to keep the case open, but fighting the medical examiner's findings is difficult without evidence."

"So this isn't a case that's been assigned to you."

"Are you going to help or not?" he demanded.

"Are you going to answer my questions?"

"That wasn't a question."

"I asked how involved you were."

"As in, am I emotionally compromised?" He curled his lip derisively, his hands still clenched into fists.

"As in, are you fucking the dead girl's grieving mother?"

He reared back, utterly affronted. Though I wasn't certain if it was my language or the accusation that bothered him.

"Unbelievable," he snarled. "I come to you as a friend and—"

"Did you?" I asked, not remotely believing him. We weren't friends. We were barely friendly. "Come to me as a friend?"

Liam ran his hand through his hair, looking momentarily confused. Flustered, even. And completely adorable.

I had the utterly insane urge to press myself up against him and tease my tongue into his slightly open mouth. "I really need to get some sleep," I muttered.

"I know her father, okay? He also works for the VPD. And yeah, therefore it's not on the up and up. I'm not fucking his grief-stricken wife. I would, however, like to try to get them some closure. Only three people in the city think their child was murdered. I'm one. Which is why I've been waiting for you, Mory. To ask a favor of a friend. We've had each other's backs. When everyone else had fallen. We had each other, didn't we?"

A pinpoint of darkness opened up in my chest at his emotionally laden declaration. At the reminder of what we'd been through together—the epic battle, me inside the stadium with his sister Gabby, and him outside, protecting the city. I'd lost count of how many elves I slaughtered that day. I could only imagine he had too. But I didn't try to stuff that dark remembrance away, or swallow it, or smother it. That never worked. I acknowledged it, then went about the business of bringing some light back into the world.

I tucked my knitting into my satchel, hopping off the gravestone and scooping Ed up from the grass. The turtle wiggled happily in my hands. He liked the feel of my magic.

Liam's earnest expression flattened, his gaze cast to the ground.

I stepped toward him, smiling. And for some weird reason, I lifted up on my tiptoes—he was over a head taller than me—and brushed a kiss against his cheek, savoring the feel of his stubble against my lips. I hadn't ever done that before, not to anyone, but he looked as though he needed it. "It'll be okay, sorcerer."

He raised both eyebrows. "Will it?"

"Yep. You can't officially hire me, of course. But one friend can go for a walk with another friend in a graveyard."

"Even a sorcerer and a necromancer?"

"Sure. Especially if the necromancer makes a habit of keeping track of all the people interred in said cemetery, and she's just gotten back into town."

He laughed quietly, stepping forward to pick up my duffle, then offering me his arm.

I snorted, tucking Ed into my satchel and curling my hand around Liam's bicep. I tried to force myself to ignore the shift of the sorcerer's muscles under my fingers. Unsuccessfully.

Liam steered me toward the nearest pathway. Our strides didn't match. He slowed and I picked up my pace. We wound through trimmed cedar trees and broad red maples, carefully skirting interment sites.

"Don't the mundanes stare at Ed?" Liam asked.

"They don't see him."

"How's that?"

I laughed. "Magic, sorcerer. Magic."

He laughed quietly, shaking his head. "I remember, 'Shut up and listen.' "

He was quoting me, back from when he'd done a lot of demanding of a magical nature—including potentially putting Ed in danger—and I had balked.

"That feels like a long time ago," I said.

Silence stretched between us as we hit the paved path and Liam navigated us to the right. Then he finally said, "It does. And also like it happened yesterday."

I knew exactly what he meant.

ODDLY, I DIDN'T SENSE ANY PRESENCE FROM THE SITE THAT LIAM directed me toward. Standing in a cemetery I had claimed for myself, I shouldn't have needed a focal, but I pulled a snubbed, half-melted candle out of my satchel and set it on one corner of the practically pristine dark-granite headstone. The girl's remains had been cremated, but her parents had still opted for a belowground interment. Expensive.

I dug through my satchel for a lighter and lit the candle—ignoring the name and dates on the headstone as I did. I really loathed fresh gravesites and recent deaths, especially involving children. And

I didn't need my emotional response muddling my casting.

Ed watched me from the strip of green grass to my right, following the movements of my hands. All necromancers glowed to the undead—to all aspects of undeath. I'd been told by more than one vampire that I glowed brighter and lighter than most. That radiance would increase when I cast my magic, and Ed liked to watch.

"Something wrong?" Liam asked. The sorcerer was standing just within my peripheral vision. Set far enough back to give me space, but with his arms crossed and a no-bullshit-tolerated set to his shoulders.

Guarding me. As I'd figured out through my friendships with his siblings, that was pretty much the sorcerer's long-standing gig—never mind that the gig was most often redundant in heavily magically fortified Vancouver. I'd already reminded Liam that the power that connected me to the cemetery would cloak us from the sight of most nonmagicals. But some habits were hard earned. Over the many long days that I was mostly blind as I moved Ed through an enemy fortress, Liam had stood over me similarly, letting me map that fortress so we could find our missing warriors.

"Nothing," I said, settling on my knees. The damp grass would soak into my jeans, but I was currently carrying multiple changes of clothing with me. Or rather, the sorcerer was, since he was the one currently holding my duffle bag. "It's just unusual for me to need to set a focal in order to pick up a presence. Or pick up minor details from remains. Especially in this cemetery."

Liam nodded but didn't ask me to elaborate. The Adept rarely questioned each other about personal magic—to do so was actually considered rude—though it wasn't out of line when actively working with someone. Adepts in general, the older subset at least, were notoriously close-mouthed. About everything.

Despite having not yet celebrated his twenty-fifth birthday, and therefore technically being among the younger crew, Liam was a stickler for the rules. Born at the end of December, the detective was a Capricorn through and through. Which I knew only because his sister Peggy was into astrology, not because I had a thing for the sorcerer.

I closed my eyes for a moment, settling myself in place. I felt the deep pool of power that lay under me, spreading in all directions across the entire property. Capped by neatly defined sharp edges on all its sides, exactly where the cemetery ended. That ocean of power didn't bleed over the edges, not even to include the sidewalks where they marked the boundary of the property. It likewise thinned across the two streets that cut through Mountain View—the pedestrian-only Thirty-Seventh Avenue where I'd entered, and Thirty-Third Avenue that was still open to traffic. The City of Vancouver had purchased the property hundreds of years ago. There were legal documents to support that, and the centuries of accumulated death magic mimicked that claim of ownership. One foot outside any of the gates, and I would no longer be standing on the cemetery grounds. No longer able to pull power from it.

I opened my eyes and focused on the flickering candle. When a casting was difficult, I often pulled out my knitting, using it as a guide and a second focal. But for now, I simply reached a tendril of my magic out toward the candle, using the half-melted votive as an anchor, then sinking that questing lick of power into the interment niche set beneath the headstone. I immediately felt the presence of remains. I could tell that Liam's victim had been cremated. Ashes felt different than a body—less substantial but more condensed.

But I couldn't pick up anything else…

I listened for any whisper, any hint of energy. I should have been able to feel a spark from the remains, cremated or not. A shade should have had to respond to my magic almost instantly.

Nothing.

"What's wrong?" Liam asked.

I shook my head, pulled my focus from the candle, and raised my hands to the sides. I cast my other senses out all around me, searching gently so as to not unintentionally disturb any of the shades slumbering within the remains in the immediate vicinity. Or, even worse, accidentally reanimating any corpses.

The walking undead always pulled too much attention my way. And being under siege—twice now—by the warriors who called Vancouver home and made it their business to enforce that territory had been terrifying enough. Sure, I adored most of those warriors. I wore the protection of the dowser herself strung around my neck. But they were scary as hell even before the weapons started being wielded.

Plus, I didn't imagine that the gun-toting sorcerer at my side would react well to zombies, even if they were under my control.

I immediately picked up various imprints from all the nearby gravesites, too many to sort through. I pulled back, concentrating on the five interments surrounding me. I gleaned clear impressions from four of the five without even really trying. But the ashes of the child Liam needed to question were…blank.

I pointed to my left. "Male. Died when he was…seventy-six."

Frowning, Liam leaned over, silently reading the gravestone. He nodded.

I pointed in front of me, over one row. "Two women. One died at forty-eight. Breast cancer. She had chestnut hair and loved to laugh. One was sixty-seven. She loved sucking on hard caramels and died from…the flu? No, complications after surgery…pneumonia."

His frown deepening, Liam uncrossed his arms, stepping past me and the child's headstone to check the names and dates from the next row over. He nodded, then looked at me questioningly.

I pointed at the headstone I was kneeling in front of. "Blank."

"Blank?"

"Some of the graves in Mountain View are actually empty—"

"She's buried here," he snapped without letting me finish my thought. Then he rubbed his face. "Sorry. I just…this case. I attended the interment."

"As I was saying…"

He huffed a laugh, waving his hand for me to continue.

"A few graves in Mountain View are empty. Like, if a body was never recovered."

"Makes sense."

"When I try to read an empty interment, there's just nothing there. Nothing to connect me to the person who's memorialized at the site. But…" I shook my head, confused. "These remains are present but just…blank. Without any spark. No soul imprint."

"Okay…"

"That's all I've got."

He sighed heavily, casting his gaze around but not really looking at anything.

I watched him, backtracking through our conversation in my mind. "So you're friends with the parents, not just work acquaintances."

"Does it matter?"

I shrugged. "It…defines you. More."

He narrowed his eyes at me. "Because you thought me so prejudiced that I couldn't have mundane friendships."

"No," I snorted. "I know you have nonmagical friends." I emphasized the word friends. Heavily.

Liam stilled, suddenly watching me a little too closely. Then a smile ghosted over his face. "Girlfriends. Yes."

I lifted my chin haughtily. "I think you have to date them to actually give them that title."

His grin widened. "Why do you suddenly care?"

"That you're disrespectful of women? I care."

His tone was deceptively cool. "How do you know it's by my choice?" He flicked his fingers offishly. "The parting of the ways."

"Well, I was willing to give you the benefit of the doubt, but if you're saying you suck in bed…" I shrugged, smirking.

He laughed. The sound was still edged with darkness. I hadn't managed to tease him all the way out of his mood. But he'd allowed me to ease it for him.

Liam stepped closer, crouching beside me, near enough to touch, pinning me with his dark-eyed gaze. I could see that the brown base of his iris was shot through with blue and green. He opened his mouth, perhaps to continue teasing me, but then closed it, grimacing.

Ed wandered over and perched on the tip of Liam's black dress shoe.

The sorcerer sighed, then got back to business. "What do you mean by blank? Because she was cremated?"

"No. I might not be able to pull a shade forth from older cremated remains." In fact, I probably could. But it was always a good idea to underplay magical prowess, especially for necromancers. Death magic creeped other Adepts out. "But I'd at least get similar impressions to the ones I pulled without a need for a focal from those other sites." I gestured toward the still-lit candle. "These remains have been…I don't know…tampered with somehow, maybe? Replaced with something that reads like cremated remains but…isn't?" Yeah, that sounded just as lame in my head as it did coming out of my mouth.

Liam shook his head. "They haven't."

"I know what I'm doing. I can show you my freshly inked certification from the Academy to prove it."

He shook his head. "I don't doubt you…and congratulations."

"Thank you."

He nodded, still all business. "I know the child's remains are here. I saw them interred. I know that Dwayne visits regularly and Maria…can't. Neither of them would have the remains removed or replaced. And why would anyone else? Is there a black market for that sort of thing?"

"There sure is. Black witches are especially fond of children, cremated or otherwise."

"Jesus, really?" Liam muttered.

"Yep. But why would someone go after the remains of a nonmagical? And in Godfrey territory? Doubtful."

"I agree." He pinned me with a look filled with epic amounts of expectation. "So what else could a blank spot mean?"

I sighed, suddenly weary again even though the rush of power I'd taken from the cemetery upon entering had buoyed me. "I don't think there is any other…logical explanation…"

Wait…

I had come upon a blank spot before. More than one, actually. In this very cemetery.

"What did you just remember, Mory?" Liam asked. His tone was thoughtful, almost beguiling. Persuasive.

I narrowed my eyes at him. "Don't use that magic on me, sorcerer!"

He looked startled. "I wasn't…"

"That suave persuasion thing…I know that Rochelle asked Jade to embed that in your police badge." Rochelle was the wielder's oracle. She'd foreseen Liam needing to redirect any nonmagicals that wandered too near during the confrontation with the elves two years ago. As I understood it, the sorcerer's badge now amplified his own natural power of persuasion.

Liam's lips quirked, curling at the edges. His bottom lip was slightly fuller than—

I probably shouldn't have been staring at his mouth. I jerked my eyes upward. He looked amused. Really amused.

"I have to be wearing the badge, Mory," he drawled. A much, much heavier layer of suggestion was slicking his words now. "Touching it. To harness the power of the artifact."

Wait…what? I touched my own powerful artifact through my poncho. I couldn't harness the power of the necklace consciously. It just existed. It repelled harmful spells and malicious magic. Someone could still punch me, of course. But if they laid hands on me for any amount of time without permission, they got a nasty surprise—and singed fingers were the least of the ramifications. It had actually made for two somewhat awkward sexual encounters and one hilarious attempt at harassment while I'd been at the Academy.

All right. The awkward parts of the sexual encounters might have just been me, specifically refusing to remove an artifact that radiated power while having sex.

Liam dropped his gaze to my hand, raising his eyebrows. "Exactly."

"Exactly what, sorcerer?" I snapped, trying to get on top of the conversation again. I had an inkling that I had just admitted being entranced by his voice alone, and that was…well, disconcerting.

Yes, I could raise all the corpses occupying all the gravesites over the more than one hundred acres of the cemetery. But admitting I might be attracted to a sorcerer—purely on some surface level, of course—was throwing me.

He nodded toward my hand. My fingers still rested on the ridge of my necklace. "Your artifact repels magic."

"Malicious magic," I said snottily.

He tilted his head. "And me…you wouldn't consider me being…persuasive…as malicious?"

My cheeks flamed. Oh, damn. Now I was blushing! I looked away, reaching for the candle and blowing it out so the wax could dry. Ed had wandered off, but the tie eternally anchoring him to me was as taut and tight as ever.

Liam cleared his throat. "I apologize if I was…using any undue influence on you. You were thinking about the blank spot?"

"Yes." I kept my gaze on the candle, gently swirling the wax to cool it in layers, distracting myself. "I've encountered them before. Twice. With ashes, as well. The first time, my mother suggested that the interment was empty, or that I wasn't…"

"Powerful enough to read it."

"Yes."

He glanced at the headstone, his expression darkly thoughtful. "But that isn't the case now. Not after…all your recent training."

I thought Liam's hesitation might have been a reluctance to mention the elf invasion. Again. When his own sister, Gabby, had amplified me so much and for so long while I was trying to close the other-dimensional portal that she'd drained almost all of her magic. It had taken her months to recover.

It had taken all of us months to recover. Mentally more than physically, since we had access to the most powerful healer in the world at the time. And magic often made up for that level of draining, of being near death, by doubling or tripling in power.

"No," I finally said. It was possible that I was actually more powerful than my mother now. Though she had more skill and experience, and typically necromancers grew more powerful with age. "The second time was actually on the day I left for the Academy. I stopped here before catching my flight—"

"Of course you did."

I gave him a look.

He grinned unrepentantly. Unfortunately, the expression slipped from his face as quickly as it had appeared.

I'd been questioning my decision to attend the Academy, and wandering through Mountain View a final time before departing had settled me firmly into the choice. I had stopped by my favorite headstone and allowed my unfocused magic to reach across the expanse of the cemetery, caressing the gravesites—as creepy as that sounded, even in my head. Saying farewell but not goodbye.

Mountain View was part of me. A huge chunk, really. Our magic forever intertwined. Till death do us part.

Realizing I was just sitting in front of Liam, lost in the remembrance and my concern over leaving the cemetery behind for any length of time, I cleared my throat. "It was an interment from 1945. Unmarked, except for the date. I actually texted the info about both blanks to Tony, but then got busy at the Academy and never followed up with him."

"So?" Liam sighed. "The ashes are likely…corrupted somehow? You won't be able to speak to the shade?"

That didn't sound right or feel at all possible, especially when dealing with nonmagicals. And it certainly hadn't been covered in my Academy training. But I had no other explanation. "I'll look into it further. I really had just assumed my mother was right. That I wasn't powerful enough to pull an impression."

Liam nodded, still looking at the headstone. Possibly only half listening.

I deemed the candle solid enough to tuck into my satchel, then I stood. My jeans were wet from the knees down.

"I'll drive you home," Liam said gruffly. Then he stepped away before I could refuse.

I scooped Ed up. But before I walked away, I glanced down at the headstone.

I knew I shouldn't have, but I did. I couldn't not at least look. At least know her name.

Tanya Atkinson
2008 – 2017
Beloved Daughter
Never Forgotten

Tanya. A sharp pain arced through my chest. I pressed Ed against it. He wiggled, but I held him tightly. Hot tears spiked, and I fought them back. I was tired, jet-lagged, and a little overwhelmed about returning home after pretty much running away. No matter how legitimate the choice to get the training and education had been.

I didn't have dominion over life and death. I hadn't hurt this child. But someone might have.

I looked over at Liam.

He was watching me from two rows over. Hands shoved into the pockets of his suit pants again.

"I'll look into it."

He nodded. "We both will. Come. I'll take you home. You need to sleep."

I stepped toward him, still holding Ed like a tiny, rounded shield against my heart. "I should check in with Tony first."

He shook his head. "He's on duty for a couple more hours. Grab a nap, some food, and meet him later."

Liam reached for me. And as if it were the most natural thing in the world, I wrapped my arm around his again, leaning into him for comfort.

"Thank you," he murmured. "For breaking the rules. For me."

"Misfits unite!" I declared quietly, trying to jest but not quite making it work.

He snorted. "Misfits. Right. I'm not sure how I got grouped in with the rest of you, though."

"I didn't write the club guidelines," I groused. "I just enforce them. Hence, having your back."

"If your mother hasn't encountered the blank spot phenomena…" His tone was distracted again, remote. As though he could hold onto the present only for a few moments before getting sucked back into his own head. And possibly caught in an endless loop about Tanya's mysterious death. A case that might have no solution because nothing untoward had happened.

"I have access to an extensive library. I can ask Teresa Garrick. I can search the Academy online database, though admittedly it's thin. Jasmine was working on adding to it."

Liam grunted. "With Tony."

"Right. And Benjamin."

Liam's arm tensed under my hand. "Yeah," he drawled. "And the chronicler."

"He's been bugging you, eh? Pestering you with questions?"

"He doesn't pester."

No, Benjamin Garrick was epically polite. Detached even. Sharply focused, but not aggressive. I shoved thoughts of the vampire out of my head and glanced around. "Where did you park?"

"On Forty-First."

"But you came in on Fraser."

He went quiet for a moment, then asked in a deceptively casual tone, "How did you know?"

I laughed. "That's for me to know, sorcerer."

"And for me to find out?"

I grinned, feeling myself starting to flush again. What the hell was going on with my hormones? "I'm cultivating an air of mystery."

He cocked an eyebrow at me. "With the undead turtle, the knitting, and the…" He peered down at the colorful fringe of my poncho. "…beads clicking and clacking while you walk?"

"Yes," I said haughtily. "You have absolutely no idea where to even start figuring me out."

He laughed, a little uproariously for my taste. He sobered quickly, though, murmuring absentmindedly, "Mysterious through and through."

I didn't press my point.

Mysteries didn't explain themselves, after all.

WE PULLED UP TO THE CURB BEFORE A HEAVILY WEATHERED, cream-colored grand Georgian manor. The front gardens were out of control. The laurel hedge was easily three meters tall, as well as completely encroaching on the sidewalk. I was surprised my mother hadn't gotten a notice about it from the city. But then, she might have received a fine and not even opened it. Or cared.

All the other houses—mansions, really—in the immediate area were pristinely kept. Stone walls topped by wrought-iron railings were scrubbed clean of any encroaching moss. Cedar hedges and trees were pruned into symmetrical shapes. Gated circular driveways were sharply edged in brick or neatly trimmed lawn.

But not our home. At least not since my father had died.

I didn't get out of the car. After a moment, Liam turned off the engine.

"No one home?" he asked quietly, glancing up at the dark house. The closed wrought-iron gate that bisected the front path was wedged into the overgrown hedge.

"No lights," I said. The statement came out more resentful than I'd intended.

"Well," he drawled, "necromancers live here…"

I laughed despite myself. Then I laid my hand on the latch, opened the door, and forced myself to climb out of the warm car. Liam tugged my duffle from the back seat, passing it to me.

"Thank you," I murmured, settling my free hand on the top of the passenger door with the intention of closing it.

"Lunch tomorrow?"

I nodded. "Sushi. I've been craving it for months. Text me a time. I'll text Tony and remind him about the info I sent him. I'll see what we can cobble together about the blank spots before then." I shut the car door. The house was looming behind me, and I wanted to confront it, to sever the strange, stifling power it apparently had over me.

I really was jet-lagged.

The front gate was actually stuck. I had to shove it with my shoulder. The bricked front path was overgrown, half covered in spreading veins of moss. The place practically screamed 'creepy dark magic.'

And the massive set of wooden double front doors were unlocked.

So typical.

Liam didn't pull away from the street-side curb until I stepped inside, crossing into the darkness awaiting me. I closed the door behind me, resolute—but heavy with the sadness I'd brought with me from the cemetery.

I pressed back against the door, suddenly wishing I'd invited the sorcerer inside with me. Or, even better, had gone somewhere else with him instead. Shared a meal, surrounded by the comforting chatter of the other restaurant patrons. Then wandered out into a city awash with lights, shoulders and maybe even fingers brushing.

Just comforted by being together.

I remembered that feeling. The sense of being watched over by Liam, even though I'd spent the bulk of our days together drained of magic and scared of losing everyone I loved or cared for. That was a short list. Really short. And almost all of them had been in perpetual danger during that dark time. Jade, Kandy, then Benjamin and Jasmine...

But as he'd said only an hour ago, Liam had had my back.

The empty front entranceway stretched before me, a vast marble floor leading to a sweeping staircase. The house felt chilly. Abandoned.

I sighed as I pushed off the door, turning the heavy bolt and dropping the security bar in place. If my mother came home, she wouldn't be able to enter

TWO

MY FEET WERE DRAGGING BY THE TIME I MADE IT TO THE TOP OF THE stairs, so that I nearly tripped on the final step. Weariness mugged me, but not quite enough for me to completely ignore the closed door to Rusty's room. Crossing by the door—the last resting place of the only items that remained to document my brother's life—felt like rubbing sandpaper over the wound he'd left on my heart. Or, more accurately, a cheese grater.

I had thought that rawness might have healed in the time I'd been away. I'd thought that returning to the house, to my darker memories and moments, wouldn't be quite so painful.

Except painful wasn't the right word.

Disturbing. Disjointed.

I fought a weird urge to throw open the door, exposing my brother's eternal memorial. Rusty had been dead for over six years. He hadn't even lived at the manor at the time of his murder. He'd also been completely complicit in at least three murders himself—sacrifices made to obtain magical power. That power had ultimately been harnessed by his accomplice, Sienna. Jade's foster sister. But Rusty had participated, willingly. As far as anyone knew.

I'd never had the nerve to outright ask him.

Or rather, to ask his ghost.

I could still remember the feeling of being drained by my brother, by his spirit. The feeling of him siphoning my life force. Even dead himself, he would have killed me, sacrificed me, to avenge himself on his murderer.

I hadn't known him at all.

Rusty's death broke my mother. She'd already been shattered from losing my dad, not that I'd known it. I'd been too young to understand.

I kept walking down the long hall of what I still thought of as the family wing of the house—though I could state without any irony that a family didn't actually reside in the manor at all. Despite the eight bedrooms, living room, parlor, recreation room, library, massive dining room, and kitchen. Despite the perpetually empty pool and decks meant for entertaining, including an outdoor kitchen.

A mansion. Filled maybe every few years if my mother hosted a gathering of necromancers. Not a home.

The door to my room was closed. I opened it, expecting the air to be musty. It wasn't. The room was also tidier than I'd left it. Queen-sized bed neatly made, sheets and duvet tucked in, pillows plumped.

Hardwood floors polished. The cleaners had been through enough times to keep it freshened.

But it still felt empty. A smaller reflection of the larger house surrounding me. And for a moment, I had no idea why I'd come home. I wasn't needed, not by the coven—they had two powerful necromancers. Not by my mother.

I dropped my duffle on the upholstered bench at the foot of the bed, tugged Ed out of my satchel, and placed him in the large glass aquarium, long since dry, that sat on a wide bureau set against the opposite wall.

I'd never quite realized how huge the bedroom was, including the full-sized en suite. I'd never really realized how huge the house itself was. All that wasted space…

Ed rubbed his belly in the thick layer of sand that covered the bottom of the aquarium. A skull of a mouse was perched on one of his flat, smooth rocks, and he immediately trundled over to investigate it.

That was odd. I didn't remember adding a skull to Ed's other furniture—rocks, a piece of gnarled wood, and a series of colorful glass marbles that he liked to rearrange. He didn't need sleep, so I made certain he had things to occupy him while I slept.

I crossed to the corner window, dropping my satchel on the desk that sat to one side. The window was sticky, swollen from the seasonal rain, but I managed to wrench it open an inch.

A shower would be a good idea. I headed back toward the bed, intending to pull my toiletries out of my duffle. Then I ended up facedown on the duvet instead.

About twenty minutes later, I woke up enough to remove my boots and poncho, burrow under the duvet, and set an alarm for midnight.

I had a self-proclaimed tech sorcerer to see.

Sleep muffling my thoughts, I blinked up at the dark ceiling, listening to Ed wander around in his aquarium and the muted breeze coming through the open window. I thought it was odd that Liam had seemed so different, beyond the fact that he was obviously distracted. And frustrated. And angry.

I had never believed that people could change that much. Not quickly, at any rate. The sorcerer had always felt distant to me, holding himself on the edge of things. Protective but remote. And I'd been just fine with that.

But I'd somehow seen more of him in this one afternoon than I had in the previous couple of years of vaguely knowing him. Today, he'd been everything I thought him to be, plus more. Playful, sad, frustrated, confused…and he'd smiled.

I liked him better for it.

I fell asleep remembering holding Liam's arm, strolling through the cemetery with him matching my stride. I remembered feeling the need to tease away his frustration, his underlying sorrow.

Because I had liked the way it felt when he focused on me, whether smiling or frowning.

And that wasn't like me at all.

I was a powerful necromancer holding onto the light while straddling a dark abyss.

I wasn't playful.

And I didn't like sorcerers.

As petty as that was, it was a pretty definitive rule for me. Because sorcerers didn't suddenly go dark. They actively moved that way their entire lives in the hunt for power.

But I had really, really liked being playful with Liam Talbot.

That was weird.

I WOKE, PULLED FROM SLEEP BECAUSE A PRESENCE HAD SETTLED deeply within the house. The steady pulse of energy was muted by the distance between us, but more powerful than it had been the last time I'd felt it.

A vampire was waiting for me. In the library, at best guess.

So maybe he was just doing some research.

I never knew one way or the other.

In the aquarium, Ed was perched crookedly on his log, wearing the mouse skull as a hat. Except given the shape of his head, it was more of an all-encompassing mask.

I snagged my phone from the side table and took a picture. I could have totally rocked an Instagram account if I wasn't worried about getting murdered for exposing the magical world to the nonmagical.

"You're insane, you know," I whispered to the undead turtle.

He turned invisible.

The mouse skull remained, hovering above the thick layer of sand that covered the floor of the aquarium.

"I can still see you."

Ed appeared, dropping his jaw down in a smile. Though I could only see the bottom half.

I clambered out of bed. "Do you want to go for a walk downstairs?"

He shifted a little, turning the mouse skull away from me. That was a no. Our ability to communicate was limited, but I tried to not just cart Ed around without permission. I ran my fingers down his bumpy carapace, feeling the magic that coated him tingle under my fingertips. Magic that allowed him to turn himself invisible at will, even though it shouldn't have been possible for him to function in a way that wasn't ultimately sourced from my magic. And that was just one of the reasons I'd had to register him with the Academy.

I wandered into the bathroom in a vague attempt to make myself presentable. Not that the vampire in the library cared what I looked like.

I doubted he would even notice.

I SHOWERED, THEN SENT A SERIES OF TEXT MESSAGES. I FIGURED that if I gave them too much time to think about it, people would decide it was weird that I'd come home without telling anyone, and then hadn't even checked in.

I didn't expect to hear back from anyone, except maybe for Tony. It was close to midnight, though I wasn't actually certain when the tech sorcerer slept. But my phone pinged back almost immediately with a text message from Pearl Godfrey. Pearl, Jade's grandmother, was the head of the Godfrey coven as well as the chair of the witches Convocation. She was also my mentor. Which meant that until I'd left for the Academy, we used to sit around at Jade's bakery and knit for an hour every week. And while doing so, the elder witch would somehow make certain that I hadn't gone dark yet.

Also—and it had taken me far too long to put this together—the knitting had taught me more about wielding my magic than anything else I'd done training-wise up to that point. My mother wasn't a teacher. She also didn't believe I was worth her time, not until I was at least thirty. So I had learned by watching. And by screwing things up.

I read Pearl's message.

>*Welcome home. Please meet me at the bakery tomorrow at 9 A.M. We have a lot to discuss.*

All right, then. That wasn't ominous at all.

I sighed, texting back a thumbs-up emoji. Then I grabbed a bowl of cereal—granola with almonds and raisins that I hoped wasn't completely stale—before I headed into the library. The unopened skim milk in the fridge was a week past its best-before date but tasted fine.

Which made me wonder how long the front door had been unlocked. Again.

A dark-haired, slight-framed man in a black sweater and dark jeans was seated at the far table by the back windows of the library, near the shelves that held the necromancy texts and my mother's impressive collection of animal skulls. His head was bowed over a pile of books as he made copious notes in a black leather notebook with a gold fountain pen. He had turned on a couple of desk lamps, casting golden light over just some of the thousands of books housed in the dark-stained oak bookshelves, over the oak reading tables and the polished oak flooring. The overhead lights were off.

Even when dealing with the handwritten—and often close to indiscernible—text of the library's fabric- and leather-bound books, the vampire didn't need much light to read by.

My stomach squelched with sharp anticipation at the sight of him.

Damn it.

Benjamin Garrick.

Dark-brown hair fell forward over his wide brow. His pale skin held an olive undertone, and his fingers were long and dexterous. He appeared to be in his very early twenties or late teens. He was, using human years, almost the exact same age as me. Twenty-one. But in vampire years, he was still considered a fledgling. He'd been remade three years ago.

Benjamin's cheekbones were more edged than I remembered. His jawline more sharply defined, heading into chiseled territory. The vampiric magic that reanimated him was slowly molding him into the perfect predator. Sleek, otherworldly, beguiling…

I was halfway across the library before he looked up. His eyes were pools of darkness in the dim lighting. He smiled, revealing only the tips of his teeth. The expression transformed his face even further. And, suddenly, he was more—more vibrant, more real, more deadly. The beckoning pulse of his power expanded.

I always had to stop myself from reaching for Benjamin's magic, from coiling it over my heart. From claiming it…and him.

I didn't have as much trouble when Jasmine was near. The tenor of the golden-haired vampire's power was different—lower, deeper, more dangerous. And the magic of Kett, the master of them all, was a dark ocean of death and destruction. Him, I avoided—because I occasionally had to stop myself from running screaming from the room when Kettil, the executioner of the vampire Conclave, was near.

Benjamin's magic reached for me—his ability to ensnare was naturally carried in his smile—beckoning me forward.

I didn't resist it. That would look weird. And the vampire wasn't doing it deliberately. But I did shove a spoonful of cereal in my mouth in the hopes of distracting myself—and managed to bite my tongue in the process.

Ow! Ow! Ow!

"Mory?" Benjamin was up and across the library, reaching for me before I'd even seen him straighten from his chair.

I flinched, one hand over my mouth, the other holding the bowl. Milk sloshed over my thumb and the back of my hand.

He had moved too quickly. Quicker than I thought he could. Another adaptation.

"I'm sorry," he murmured. "I didn't mean to startle you."

The cloying pull of his magic had disappeared. I shook my head as I switched the bowl to my other hand, trying to suck on my wounded tongue and wipe the spilled milk on my jeans at the same time.

Benjamin stepped forward, moving deliberately slowly. I almost snapped at him, telling him he had no reason to treat me as prey. Other than the fact that I had just acted as though he scared me. He gently took the bowl of cereal from me, then crossed steadily back to the table he'd commandeered.

I scrubbed my sock foot over the droplets of milk I'd spilled on the dark hardwood floor, then followed him. I wasn't supposed to be eating in the library. But since no one was ever home to enforce the rules, I ignored them whenever I felt like it.

"What are you researching?" I asked as I drew close.

The corner of his mouth curled up teasingly. "Hello. I've missed you. Welcome back."

I huffed. "We text practically every day."

"Not today," he murmured.

Some sort of condemnation edged his words. I ignored it. I hadn't told anyone I'd gotten on a plane, so I wasn't going to be reprimanded by someone who only really spent time with me because I knew things he wanted to know and record about the Adept world. And now about the Academy. Benjamin had continually peppered me with questions about my training all the time I was there.

He gestured toward three leather-bound black notebooks on the corner of the table nearest me. "I've compiled an early draft of the necromancy section of the chronicles. I was hoping you'd look over my notes and make suggestions, corrections." He'd returned his attention to the book he was reading before even finishing his request.

Typical.

"I doubt I need to correct anything, Benjamin," I said, sliding into the wooden chair opposite him, reaching for my cereal, and taking a bite.

"Suggestions then, for additions…"

He went very still suddenly. Then he slowly raised his gaze to me. His magic rose, tendrils of power licking toward me. The tone of his voice deepened in a way I'd never heard from him, as he whispered, "You're bleeding, Mory."

"Oh," I said, sticking out my tongue. "I bit—"

Benjamin was standing before me. One hand flat on the table, one on the arm of my chair. Caging me in with his body. His face was now only centimeters away from my still-extended tongue. He had stood, crossed around the table, and physically turned my chair to face him, all without me seeing more than a blur as he moved.

I slowly retracted my tongue, steadily meeting his dark-eyed gaze. "I didn't realize," I murmured, knowing I shouldn't have been looking him in the eye, yet unwilling to drop my own gaze. I wasn't certain if I was scared or thrilled. The two possibilities felt one and the same. And I hung there, on that precipice, waiting to see which side I dropped over.

Tension ran through Benjamin's jaw. He was gripping the arm of my chair. Magic welled. But not from either of us.

A necromancy working. Ongoing.

Benjamin was still on his mother's tether. Still wearing a working composed from bird bones and embedded into his skin. It was supposed to keep him in check, to quell his magic. But the last time I'd known him to be wearing it, it had also almost killed him. Because it wouldn't allow him to feed when he was seriously hurt, and vampires needed to consume blood to heal.

He hissed quietly as he straightened, wrapping his right hand over his left wrist. The sleeves of his thin black sweater hung over the back of his hand, covering from sight the seething magic I could feel. He hovered, looking down at me. I couldn't read his expression.

I picked up my bowl of cereal and took an exaggerated, slurping bite.

Benjamin sighed, turning and crossing to the window overlooking the overgrown backyard. It was slightly open. The vampire didn't use the front or back door to come and go from the house. He preferred to enter clandestinely, thinking he was avoiding my mother that way, even though he had to know that any necromancer within the house could feel his magic the moment he stepped on the property.

"I'm sorry," he murmured for the second time in the previous ten minutes.

"Why are you still wearing that bracelet?" I asked.

"I think you just saw why."

"No, Benjamin. You wouldn't have hurt me."

"I would have tried to take you, Mory."

My heart thumped. I forced myself to ignore my reaction, eating another mouthful of cereal. His version of 'take' wasn't the same as my raging hormones' version of 'take.'

"See," he said, still turned away. "You're scared of me."

"I'm not scared."

"I can hear your heartbeat, Mory. Remember what I am."

I contemplated telling him that he was misinterpreting what he was picking up from me. But I just couldn't do it.

I couldn't expose myself.

I had stayed away for over a year and a half in order to quash this crush. I found Benjamin's magic beguiling. And I liked him as well. Too much. His sure-to-be gentle rejection of that misplaced affection would be worse than him trying to bite me.

"You can't hurt me," I said, my tone firm. "My necklace…my own power…keeps me safe."

He sighed. "You're right, of course. I just haven't fed enough tonight. I hadn't realized you were home until after I was in the library."

I frowned. "You didn't come here to—" I swallowed the question, realizing what I was saying. "You've been sneaking in? Because my mother is gone?"

He laughed quietly, striding back to the table as if nothing had happened. "She's been gone for almost two weeks. I'm surprised she hasn't had the house warded against me."

"Kind of hard to explain it to your mother," I said wryly. "Her best friend."

Benjamin shrugged. "There are two other vampires in town."

I snorted. "Even combined, the three of us couldn't ward the house against Kett. He'd eventually break through."

"He's not as nefarious as you make him out to be."

"He's very old and very powerful."

"Yes."

"That in and of itself is nefarious."

He huffed out a laugh. "Please."

"Does your research into vampires tell you differently?" I waited for him to answer, already knowing that the older a vampire was, the more steeped in darkness they became.

Benjamin remained silent, going back to whatever he was researching.

I let it go, finishing my cereal smugly—or as smugly as I could while spooning milk and mushy granola into my mouth. Then I set the bowl aside, reaching for the topmost of the black notebooks Benjamin had asked me to look at. I opened it, reading the neatly inscribed title inked in the vampire's cramped but deliberately neat handwriting.

The Garrick Chronicles, part one.

Necromancy and the necromancers of the Pacific Northwest.

"You could have typed these up and sent them by email," I said.

"Chronicles are meant to be handwritten." Benjamin made a note in the half-full notebook splayed open on the table to his right. "Jasmine will transcribe them when they're finished. She thinks the information should be readily available."

A painful knot of jealousy lodged in my throat.

Damn it. I'd really thought I was over this idiotic crush. I forced myself to speak normally. It didn't come out quite right, but Benjamin wouldn't notice the difference. "She's working through the Academy's archives right now. Jasmine is, I mean. Digitizing it."

Benjamin nodded. "Private collections are more diverse. You'd think more lore would get duplicated, shared, or donated, but…" He waved his hand, encompassing the library. "It just sits, collecting dust."

"It's not dusty in here," I snapped.

Benjamin glanced up at me.

I flipped a page in the handwritten chronicle, but couldn't focus on the words.

"You're mad at me," he said, incredulous. "How…why would you be mad? Because I almost…because I just—"

"No." My tone was hard. I softened it and changed the subject. "I can read these and make notes over the next few days."

"Thank you."

"What are you researching now…if you think your necromancy section is complete?"

"Well, just the Pacific Northwest edition is complete," he said. "I'm working on the section on the witches of the Pacific Northwest tonight."

My phone pinged with a text message.

> *I'm home. I got the data pulled up. Been working on it a bit. Come by whenever.*

Tony Talbot. Even though I'd texted him less than an hour before, he was apparently already working on the cemetery-blank-spot issue, which was cool of him. But then, the tech sorcerer did love a puzzle.

"Burgundy said you had an extensive collection of witch magic texts as well," Benjamin continued. "Books that the Godfreys don't even have. Not that Pearl has been terribly open to sharing what she does have. She'll lend me only one book at a time, on a set weekly schedule. And she picks them, seemingly at random. I can't remove it from the bakery, so I read perched on a stool." He grinned to himself. "Though that's a bit of a bonus. Lots of interesting things happen in the bakery after hours."

"I'm sure." There was a portal in the bakery basement, after all.

I sent Tony a thumbs-up, then focused on the conversation. Adepts weren't big on sharing their knowledge with anyone who didn't share their magic, hence Pearl—a witch—restricting what she'd allow Benjamin—a vampire—to read. I also had no doubt that the head of the Godfrey coven would withhold any texts she deemed too sensitive or too explicit in the ways of witch magic.

I rolled the conversation back to where it had begun, or at least the current branch of where it had begun. "Burgundy has borrowed some books," I said. Burgundy—also a witch, though not a full-blood—was studying medicine at UBC and magical healing with whoever was available to train her. Usually that meant Pearl or Scarlett Godfrey. She was away for a few days at a Convocation-sponsored retreat.

"From your father's family, right?"

"Yes. My mother inherited the collection when he died. He was the last of his familial line."

"No," Benjamin said reasonably. "You're the last of his line."

"Rusty was the witch," I snapped. "I'm a necromancer. I belong to my mother. And she's an orphan."

Benjamin looked at me steadily, as if he were trying to figure me out. His tone was carefully modulated when he spoke again. "I know, Mory. But relationships aren't just about what inherent magic you carry."

I sighed. "I'm sorry. I'm still tired. And I have to go see Tony."

"Have to?"

"Yes."

He nodded, his attention already pulled back to his research. "Do you want me to go with you?"

The question was completely casual, rote. The sort of way old friends talked to each other. But I knew Benjamin wasn't a fan of hanging out in the Talbots' basement. Not when he could be surrounded by hundreds of years of magical history and spellbooks instead.

"I'm fine," I said. "I'll text you when I get there."

"Take a taxi," he said. "Don't drive." Then he grinned as if he'd just remembered something delightful. "That way you can knit. I'm still waiting for my socks. Striped, you said."

I scooped up the three notebooks he wanted me to look at. "Your feet don't get cold."

"I think I'd look good wearing them."

Oh, God. He really would. But then, I had a thing for knitwear. A deeply abiding love. I would trade almost any favor for a skein of cashmere. Any color, any weight, any fiber mixture.

Still grinning, Benjamin lifted his hand, twisting his wrist as if examining it. "And maybe wrist warmers. I saw the ones you made for Tony last Christmas, with the computer icons on them." The light from the desk lamps glinted from his gold fountain pen. I knew the antique writing instrument teemed with magic, but it wasn't my kind of power so I couldn't feel it. "I think it should be skulls for mine," he said.

"Skulls. Right." I kept my tone as neutral as possible, looking at the notebooks instead of meeting his gaze so he couldn't accidentally ensnare me with the magic that accompanied his simple smile. My tolerance was ridiculously low. Probably because I was still tired. "A little on the nose for you, though."

Benjamin frowned, his magic ebbing with the dour expression. "Are you sure you're okay? You don't actually need to meet with Tony, right? Could you just email?"

"Some requests should be made face-to-face. You know that."

He nodded. "Even trades."

"Yes."

There was a certain protocol in asking a favor of other Adepts. As in, it wasn't done unless you had something of equal value to trade. Asking for favors created power imbalances. And the last thing I wanted was to inadvertently create more bonds and ties than the ones I already carried. Of course, if Liam had actually hired me—if this case had involved an

Adept child mysteriously dying, rather than a non-magical kid—then I could have simply hired Tony in turn.

Benjamin skirted the 'even trade' rule by having been officially declared a chronicler. Though honestly, I was pretty certain that the entire job—and the title that came with it—had started out as a joke between the more powerful Adepts who called Vancouver home. A joke that Benjamin's mentor, Kett, had taken full advantage of, ensuring that Benjamin had express permission to ask any question of any Adept in the city. The Adept being interrogated didn't have to actually answer, of course. But they couldn't outright murder the junior vampire for asking.

And yes, some Adepts were that touchy.

I stood, balancing my empty bowl on the stack of notebooks so I could text Tony with one hand as I exited the library.

Heading your way.

The vampire's answer to my question about what he was currently researching filtered through my distracted, overtired mind. Witches. Specifically, the local coven. I turned back at the doorway that led into the marbled front entrance. Benjamin was still deeply engrossed in his books. He had a third one open, as if comparing texts.

"Hey, Ben?"

He looked up.

"You'll tell me, won't you? If you find out anything about my dad? About how he died?" I left out all the other questions the vampire already knew I had, because we had discussed it. At least as much as I could discuss something I knew nothing about. Questions such as why the Godfrey coven didn't have any male witches at all? Did Pearl Godfrey's husband die at the same time as my father? Was that death by magical means?

And why wasn't anyone willing to talk about it?

He nodded. "You know I will."

And I did know that. No matter what personal conversations we avoided, Benjamin would never hold back information. I just had to ask.

"I'll join you in a bit," he said. "I'll set a timer so you don't stay too long. You need more sleep. It's midmorning in Latvia, so you've pretty much stayed up all night after traveling all day."

"Okay." The chance of Benjamin not just shutting off that timer, or snoozing it over and over until he had to leave to avoid the rising sun, was slim. But the thought was nice.

"What are you researching?" he asked, frowning as if just realizing he'd forgotten to collect an important piece of information.

"Those blank spots at the cemetery," I said. "Do you remember? I found one for a young girl while looking for Rochelle's mom's interment. Then just before I started at the Academy, I found an unidentified niche from 1945. I assumed they were just empty, or I was misreading them somehow. But I found another tonight. I can sense the remains, but none of the energy that should be easy for me to pick up."

"I do recall. I haven't found any mention of such an occurrence in any of your mother's books. I left a blank page in the chronicle to fill in when you figure it out." He nodded toward the stacked notebooks I held.

"It might be nothing."

Benjamin tilted his head thoughtfully, twirling his pen through his fingers so quickly that it was just a blur of gold. "You've already been to the cemetery?"

"Yes." I held off mentioning Liam and his request. The sorcerer hadn't sworn me to secrecy, but I felt oddly protective of the moments we'd shared at Mountain View. Normally, I would tell Benjamin anything just in the hope of drawing his attention. Which was utterly pathetic, even if admitted only to myself.

"Let me know what you find," Benjamin said. "It's not too late to make additions to this edition of the chronicle. I'd like to flesh it out as much as possible before I hand it over to Jasmine."

Right. The chronicle. The accumulation of knowledge, the gathering of resources. That was what was important to the vampire. It was easy to assume that he wasn't power hungry like some of his kind. Except he was. Just in a different way.

"Right. Sure." I headed toward the front entrance again, then hesitated. Another idea had occurred to me.

Certain Adepts would do anything to accumulate power, yes. But the kind of power they sought was specific to the kind of magic they wielded. Sorcerers sought out artifacts and rare spells. Witches turned to black magic and blood magic. Necromancers collected remains, such as the extensive animal skull collection that occupied the bookshelves to the vampire's immediate left.

"Hey, Ben?"

He made a thoughtful noise in the back of his throat, but his attention remained glued to his notes. Again.

"Do you know of any Adept, or any magical creature, that can steal souls?"

"Other than you?"

I stiffened. "I don't…that's not what I do!"

He looked up, blinking. "I was joking, Mory."

I glared at him. My shoulders were suddenly tight, gripping the damn notebooks and my empty bowl.

Benjamin's expression went carefully blank. His tone was once again measured. "Some would say that a vampire is soulless. That when we are remade, our soul departs."

"The blank spots in the cemetery aren't from the graves of vampires," I said, still in pissy mode. Though I could have said more. I could have told Benjamin he was wrong.

The energy that filled him—that had remade him—pulsed with life force. And, in my opinion, that life force equaled a soul. That energy was what pulled me to the vampire. Continually. Because it felt as though it belonged to me. Or, maybe, belonged with me.

He shrugged and went back to work.

I wavered, once again worried about saying too much. Worried about exposing myself and my obviously still-engaged feelings. Magic had a way of mixing everything up. "You know that's not right, Benjamin? That soul thing?"

He looked up at me.

"I can feel you…" I forced myself to continue, to keep my tone steady. "Your life force."

He frowned, just a slight crinkling of his forehead. "And Jasmine? And Kett?"

"Yes. Different for each of you."

"Then it's just the magic that animates us that you feel," the vampire said tonelessly.

"I'm not going to argue about it with you," I said, still edgy. "I'm the expert here."

A smile ghosted over his face. "Fine. We shall discuss it further when you're not otherwise engaged. I'll bring yarn to make it an even trade."

Something about that smarted. I was a massive fan of yarn, of course. But my magic was rare, powerful. And he was being flippant about it. Or at least as flippant as Benjamin Garrick was capable of being. "Fine."

He tapped his pen against his phone. "The timer is running."

I exited the library without another word. In the kitchen, I rinsed my bowl and dropped it into the empty dishwasher. Then I headed upstairs to collect my satchel and Ed.

THE WINDOWS OF THE RED CRAFTSMAN IN WHICH THE TALBOTS— minus Liam—made their home were dark except for a blue-tinged light emanating from the windows of the partially belowground basement. It was past midnight, after all. Most sane people were asleep on the dark side of the morning.

Liam lived in an apartment. Downtown, I thought, though I'd never been there. He'd moved to Vancouver a couple of months before the rest of his family, to get established at the police department. He'd had to do a year of probation. Then he'd pulled some strings—magical and nonmagical—to achieve the rank of detective in the homicide division while still in his early twenties.

The rest of the Talbots rented the house from Pearl Godfrey. The Godfrey witches were mini real-estate moguls, which was good for the Talbots. Houses in Vancouver were otherwise insanely expensive, either to purchase or rent.

I took the front path, then veered with it around the side of the house to the back concrete steps. Someone—presumably the gardener who took care of all the Godfrey properties—had made an effort to tame the wild garden that occupied every bit of the small lot excepting the house and two tiny rectangles of lawn, front and back. But the rhododendrons still brushed my shoulders as I passed, as did what I thought was a lilac that still had a few of its leaves.

The beads on the fringe of my poncho clattered as I jogged down the stairs to the back door, finding it unlocked as usual. I unlaced and tugged off my boots, crossing through the laundry area along the open-stud hall without turning on the light. Six bikes hung from hooks against the walls, along with just as many sets of skis. I paused before opening the door to the recreation room. The basement room doubled as Tony's lair when it wasn't game or movie night. I knocked quietly.

My phone pinged. I pulled it out, finding a text from Tony.

>*Knocking? Really? Just come in.*

I grumbled. Who took the time to text when he could have just called out to me?

Tony. Tony Talbot. Tech sorcerer. That was who texted instead of speaking.

I opened the door, stepping into the large room. The light I'd seen through the windows emanated from the four screens in the far corner—two mounted to the wall and two on either side of the corner desk.

A darkly shadowed figure sat in a swivel chair, facing the monitors, fingers flying over two separate keyboards. He had a laptop balanced on one knee. What looked like thousands of numerals scrolled upward on the screen to his immediate left. The top right screen was currently cycling through pictures.

Tony Talbot. In his tech lair.

As I shut the door behind me, a charcoal sketch depicting me perched on my favorite tombstone in Mountain View filled the screen. It had been drawn by Rochelle, the oracle, two years ago. But I wasn't going to read anything into the fact that Tony still had a copy of it. All sorcerers collected artifacts of power. Tony just did so digitally. And Rochelle was epically powerful.

"I expected you sooner," Tony said, not turning from the monitors. His American accent was more pronounced than his brother's, probably due to the fact that he rarely left the basement to speak to anyone other than his siblings or parents. "Saw you arrive."

He gestured toward the upper wall screen on the left, which displayed a grid point map showing a large portion of Vancouver. It was a view of the magically crafted map located in Pearl Godfrey's basement, which picked up and tracked magical occurrences within a boundary that the witches had erected around the city. Somehow, because that was how their tech magic worked, Tony and Jasmine had built and programed a digital version. And someone was assigned to keep an eye on the map twenty-four hours a day, either digitally or in Pearl's basement. Tony was either pulling two shifts today—or more likely, he always had the map open when he was in his lair.

"I needed some sleep before I checked in." I crossed around the massive sectional couch that occupied the center of the room, along with a broad square coffee table and a huge wall-mounted TV. Setting my satchel down on the section of the couch nearest Tony, I pulled Ed from its cluttered depths. I already had my phone in hand.

"After you met with Liam," Tony said.

What looked like a multitiered chat of some kind was taking place on the tech sorcerer's fourth monitor. Despite also conversing with me, Tony was typing on two keyboards. His left hand was doing whatever programing—or hacking—he was working on, and his right hand was responding to the chat. Like me, Tony occasionally worked for the witches Convocation. But he had other employment that was more…unofficial.

"Mory?" Tony grumbled. "Am I speaking to thin air? You met with Liam right off the plane? Is that why you came back? For him?"

Wait…what? "He found me at the cemetery and asked me to—"

"Speak to a ghost, yeah, yeah, blank spots…" He set the laptop on the desk, angling it so I could see the screen. "He texted."

"Why ask if you're just going to be an ass about it?"

"So I can be an ass about it."

"Welcome home to me," I muttered.

He snorted, gesturing toward the small black fridge situated at the bottom right of the desk. "Want something to drink?"

"No, thanks." I set Ed on the desk. He liked to play around in Tony's wiring if I put him on the ground, and the detritus that covered the desk was almost as interesting.

"Hey, undead buddy!" Tony crowed. He swiveled to his right, hooking a second desk chair with his foot, and pushing it toward me. He then grabbed and upended his trash can over Ed. And the laptop. Empty packages of salty treats, including corn nuts, Doritos, and Lay's salt-and-vinegar chips, rained down over the undead turtle. Ed immediately started climbing around in the garbage.

"Really?" I sighed. I grabbed an empty wrapper for licorice allsorts that had settled on the laptop keyboard, tossing it back in the trash can.

"Really." Tony flicked his fingers over the trackpad on the laptop, and another image popped up on the screen. "I added Liam's dead kid." His attention returned to his main keyboards and the two other active screens.

I sat in the second chair, scooting closer. Ed had managed to wedge his head and shoulders in a package of Ruffles all-dressed chips, and I wasn't certain yet if he needed help or if he was perfectly happy.

"It's a map..." I said, moronically blinking at the laptop screen as I recognized the layout of Mountain View Cemetery. Three spots were highlighted. "You made a map of Mountain View?"

"Makes sense, right?" Tony said, his attention divided between his programing and the chat screen. "You sent me the info about those first two blank spots…" He shrugged off the rest of whatever he was going to say.

"I'm sorry I didn't follow up on that right away. I got to the Academy and just…there was a lot going on. Getting set up, then just figuring out where the hell I was supposed to be. You know."

"Yeah, sure. Cool. Cool." He nodded toward the laptop. "I figure now that you're back, you'll want to keep mapping the entire cemetery, like systematically."

"Wow, great. I love it. Thank you!"

He touched his forehead in a two-fingered salute. "At your service, my lady of the dead."

I snorted, peering at the laptop screen. The currently marked gravesites didn't appear to form any sort of pattern. "Is this like a PDF?" I asked. "Can you send it to me to fill out?"

"Is it like a PDF…" he muttered, chortling under his breath.

"So that's a no?"

Tony turned his attention—well, his left hand at least—to the laptop, clicking on one of the dots. An info box appeared. It contained a half-filled-out form about Tanya, from Liam's case. Her name, date of birth, date of death, and the names of her parents had been filled out. But Tony had added extra spaces for occupation, description, and a note section at the bottom. "It's an interactive database. I can load it on your laptop—"

"I don't have a laptop."

"You don't have a computer?" Tony sounded utterly aghast, as if I'd just informed him I had only two weeks to live.

I waved my phone at him. My very nice, very expensive phone. Necromancy didn't erode tech like the magic of most witches and sorcerers did—with Tony, the tech sorcerer himself, being a notable exception. But other than using the computers at high school to write English and history papers, I hadn't really needed anything more than a phone. The necromancy branch of the Academy really hadn't been big on tech.

Tony curled his lip derisively at my phone. "That was out of date last month."

"It has the latest operating—"

"Please. I'll get you a new one tomorrow. And a laptop."

"I can't afford—"

"I'll bill it to the Convocation. It's my job. You're on their payroll, Mory. They have to be able to keep in contact with you. By which I mean me. I have to be able to keep in constant contact with you."

"I like this phone," I muttered. And the 'constant' part sounded a little clingy for my tastes.

"The new one is exactly the same dimensions. So you can use the same case. Just comes with extras, built in by me." He flashed me a grin, managing to keep his gaze mostly on his monitors while doing so.

Tony looked a lot like his brother, Liam. Slightly shorter and way less toned. His skin was tanned, though he never saw the sun. Currently, it was tinted with all the different light coming off the monitors. But his face didn't quite have the same…strength? Not as chiseled as Liam. And certainly not as arrogant or bullheaded or pushy.

I freed Ed's head and shoulders from the package of all-dressed chips, taking the opportunity to transfer the salt-crusted wrapper to the trash can.

"Anyway…" Tony drawled. "You can add other details and flag the gravesites in different colors. I used gray for the blank spots you've already identified, but left the other categories up to you."

"This must have been a lot of work, Tony."

"It's nothing."

"You can't bill it, though. And I can't officially hire you. Liam's case doesn't have anything to do with the Adept. The victim was a nonmagical. We should negotiate a trade."

"I can bill it through to the Convocation because I'm getting you set up. How you handle it on your end is your choice."

"It shouldn't be a favor, though."

"Fine. Would be nice if my own family members thought that way too."

"They probably think that anything you do for them is covered under room and board."

He shook his head. "I'll bank it. What tech sorcerer wouldn't need the services of a necromancer? Eventually."

I snorted, unable to fathom any reason why Tony would ever need my help. "I'll see if I can come up

with something of equal value. Like…something…"
I had absolutely no idea what I could possibly offer a
tech sorcerer. Certainly not a magical tome from the
manor library, which would thrill Benjamin. Tony
would freak out if I even suggested he touch paper.

"Fine, fine. Now for the older blank spots, I
couldn't dig that deep on my end. But as far as I can
see, no one has officially removed the remains from
the sites, and definitely not from Liam's site. No work
records."

"Yeah, I can sense the remains," I said. "Just
not the energy that should be connected to them.
It could still be some sort of grave robbery scheme,
though…or someone tampering…"

"That's your end of things," Tony said with dis-
taste. "But I got you started with identifying your
John Doe." He nodded at the laptop. "A solid guess,
at least, based on newspaper articles around the time
of his death." He clicked one of the gray dots on the
map of the cemetery.

An information panel opened. Most of it was
blank except the month and year of death. Tony
scrolled, then clicked on a link in the notes section.
Another screen opened, revealing a scanned copy of
an old newspaper article. About a boy found in Stanley Park in September 1945. The blank spot I'd found
the day I left for the Academy.

"Eight or nine years old…" I murmured. "Unidentified. Cause of death…no foul play…"

"Yep. Same as the girl from 1956. I found an obit
for her. It's attached to her entry."

I sat back, grinning at Tony exuberantly. "You rock!"

He blinked as if I'd just blinded him with a bright light, then turned away with a shrug. "It's barely anything. You're the one who's going to have to figure out why the remains are reading as blank."

"Or if it's connected to anything at all."

"Right."

"I couldn't find anything in my mother's library when I looked before, and Benjamin's gone through all the necromancy books for his chronicles. But maybe I'll try checking the Academy database. Jasmine's still digitizing it, right?"

"Yeah, though I hear it's becoming a point of contention. The witches Convocation doesn't want to share their information, but the Academy is open to all Adepts. Except vampires, I think. As long as they have someone on staff who can train whatever specialty is needed. They had to bring someone in for you, hey? Peggy mentioned it."

I nodded, clicking through the dots for the other gravesites and scanning through the little information Tony had gathered. "Yeah, a retired necromancer professor," I said. "She had a family member, an aunt, who was a soul seer. Dead now. But the niece had access to her aunt's diaries, and we worked together privately in the afternoons. Regular necromancy classes in the mornings."

"I bet Benjamin would love to get his hands on those diaries," Tony said. His tone was oddly pitched. But what, if anything, he was implying, I didn't know.

"I'm sure he would." I had, in fact, taken more than a few pictures of the diaries' contents, though I hadn't shared them with the vampire yet. "But they're personal property. Not part of the Academy's collection."

Tony made some sort of agreeable noise in the back of his throat. "So…have you seen him yet?"

"Benjamin? Yeah, he's at the house, reading his way through the library. Why?"

Tony shrugged. "We barely see him. He's, like, the same age as us. He's a gamer. Or he used to be."

"Huh. I didn't know that. I guess he's just focused on his research." I peered at Tony's larger screen, really unable to decipher anything. "What are you working on?"

"Bunch of stuff. All hush-hush and top secret."

Okay. That effectively thwarted that avenue of conversation. "I'd better go. I need to drop by the bakery early to see Pearl."

"The head of the Convocation." Tony waved his hands in the air. "Fancy."

"I thought you still hung out in her basement running the map room, like three times a week. Liam said you were on shift today."

"Doesn't mean Pearl Godfrey meets with me." He pronounced the elder witch's name with some sort of accent, possibly mangled British. "And I do most of my monitoring from here unless I'm reinforcing the connectivity. Which you'd know if you'd bothered checking in with me while you were gone."

"Yeah, well," I scoffed, "Pearl meets with me because everyone is still waiting for me to go crazy dark, so be happy that…"

Tony was eyeing me oddly.

I stopped talking.

His next question was almost a whisper, all his previous humor buried under an unusual layer of concern. "What do you mean 'crazy dark'?"

"Like, you know…"

"I don't know."

"I'm not some puzzle or program for you to figure out, sorcerer."

"Whoa, babe. You brought it up."

"I'm also not your babe."

He wagged his eyebrows at me, grinning. "Any time you want to rectify that."

I huffed out a laugh, freeing Ed from the pile of trash he'd built into a nest. "Hilarious."

"Yeah," he grumbled, turning back to his screens and keyboards. "I'm just sooo funny. Come back after two tomorrow for the phone and the laptop."

"In the afternoon?"

"I do need to sleep, you know."

"Yeah, that's why I was surprised you meant afternoon."

He just grunted in response.

I picked up my satchel, choosing to carry Ed. "Thank you."

"Keep me posted on what info you gather. I'll keep your map synced with mine."

"Thank you." I headed for the door, actually laying my hand on the handle before Tony spoke again, delaying my exit.

"Are you happy to be back?"

I glanced over my shoulder. The tech sorcerer was still fixated on his screens, his back to me. "I'm not sure yet."

"Yeah, I get that."

"It's a little inappropriate, given that it involves a dead girl, but it's good to have Liam's case to focus on."

"Yeah," Tony said wryly. "Liam can always provide a good distraction."

"Thank you for your help."

"Thanks for actually coming by. Everyone else just emails."

I opened the door, stepping through into the dark hall beyond.

"Dinner," he blurted.

"What?"

"The favor you owe me…could be dinner? Say this week sometime."

I laughed. "I don't think you want to clear this level of favor for a couple of pizzas, Tony."

"Right." His tone was different again, like it had been when he was asking about Benjamin.

"Goodnight."

"Night."

I shut the door behind me, slipping through the darkened basement and out into the cool evening air.

THREE

CAKE IN A CUP OFFICIALLY OPENED AT 10 A.M. EVERY DAY EXCEPT Sunday. For customers, that is. The back door of the bakery, off the alley that ran behind West Fourth Avenue, was always unlocked. Though only if your magic was keyed to the heavy-duty wards that protected the steel door, just as they did the entire two-storey building. Like my magic was.

At 9:07 A.M., already late for my meeting with Pearl Godfrey, I was worried the door wouldn't open at my touch. That I'd been gone too long. That I'd been forgotten by the impenetrable layers of power that protected the heart of the Godfrey coven—Jade's bakery.

But as I reached through that barrier of magic to turn the handle, I felt the wards reach back—then lick me, toes to forehead. The door swung open under my hand and all the delicious scents of the bakery hit me—icing sugar and cocoa and cinnamon and more.

Tears flooded my eyes. I swiftly blinked them away, not certain if I was sad or happy.

A willowy blond appeared in the doorway, towering over me and scowling. Her sky-blue eyes were thickly lined in black. "What?" she snapped. "Waiting for an invitation?"

Sliding one foot behind her while twisting her body, she swept her arm before her dramatically. Her hair was cinched in a tight bun high on the back of her head. She was clad in worn black jeans, a black Cake in a Cup T-shirt with a white logo, and black-and-white sneakers. A streak of cocoa marred the smooth, creamy skin of her right cheek.

And she was most definitely mad at me.

Gabby Talbot.

An amplifier. Twin to Peggy. Adopted sister to Liam, Tony, and Bitsy.

I stepped inside, tugging the door shut behind me. Gabby sauntered over to the middle of a long stainless steel table that bisected the bakery kitchen. The huge Mixmaster in the far corner was churning away. The ovens were full, each glowing timer in some stage of counting down. I'd interrupted Gabby in the middle of icing a batch of cupcakes.

The disgruntled amplifier picked up a lemon cupcake base, slapping chocolate buttercream on it with a flick of a bright-pink spatula.

I didn't recognize that flavor combo, though I'd had the menu memorized before I'd left for the Academy, including the seasonal additions. Weirdly, that missing info—coupled with Gabby's attitude—put me further on edge.

Gabby carefully set the now-frosted cupcake on a half-full tray and picked up another yellow cake base. Her hands were gloved, but I could see that her fingernails were painted black.

I opened my mouth to speak.

But she cut me off, launching into a diatribe replete with changes in tone and accent. "Hey, Gabby. Guess what? I'm flying back today! Yay, Mory, fantastic! Would you like us to pick you up from the airport? Cool, great. I'd love to see you. What's your flight number?"

"You've never said 'fantastic' like that in your life."

"That was Peggy's contribution to the imaginary text messages we should have exchanged with you yesterday."

"Do you need me for this conversation? I've only had around four hours sleep, and I have to meet with Pearl."

"Really? You didn't sleep well?" she asked, completely faking surprise. "Why would that be? Because you not only hung out with Tony last night, but you had a secret rendezvous with Liam!?"

I rubbed my forehead, any hope of being fed cupcakes for breakfast fading fast. The pinpoint of pain that had lodged in my upper chest upon discovering that Gabby was baking instead of Jade sharpened. Weird, I know. But I'd built myself up on the drive over, readying myself to be smothered and babied by the dowser. And now all I had was Gabby griping at me.

Gabby iced another of the mystery cupcakes. Her lips were thinned with tension.

So now I was angry too. Angry that she was angry at me. "What do you want me to say?"

"Well, obviously you aren't even sorry. Off gallivanting around, learning things, traveling the world…then randomly showing up without even telling any of us." Gabby set another cupcake on the tray, then stepped around the workstation to the nearest oven just as the timer went off. She reset it, shoved her hand into a thick pink oven mitt, lowered the door, and carefully rotated the trays of cupcakes within.

"I'm sorry you couldn't come with me."

The twins—Gabby and Peggy—had been wanting to attend the Academy for a couple of years now. But for reasons I didn't quite understand, they couldn't. Or maybe they hadn't been accepted. It wasn't a financial thing, because the Convocation covered tuition, plus room and board. Though my mother had made a large contribution—as families that could afford to do were encouraged to—after I'd been accepted.

My mother, true to form, had actually had no idea I'd applied. I'd asked Pearl and Scarlett Godfrey for references.

The twins might not have been way off the power charts or anything, but they both wielded valuable, rare magic. So I had an idea that the reason the Talbots had relocated to Vancouver from Boston might also have had something to do with why the twins weren't currently attending the Academy.

Though Gabby was an amplifier and her twin, Peggy, was a telepath, they were part of a family of sorcerers. And sorcerers rarely joined covens. I hadn't asked for clarification, though, because I didn't go around chatting about the darkness in my past either. And fair was fair.

Gabby glanced at me, grimacing. "I'm sorry too." She crossed back around the long steel counter, snagging an already frosted cupcake from one of the half-dozen baking sheets set into a tall, steel rolling tray as she did.

She handed the cupcake to me. I knew it by sight. *Cozy in a Cup*—banana-and-chocolate-chip cake topped with dark-chocolate buttercream.

The breakfast of warriors.

Literally.

And one of my favorites. It was the touch of cinnamon I craved. I blinked down at it stupidly. Overwhelmed. Again.

"Are you okay?" Gabby asked in a whisper, narrowing her dark-lined eyes at me. A furrow of concern was fixed in the center of her brow.

I peeled the paper lining from the cupcake, taking a bite. "I am now."

She laughed. A quiet, sad sound.

"Are you okay?" I asked around the mouthful of deliciousness.

"I'm good, actually. But we all missed you."

I nodded. Even though I couldn't say the same. Not wholeheartedly.

I had needed the break, the space. After almost dying, after wielding massive amounts of magic—amplified by Gabby's own power—I had needed to figure out who I was. I wasn't certain how I fit among the warriors and the mixture of magical misfits who called Vancouver home. I still wasn't certain.

"What's the new flavor?" I asked, nodding toward the cupcakes she was icing.

"The lemon cake and chocolate buttercream?" She grinned at me saucily. "*Allure in a Cup*. A personal addition to the bakery menu."

I clapped. Carefully. I didn't want to lose a single bite of my cupcake.

"Thank you," she said, still grinning as she took a playful bow. "Bryn added it to the Whistler menu after she tasted it."

"Nice!"

Gabby laughed, quietly pleased. Then she resumed her frosting.

I systematically mowed my way through the *Cozy* cupcake while also trying to savor every bite. Gabby's baking was almost as good as Jade's. Same recipe, of course. But Jade put something extra special into hers. Magic, maybe. But love, definitely.

"Will you be staying?" Gabby asked without looking at me.

"I'll probably have to travel a bit," I said. "For work. But yeah, Vancouver is home."

"Peggy was worried you'd meet some sexy necromancer and abandon us."

"There are no male necromancers," I said. "Or at least none powerful enough to attend the Academy. Necromancy usually only manifests in the female line."

"Witch or sorcerer, then. If it's a guy you want." Gabby waved offishly. "Someone new and exciting."

I shrugged. "I might have dabbled."

A huge smile split Gabby's normally reserved visage. "Details!" she roared.

I laughed, but got distracted when I almost lost hold of the remnants of my cupcake. "I have to meet with Pearl."

Gabby glowered, only half faking. "She's out front. Peggy is setting up today, covering for Todd. He's at some comic convention thingy."

I deposited the paper wrapper in the compost can, carefully picking crumbs from my poncho as I stepped toward the swing doors.

"Lunch, then?" Gabby asked, her tone casual.

Damn. "I'm supposed to check in with Liam about lunch."

Gabby made a snarling face. "I hate brothers."

"You don't."

"Fine. I don't. But I am still pissed at you."

"So noted."

"So do something about it."

"How about manicures? After your shift? Or tomorrow?"

"Really? You? You want to get your nails painted?"

"No. But you like getting your nails painted, and I'm making up for not telling you I was coming home."

"Quite right." Gabby lifted her chin snootily. "So it should be. We'll go right before games night, so you can pick up the pizza after the manis. That might be enough to get you off the hook. But I'm emphasizing the 'might' in that statement. I'll let Peggy know."

I hadn't attended games night for over a year and a half, but my presence was obviously assumed. And that pleased me for some reason. Except for text messages and the occasional email, I had pretty much abandoned the Talbots. But they weren't going to leave me on the outside in retribution. "Did you invite Benjamin?"

"He's always invited. Never shows."

"I'll mention it again."

"I'll text you the time for the manis and the pizza order." She waved me off, still playing at being snooty.

I laughed, crossing toward and pushing through the double swing doors. And even as I did, I realized that I had slipped into a thing I'd found myself doing constantly before leaving for the Academy—trying to include Benjamin in activities with the others. Because I'd wanted the excuse to see him, talk to him.

Damn it. I'd been trying to break that cycle. But Benjamin was my friend, and I really didn't like that he was obviously still avoiding being around people. I didn't think it was healthy.

Of course, I could have been accused of doing the same thing by running away to school. Except I'd spent every day surrounded by people. Just…new people. People who knew only what they needed to know about me. That I was Mory. A necromancer with a specialty. Not that I had a dark history that any Adept a decade older than me thought I was doomed to repeat.

And speaking of which…

A SILVER-HAIRED WOMAN WAS PERCHED ON A TALL STOOL AT A round bistro table, set midway along the street-side French-paned windows that ran the length of the seating area of the bakery storefront. Her hair was smoothed back from her face and coiled in an intricate braided bun. She wore an elaborate light-gray knitted Estonian lace shawl with a beaded edging, over a silk blouse and gray wool pants.

She pecked away at a laptop with a finger of each hand, peering at the screen through black-and-silver-rimmed reading glasses.

Pearl Godfrey.

Aka the head of the witches Convocation and the Godfrey coven.

The seating area of the bakery was otherwise empty. Which made sense, since the bakery didn't open for another forty or so minutes. Trinkets composed of various bits of things—coins, pieces of broken pottery, jade, sea glass, et cetera—hung in all the windows, strung on lengths of silver chain. According to their maker, Jade, each held residual magic that the dowser collected and transformed into what looked like wind chimes—but which were actually potentially dangerous magical artifacts. In the wrong hands, of course.

A sharp squeal emanated from my right, exploding from somewhere behind the huge glass display case. Then I was attacked without further warning. The swing doors to the kitchen hadn't even closed behind me yet.

Arms latched around my neck and shoulders, and a thick, pale-blond ponytail slapped me across the face.

"Oh! Oh! Mory!" the person attempting to choke me with affection cried. "I've been practicing my shielding, and I didn't know you were here yet."

Pearl scoffed without looking over at us. An utterly derisive yet regal sound. "The goal is to selectively filter your surroundings, Margaret. Not to shut everything out completely."

Peggy Talbot released my neck. Stepping back, she grinned at me madly, blithely ignoring the admonishment from the older witch. Pearl didn't like sloppiness. She firmly believed that screwing around with magic led to dark deeds. And she wasn't at all wrong.

But there was absolutely nothing dark about Peggy. Completely identical to her twin, Gabby, in looks, the telepath was different in every other aspect—including the fact that she was currently glowing with glee. She was also wearing a Cake in a Cup T-shirt with a white logo over dark-wash jeans, but her shirt was baby blue.

She had abandoned a tray of strawberry-buttercream-iced cupcakes on the counter behind the glass display case, which she'd been loading up in prep for opening. The case was currently about three-quarters full. And seriously looked like heaven to me.

"Hey, Peggy," I said. "You look great." Both the twins were equally lovely. Tall and slim, with creamy skin and bright sky-blue eyes.

"We only have a few minutes, Mory," Pearl said. "Please join me."

Peggy tilted her head as if listening to something. Then she said, "We're going for manicures later? Cool!"

She and Gabby were telepathically linked. Continually, I thought, though Peggy wasn't a strong enough telepath to speak mind-to-mind with anyone else. Not that I knew of, anyway. But as I vaguely understood it, the talent the Godfrey coven was most interested in helping Peggy develop was her truth-seeking abilities.

Yeah, she could tell if someone was lying with a crazy level of accuracy. Like, 98 percent or something.

Peggy winked at me, then rolled her eyes in Pearl's direction before spinning off to load more cupcakes into the display case.

Peggy and Gabby usually worked opposite shifts. Likewise, Pearl usually conducted meetings in the afternoons. Presumably, the older witch had set up her mobile office early to oversee the twins getting the bakery open on time.

I crossed to and clambered up on the high stool opposite Pearl. As always, I felt like a child when doing so, because my toes could only brush the stool's lowest crossbar. Pearl wasn't all that much taller than me, actually, but she looked perfectly poised.

I straightened my back, tugging my knitting project bag out of my satchel. The bag was decorated with characters from Harry Potter, and I had brought a set of self-striping arm warmers to knit instead of the marled hat I hadn't finished the previous day. A single strand of fingering-weight yarn was far easier to deal with when being interrogated.

"You've returned." The older witch pinned me with her sharp blue eyes over the laptop screen. "I'm pleased."

My chest went all warm. I really was a total idiot for the faintest bit of praise or hint of affection.

"Would you prefer that requests for your services go directly through you, or be filtered through your mother…or through me and Scarlett?" Pearl added the third option with just a brief hesitation. Perhaps she was concerned about stepping on my mother's toes?

I blinked, almost dropping a stitch as I swapped one double-pointed needle out for another. I had expected some sort of chastisement about returning without warning. "How is it normally done?"

"Normally, you'd have someone vet clients for you for a couple of years. Though some Adepts prefer to have all of their contracts ratified by their coven. If Scarlett or I look over your requests, we can then also assign you a partner, if needed, on a job-by-job basis."

I really hadn't thought any of this through. I'd simply gotten the email notice about my certification and had jumped on the next flight home. "A partner like Burgundy or…Benjamin?"

Pearl raised her eyebrows. "You believe the vampire could be useful to you?"

"Well, I don't know. If someone attacks me during an investigation, he's pretty strong."

Pearl frowned. "The reason to vet the requests is so that we don't put you in a situation in which you'd be attacked. Normally, you'd be called in to consult with an already established team."

I nodded. "That's how it worked on my three work-study cases."

"Yes…" Pearl returned her attention to the screen of her laptop, scanning it. "I have the reports here. The first two were child's play for you…" She waved her hand offishly. "Good money, of course, but not at all a challenge. But Latvia…" She pursed her lips, reading.

That prickle of warmth in my chest expanded. 'Child's play?' We were having an adult conversation. I'd brought my knitting because I assumed that the meeting would be like every other mentoring session. That I would knit while Pearl worked, and then at some point, she'd watch me for a while before finally giving me some tiny bit of advice. Mostly about the knitting.

Of course, teaching me how to knit in the first place had actually been all about showing me how to control and wield my power. So when Pearl sat quietly across from me for an hour, she was actually making certain I was okay. And that my magic was behaving normally.

"You solved a centuries-old haunting," Pearl continued. Then she smiled at me. Like, with pride.

"A soul had been trapped on our plane of existence," I said.

"Yes." Pearl was still smiling.

I wasn't certain how to respond, so I just grinned back at her before saying, "They have a cool knitting exhibit at a museum there."

"Do they? Hmm." Pearl started finger pecking at the laptop again. "Your mother is on assignment."

"I noticed."

Pearl twisted her lips in disapproval. But…maybe of my mother rather than me.

I turned my attention to my knitting, working a few rounds before Pearl took up the conversation again. The light-gray stripe turned red under my fingers, which pleased me, as it always did. That was a sort of magic itself. The power of math and perfectly placed dye.

"Is that the self-striping yarn that Jade got you for Christmas?" Pearl asked.

"It is. From Mudpunch. A local small-batch dyer. This colorway is black-hearted brimstone."

Pearl laughed quietly. "Perfect. Shall I send the requests I've received to you, then?"

Wait…what? "I have requests? Like, already?"

"You're the first necromancer to specialize in soul magic in over a quarter of a century. You have requests. Two consultations and three active cases. I believe the cases were put into the queue as soon as you declared your intention to study at the Academy."

"That…um…that's…"

"A little overwhelming?"

"Yeah."

"I don't believe any of these are a rush. I'll go through them, make some notes, and email them to you. If anything needs more than your basic contract, Ember Pine can modify it for you. Have you met Ember?"

I shook my head. I actually wasn't aware I had a basic contract either. It was probably among the pile of info the Academy had forwarded along with my certification. I'd only opened the main email the previous day, not the attachments, and then had been hit with an overwhelming urge to get on a plane. Or maybe that was technically two days ago now. International travel was hard on timelines.

Pearl hummed thoughtfully. "Ember is a lawyer working out of the Seattle office of Sherwood and Pine. I'll send you her contact info. I met her through Rochelle, and she also works with Jasmine. She's highly skilled in contract law. And has a number of... special clients."

More unsolicited praise from Pearl Godfrey. Amazing.

Peggy planted herself by the table with a cute little jump. "I've opened the register, but don't need to open the doors for..." She checked her nonexistent watch with some exaggeration. "Twelve minutes."

"Tea would be lovely," Pearl said. "Earl Grey. Sugar and milk, please. Mory? May I treat you to a hot drink and a cupcake?"

"For breakfast?"

Pearl's lips twitched playfully. "Well, just this once."

I laughed. "I already ate one."

"Well..." She waved her hand again, this time possibly playing at the affectedness. "Just this twice."

Peggy grinned, clasping her hands together. Then with another little hop, she took off back around the display case as if she lived to make hot drinks and serve cupcakes.

"Don't you need the rest of our order?" I called after her.

"Got it," the telepath crowed.

Right. She'd plucked what we wanted out of our heads. I opened my mouth to ask Pearl more about the job offers, but the older witch's attention was trained over my shoulder, looking with a bright smile toward the swing doors that led to the kitchen.

I followed her gaze.

Jade Godfrey walked through the doors, all golden and blue flashing eyes and toothy smile. She had her wedding-ring-laden necklace twined twice around her neck, and was wearing her leather armor. Presumably, she'd left her katana in the back office. The dragon slayer. The wielder of the instruments of assassination.

The dowser.

In all her glory.

"Mory!" Jade flung her arms forward.

And, moron that I was, I leaped off the stool and ran to her.

She swept me up like I weighed nothing, twirling me around.

Pearl clucked her tongue, presumably admonishing her granddaughter for the display of strength in full view of the glassed front door. Though I would have expected that the exterior wards would obscure anything magical that occurred in the bakery—and everything Jade did was definitely magical. So perhaps Pearl was actually just disapproving of Jade treating me like a toddler.

But I didn't mind. Just this once.

Jade set me down, smoothing her hands through my hair. Then she tugged my necklace out from under the neckline of my poncho, setting it across my collarbone. She ran her fingers along the woven gold chains and the various antique coins attached to it. "I've missed you, my necromancer. You look well."

"You look tired," I groused playfully. Because if I'd told her that she looked effervescent, she would have thought something was wrong with me.

She threw her head back with an exaggerated groan, golden curls bouncing around her face and neck. "Elves."

"You're still doing that? That peace negotiation thing?"

The dowser huffed out a sigh. "It takes them freaking months to agree to any little thing, but thankfully we rotate shifts. Though how I got lumped in with the dragons..." She trailed off, narrowing her eyes at me as if just putting something together. "What do you mean...still?"

I didn't answer her.

"What month is it?" she snapped.

"Um...October." Though it was technically almost November...

"October!" she cried, glancing over my head at Pearl. "What?"

"Have a cupcake, my Jade," Pearl said soothingly.

"I'm going to have more than one damn cupcake if it's freaking October!" Then she glanced over at the display case, spotting something that appeared to give her an instantaneous heart attack. She pressed a hand to her chest, then cried out, pointing emphatically. "What is that!?"

Seemingly frozen next to the complicated espresso machine beyond the cash register, Peggy had gone pale. Presumably the telepath was in the middle of making the mocha I'd wanted. "Um…" She darted a glance at Pearl.

The elder witch shut her laptop. "Best to just tell her."

Peggy swallowed, grimacing. "Pumpkin spice with—"

"Pumpkin spice?!" Jade cried. Energy brushed through the dozens of trinkets hanging in the windows, setting them tinkling and chiming.

No. Not just any energy.

Magic.

Jade's magic.

As with the wards on the bakery or the necklace hanging around my neck, I could feel Jade's power as it was unleashed, even though I generally couldn't pick up magic at all when I wasn't on cemetery grounds. The dowser was just that powerful.

"It's Bryn's recipe," Peggy said courageously, speaking against the daunting brush of power still lightly rattling the trinkets. Jade's business partner, Bryn, ran Cake in a Cup Too in Whistler. "Last time we spoke, you said that we should consult with her about the fall menu—"

"That was two days ago!"

Peggy grimaced. "More like…five weeks."

Jade went very, very still.

"There is no one to kill, darling girl," Pearl said.

"The elves," Jade said tonelessly. "I could slaughter all the elves. Then there would be no one left to negotiate."

"You already tried that, Jade." Pearl patted an empty stool tucked next to her table. "Let's sit. Mory and I are having cupcakes for breakfast."

"I can't stay," Jade said mournfully. "I snuck away. I'm going to need cupcakes to placate Warner and Alivia. I just…" She abruptly pivoted and crossed back into the kitchen.

"I need to open now," Peggy mock-whispered, tying on a pink ruffled apron and nodding toward the front door.

Pearl made a shooing motion to the telepath. Then, grabbing her laptop and bag, she followed Jade through the swing doors.

"What the hell?" I asked quietly.

Peggy grimaced, crossing around me to unlock the French-paned front door. "They're rotating shifts for the negotiations. And they meet in some sort of dimensional pocket, neither here nor in the elves' dimension. And…" She shrugged. "I guess time slips. Mostly it's the other way. Jade feels like she's been gone for too long, but it's only been a couple of days."

She opened the door, smiling at the few customers who had already lined up.

Grabbing my knitting and my satchel, I stepped back into the kitchen, letting Peggy get to work. Gabby, now also sporting a pink apron, passed me with another tray of cupcakes. Then she stayed out front to help Peggy with the morning rush.

To my left, the door to the walk-in pantry was flung open. Jade was standing within, just breathing. Taking deep, full breaths. Her katana was sheathed across her back.

And yeah, it smelled amazing in the bakery pantry. I'd stood there, trying to just breathe, more than a few times myself. Mostly when I'd been the one wearing the gold necklace currently twined around Jade's neck. The wedding rings that decorated that heavy gold chain held more than just the dowser's power.

My necromancy was constantly 'on,' constantly seeking out death, which was why I carried Ed with me everywhere to ground me. The dowser's main power was the same. She sensed, tasted, and collected magic just by being present.

But the wedding-ring-laden necklace also held the instruments of assassination. Jade was their sole wielder. And she had entrusted the necklace to me, to save me, even while she'd been dying.

I stood frozen for a moment, just inside the swing doors, breathing deeply myself. Breathing through the remembrance of that day. Of the stadium collapsing over me. Over us. Both of my legs and one arm had been fractured. Jade had been pinned, and no matter how hard I'd tried to help, to pull her free, I hadn't been strong enough. So she had looped her necklace over my head even as she lay dying, then had triggered a teleportation spell.

Sending me to safety before the rest of the stadium roof crumbled, burying her alive.

Saving me. And almost dying herself.

And not for the first time.

Because that was what warriors did.

Then I'd worn that damn necklace—and the instruments of assassination had fed off my life force—even though I wasn't one of the warriors. Until Jade had been strong enough to reclaim it.

A murmured voice pulled my attention through the open door to the small back office. Pearl was making a phone call, standing with her back to me.

"Mory," Jade whispered from the pantry, holding her hands out.

I crossed to her, becoming immediately enrobed in an invisible cloud of spices and chocolate. Jade pressed an ancient-looking gold coin into the palm of my right hand. I flipped it over, noting some sort of runes pressed into the age-darkened metal.

"For later," she said.

I nodded, knowing that it made Jade happy to collect magically imbued coins for my own necklace. Not that I could feel any of the residual that the coin likely held, at least until after Jade added it to my necklace. I tucked the coin in the front pocket of my jeans.

Jade nodded, seemingly satisfied. "You text me if you need me."

"Do text messages get through to…wherever you are?"

She shook her head. "I pop back to sleep here, though. I want to be in my own bed. I just hadn't gotten tired yet…" She released a heavy breath. "Five weeks is too long to be away from the bakery. I'm not interested in ruining everyone's lives because the elves need an equal number of representatives to witness every long-freaking-winded diatribe. Alivia jumped up and cut some guy's tongue out a couple of hours ago, and we took a break. I needed cupcakes."

Jade frowned thoughtfully. Alivia was an elf. But she'd helped us, freeing Jade from the portal after the roof had collapsed, even though that meant she might have trapped herself in our dimension. "I think he might have been her uncle." She shook her head. "Point is, I'm freaking done. I'll be home to-night. Or maybe tomorrow…soon. Then I'll add the coin to your necklace."

"You know it's pretty heavy already, Jade…"

"I can fix that too."

I didn't doubt it.

"Missed you, babe." She snatched a large bag of chocolate from the middle shelves at my left—like at least three kilos worth of dark chocolate, cradling it as if it might have been a baby. Then she took a step back, winked at me, and disappeared.

Right. Teleportation.

A nasty way to travel.

I knew. When Jade had saved me from being crushed by teleporting me out of the stadium, it had felt as though my insides were outside for days after.

I sighed. The pantry still smelled amazing, but Jade had taken all the energy with her.

Pearl didn't appear inclined to continue our conversation, so I got my mocha to go, plus a *Serenity in a Cup*—carrot cake with cream-cheese icing—and headed back to Mountain View Cemetery. I would have preferred to crawl back into bed, but I had blank spots to figure out. Hopefully before lunch. I didn't want to show up empty-handed and disappoint Liam. The sorcerer was already wound far too tightly about his case.

THE GRAVEYARD WASN'T EMPTY ON THIS SUNNY BUT SLIGHTLY chilly Wednesday morning. A landscaping crew was working over near the corner of Fraser and East Forty-First. Joggers and dog walkers were crisscrossing the green grounds. Interspersed among the large cedar trees that dotted the property, the deciduous chestnut and maple trees were a riot of color, steadily blanketing the gravesites with their leaves.

No one paid me any attention, even in my bright-red poncho. A side effect of being a necromancer on her claimed territory, even by daylight.

Buoyed by mocha and cupcakes, I had grabbed a car share and made it to the cemetery. But, perched now on my favorite tombstone and sipping my still-warm drink, I found myself stymied, pondering the overwhelming task of checking every single gravesite for blank spots.

Over a hundred thousand sets of interred remains occupied the vast sprawl of Mountain View.

It would take days to systematically check every individual interment. And simply casting wide and far would be ineffectual, because the blank spots were just that—blank. Even if I could sense the interred remains while focused on an individual site, I didn't think they would put off any more feedback at a distance than say, the path. Or a building. Or a car. Or a memorial site, for that matter.

Which meant I needed to be mobile, pulling quick and fast impressions as I walked a grid. Or, better yet—since I was already situated near the center of the property—a spiral. If I hit a blank spot where I could easily see a marker, then I could pause, figure out if it contained remains, then note the name and dates. Of course, I'd also have to figure out some sort of way to keep track of it all without Tony's interactive map.

I sighed, taking another sip of my mocha. Peggy had been liberal with the chocolate, which was cool with me since I only drank coffee for the caffeine. Being in the cemetery might invigorate me magically, but spending the next couple of hours continually scanning while walking was going to result in one exhausted necromancer.

I abandoned my comfy perch, pulling out my phone and opening a new note. I had no other idea what to do. I could dig through more books in the manor library, but they weren't catalogued or indexed. And I'd already scoured the few I deemed relevant the first time I found a blank spot. I could log into the Academy database, but again, it was a work in progress.

For now, trying to map the phenomenon seemed like the best use of my time. Maybe there was some sort of pattern?

Sighing, I downed the last swig of my mocha, tucking the paper cup in my satchel. I reached out with my magic. Not enough to call any shades forth, but just enough to pick up quick impressions. Then I started walking.

NOT INCLUDING TANYA AND THE TWO INTERMENTS I'D PREVIOUSLY identified, I found six more blank spots—places where I could sense remains but no soul energy—before Liam texted a location and time for lunch. That made nine blank spots in total, in addition to a few sites that were well and truly empty for other reasons. Memorial burials, most likely.

Fresh flowers and a crystal-cut glass sea turtle now marked Tanya's grave, and I wondered if I had just missed Dwayne Atkinson, since Liam had indicated that Tanya's mother didn't visit the cemetery. Another of the blank spots—James Wu, who'd died in October 1996—had a ceramic Asian cat perched next to the headstone. It looked fairly new.

Nine blank spots.

Nine somehow-corrupted remains?

Making note of the locations of each spot as best I could, I texted all the names and dates I'd collected to Tony as I headed for the car share I'd reserved over on Forty-First Avenue.

It was possible that the cremated remains I could sense but not read had been divided among family members for their mantels or whatever—leaving only a small portion to be interred. But even then, I should have still been able to pick up soul energy from those interments. Sure, I considered the possibility that maybe I just couldn't. Maybe I wasn't as capable as I'd thought. Maybe the jet lag was affecting me adversely.

Except that among the blank spots was a second one marked as containing unidentified remains, from December 2005. No name on the niche, the same as the blank spot I'd noticed from 1945, just before I'd left the city. So if it was a case of ashes being too small a sample for me to fully read, how would unidentified remains, presumably unclaimed by anyone, possibly fit that profile?

Additionally, four of the blank spots were in-ground gravesites, which had actual bones and probably a coffin buried within. And there was absolutely no way that any family member took the majority of a desiccated corpse of a child home for display.

Frustrated, I scrolled through my notes, re-arranging them chronologically. The dates of death ranged from the unidentified eight-year-old in 1945 to Tanya in 2017.

And yes, every blank spot appeared to be the grave of a child.

Unidentified 8-year-old—DOD Sep 1945
Jean Sadler—DOD Nov 1956
Misty Dean—DOD Nov 1965
Anna Campbell—DOD Oct 1976
Danny Pim—DOD Jan 1987
James Wu—DOD Oct 1996
Unidentified 11-year-old—DOD Dec 2005
Tanya Atkinson—DOD Jan 2017

At the Academy, I had tested in the highly sensitive range. Which meant I could pull impressions—sex, gender, age at death, height, hair color, and more—from a single finger bone. I didn't even need the entire finger. I'd only failed to pull an impression when testing on a skin sample, a tiny vial of ashes that I'd later learned weren't human in origin, and a preserved eyeball. Though one necromancer from India—Arya Kapoor—had pulled correct impressions from all three.

I was willing to bet that Arya had more than three active cases waiting for her when she got certified. Not that I was jealous. Even I found caressing eyeballs and skin samples with my magic creepy as hell.

So why were these nine sets of remains reading as blank?

If the sites I'd identified hadn't been a mixture of embalmed, cremated, and what I assumed were natural burials, I might have guessed that some sort of obscure medical procedure was an underlying cause. Intense radiation treatment, maybe? Except the range of dates and Tanya's official cause of death didn't support that theory.

Blank spots…

Missing shades…

Misplaced souls…

Souls…

Wait…

Was that even possible? Could souls go missing or be removed? Even though I'd posed a similar idea to Benjamin the night before, it sounded utterly crazy by light of day. And I was a necromancer.

But if it wasn't just a crazy idea, then why? And how?

No. The remains just had to have been corrupted somehow. That was the only thing that made sense given all the circumstances. That was the logical assumption.

Unless some sort of magic was involved.

I crossed the invisible barrier between the exterior boundary of the cemetery and the edge of the sidewalk. Weariness washed over me. I stumbled.

Right.

I had just expended a lot of magic in a thin but continual stream. And I hadn't had much sleep to begin with.

I glanced at the time. I could grab a fifteen-minute nap in the car share before I needed to leave to meet Liam. Hopefully no one noticed the necromancer snoozing in the front seat.

IN THE END, I WAS TEN MINUTES LATE FOR LUNCH. BUT I'D GOTTEN in a nap and had texted ahead to tell Liam, so I felt okay about being tardy. Unfortunately, though slightly more rested, I was still completely confused about how remains could be corrupted or altered to render them unreadable. Hopefully, the consumption of sushi would help my beleaguered brain.

Liam was sitting next to the window near the middle of the restaurant. He stood to draw my attention when I pushed through the glass door. He was wearing another navy suit. The presence of a tie perfectly cinched around his neck informed me that he was on the job. I crossed to him, peeling off my satchel and poncho. The restaurant was warm and full of patrons and quiet chatter. Two sushi chefs worked behind an open counter, while various serving staff carrying trays of rolls, sizzling pans of teriyaki, or individual pots of tea wove between the tightly spaced tables.

I slid into the chair across from Liam, catching him dropping his arm from the corner of my eye, as if he'd expected to shake hands. I tucked my satchel against the wall, reaching into it to make sure that Ed was comfortable.

"Sorry I'm late," I said.

Liam sat back down. "You texted."

He had already ordered a California roll. And I was absolutely starving. The Academy claimed to serve sushi on Friday evenings, but it was total garbage in comparison to the quality to be found on practically every street corner in Vancouver. I reached across, stole a piece of his roll, and dipped it in his full soy sauce dish.

"Wait…" he said.

I popped the roll in my mouth, chewing as I readied a flippant comeback about stealing food from a police detective—and then heat exploded in my mouth, streaking back and through my throat and nasal passages. The sensation filled my head. I choked, chewing frantically.

Liam tried to press a glass of water into my hands. I waved him off, swallowing, then attempting to drown the heat with a large swig of his green tea instead.

The tea was too hot, singeing my tongue. My eyes watered.

Liam grimaced in commiseration. But the sorcerer was also blatantly trying to not laugh.

I glared at him, dabbing at my weeping eyes with a paper napkin. "You put wasabi in your soy sauce."

"I do." He grinned widely, giving up on suppressing his amusement.

"A lot of wasabi."

"Yes."

I tried a sip of water. "Well, my sinuses have never been clearer."

Liam laughed, a warm, deep chuckle. His dark-hazel eyes rested on me with an open, friendly expression.

"I'm glad I amuse you, sorcerer."

"That makes two of us."

I poured some unadulterated soy sauce into my empty dish, then stole a second piece of Liam's California roll. It was far, far tastier without the wallop of wasabi.

Liam, still grinning, dipped just the edge of a piece in his own soy mixture—not allowing the entire end to soak like I had—then popped it in his mouth. I really should have noticed the green tinge to the liquid. He winked at me, chewing.

I pulled my phone out of my satchel, leaning across the table toward him. "I found more blank spots."

He blinked as if confused by the topic change.

"At Mountain View," I said. "That's nine in total."

Liam took a sip of his tea. "You went back this morning and scanned the rest of the cemetery?"

I nodded, glancing over the names and dates I'd jotted down in my notes app.

"No wonder you needed a nap."

I shrugged. "Picking up impressions is a mostly instinctual-level casting."

"You need to eat." He raised his hand, and one of the serving staff popped over to our table. The place was chock-full with the lunch crowd—lots of singles—including the sushi bar. "Do you want to share a couple of boxes?"

Boxes were the best way to get a mixture of dishes on a small enough scale for two people to share. "Yeah. As long as one has teriyaki chicken and the other sashimi. No pork or beef. Unless you want it."

Liam shook his head. "I'm fine with chicken or fish."

"Box A with chicken," the server said, jotting a note on her pad. "And box C."

"Thank you."

The server hustled off. Another of the wait staff crossed by the table, pausing to pour me tea and water, then to top up Liam's drinks.

"This is one of my favorite sushi places."

"I know," Liam said, eating another piece of his roll. "I asked Peggy."

I glanced up from my phone, eyeing the sorcerer. That was odd. I had assumed he'd picked the location because he was working in the area, since it was a little out of the way. The restaurant was, however, easy to get to from my mother's place in Shaughnessy, so if it was my turn to pick up takeout for games night or movie night, I usually ordered from here, then drove down the hill to the Talbots.

Liam smiled, then nudged the last three pieces of his California roll toward me. "I hadn't actually eaten sushi until coming to Vancouver."

The navy suit brought out the blue shards in his eyes. Or maybe it was the filtered sunlight through the window. The leaves of the oak trees lining the street were a deep golden brown, still half clinging to their branches. If the wind picked up anytime soon, it would strip the last of them.

"Eat, Mory," Liam said. His tone was low, intimate. "You just expended a lot of magic on not much sleep."

I shook my head—not disagreeing with him, but so that I stopped staring at him. I took another piece of the roll, chewing thoughtfully as I passed him my phone with the note open on the screen. "The spots I found range over the last eight decades. Which is super odd."

"Another one unidentified," Liam murmured, running his thumb up the screen to scroll.

"Yeah. And one blank per decade."

"Tanya's parents didn't do anything to her remains that might have altered them."

"What? Really?"

"And I tell you…" He grimaced, his attention still fixed to my notes. "That wasn't awkward to bring up at all."

The server abruptly appeared beside us, holding two black-and-red box trays. We both shifted back. I hadn't realized I'd been leaning toward Liam so intimately. And he to me.

The server set the meals down, along with miso soup and a bowl of white rice each. "Enjoy!"

"Thank you," we murmured at the same time.

I took inventory of the bits of bounty arrayed before me. Teriyaki chicken, another California roll, two mini spring rolls, a green salad, and three pieces of sushi—tuna, salmon, and ebi. Liam's box had mixed veggie tempura, tuna-and-salmon sashimi, gyoza, and the green salad, as well as what looked like a dynamite roll.

Liam turned his attention back to my phone. "Do you mind if I email this to myself and Tony?"

"Go ahead. I already emailed Tony." I freed my chopsticks from their paper wrapper, cracked them apart, and rubbed them together to remove any shards. "He's got an interactive map of the cemetery he programmed. So once I pick up a laptop from him, I can make notes all in one place, for each interment."

"He created a map? Of the cemetery?" Liam narrowed his eyes thoughtfully. "In a single night?"

"Um…no? I think he's been working on it since I first talked to him about the blank spots. Back when…" I waved my chopsticks, feeling too tired to dredge up and hash through the past.

"Right." He set my phone on the corner of the table near my left elbow, then selected a piece of raw salmon. He dipped the sashimi into his souped-up soy sauce.

I pulled my phone closer, scanning through the dates again. The unidentified eight-year-old male in September 1945. Tanya in 2017. Seven other children in between. I nibbled on some of the bean sprouts tucked under my teriyaki chicken as I looked up to gaze out the window.

Outside, a tall, slim woman in her midthirties was standing underneath the nearest oak tree. Tucked into a green knit beret, her red hair was practically orange. She turned away as I glanced toward her. Her eyes were hidden behind huge, reflective tortoiseshell sunglasses. But I would have sworn she'd been staring at Liam.

"Friend of yours?" I muttered, eating a piece of ebi sushi and sounding a bit more put out than I'd intended.

Liam followed my gaze, cranking his head over his shoulder to do so. The woman crossed toward the front entrance of the restaurant. "Never seen her before."

"Bit old for you anyway."

Liam's tone became suddenly clipped. "Oh, yeah? You think I just line up my secret liaisons out the door, just in case one falls through?"

I snorted. "Probably. Though as far as I know, you aren't terribly secretive about it."

Liam's gaze flicked over my shoulder. I caught the sound of the door closing, presumably behind the red-haired woman.

I felt bad about poking at him. His sisters teased him about his 'come-and-go harem' all the time. And I'd been teasing as well, but it hadn't come across like it. At least I was fairly certain I'd been teasing.

"It's none of my business."

"There's nothing going on that…" Liam shook his head. "I'm not currently dating anyone."

"Sorry. I'm not…we're trying to talk about the case, and I'm distracted by exhaustion and hunger."

He nodded, letting the topic drop. Though his expression remained tight as we ate in silence for a while.

Liam reached across with his chopsticks and stole a piece of chicken. "We're sharing, right?"

"Right. I'd like that piece of tuna."

"It's yours."

I took a slice of his sashimi, soaking it in soy, then letting it practically melt in my mouth.

Liam smirked at me, then took the second mini egg roll from my box. Which was fair, because I'd already eaten the first.

"The ten-year spacing is weird, though. Right?" My thoughts were circling back to the annoying mystery of the blank spots. "I mean, it isn't a perfect ten years. But if Tanya's parents insist they didn't do anything to her remains, I should have been able to pull an impression from them. I'm ranked highly sensitive. One level below top tier."

"There are rankings for necromancers?"

"According to the Academy."

Liam grunted thoughtfully.

"So it's, like, almost a pattern."

"From September to January? That's a five-month range." So he had noticed the spread of the dates already. "Probably just a weird coincidence."

I looked at him, a sudden and completely un-welcome thought occurring to me. "You know when coincidences aren't weird?"

Liam grinned at me as if playing along. "When?"

"When magic is involved."

He shook his head. "Tanya didn't have a drop of magic in her. Neither do her parents."

"I could argue that you might not be sensitive enough to pick it up."

"Fine. I'm 95 percent certain. I've shaken their hands. Someone would have to be a hell of a lot more sensitive than me to pick up anything in that 5 percent gap."

"There are more sensitive Adepts. Jade…the vampires…"

The vampires.

An uncomfortable shock zinged down my spine. Could a vampire drain a soul along with a person's blood?

"What is it, Mory?" Liam whispered. He glanced around us, suddenly on high alert. Both his hands were under the table.

He'd thought I was reacting to an exterior threat. I didn't know Liam well, but I wasn't certain I'd ever seen him quite so keyed up as he had been the last two days. This case was eating at him. Maybe it was just his ego being tweaked by not being able to solve the murder of Tanya Atkinson. But I had a feeling it was something more to do with his protective in-stincts being in overdrive. Instincts honed by years of looking after his adopted sisters, Bitsy, Gabby, and Peggy.

And I had no doubt that my return was adding to that. Just as he'd watched over me through the entire incident with the elves.

"It was just a nasty thought," I whispered, pulling his attention to me. "One that results in a question needing to be asked of one of the only Adepts I make it a habit to avoid bumping into."

Liam grimaced. "Can you relay it through Jasmine?"

"How did you know I was talking about Kett?"

"You're a necromancer," he scoffed. "The only Adept who could possibly creep you out is a master of the undead."

"That's not a compliment. Like, not in any way."

He laughed quietly, chopsticks back in his hand now. Rather than the gun that I was fairly certain he'd pulled under the table.

"You can't ask a powerful Adept questions about their magic via email. Hell, you're not supposed to ask them face-to-face. You might have to officially hire me?" That came out as a question, though I'd meant it to be a statement.

Liam grinned teasingly. "I'm not sure about working together officially, Mory."

I frowned. "Why not?"

He lost the smile, shaking his head slightly while he snagged a piece of the dynamite roll and dipped it lightly in his wasabi-soy-sauce mixture.

I had clearly missed something. I was way better at communicating with dead things than I was with people. Plus there was something about Liam Talbot that rattled me in general.

"Someone could be blocking you, right? That's the other possibility with the blank spots." He popped the roll in his mouth.

"Sure. Total possibility. But why would an Adept go out of their way to block a necromancer? And to only block me from reading nine graves? That's super specific. And again, that suggests magic is part of the equation."

He stilled, looking at me for a moment as if testing out my haphazard theory in his mind. Then he nodded, grimacing. "You think we have a serial killer."

I did. That was what my gut had been screaming at me. Because as soon as Liam had voiced the possibility, an annoying buzz settled—a buzz that had been dogging me since I'd tried to touch Tanya's essence and failed. "Yes. And you do too. That's what's been bugging you about Tanya's case. That's why you're all riled up."

"I'm not all riled up."

"You so are."

"Mory," he said, exasperated, "you'd know if I was riled up."

That gave me pause. I wasn't totally sure we were still talking about the blank spots, or murdered children.

He cleared his throat. "You were saying…?"

It took me a second to pick up the thread of the conversation. "I was saying I'm not infallible. But someone is either sneaking around and doing something to somehow corrupt remains in the cemetery…like some sort of weird scientific experiment…with, like, I don't know…radiation?"

"Something to investigate."

"I'm sure we can look into more than one possibility at a time."

He ate another piece of salmon sashimi, waving his chopsticks as if prompting me. "Or…"

"Or…" I said grimly, glancing at the notes on my phone again. "About once a decade, an unknown Adept is hunting children in Vancouver, stealing their souls, and somehow staying under the witches' radar."

"And what kind of Adept consumes souls?"

I shook my head. "I have no idea. It's not a necromancer. I just trained for eighteen months, learning as much as I could about soul magic. Some of it's frowned upon, but it's the exact opposite of consuming."

"Summoning a soul is frowned upon? Or tying a soul to another corpse, or…" Liam left that line of questioning open-ended, perhaps not wanting to articulate any other possibilities of what I was capable of conjuring.

My stomach soured. Yes, even I got creeped out by the abilities I could wield—at least in theory. "Yeah. But the corpse…the body that soul was originally anchored in, still retains enough energy that a necromancer could read it on a basic level at least. Maybe even pull up a shade."

"Because a shade or a ghost is different than a soul or a spirit."

"Yes."

Liam sat back, chopsticks idle in his hand. "Well, it's not a sorcerer either. Even black magic…" His gaze flicked to me.

Yeah, I knew all about dark sorcerers. "I know. We're looking for an Adept who strips every last imprint of a spirit from a corpse. As if that person never existed."

"Jesus," Liam muttered.

I didn't like the sound of that either. "Maybe…maybe the deaths of the children are happenstance. Maybe it's the remains that have been targeted, after death. Like…" As I spoke, my mind flashed back to the crimes that my brother and Jade's sister, Sienna, had been convicted for. "Like maybe an unknown ritual, or old magic that's been suppressed. Witches are big on hiding black magic spells and dark artifacts, right? You know that Pearl has books she's never going to let Benjamin read, or even index." I personally knew of at least one spellbook that Sienna had gotten her hands on—and over a dozen people who'd paid for that security breach with their lives.

"There's only one way to confirm that."

I nodded, understanding what he was thinking. We would need to enlist a witch, dig one or two of the interments up, and test the remains for magic that

I, as a necromancer, couldn't pick up. "Not Tanya," I said.

"No." Liam's agreement was immediate and brusque. He glanced at his watch—he still wore the old-fashioned kind—then tossed his napkin to the side of his plate, raising his hand for the bill.

"So that still leaves a witch as a possibility."

He shook his head, pulling out his wallet. "We can confirm with Pearl, but it's not a witch."

I was pretty certain he was right. I picked up my phone and tapped out a text to Jasmine.

I need to meet with Kett. As soon as possible. It's work related. I think some asshole Adept has been killing kids in Vancouver for the last eighty years.

Then I edited the text, deleting Kett and replacing it with the ancient vampire's titles—elder and executioner of the Conclave—instead. That seemed more official. I hit send. And only then realized I probably should have added a personal note. I sent a second text.

Oh…and hi! I'm back in town.

"I'm going to need a contract," I said. "Kett will definitely be a stickler for that sort of thing. Assuming he even lowers himself to meet with me at all."

Liam thrust his hand across the table. "Morana Novak, I'd like to hire you to investigate the death of Tanya Atkinson. I believe she was murdered by an unknown Adept, possibly a serial killer."

I wrapped my hand around his. I'd had no idea he knew my full name. His skin was warm, numerous shades darker than my own, and his grip firm. "I'd be happy to help you. My standard rates will apply."

I had no idea what those rates were, actually.

Liam nodded, and then some sort of energy shifted between us, settling over the back of my hand and wrist. That was surprising.

"Magic?" I whispered. "A magical binding?"

He nodded. "I'm surprised your necklace allowed it."

I sat back in my chair, belatedly remembering to release his hand. My skin felt chilled after I let go of him, so I tugged the sleeve of my sweater down, fisting it in my hand. And, yes, I was in layered knits. The thin, mostly dark-purple sweater I was currently wearing had taken me months to knit. The colorwork yoke and cuffs—a wrought-iron gate pattern in teal with a pop of fuchsia for each of the four petal flowers—had actually been the easiest part. It was the body and arms that had bored me nearly to death. Mind-numbing, seemingly endless rows of fingering-weight stockinette stitch. Thankfully, the Academy had Netflix.

My phone vibrated. I glanced at the screen as a series of messages popped up. "Text from Jasmine…"

>*6:15 P.M. The penthouse.*

>*Welcome back.*

>*:P*

I snorted. "Kett has agreed to meet. Tonight."

"I'll come with you."

"You better believe you will." I was not suffering through an audience with the executioner on my own. Necromancers didn't willingly wander into the lairs of ancient vampires without backup. And a spelled silver stake. But I didn't have a stake, or any ability to use one. I had no doubt that Liam Talbot carried spelled silver bullets, though.

Neither would work on Kett, of course. But there was some comfort in pretending we could fight back if we pissed him off with our questions and he decided to drain us.

The server popped by with the portable Interac machine. Liam glanced at the bill, tapped out a tip on the keypad, and paid.

"To go?" the server asked, gesturing toward the unfinished food.

Liam glanced at me.

"I'm not in a rush," I said. "I'll stay and pick a bit."

The server ripped a receipt free from the machine, handed it to Liam, and took off.

"You need to go?" I asked, though the answer was obvious. Apparently, I liked the sorcerer's company. I blamed my lapse in judgement on having eaten too many meals alone. If cereal could be classified as a meal.

"I do. Sorry."

"No worries. I'm sorry I was late."

I tugged my wallet out of my satchel.

"No," Liam said bluntly.

"Thank you."

He nodded. "How much protection does the necklace give you from the vampires?"

"They aren't going to hurt me. Jade would carve out their hearts."

He leaned forward, his gaze intense. "And if vampires do consume souls along with the lifeblood of their victims?"

"Then Kett will tell us," I said with an extreme lack of conviction. I shored up my resolve. "And if there is a rogue vampire hunting in Vancouver, the executioner is going to want to know. It's his job."

Liam nodded, though he didn't look wholly convinced.

I sighed, relenting. "The necklace blocks all malicious magic. The vampires can't hurt me. No Adept can hurt me. Magically. I can tell you in no uncertain terms that if you grab my ass and I don't want you to, the necklace will try to burn your hand off."

Liam looked impressed, and a little amused. "Personal experience?"

I grinned at him.

"That's a hell of an artifact."

"Yeah, well. We all have our burdens to bear. Mine is being under the protection of the dowser."

He glanced at his watch again.

"Go."

He nodded. "What are you going to do?"

"I'm going to ask Tony to get me as much information on the names on my list as possible."

Liam nodded grimly. "I'll do you one better. I'll pull any case files I can find."

"Email them to me and Tony. So he can include them in his search. He's quicker at compiling than I am."

"I will. But if there's an Adept involved and the witches don't already know it…"

"I know."

He stood, doing up the top button of his suit jacket, then stepping by me. I lifted my hand and touched his forearm. He paused, towering over me.

I tilted my head back so I could meet his gaze. "Thank you for lunch."

He nodded. His expression was tight, distant. Already focused on other things, perhaps. Then, inexplicably, he leaned over as if to kiss me—then caught himself. "You're welcome. Text me the address."

"I will."

Then he straightened, striding down the aisle toward the front door.

The woman with the practically orange hair, who had apparently taken a seat at the sushi bar, watched Liam exit. I did as well. It was a great view, after all, and I wasn't blind. But I also wasn't some random stranger staring at another random stranger. The woman just sipped her tea when she was done, making no move to follow the sorcerer out of the restaurant. Not showing any sign that she actually cared. So apparently, I was so messed up with what I might have been feeling that I was projecting onto random strangers now.

I turned back around and finished off the rest of our lunch. Good food should never be wasted.

FOUR

MY PHONE VIBRATED. ON MY CHEST. I BLINKED SLEEPILY. I HAD fallen asleep on the sectional in Tony's tech lair with a laptop open on my stomach, though the screen was currently in sleep mode.

I groaned, trying to focus on the screen of my phone.

>*Causes of death all listed as heart attacks or undetermined natural causes. In all the files I've found so far.*

"Liam?" Tony asked without turning from his workstation.

"Yep." I texted back, my brain still playing catch-up. I couldn't remember whether I'd been in the middle of a text conversation with the detective or if he'd just started a new thread.

Heart attacks? In children all under the age of eleven?

>*It happens.*
But they'd all been kidnapped?

>*They all appeared to have gone missing for a short period of time and were found dead. Away from home.*

I stared up at the ceiling, working through my muddled thoughts out loud, "Could…I don't know…could the trauma of being kidnapped somehow trigger a heart attack for a kid?"

"Without any physical signs of trauma or injury?" Tony's fingers flew over his keyboards, tapping out different rhythms. "Not sure. But I'm collating the reports as Liam scans them, so we'll have a better overview soon."

I sighed, forcing myself to sit up. I'd apparently fallen asleep in the middle of figuring out how to work with the map of the cemetery that Tony had programmed for me, inputting all the data I'd collected from Mountain View. Tony had bestowed the new laptop and phone on me moments after I'd arrived. A glance at that new phone, which to my mind had looked and worked exactly like my old phone, informed me that it was just after four in the afternoon. So I couldn't have been asleep for long.

Ed was perched on the edge of Tony's desk, looking as though he was contemplating leaping off to get to me. He was wearing what appeared to be a tiny pirate hat on his head. I peered closer. The hat had been meticulously folded out of a bubblegum wrapper and secured with an elastic band.

"Tony," I groaned.

Tony swiveled, glancing at Ed, then at me, grinning. "He likes it."

Ed launched himself from the desk. Immediately plummeting. Tony grabbed him before he hit the floor.

"Dude," the tech sorcerer said, "you ain't a jumper."

I scrambled upright, kneeling on the couch and reaching over the back for Ed. Tony deposited the undead turtle into my hands. Ed wiggled all his limbs. Happily, I thought, though he'd lost the pirate hat during his ill-conceived leap.

"You haven't answered Liam's last text," Tony said, turning back to his keyboards and monitors. "Way to leave a guy hanging, Mory."

I snorted. "Liam isn't a guy."

"Ouch."

"I mean, he's like officially contracted me." I settled Ed in my lap, retrieving my phone to see where I'd dropped the conversation with Liam.

"Even worse," Tony said.

"Have you got all the files now?"

"Five. Liam's still looking for the others." He gestured toward a stream of words running slowly up his top left monitor. "I'm running word recognition software to compile all the terms the files have in common. I keep getting errors, though." He grimaced. "Handwriting," he spat, like that was some hideous disease doomed to kill us all.

"Wow," I said. "That's super useful."

"Please. That's super basic."

I texted Liam.

Tony is compiling a list of common words from the files you've sent so far.

I peered at Tony's screen. A box containing a shorter list was open at the bottom left corner. Most of the words contained there were common, like 'if,' 'and,' and 'but.' But ten or so words were set out in bold. A number at the end of each entry indicated how many times the particular word had been noted so far.

I texted the top seven words to Liam.

Child, natural, causes, coroner, police, officer, investigation…

>*Yeah, T is keeping me in the loop. Thx.*

>*I'll pick you up in an hour and a half. We'll go over our questions before the meeting.*

He was referring to the sure-to-be-utterly-terrifying chat with the executioner of the vampire Conclave, which was scheduled for just after dark. Normally, I wasn't remotely scared of the dark, and Kett could walk during the day anyway. But he was also an ancient, powerful being. I wasn't sure I'd ever exchanged more than two words with him directly. Being in the same room as the executioner made my teeth ache.

But since it was my brilliant idea, I couldn't act like a baby about it. At least not outwardly.

Okay.

I set my phone aside, distracting myself by watching words being added to Tony's scroll. I read the stationary list a second time, noting the tallies ticking steadily upward for each entry. Coroner remained in the fourth spot, after the incidental entries.

Coroner…

Vancouver had had some coroners with long tenures. A TV show had been made about one, years ago. "Hey, Tony. Do any of the cases share a coroner?"

He grunted, shifting slightly in his chair as he tapped a few keys on his left-hand keyboard. He grunted a second time, sounding mildly impressed. "Yeah. A bunch."

"What about the oldest cases?"

He mumbled to himself for a moment. "Charles Wells comes up for the 1956 and 1965 cases…wait…and he was an assistant in 1945. He's dead, though, so you can't talk to him. Plus, since it isn't an official case for Liam, you can't really speak to anyone alive. You don't want to get him in trouble."

"Where is Charles Wells buried?" I asked, mentally crossing my fingers that his family hadn't scattered all his ashes at their cabin or off a favorite fishing pier.

"Buried? What?" Tony asked. Then, apparently remembering who he was talking to, he hissed excitedly. "Right!" His fingers flew over the left-hand keyboard, using all ten digits this time. Windows flashed open and closed, until what looked like a scan of a newspaper article filled the screen. Tony raised his arms in the air and howled, "Mountain View for the win!"

I snorted. "I don't know what you're so excited about."

"I'm totally coming with you."

"You're not going to be able to see anything. Just me, talking out loud."

"What!" Tony swiveled around in his chair, distraught. "I can't see the coroner ghostie?"

"The fact that you call him a ghostie is worth a lifetime ban from Mountain View."

Tony clutched his chest dramatically, feigning pulling out a knife. Then he pointed a finger at me, faked a laugh and slapped his knee. "Lifetime ban from a graveyard…hilarious."

I sighed. "Shades won't manifest unless I lend them a bit of my energy. So I'm the only one who can see them." Except if the tech sorcerer did come along, I could have also held his hand, looping him in on my summoning. But for some reason, I felt reticent to suggest that as an option.

"Oooo, yes. Let's go do that. And film it! I could use some easy money."

"You can't capture a shade or ghost on camera."

"No. *You* can't capture a shade or ghost on camera." He started pulling devices and other electrical things out of his desk drawers. Wires and such.

"I need to shower." I looked down at my crumpled clothing. "And to change before my audience with Kett."

"Your new phone has an excellent camera—"

"I'm not filming the executioner of the Conclave."

"And a recording device," Tony continued, completely ignoring me. "The microphone is sensitive enough that—"

"No, Tony."

"Seriously?"

"Liam will be with me." I tucked my new laptop and Ed into my satchel, squishing my yarn and knitting. I was going to need a bigger bag. "Get him to type you up a report of the conversation."

Tony muttered something under his breath. It sounded mocking.

"What was that?"

"Fine by me. I'm billing Liam for the hours anyway."

That wasn't what he'd said, but I didn't bother pushing him. "Bill me. I'm not sure who's paying yet. But once we figure out what type of Adept we're dealing with, the witches, and possibly the vampires, can fight over jurisdiction."

"Fine."

Pissy much? Geez. "See you later for games night?"

"Where else would I be?"

"Hopefully getting an attitude adjustment."

He snorted. "I want pineapple on my pizza."

"Fine." Apparently, Gabby had texted to tell the tech sorcerer that tonight was my treat.

I took off, already looking for the nearest car share on my phone app. I was slightly worried I was actually going to need to iron something in order to meet with Kett. Like…slacks. I might have to borrow something from my mother.

Ugh. I hadn't thought this career thing through at all.

I WAS BLOW-DRYING MY HAIR WHEN I REMEMBERED I WAS supposed to meet Gabby and Peggy to get manicures before picking up the pizza. I groaned, snatching up my phone just as a text message came through from Liam.

>*I'm here.*

I dashed off a reply.

I left the front door unlocked. I need about another ten minutes.

Then I opened the group text I shared with the twins.

Sorry. Work. Will need to skip the mani but still on for pizza.

I abandoned the hair dryer, racing out of the en suite into my bedroom to tug on the black skirt I'd lifted from my mother's closet. It was a little loose around the waist, but my hips were wide enough to stop it from falling down. I layered a delicate, dark-gray cashmere sweater I'd knit while at the Academy over a black tank top. My gold-coin-laden necklace sat just above the scooped neckline.

Standing in front of the full-length mirror on the wall next to my bureau, I twined an asymmetrical triangle shawl around my neck. The shawl consisted of three colorways—the garter stitch transitioning through sections of textured slip stitches from dark purple into a light blue, with a purple-and-pink speckle in the middle, then back out to a sky blue. The shawl was huge, almost three meters from tip to tip. But it layered nicely around my neck, hanging past my—

A sorcerer was standing in the doorway to my bedroom, leaning against the doorjamb and staring at me. His mouth was slightly open, as if something had thrown him. He was cradling Ed in his hands.

I blinked at Liam, still fiddling with the scarf in the mirror, knotting the longer point so it didn't drag too much on me. "Everything okay?"

The sorcerer shook his head as if waking up. Then he seemed to remember he was holding an undead turtle. "Ed was contemplating the stairs. You look…nice."

I grimaced, crossing to take Ed from him. "I had to borrow a skirt from my mother. I didn't have anything this plain."

His fingers brushed mine, as if he was reluctant to completely let go of Ed. "The skirt isn't plain. It's…" He frowned thoughtfully, then didn't bother finishing the thought.

I shrugged. "Even I know that Kett being an elder of the Conclave is a big deal. Plus executioner. Dressing nicely will make it seem like I…"

"Give a shit?"

I laughed. "Yeah. Professional. You know."

Liam nodded, straightening and smoothing a hand down his jacket. He had changed as well, into a medium-gray suit that hugged his shoulders and tapered to his slim hips. He'd paired the suit with a white dress shirt and a deep-blue tie. His skin looked more golden, his eyes showing more blue.

I looked away, hoping he hadn't noticed me staring. Though it was probably hard to miss, since he'd been looking steadily back at me while I checked him out.

"So…" He cleared his throat. "Your house is really big."

"That it is." I set Ed on the bed next to my satchel. "I just need to finish up."

"No worries." He glanced at his wristwatch. "We have time."

I crossed into the en suite. Liam stepped into the bedroom, then followed me as far as the doorway of the bathroom.

He glanced around, murmuring, "So…questions to ask the master vampire…"

I saw Liam taking in the expanse of the bathroom, which like the house, was huge. Marble flooring and counters. A standalone clawfoot bathtub that I never used. Walk-in shower big enough for two.

Big enough for two?

That was…that idea had never occurred to me before…

I turned to the counter, quashing the misplaced thought as I surveyed my meager collection of makeup—two eyeliners, a pink blush, and three shades of lip gloss. I selected the lighter shade of eyeliner—dark brown—and leaned forward over the counter, peering into the mirror to apply it.

Liam was watching my reflection. He still hadn't finished his thought.

"I think we should just systematically lay out what we've discovered," I said. "As briefly as possible. Kett…um…gets bored easily. I think."

"You know him best."

I sighed. I'd lined one eye darker than the other. I was used to going all in when applying makeup. Bright and bold and not caring what anyone thought. "I don't really know him at all." I smudged the line on both of my eyelids, then gave up. I brushed on a hint of blush, then selected the lightest color of lip gloss—orange. I blinked at the color, then looked at Liam. "This is going to clash, eh? With the hair and the scarf?"

Normally, my dye jobs came out of a box, but I'd made a couple of witch friends at the Academy. One of those—Honey Sherwood—had loved dyeing my hair, hence the multicolored do in purple, pink, and light blue. And yes, it pretty much matched my scarf.

Liam glanced at the lip gloss, then up at me. Then he sort of…paused. Staring at my lips. He cleared his throat, stepping fully into the bathroom to peer down at the two other shades on the counter.

And suddenly the obscenely huge bathroom felt too small.

Liam's shoulder brushed mine, and I became epically aware that I'd never had anyone—let alone anyone of the male persuasion—in the bathroom with me. Or in my bedroom at the manor, for that matter.

"All too dark, I think," Liam finally said. "Good for dinner or clubbing. Your natural color is...I mean, do you have a clear gloss?"

"No." My voice caught in my throat. "Um...lip balm."

"Good enough." He looked at me again, gaze lingering on my lips.

His eyes were darker again. Likely due to the different lighting in the bathroom. But I noticed.

And then I continued noticing. Continued staring...

Something thumped in the bedroom.

Liam spun around.

"It's just Ed," I said. "He's decided he can jump." My heart rate was amped up. My chest felt a little tight. And warm. It wasn't uncomfortable, but it was weird.

I was attracted to Liam Talbot.

And I couldn't blame being sleep-deprived for my reaction anymore.

I was sexually attracted to a sorcerer.

A sorcerer.

about school with someone who was years away from any of the formal training he must have taken felt childish.

"When you were studying," Liam prompted. "Soul magic."

"Yeah." But I changed the subject. "You didn't go to the Academy."

"No. Tony could have, but he's got Jasmine now. As I understand it, she could have taught tech magic at the Academy if she'd wanted to. Before."

I snorted. "Before her special dietary needs." The Academy wouldn't be interested in a vampire wandering their halls now, no matter how talented she was. Not one bit.

"Right. Though I think she's unusual for a fledgling. Especially compared to Benjamin." He glanced over at me, rolling to a stop before the red light at Burrard Street and Broadway. "And Benjamin is different because of his mother."

"Yes." Teresa Garrick was a powerful necromancer. The bone bracelet she'd crafted was designed to help her son control his urges. It had almost killed him once in order to do just that. The sips Benjamin had taken of his mentor's blood had changed him as well. Though I hadn't witnessed the actual exchange of blood and magic, I'd felt the results. Which was something else I hadn't mentioned to anyone, especially not to Benjamin.

"Right." Liam cleared his throat, lifting his foot off the brake to roll forward as the light changed to green and the traffic ahead of us started moving. "My formal training was actually easier to get within the mundane world."

"To be a police officer."

"And then again to make detective. Twice."

I grinned at him. "Still sore about having been on probation, are you?"

He chuckled quietly. "I picked up some stuff, so it wasn't all bad. Plus, the VPD offers lots of additional training. I do what I can without drawing too much attention, taking on cold files, and…"

"And not using your badge unless absolutely necessary," I said teasingly when he didn't elaborate. The persuasion magic layered into Liam's badge was something he wasn't really supposed to use unless the situation was dire. With him being a detective, I suspected that must have been a hard line to draw, especially considering his need to protect everyone.

He snorted but didn't answer. Presumably he didn't want to incriminate himself.

I wasn't quite done with the teasing, however. "Do you have to deliberately miss when you're doing any kind of gun stuff?"

He laughed more robustly. "I'm careful to not surpass the guidelines."

"Like not shooting around corners?" I asked, joking.

"Yeah, like that."

"Wait. You can shoot around corners?"

"Bend the trajectory of bullets?"

"Yeah."

He hummed thoughtfully, driving steadily down the hill toward the Burrard Street Bridge. "You were telling me about soul magic and the transitory hours of the day."

I laughed. "Are you negotiating? A question answered for a question answered? Is that like some interrogation technique?"

"Some people refer to it as being a good conversationalist."

"Who told you that? Your mother?"

He laughed, seemingly involuntarily, as if the reaction had been torn from him. And I couldn't help but grin.

"She also tells me I'm handsome and charming," he added, still laughing. "So I shouldn't believe her about that either?"

Danger. Danger. Trap up ahead, turn back. Turn back.

I glanced out the window, watching the city slip by but not really looking for anything. "There are some Adepts who believe that the energy that fuels us…our spirits, our souls…fluctuates with the time of day. Closer to the surface at dawn and dusk. Like the moon controlling the ocean tides."

Liam didn't say anything.

I toyed with the strap of my satchel, feeling Ed's comforting energy humming away inside the bag.

"This was in a course?" The sorcerer held his hands evenly spaced on the steering wheel. His grip appeared light but sure.

I shook my head. "There really isn't a course for what I do. But I had access to lots of books and guidance. The idea was in the diary of a necromancer who specialized in soul magic, like me. She preferred to cast just before dawn, rather than midnight. She thought that souls would be slumbering through the dead of night." I fell silent. Articulating the idea out loud made it sound really hokey.

"Have you tested her theory?"

"By casting at dawn? Yes. On my last case. In Latvia. A haunting. But it wasn't a ghost."

"A trapped soul?"

"She wouldn't speak to me the first two times I approached, so I went back alone at dawn. Three days ago now. She came to me then. She looked anchored, substantial. We didn't speak the same language." I laughed quietly, the memory still sharp in my mind. "But she took my hand and I told her..."

The car had stopped moving. I hadn't realized we'd arrived. Liam reversed to parallel park, guiding the car into the tight spot effortlessly. I glanced around as people hustled up and down the sidewalks. Kett's apartment building was situated on the downtown side of False Creek.

"You told her?" Liam asked encouragingly. His tone was low and warm. He'd turned in his seat, car keys dangling in his hand, watching me intently. As if what I had to say was important to him somehow.

But then, all sorcerers were collectors in some fashion.

I looked away, shaking my head and reaching for the door latch. "We'll be late."

I climbed out of the car. Stepping over to the meter, I paid for an hour of street parking with the app on my phone before Liam could say anything. He didn't protest, simply locking the car and joining me.

"Ready?" I asked, more for myself than him.

"To officially meet an elder vampire? Why not?" he drawled, thickening his American accent with a wallop of bravado. "It wasn't like this case wasn't already frustrating in the extreme."

I crossed toward the carved-glass entrance of the building. It loomed over us, but more beautiful than intimidating. The panels inset beside the double door were First Nations art, I thought. But I didn't know what animals were depicted there. Ravens? Or maybe eagles? I pressed the buzzer for the penthouse, then stuck my tongue out at what I was pretty certain was a camera.

Jasmine's voice filtered over the speaker. "Don't make promises you can't keep, little necromancer."

Liam snorted from behind me.

The door clicked, allowing us to enter. Liam swept it open, and I crossed past him into the marbled lobby.

"What are the chances this isn't a waste of time?" the sorcerer asked quietly.

"The chances are good," I said, pressing the button for the elevator. We stood, side by side, reflected in the polished steel doors. Him—tall and darkly handsome. Chiseled. Focused. Me—bright haired and wearing my mother's clothing, clutching my satchel. "We just need to intrigue him. He's a collector." I glanced sideways at Liam. "Like you."

Liam's reflection in the steel door frowned. Then he glanced at me questioningly. But the doors whooshed open and I stepped within the elevator. Liam closed his mouth on whatever retort he'd been going to voice, stepping in with me.

I pressed the button for the penthouse. And we instantly sped upward.

Kind of like two tasty appetizers on a serving platter, about to be placed before a prince of darkness. Or maybe the *Emperor of Blood and Annihilation* was a better title for Kettil the executioner.

THE ELEVATOR SLID OPEN TO REVEAL A BRIGHT WHITE HALLWAY. Seemingly endless white walls stretched along a white granite tile floor. A large oil painting hung directly across from the elevator, providing the only color in the immediate area—an unframed, pure white canvas covered in thick, liberally splattered deep-red paint.

"Well, that's not disconcerting at all," I mumbled, stepping out.

Liam followed, standing so close that our arms brushed.

"Really?" Jasmine flowed around the corner to my left. Long dark-gold curls swirled a luxurious riot around her head and shoulders. Her generous curves and creamy-skinned bare legs were barely contained within a brown wrap dress. Silk, I thought, judging by the way it moved with the vampire. Her bright-blue eyes twinkled with mischief. "I thought it was…amusing." She laughed huskily. "Totally on the nose, of course, but hilarious."

If I hadn't known her, that laugh would have had me muttering prayers and reaching for a silver cross. And since neither prayers nor a cross worked against a vampire, it was good I needed neither with Jasmine.

The golden-blond vampire closed the space between us, completely ignoring Liam. She paused with both hands extended toward me, palms down. Her fingers appeared to be tipped in blood, their color a deep, dark red similar to the paint slashed across the painting. Nail polish, I assumed. Though it looked thick…and sharp.

I reached forward obligingly, sliding my hands into hers.

Liam tensed beside me.

Jasmine's grin grew more wicked.

I sighed. She was going to play a round of 'rattle the sorcerer.' A favorite game of hers, and Liam never seemed to catch on to the vampire's deliberately antagonistic performance.

Jasmine drew me forward. The bright pulse of her magic shifted, becoming almost fluid. Seductive. "I've missed you, little necromancer," she said, her voice deepening. She inhaled, her nose only a hand's width from my forehead. She was taller than me, even though she was barefoot and I was wearing my boots. "I've forgotten how good you smell."

A low noise emanated from somewhere in the depths of Liam's chest. He silenced himself a moment after vocalizing the involuntary snarl. Jasmine flicked her gaze over my head, smiling impossibly wide now. Her pupils were blown out, laughing at the sorcerer.

"Tell me you've missed me," she mewed playfully, returning her intense gaze to me. Staring deeply into my eyes as though she were trying to entrance me.

She wasn't, but the sorcerer at my side wouldn't have known that. Not for certain.

"Jasmine," I chided. "You texted every couple of weeks. How could I have really missed you?"

She rocked back on her heels, pouting sexily. She was still holding both my hands, but so gently that I could barely feel her touch. "Nasty, necromancer. You could at least play along for a little bit. I love it when the sorcerer gets his boxers in a bunch."

"How would you know if I wore boxers or not, Jasmine?" Liam asked, his voice chilly.

She flashed him a smile that looked a lot like a predator baring its teeth in anticipation of a great meal.

Apparently the sorcerer and the vampire were working out who was on top in the pecking order of Vancouver's Adepts. Still. Ugh.

Before I could distract them from their seemingly endless 'who is the bigger badass' game, Jasmine cranked her head to the right as if listening to someone. Then she grimaced exaggeratedly. "His majesty is waiting."

"Emperor," I muttered under my breath, indulging in way too much trepidation while lingering in the front hall of a predator's den. My fear, or at least my disconcertion, was probably an aphrodisiac to bloodsuckers. "That's a better title for him."

Jasmine's burst of amused laughter ran up my spine, prickling across every nerve ending. I forced myself to remain motionless. Still chuckling huskily, she dropped my hands, spinning away.

I had to turn my head to avoid getting a face full of golden curls.

The golden-blond vampire disappeared deeper into the penthouse to our left. Liam was standing rigidly beside me, staring after her. A little too fixated for my liking. He really needed to be calm and collected around vampires. As did I. Normally, it took a lot more to rattle him. Jasmine had let him off easy.

I brushed my fingers against the back of his hand, silently asking him if he was okay.

He started, then met my questioning gaze. He answered me nonverbally by capturing, lightly squeezing, then immediately releasing my fingers. "I'm here. I'm just not looking forward to the potential fallout."

"We can hear you," Jasmine called from farther into the penthouse.

"We know!" I yelled back.

She laughed.

I turned my attention back to Liam.

He was smiling slightly now. "How long have you been so fearless?"

"I'm not. I'm just more worried about murdered children than the vampires of the Godfrey coven. A coven that numbers us among their valued members as well."

Liam snorted quietly. Presumably at the thought of a sorcerer being part of a witch coven.

Ignoring him, I tugged off my boots and the hand-knit socks that didn't really match the rest of my outfit, setting them within the otherwise empty hall closet. I had to push on the paneled wall in a few places to figure out how to open it. Then I hung up my wool coat, also pilfered from my mother's closet, slinging my satchel back over my shoulder.

"You know it's only Canadians who do that, right?"

"What? Have hallway closets?"

"Take off their shoes." Liam tugged at the laces of his dress shoes. Oxfords, I thought, but I really wasn't up on men's fashion. Or any fashion, really. Except for the latest trends in handmade knitwear.

"Really? Aren't you just trampling dirt through every house you visit?"

"Yeah," Liam said, amused for some reason. He toed off his shoes and tucked them beside mine in the closet.

I didn't wait for him. The granite tile was cold under my bare feet. I really should have been wearing nylons, but I didn't own any. Nor did I own dress shoes, and my mother's feet were bigger than mine. I presumed that the vampires didn't even notice the chill.

The hall opened up into a grand room, white tile giving way to almost-black hardwood flooring. An open, spotlessly clean kitchen sat to my immediate right, a large glass dining room table ran the length of the floor-to-ceiling windows beyond the kitchen, and a huge living room took up the rest of the open space.

A hypermodern sectional couch in light-gray leather, a number of off-white U-shaped armchairs with uniformly low arms and backs, and a thick white rug that was probably worth fifty thousand dollars on its own made up the primary seating area. The coffee and side tables were glass with just enough metal to hold them up. A huge crystal chandelier coiled down from the vaulted ceiling in the center of the living room. A white grand piano occupied the far corner, and a huge TV hung on the only other windowless wall.

Directly across the room from me, the executioner of the Conclave sat in a dark-gray leather designer recliner. He held a newspaper spread from hand to hand, blocking my view of his head and chest. Like Jasmine, he was barefoot, wearing weathered blue jeans and what appeared to be a navy cashmere sweater—so dark it was almost black. The weave was thin, delicate. What I could see of his skin was beyond pale. As usual.

Other newspapers were neatly folded and arrayed on the coffee table near Kett. At least a dozen in various languages.

Benjamin Garrick sat at the end of the dining room table, a half-dozen leather-bound notebooks spread before him. I was surprised to see him, since the sun was only newly set.

Seated as near to Kett as she could be without sitting on the floor at his feet, Jasmine perched in the sectional, cross-legged, with her laptop balanced on the arm of the couch. A tablet and three phones sat on the leather cushion to her right.

The magic of the vampires seethed in completely disparate ways. Benjamin's power was a bright beacon—one that I usually had to struggle to ignore when we were alone together. Jasmine's energy was a lower, deeper, fuller pulse.

But Kett. Kett. The executioner emanated a dark vortex of power, achingly chilling.

"What murdered children?" Kett asked. His tone was the opposite of warm, but somehow not condescending. More of an absence of emotion. Though he appeared Scandinavian in origin, his English was unaccented.

My brain stumbled, clicking over the events and conversations I'd had since arriving back in Vancouver. I couldn't remember mentioning anything specific about the investigation to Jasmine...ah. Kett had overheard us in the hallway.

"It's a bit of a story," I said, crossing close enough that I could curl my toes into the thick-looped wool rug.

"Do tell."

Benjamin rose smoothly from the dining room table, carrying a notebook and his pen at his side as he drifted into the living room area, pausing just behind Kett's left shoulder.

Liam stepped up next to me. His gaze flicked from vampire to vampire, but he seemed more relaxed than before.

"Might I introduce you?" I asked, floundering around with the expected formalities when addressing an elder Adept of the executioner's power and position.

Kett carefully and precisely folded the newspaper, which appeared to be written in some sort of Asian script. Based on the other papers arrayed on the coffee table, the ancient vampire spoke at least a dozen languages. But then, according to the rumor mill—aka Benjamin Garrick—Kett was over twelve hundred years old.

The executioner's hair was so pale that it was practically white. His eyes were a silvered blue. But I'd seen his other face—all whirling red eyes, long fangs, and sharp claws—so I knew what perpetually lurked just beneath the vampire's icy, chiseled surface. He laid the newspaper over his crossed knee, then tilted his head toward me, ever so slightly.

"Liam Talbot," I said, turning slightly toward my silent companion. "Sorcerer. Weapons specialist. Detective for the Vancouver Police Department."

"Wielder of the shield of persuasion," Kett added dryly. "Bequeathed by the dowser at her oracle's request."

It was totally possible that the vampire was mocking me, amused by my attempt to be formal, professional. But that was difficult to assess, because he otherwise appeared to be carved out of the same white granite that tiled his entranceway.

Benjamin twitched, then flipped open his notebook and jotted something down. Most likely the title that Kett had just given Liam's police badge, which was now technically also a magical artifact.

I ignored the ancient vampire's amusement. A twelve-hundred-year-old Adept of power could trample all over the rules if he wanted, but I wouldn't get far doing so. "Kettil, elder and executioner of the Conclave," I said. "Sire of Jasmine, mentor of Benjamin."

Jasmine laughed quietly. "Oh, the bindings of blood, how they do chafe."

I had no idea what she was talking about.

"Pleased to finally meet you, Kettil." Liam nodded his head in a slight bow, but didn't step forward or offer to shake hands. As a rule, Adepts didn't touch each other. Magic passed too easily skin to skin.

"Likewise." Kett flicked his disconcertingly flat gaze to me. "The murdered children?"

"I'll have Tony send Jasmine the exact details of the cases we've linked together. But to give you the short version, I returned home yesterday and Liam asked me to raise a shade at Mountain View cemetery."

"A nine-year-old girl." Liam picked up the narrative. "The child of a colleague. She died in 2017."

"Of?" The vampire arched one pale eyebrow. "Exsanguination?"

"No," I said. "The coroner listed natural causes."

"But you know differently."

"The gravesite is blank."

Kett stared at me, expressionless.

I waited, hoping I'd baited the hook just the perfect amount. Getting an elder's attention was one thing, but holding it was near impossible sometimes.

Benjamin looked up from his notebook. Jasmine's fingers tapped lightly on the keyboard of her laptop.

Kett flicked the neatly folded newspaper onto the coffee table. It landed—quite impossibly—perfectly in line with the others arrayed there. "And you are certain the remains haven't been removed."

I suppressed a shudder over the casual display of power from the master vampire. "As far as I can tell," I said. "They could have been corrupted somehow, though…maybe by magical means? We're thinking of checking the older sites for residual."

Kett's lips twitched. "Grave digging? How oddly appropriate." His gaze flicked to Liam. "And highly illegal."

The sorcerer's lip started to curl as he formulated his retort.

"Yes," I interjected before Liam could piss off the ancient vampire. The elderly liked to be right. About everything. "And I've identified the coroner on three of the oldest cases. I'll raise and question his shade tonight as well."

"Explain what you mean by 'blank,' necromancer." The command in Kett's tone was laced with magic. It settled over my shoulders and collarbone. And then the magic of the coin-laden necklace hidden under my tricolor shawl welled up and…ate it. That was how it felt, at least.

Kett laughed quietly, as if he'd also felt the necklace's response and it delighted him. "My apologies," he murmured. "When you surround yourself with powerful beings, it is easy to forget how vulnerable others can be. I will watch my tone. Please continue."

Okay, then. "When a necromancer focuses on a gravesite, or any set of remains really, she should be able to easily discern basic information about the deceased."

Benjamin interrupted. "Including animals?"

Kett flicked his gaze to the dark-haired vampire. "Not germane, Benjamin."

"No. I'm sorry."

"It depends on the necromancer," I said, keeping my gaze on Kett steady, even though Benjamin's focused regard prickled intriguingly across the right side of my face and neck. "I'm ranked highly sensitive. I can pick up, at minimum, cause of death, sex, gender, and age for most organisms. Whether the whole corpse remains or simply a portion, including ashes. Spiders give me trouble. And I can't read bugs or invertebrates at all."

Kett leaned back in his chair. One hand on his crossed knee, languid. Poised.

Interested.

That was good. I had his complete attention. I just needed to keep it.

I felt the moment Benjamin looked away from me, returning his attention to his notebook. I almost swayed toward him, but I was also instantly relieved to be released from the magic that underlaid his focused regard. Now that was odd.

"There are nine blank spots at Mountain View cemetery," I continued. "Nine children. All of whom, as best we've pieced together, went missing from their homes for a short period of time, or were never actually identified. And then died, of supposed natural causes."

Kett flicked his fingers. "Heart attacks and the like."

"Yes." Liam's resonant voice was a sharp contrast to the smooth icy tone of the vampire.

"I can sense remains of some sort within the interments," I said. "But no energy imprint. Their souls are missing."

Kett nodded, a quick dip of his chin. "Or misplaced."

Misplaced, yes. I'd had the same thought. My heart started beating faster, anticipating Kett's next words and the confirmation that I wasn't just making things up, or misinterpreting the situation. Apparently, I still craved the validation of my elders.

Benjamin's pen stilled. His head tilted toward me, though his attention remained on his notebook. Most likely transcribing our conversation, but pausing to home in on me. Which didn't help with my heartbeat issues.

I cleared my throat. "What do you mean?"

Though he was still looking at me, Kett didn't answer. Instead, he flicked his gaze to Jasmine.

She nodded. "I've got the files and the initial breakdown from Tony. I'll read through it."

Kett nodded, returning the full force of his attention to me. My skin didn't prickle under his regard. Either Kett's control was just that much better than Benjamin's—and I would have been surprised if that wasn't the case—or their magic was different.

Speaking of magic, apparently Jasmine and Kett could communicate telepathically. Or Kett had been, at least. Jasmine had answered her master out loud, just as when she'd been listening to something while we were in the hall.

Before picking up on that little nugget, I would have said that nothing could possibly be worse than being hunted by an invulnerable, ridiculously strong predator who could move faster than I could see.

But knowing that vampires could also communicate telepathically while hypothetically hunting me down ratcheted that little nightmare right up.

And there was that necromancer-ingrained prejudice. Again. I knew better. I knew that these three vampires would never hurt me. That, in truth, they valued me in different ways. But my instinctual magic informed me that my rational mind was a moron for believing I could stand in the same room as three vampires and survive.

My heart had a completely different spin on it all as well. But only because Benjamin was among the three.

We were standing in silence. Liam was a warm presence to my right.

"Executioner…" I started, then faltered. I should have used his other title—elder—given what I was about to say.

"Ask me what you are here to ask, little necromancer," Kett said.

I nodded, meeting his gaze steadily, though I knew a vampire could ensnare with mere eye contact. But not me, I reminded myself. My necklace warded my mind against the vampires. "When a vampire drains a victim…"

"Murders," he said wryly.

"Yes. Though I know that's not your way."

"Do you?"

"Yes." I firmed my tone. "I'm not some ignorant witch or prejudiced necromancer." My gaze flicked to Benjamin. "I know that vampires don't kill indiscriminately."

"Some vampires," Jasmine muttered darkly, not looking up from her laptop.

Kett settled his gaze on her bowed head. "What vampire do you know who is killing humans?"

She waved her hand. "You know, all the ones you murder in return."

Kett sighed, a noise that contained as much emotion as I'd ever heard from the ancient vampire. "Please continue, necromancer."

He bit off my title sharply, presumably indicating he'd accept no more interruptions from his vampire crew.

"When a vampire wholly drains their victim, do they somehow also consume their soul?" I asked steadily. "Their life force, their energy, if you prefer."

"Soul is fine for the purposes of our discussion."

I nodded. "Soul, then. The murders are spaced about ten years apart, the victims all within three or four years of each other in age. All went missing, or were never identified, before their deaths. Of seemingly natural causes. But I should be able to pick up something, anything, from the sites. From their remains."

"But they weren't bled out."

"I'm not…I'm not accusing a vampire—"

"Why else would you be here?"

I shrugged. "The consumption of blood seems to me…seems to be the same as the consumption of life force."

"I see the parallel you've made."

"I'm just trying to eliminate possibilities. To focus the investigation. And you are the oldest Adept I know." I made a bit of a mental leap, pressing forward. "You would know, for example, if every ten years, a vampire would…need to take a soul, not just blood. To feed, to survive."

Kett went still. Utterly statue still. Not moving, not breathing, not even blinking. All his power, which I would have expected he was already holding tightly reined, folded in on itself.

Jasmine looked up from her laptop, then over at me. "I hate it when he does that. I'd get something to drink. This might take a while."

"What?" Liam asked. "Really?"

"If you had twelve-hundred-plus years of knowledge stuffed in your head, and a little necromancer came along asking obscure questions, how long would it take for you to access that database?"

"I'm not that little," I grumbled.

Jasmine flashed me a toothy grin. "There's water and…well, water."

Kett still hadn't moved. I set my satchel on the section of the couch nearest me and pulled Ed out to let him wander. He would love the rug.

Liam was looking a little lost, casting his gaze around. Benjamin was bent over his notebook.

Jasmine was managing her laptop, a tablet, and a phone at the same time.

I wandered into the kitchen, where the dark hardwood flooring transitioned to more white granite tile. I had to open up three empty cupboards before I found a set of heavy crystal wineglasses.

Liam had followed me into the kitchen. I stepped over to the huge stainless steel fridge, trying to decipher the instructions for retrieving ice and water from it.

"What the hell?" Liam whispered, leaning close. His breath warmed my temple and cheek.

"Fugue state," I murmured back. "Also...there's the possibility he knows the answer but won't tell us. You're prepared for that, right? He is the executioner of the Conclave. If we are hunting a vampire..." I trailed off, meeting Liam's gaze.

He nodded his understanding, though he didn't look happy about it. No, Liam Talbot wanted to kill the monster we were hunting. Or if it was somehow a regular human who'd murdered Tanya Atkinson, then he wanted to be the person who incarcerated them.

I, however, wasn't an executioner. Or a judge. Or a jury. I was simply a highly specialized investigator. And happily so.

If Kett wanted to solve my case and deal with the bad guy, I had absolutely no issue with that. The nine dead children would be avenged. I'd eat pizza and hang out with everyone at games night, then go home and start figuring out my immediate future.

I turned back to getting us something to drink. "Ice?"

"Yes, please."

I clicked the button for ice, releasing a few cubes from the dispenser, then filled the heavy wineglass with water, offering it to the sorcerer. I poured myself a glass as well, no ice.

Liam drained his glass, then started chewing on a piece of ice.

Phantom nails scored the back of my neck. I nearly spit out a mouthful of water. "Ew, sorcerer! Stop that."

He paused, staring at me in disbelief. "Really? Me chewing ice is what puts you off in this situation?"

I huffed. "At least suck on it quietly."

A wide grin spread across his face. "Oh, I can suck quietly."

I snorted.

Jasmine laughed.

I glanced at her—all the way over to the other side of the large suite where she could still hear our quiet conversation—then back at Liam. Pointedly. "Teasing about sucking in a penthouse full of vampires might be in bad taste, sorcerer."

He laughed. "Well, you know I'm still learning the rules. Is talking about sucking—with you—permissible elsewhere?"

Jasmine actually looked up from her laptop—it was usually impossible to pull her attention completely away from any tech—laughing at us quietly.

I bumped Liam with my shoulder. "I'm trying to be professional."

He raised his hands in surrender, still holding the wineglass. Then he made a show of tipping another piece of ice into his mouth.

And sucking on it.

While looking at me.

His gaze dropped to my mouth, which was…possibly…hanging open slightly.

I stared at him. Sucking on a cube of ice…

I was staring.

I needed to stop staring.

I forced myself to look away, taking a sip of my own water. Then, once I had myself under control, I wandered back into the living room area. I wasn't interested in the sorcerer's teasing. I was serious about being professional. If Kett was willing to share information, either directly or through Jasmine and Benjamin, he would be a valuable resource for any necromancer.

The fact that that was only true because vampires had systematically attempted to wipe necromancers from the face of the earth, completely snuffing out entire bloodlines centuries ago, didn't change the present circumstances.

I started to settle on the sectional beside Benjamin, but Liam nudged me toward Jasmine's side of the coffee table.

The golden-blond vampire laughed at the sorcerer. "Really? You think I'm less likely to bite Mory?"

"No." Liam's tone was stiff. "I think there's a better chance you'd put yourself between Mory and Kett. If it came to that." He sat one couch cushion away from Benjamin.

The dark-haired vampire didn't appear to be paying attention to the conversation, but I knew he was storing every word, every sentence in his mind even while not actively transcribing them into his notebooks. Obsessively, perhaps. But there were worse things for a vampire to obsess about.

Jasmine flicked her gaze to Benjamin, then eyed the sorcerer. "The only person in this room who has any possibility of hurting Mory is you, sorcerer."

"I think I've proven myself to you enough for one lifetime, vampire."

She shrugged belligerently. "One lifetime perhaps. But I'm currently on my second go-around."

"Okay," I interjected. "Enough. You are all big and bad. I'm the tiny vulnerable one. You all protect me. Equally. Fine?"

Jasmine smirked. "Argument won. Point to the necromancer."

Benjamin flicked his eyes toward me, head still bowed, dark hair falling across his forehead. A smile ghosted across his lips. I returned it.

Liam followed the direction of my gaze, frowning. Then he tipped his glass back and started chewing on ice again.

Asshole.

"So, the Academy." Jasmine's fingers flew over the keyboard of her laptop. "Did you enjoy it?"

"Totally." Ed came over to sit on my foot. I wiggled the toes of my other foot, and he playfully snapped at them.

"Did they make you register Ed?" she asked.

"Yeah. But the records are sealed."

Jasmine snorted.

"Okay, well…the records are sealed except to people like you."

"It's a good thing there aren't many of me in the world."

I scooped Ed up and placed him on the couch between us. He immediately made a beeline for Jasmine's thigh, which he was unsuccessful in scaling. The golden-blond vampire tickled him under the chin.

"Who'd be interested in me?" I asked.

"It's the dowser the Adept world is interested in," Jasmine said. "You had to register your necklace as well, yes? And they made you declare the maker?" She touched the long gold chain that hung around her own neck, decorated with a cluster of tiny cubes at the end.

My witch friend Burgundy had told me that those cubes glowed with blue witch magic, but I couldn't see it. They were reconstructions—tiny magical recordings. How they were significant to Jasmine, I didn't know. The dowser had added magic to the necklace itself, at the behest of the oracle prior to all of us laying siege to the elves' stadium stronghold. With that magic, the golden-haired vampire could render herself practically invisible.

"We all expose her," Jasmine added thoughtfully.

"Jade can't walk through this world without people noticing," Liam said chidingly. "That isn't Mory's responsibility."

Jasmine opened her mouth, possibly to bite the sorcerer's head off. But Kett abruptly turned, pinning his silvered gaze on me.

Everyone else went very still.

I settled Ed on my lap, laying my hand over him, grounding myself in the magic embedded into every one of his undead cells. Then I scooted forward on the couch, perching on the edge and bowing my head slightly under Kett's disconcertingly fixed gaze. "Your counsel is greatly appreciated, elder."

He inhaled deeply. He hadn't been breathing. Then he sighed quietly. "Yes. I suspect Jade would not be pleased with what I'm about to share with you. Or Pearl, for that matter. Though for different reasons."

"Okay."

"You will not hunt this creature, Mory," Kett proclaimed coolly.

"What am I? An idiot? I leave the hunting of psychopathic monsters to the…"

"Psychopathic killers?"

I swallowed. "You know. Those of you with the strength and the swords…and the…"

"Teeth?" Kett smiled, revealing perfectly even, perfectly straight teeth.

If he came for me, I'd be dead before I even saw him move. And now that my memory had been jogged by the spike of terror I was currently trying to ignore, I recalled when I'd seen Kett survive a killing blow from a knife created by Jade. What were the chances that the necklace I wore would actually protect me from him?

My heart hammered in my chest. I breathed against it, calming myself. Ineffectually. "Right."

He shifted back in his chair, settling one hand on the arm and one on his knee. "Your evidence is thin."

"Yeah. I'm still gathering it."

He nodded. "I'll have some books shipped to Benjamin, but I can tell you what little I know of this eater of souls…"

My heart was pounding again, guts churning. But for a different reason now. As if some visceral part of me didn't want to be right. Didn't want to know that there was a creature targeting children and consuming their souls.

Unchecked.

For decades.

We were all staring at Kett, hanging in the silence.

He was staring at me. His tone deepened, intensified. "You will not hunt this creature, Mory. But…" He glanced at Liam. "I will not deny you the right to collect the evidence as you have already laid it out. Pearl Godfrey and the Convocation will require it."

"And you?" Liam asked cuttingly. "Will you hunt the eater of souls?"

Kett eyed him coolly. "Not if I don't have to. A conversation might do. A…redirection."

"Out of your territory?" Liam's tone was sharp, confrontational.

"Yes. Also, as I understand it, she doesn't need to kill to feed. Though perhaps there is something in the ten-year pattern Mory has described. Perhaps she needs to kill once a decade, but can simply sip from her victims in the in-between."

"What are we dealing with?" I asked, my voice thinner than I would have liked. "And you said 'she.' Do you know her?"

Kett shook his head. "No. But, as with necromancers, I understand this magic passes through the female line."

"Not a vampire."

"A different sort of vampire." Kett's lips twisted into a sneer. "My understanding was that you just specialized in soul magic at the Academy."

It wasn't a question. More of a dig, but with no force behind it. I answered anyway. "You know I did."

Kett flicked his gaze to Jasmine. "Their training is woefully inadequate."

"Jesus, old man," the golden-blond vampire griped. "You just had to dredge the answer out of that vault you consider an educated mind." She was gearing up, as if this was an ongoing argument. "And if all the subsets of Adept didn't hoard information like…like…asshole hoarders—"

"Really?" Kett's tone was amused. "You couldn't come up with—"

"We talked about you interrupting me—"

"Jasmine." Kett's snapped command reverberated around the airy room. Though I didn't think there was any magic behind it. "You are working with Benjamin to rectify those omissions."

"But you aren't going to let us share what we compile."

"We will discuss it at a later date."

Jasmine huffed, exasperated.

"Um…" I tucked my hair behind my ear. It didn't stay. "That's great and all, but—"

"A succubus." Kett settled his gaze on me again. "You…we have a succubus in Vancouver. Though I doubt she resides in the city full time. And her inherent masking must be impressive to have avoided the witches for this long."

Benjamin flipped to a blank page in his notebook. Jasmine's fingers were flying across the keyboard. I imagined the duo working like that for days on end, asking Kett questions and recording his answers.

Except Kett wasn't usually so forthcoming. His minutes-old argument with Jasmine was only the most recent evidence of his predilection for being close-mouthed.

"Why tell me?" I asked.

A slow smile curled over his lips. "A succubus is a rare creature. I've never met one myself. But I've heard tales. Fairy tales. Morality tales. Myths."

"And you are a collector."

His smile widened. "I am."

"You think I can track him or her down."

He laughed quietly.

All the hair stood up on the back of my neck. Ed tucked his head under my thumb. Liam's hand twitched, as if he'd almost reached for his gun.

Yeah, the executioner could layer a lot of creepy into a simple chuckle.

"Yes," Kett said. "I do, soul seer."

"Because a succubus…consumes souls. And I can feel, interact with souls. But…if…" I trailed off, my mind whirling with what the ancient vampire was implying. "You think that a soul…that life force, energy cannot be destroyed."

"I know it can't." Then he gestured to himself with a flick of his fingers. "Simply transformed. As you've done with your turtle."

I met his gaze. A huge pit of fear opened up inside me at what I was fairly certain he had just implied. But I couldn't ask for clarification. Not with Liam in the room. Maybe not ever.

Some information was deadly. Such as the fact that the traditional reasoning for vampires slaughtering necromancers was that those of us with power could control vampires—but it was possible there was another reason. A reason that Benjamin's magic called to me so brightly, so beguilingly. As if it was actually my power, to have and to hold, that animated the younger vampire.

But such a history—the true connection between vampires and necromancers—would have been wiped away with all the bloodlines destroyed by the vampires.

Ed wasn't just the reanimated corpse of my turtle. He was…more.

Vampires weren't just reanimated corpses. They were much, much more. And even though Benjamin doubted he had a soul, I could feel the energy that flowed through him. And through Jasmine and Kett.

So…how had vampires been created in the first place? By what magic?

Or was 'by whose magic' the actual question?

"A conversation for another time," Kett said smoothly, as though he might have been tracking my thoughts.

Liam was glancing back and forth between the elder vampire and me.

I cleared my throat. "Please continue, elder. The succubus is a rare creature who consumes souls…life force energy…in order to survive?"

"I know little else. Likely female."

"Does she appear human like most of the Adept? Or is she different…like the elves?"

"Human, and vain about her appearance, I believe. According to the lore."

"Is she capable of shapeshifting, or using magic to disguise herself? Mind control?" I knew that vampires were capable of all those things, depending on how powerful they were. "And what about strength and speed?"

He curled his lip at me, once again amused. "Strong, but not on the scale you've come to expect. I cannot answer your other questions definitively."

"Still way stronger than me."

"Obviously. Which is why you won't go anywhere near her." He paused, waiting, then added with a hint of impatience, "I haven't heard you promise, necromancer."

"I'm not a hunter. I understand my limitations. I embrace them. I'll just follow up on those leads."

"And you will refrain from any grave digging until we have gathered more information. I'm not interested in bailing you out of jail, then explaining that I had to do so to the dowser."

I opened my mouth to snottily inform the executioner that while I was standing within the boundary of Mountain View, no one—and certainly not any nonmagical member of law enforcement—would be able to see a single thing I did.

Kett raised an eyebrow at me.

I shut my mouth.

"And," the elder vampire continued smoothly, "though I doubt it will come to that, if you do get approval to fully examine the remains, you will be backed by a witch. And not just that…friend of yours."

I huffed out a sigh. He meant Burgundy, though I had no idea what he'd been about to call her before he corrected himself. Burgundy was technically only a quarter-blood witch. The executioner was a snob. "I'll talk to the shades first, see if I can piece together common events…" I looked at Liam, realizing I was on shaky ground. Again, I wasn't actually trained to investigate murders. I just talked to the dead.

"Hopefully we can create a profile and narrow our search parameters," the sorcerer added helpfully.

"Right." I smiled at Liam for the save. "Though it all might be moot if the remains have been corrupted by other means. Like ritual magic or…something of nonmagical origin."

Kett nodded, reaching for another of the newspapers on the coffee table. "A possibility for certain. And also something easily verified when the dowser returns. Benjamin will accompany you."

"Benjamin can't stay with Mory during the day," Liam said tersely.

"That's your task, sorcerer." Kett flicked the newspaper open. It was written in what I thought might have been German.

"I need to work. I have a job."

"Confine your hunt to the evenings, Mory," Kett commanded. "If the sorcerer wishes to be negligent."

Liam clenched his hands. And his jaw.

I interjected. "That's not—"

"We're done for now. Benjamin, you will keep in constant contact with Jasmine."

"Constant?" Jasmine grumbled.

"I'll get my bag." The dark-haired vampire stood, swiftly crossing to the dining table, collecting a couple of notebooks, and stuffing them in his worn leather satchel.

I sighed. Heavily.

Kett flipped a page of the newspaper, not bothering to look at me. "Jade wouldn't be happy if something should befall you, little necromancer."

"Why does that sound like a threat?" I muttered, standing up.

Liam stood as well.

Jasmine snorted, laughing.

"And Benjamin…" Kett continued reading, ignoring us. "If you happen upon this succubus?"

"Bite down real hard," Jasmine said, cackling. "And hang on for the ride."

Kett lowered his newspaper, flicking his silvered gaze to Jasmine. She stopped laughing. The executioner then looked at Benjamin, raising one eyebrow expectantly.

"I grab Mory and run." The dark-haired vampire smiled in my direction, but the expression was tight. Joyless.

"Yes, Benjamin." Kett shifted his disconcertingly flat gaze to me. "You run. Even you can outrun a succubus."

I sighed. "You're such an asshole, you know?"

Liam went still beside me, as if all of his senses were suddenly trained on the master vampire.

Kett grinned widely. "Apparently an appealing trait for some."

I snorted. "Not me."

"Well, it's good you're off limits then, little one."

"Seriously?"

He chuckled.

Jasmine threw back her head and laughed.

Oh, my god. Vampires laughing were all creepy as hell. And I talked to the dead.

Shaking my head, I scooped up Ed. Then I paused, recalling my training. "Thank you for your time and the information, elder."

Kett flicked his fingers at me. I was more than happy to be dismissed. Though my head was filled with too many questions, and I wasn't sure where to get the answers.

"Yes," Liam murmured agreeably. "Your assistance is appreciated."

Kett ignored the sorcerer.

I was halfway back to the elevator with Benjamin and Liam tight behind me, when I realized I was walking away from another valuable resource. I didn't have to do everything myself.

I stopped midstep, spinning back. Benjamin glided around me, but Liam plowed into me, grabbing my upper arms so I didn't face plant on the granite floor.

"What the hell, Mory?" the sorcerer muttered.

"Sorry." I raised my voice. "Jasmine?"

"Already looking," the golden-blond vampire called back. "Though finding nothing."

"Email me links if you do? I can sign in later tonight."

"Will do."

"Thank you."

Liam raised a questioning eyebrow.

"Academy database." I grabbed my boots from the closet, tugging on my socks. "I only have access to the necromancy section, but Jasmine can access all of it. She's the one getting it up to date."

"As much as possible," Benjamin muttered, pressing the call button for the elevator. "There's a lot of resistance. Especially because most Adepts don't work well with technology."

Liam crouched to tie his laces, eyeing the dark-haired vampire, but didn't contribute to the conversation.

Benjamin kept his gaze on the elevator doors. Shoes on, the sorcerer and I joined him. The three of us, side by side with me in the middle, reflected in the polished steel, completely busting another myth—that vampires couldn't be seen in mirrors. None of those sorts of stories were true, it seemed.

Which meant that everything Kett knew about the succubus could be wrong as well.

Vampire. Necromancer. Sorcerer.

A study in contrasts.

I was surprised that Benjamin didn't pull out his notebook and start to sketch us. But then the elevator doors opened and I stepped inside. The other two followed a step behind.

"Succubus," I murmured.

"Yes," Benjamin said.

Liam mashed his finger on the button for the lobby. "You don't have to sound so gleeful about it."

"And there is no need for you to be frightened, sorcerer." Benjamin smiled thinly. "Frightened for Mory...of course."

A muscle in Liam's jaw twitched. "Of course."

The door slid closed, entombing the three of us within.

It was going to be a long night.

FIVE

THE FINAL RESTING PLACE OF THE CORONER WHO HAD BEEN involved in the autopsies for the first three children on my list of blank spots was surprisingly easy to find. After discovering the newspaper article indicating that Charles Wells had been buried at Mountain View Cemetery, Tony had continued digging, texting the location of the plot to me while we'd been meeting with Kett. As coroner, Wells had been involved in a number of sensationalized cases in Vancouver's history, most of which were fairly well documented.

It was fully dark and had clouded over by the time we arrived at Mountain View and followed Tony's directions to the coroner's grave. The large red-marble headstone was ornately carved, capping a double plot that held the interments of the coroner and a Lillian Wells—Charles's wife, I presumed.

Liam and Benjamin stood off to one side while I set up for the summoning. The sorcerer was fielding text messages, and the vampire was still making notes in his black leather notebook. I had no idea how Benjamin wrote so neatly while standing. A vampiric gift, perhaps.

I set my candle at the base of the gravestone, under the carved names and dates for Charles Wells. Though I'd been able to read the remains buried beneath the stone without even trying, so it was unlikely that I would need the focal. Or that I would accidentally summon Lillian instead of Charles. I let Ed out of my satchel so he could free-range in the damp grass, then knelt on the towel I'd remembered to pack earlier. The evening was chilly. Holding a shade long enough to have a conversation would leech my warmth as well. I tugged on the thick-ribbed hat I carried for emergency purposes, though it didn't match my outfit in the least, and found myself wishing I'd brought jeans to change into as well.

Normally, I would have also pulled out my knitting, but I needed both my hands free for this conversation. I closed my eyes, deepening my focus. Letting myself feel my own weight on my knees, firmly grounding myself in the now, in the present. Then I allowed a single tendril of my magic to slip down into the ground and tease the shade forth.

Charles Wells rose easily, eagerly.

I often wondered if the ease with which I could pull a shade forth reflected the personality of the person they'd once been. Had the coroner been helpful and chatty in life?

I opened my eyes. The indistinct head and neck of a balding man hovered before me—sticking out of the ground, really, as if he was standing on top of his coffin.

Well, that was unusual. And seriously creepy, even for me.

"Hi!" I said brightly. It was important to keep a shade's attention focused on me, engaged.

Liam flinched in my peripheral vision, then looked around.

"No Adept can sneak up on Mory in a graveyard," Benjamin said dryly. "No mortal can sneak up on me at all."

I kept my attention on the coroner, missing the withering look the sorcerer was sure to have cast at the vampire. The two of them hadn't exchanged more than three words since we'd entered the elevator at Kett's penthouse. "Why don't you join me up here?" I asked the shade. I really didn't want to have a conversation with just his head. "Come sit in the grass with me. Like a picnic."

"Have you got him, Mory?" Liam asked.

I nodded. The coroner kept his focus on me. Obligingly placing his hands on the ground as if he needed to pull himself up, he crawled out of his grave and settled on his knees across from me. He didn't glance around or seem at all aware of his environment. Which was good. That meant I hadn't fed too much power into him.

Ed trundled over, settling near my right knee to peer up at the ghost. I wondered if the undead turtle saw what I did. Specifically, a grayed-out, indistinct figure of an older man in a suit that might have been navy blue. His jovial face was carved with deeply etched laugh lines and marked by a small, almost square scar on his chin. Wide-spaced eyes. Rounded cheeks. He looked to be in his early sixties, though I knew—courtesy of Tony's research—that the coroner had lived well into his seventies.

That was the other unusual thing about how my particular brand of necromancy manifested. Shades summoned at a gravesite were most often simply a projection of each person's moment of death. But the shades I called forth were often presented in a form that I'd always assumed was how they best recalled themselves.

Yeah, it didn't make a lot of sense to me either. I just knew that it was unusual. More like how ghosts presented themselves, rather than just an echo of the deceased.

I knew that if I held out my hand, if I touched the shade, pumped more energy in, I could bring him forth more substantially. In trials, I had summoned forth ghosts that had remained on our plane of existence for hours afterward, even without me maintaining contact. I'd summoned forth entities so thoroughly that they'd become aware of their surroundings, their situation.

That had earned me the top ranking a necromancer can get in summoning. And it had been a terrible, terrible day. One I hoped never to repeat. To pull a shade forward so far that they understood they were dead was heart-wrenching. And just plain wrong.

I reached my hands out to the sides, offering them to Liam and Benjamin. Earlier, the idea of doing the same with Tony had been off-putting, seemingly too intimate. But now, with Kett's blessing, I could rationalize that the investigation was sanctioned. Therefore, I was working in an official, professional capacity.

And yeah, I got the irony. It was ridiculous that having a vampire's approval could make something feel blessed.

The coroner's shade kept his attention riveted to me. Liam instantly took my hand, his warmth making me realize that I was already chilly. I wrapped my magic around the sorcerer, tugging him closer. Not physically—but that was how it felt to me, as if I were sharing space with him.

"Wow," Liam murmured, gazing at the coroner—able to see him now through my magic. "Can he see us? Hear us?"

"Just me," I said.

Benjamin slipped his cool fingers into my other hand. My skin was warmer than his. His magic welled under my palm, beckoning. I ignored it. It wasn't mine to have or to hold. It settled.

I didn't need to wrap my magic around Benjamin in the same way I'd needed to with Liam. Touching him was enough. He was already almost at the same level of awareness I was. As if he was closer to the grave, for lack of a better way of describing it. Yet another thing that hadn't been mentioned in my training at the Academy. But then, what necromancer worked with a vampire?

"Amazing," the vampire whispered.

I focused on the shade. "My name is Mory. Are you Charles Wells?"

"I am," the shade said. His tone was flat.

Good.

Liam's hand flexed in mine.

"Mory," Benjamin asked, hushed. "Will a recording device work? My phone? I should have asked before."

"No. Sorry." I smiled at Charles. "I'd like to ask you some questions about three of your cases. The first was an unidentified boy that you worked on in the late summer or early fall in 1945. September? I believe he was eight. Do you remember the case?"

"Yes."

"How did the boy die?"

"It was deemed to be natural causes."

"And you didn't see any evidence of foul play? No physical trauma or blood loss?"

"None."

"Why was the boy unidentified? You couldn't find any family members or a missing person's report?"

"None. The police searched for weeks. The boy had been abandoned in Stanley Park under a maple tree. He'd been dead for at least three days before a groundskeeper found him."

Liam squeezed my hand questioningly.

I nodded, indicating that he could speak to me.

The sorcerer hunkered down beside me. "Evidence of that abandonment? Was the boy found in a makeshift camp? Was there evidence of starvation? Any reports of a child living alone in the park?"

I related Liam's questions to the coroner.

The shade's brow creased. "Not that I know of."

"Who could we question?" I asked. "Who was the lead investigator?" That info would likely be in any of the files Liam had found, but getting confirmation was never a bad idea.

"Tim McKinnon oversaw that case."

"How does he remember with such clarity?" Benjamin asked.

I shrugged. "Magic. He can answer direct questions, but he can't make guesses. In life, he probably would have tried to answer all of Liam's questions, but his shade deals in facts, not suppositions. Not emotional responses."

The coroner's figure was thinning around the edges. I fed another thread of magic into him. "We need to keep moving," I said. "If I'm going to have other shades to raise." I squeezed Liam's hand so he understood I was talking to him. "Text Tony the police officer's name? Let's see if he's interred at Mountain View."

The sorcerer nodded, texting with one hand.

"I'd like to ask you about Jean Sadler, a case from November 1956. She was eleven years old. Do you remember her?"

"Yes."

"Can you tell me about your findings?"

"Female. Age eleven. No signs of abuse or trauma. Cause of death was natural causes."

"A heart attack."

"Yes."

"That's unusual for a young child, isn't it?"

"Yes."

"Did you check the family history? Her medical records?"

"No history of medical issues."

Liam shifted closer to me, murmuring, "Was there anything about the case that bothered him?"

"He might not be able to answer that. Do you have a more specific question? Something fact based?"

Liam took a deep breath, thinking. "What was the condition of the body? Had she been left out in the elements? Scavenged? Who found her? And the lead detective's name."

I related Liam's questions to the coroner.

"The girl appeared to be in perfect health. She was found within an hour of passing away. In a field of dead daisies, according to Detective Johansen's report. Dan Johansen." The shade fell silent.

Liam glanced down at his phone, texting again.

I started to ask about the third victim, when the coroner spoke without prompting.

"It bothered him. It bothered Dan."

I hesitated. I double-checked that the tendrils of my magic were firmly anchored but that I wasn't feeding too much energy into the shade of Charles Wells.

"Why did the death of Jean Sadler bother Dan Johansen? How do you know?"

"We went out for drinks. After I ruled it natural causes. The parents were…upset, insistent that the girl hadn't run away. It bothered Dan. That field of dead daisies. No footprints, he said. No crushed flowers, except for those under the body. Impossible, I thought. But I didn't say anything. Just bought Dan another rye. He retired the next year. Still had the file on his desk."

The coroner's shade fell silent.

I shivered, cold inside and out. But I checked my connection to the shade again and pushed forward. "November 1965. Seven-year-old girl."

"Misty Dean. Natural causes, like the other two."

The shade shouldn't have been volunteering information. He shouldn't have been making connections. "I've been holding him for too long," I whispered.

"The same…" the coroner murmured, sounding thoughtful. "Natural causes. Not a mark on the body. Found in a school playground on a Sunday morning. Parents hadn't even known she'd left the yard, it happened so fast. No footprints in the sand except for the person who found her…no sand on the girl's shoes…"

He should have been toneless, not thoughtful.

The shade of Charles Wells frowned. "I was only six months away from retirement. Paul Reid was the lead. But...I should have made the connection. Three cases, each about ten years apart. Heart attacks in such young children." His gaze flicked away from me, looking at Liam, then at Benjamin.

"I have to let him go," I said.

"Wait," Liam protested.

"No, Liam." My heart rate ratcheted up. "You don't understand."

The shade of Charles Wells lunged for me, icy fingers digging into the flesh of my shoulders. He screamed into my face. "What is going on?!"

A harsh wave of grief and dread tinged with terrible understanding emanated from the shade, freezing me momentarily in place. I'd pulled him too far forward, had fed him too much power. It shouldn't have happened...I thought I'd been careful...

"Mory!" Liam's grip tightened on my hand painfully. His touch was almost searingly hot compared to the icy digits of the coroner's shade drilling into the flesh of my upper arms.

I shoved away my own fear. I could do this. I knew what I was doing. I was even good at it. I wrenched my hands from Liam and Benjamin, severing their visual connection to the summoning.

"The children!" the coroner's shade cried, trembling with need.

I brought my hands forward, hovering them by the shade's shoulders but not actually touching him. Continuing to refer to him as a shade was likely a misnomer. I had definitely made him too aware—but I would worry about that later. "It's all right, Charles," I murmured, trying to keep my tone even, though my heart was still hammering erratically. "You've been very helpful."

"The children?" he asked.

"Yes," I said. "We're going to fix it. You can rest now. Rest now."

"Rest now?" the shade echoed.

I firmed my voice, making it a command. "Rest."

The coroner's shade slid away from me. The tendrils of magic anchoring Charles Wells to me thinned. Then he slipped back into his grave.

Shaking, I reeled in the strands of magic as I reached for my focal candle. Benjamin got there first, pressing the fluttering candle into my hands. I snuffed the flame with a long, steady exhalation, visualizing severing the link to the shade at the same time. The connection between me and the grave dissolved.

"What the hell was that?" Liam asked quietly.

I shook my head.

Benjamin took the candle from me, blowing on the wax to cool it quickly.

Liam's phone vibrated in his hand. He didn't look at it, his gaze on me. "Mory?"

"I'm fine," I said.

I just couldn't stop shivering.

"What happened to that shade? He started answering questions you hadn't asked."

"Yes." I dropped my head back, looking up at the dark, cloudy sky. It was going to rain soon.

"Has that happened before?"

"Not with a shade."

Benjamin wasn't making any notes. He was crouched before me with his gaze on the candle.

I had scared both of them.

"I need more of an explanation, Mory," Liam snapped.

Apparently, I only got thirty seconds of recovery time as far as the sorcerer was concerned.

"Not everything is neat and tidy," I snarled, clenching my fists, heat flooding my face. "In trials, no shade has behaved out of the ordinary. But I'm…different. I have to be careful. I was being careful. But…" I exhaled harshly, glancing around. "This is my claimed territory."

"Different conditions," Benjamin murmured.

"Yes. I'm more powerful here." I nodded, scooping Ed up. I felt a little more grounded with him in my hands. I stood shakily, but pulled away when Liam tried to hold my elbow to steady me. "Next gravesite?"

"No," Liam said bluntly.

I turned and pinned him with a narrow-eyed gaze. Which, honestly, was a little difficult to do when he was so much taller than me. "Next gravesite," I snapped. "I know Tony texted you."

He grimaced. "Mory…"

"This is my job," I said, squaring my shoulders. "Something…a succubus maybe…is killing kids, Liam."

He clamped his mouth shut, looking away from me resolutely. As if the discussion was over.

I shook my head, glancing at Benjamin.

The dark-haired vampire's expression was impassive, his tone cool. "Mory doesn't take orders from you, sorcerer."

Liam snorted. "You just want the story, vampire. She can't trust your judgement in any way."

"It's not a game." I ran my fingers over Ed's carapace, thinking. "Five questions, then. You can write them down."

Liam's expression was hard. "Five questions."

"Deal."

He nodded, glanced at his phone, then walked away.

Benjamin brushed my cheek with cool fingers.

I flinched.

He snatched his hand back.

"I'm okay," I murmured to him.

The vampire nodded curtly, his dark eyes boring into mine as if trying to read the truth etched into my soul.

Then he opened his notebook and uncapped his fountain pen.

So that moment was over.

Still carrying Ed, I grabbed my towel and my satchel, following Liam deeper into the cemetery. Benjamin trailed behind me.

LIAM WAS CROUCHED BY A FLUSH-MOUNTED GRAVE MARKER MADE of copper, covered by a patina of green. He was reading the name and dates stamped into it by the flashlight on his phone. I kept my gaze averted to preserve my eyesight. I saw pretty well in the dark, and almost perfectly well in the dark while on the grounds of Mountain View. But bright light could compromise that magic.

My favorite headstone was only a few rows away. And I suddenly felt the utterly irrational urge to visit it. The coroner's shade had rattled me. I wasn't completely certain what I'd done wrong during the summoning, except that he'd been more present from the beginning, and I was casting on land that some Adepts would have referred to as my 'seat of power.'

I had drained my magic almost two years ago. In the fight with the elves. We all had, actually. I'd also been hurt, badly. And then…then I'd worn the instruments of assassination for long enough that they nearly killed me a second time.

I touched my necklace through my shawl, running my thumb along the edge of the lowest-hanging gold coin. I could feel a brush of the energy, the protections, that coated it. It was possible that I survived the instruments of assassination only because I'd also been wearing my own powerful artifact.

It was also possible that, already injured and drained, having my life force slowly consumed had strengthened my magic—until Jade had been strong enough to take the artifact back. The courses at the Academy had been practically effortless, even though my previous training had been seriously spotty. Most necromancers grew into their power—meaning the older they were, the more powerful. My mother wouldn't have bothered training me at all until I was in my thirties, except that everyone had been worried about me going dark. So she'd taught me enough that I could claim Mountain View and keep Ed with me when he'd died of natural causes.

"You don't have to do this," Liam said quietly, calling me back to the present. The sorcerer had straightened, presumably having confirmed that he'd found the correct site. His expression was more concerned than judgemental, though.

Benjamin stepped up behind me. I could feel his magic, rather than see him, but Liam's gaze shifted over my shoulder…and became stony.

"I'm fine," I said. "Still working through the jet lag. And before tonight, I hadn't cast here since…you know…"

Liam nodded. "I know."

"I'm not following," Benjamin said.

"Because you weren't there, vampire," Liam said. "You were too busy trying to tear Bitsy's throat out."

Bitsy was Liam's sister. Along with Jasmine and Benjamin, she had been part of a small infiltration group during our siege on the elves. Bitsy, Jasmine, and Benjamin had been tasked with rescuing the fallen warriors, while Gabby and I, along with Jade and her father, Yazi, had been part of the distraction. Then I'd closed the dimensional gateway the elves had erected while a bloody battle raged around me.

Liam had been outside the stadium with the witches and the other sorcerers, dealing with their own battle. And protecting the city from spillover.

Bitsy had gotten hurt because Benjamin had gotten hurt. He had almost died. She'd healed. In fact, there was a good chance that Benjamin actually had died that day—and had been brought back for the second time.

I had no idea that Liam still held that two-year-old incident against Ben. It made sense, given the sorcerer's overly protective nature. But right now seemed an odd time to bring it up. Again, Liam wasn't usually so easily riled, but the incident with the coroner's shade probably wasn't helping that.

A heavily weighted silence settled over the three of us. For a moment, it felt as if it was going to impede my breathing, but then I inhaled perfectly fine.

"Liam," I said. "You know that Kandy, Kett, and Warner wouldn't have gotten out without Benjamin. And Jade…" I cleared my throat. "I was there. I was on the main battlefield. We wouldn't have won without Kandy and Warner. Gabby would have died without Warner getting her out to the witches." I could have gone on, detailing the sequence of events that I was completely certain had needed to line up in that one specific way in order for us to quash the elf invasion. Even if the oracle hadn't seen it all, she'd seen enough to place the players on the board—including Bitsy and Benjamin.

My mouth soured. So many dead elves. So many injuries. Jade almost dying. Gabby almost dying.

And Benjamin…he was forever changed.

We all were.

Liam didn't speak, though his attention had shifted to me instead of Benjamin.

"I did bite Bitsy, though," Benjamin said. "I don't remember doing it. But Kandy was there to pull me off her."

Benjamin's confession only added to the weight that hung around us—the sensation strong enough for me to wonder if it was some sort of magic I was feeling.

The dark-haired vampire pulled back the sleeve of his sweater, revealing the bone bracelet embedded into the flesh of his left wrist. It looked painful—and seethed with darkly tinted power. To me, at least. "I died for it," he said softly. "If it's any consolation."

"And then you rose again," Liam snapped.

"And Bitsy is also okay," I said. "She doesn't blame Benjamin at all. She was the one on the ground, in the moment, Liam."

"I did," Benjamin said, as if I hadn't interjected myself into their argument. "I rose again. Different from before. Again."

He stepped away and over to the grave marker, where he crouched, pulling a sketchbook and a pencil out of his satchel. He tore a piece of paper from the sketchbook, pressed it over the inset grave marker, then rubbed the pencil over it. Making an impression of the design that had been carved there. Some sort of military crest, at best guess, though I didn't recognize it. The shade I needed to question next had served, possibly even fought in some war, before he'd become a police detective.

I shifted my attention back to Liam. "If you're going to hold what happens to us in the heat of battle against us—and to the people we care about—you're going to be very unhappy, Liam."

He frowned, opening his mouth to refute my statement.

I cut him off. "I could give you a list of people I've hurt, unintentionally. People who have gotten seriously injured…people who have died…because of my actions."

Liam snapped his mouth shut, grimacing. "That's not the same—"

"It's exactly the same."

Benjamin neatly folded the impression he'd made, tucking it into his notebook, then straightening.

"Shall we start with Gabby?" I asked, trying to keep my tone even and my voice steady, though I wasn't wholly successful. "She almost died amplifying me."

Liam shook his head. "No."

"Yes. Because I was the only one who could shut down the dimensional gateway without blowing the entire city up. But I wasn't powerful enough. So I needed Gabby."

"We all needed Gabby," Benjamin added softly.

"Right," I said, clearing my throat. "And once, many years ago now, I got a werewolf killed. Sacrificed to call forth a greater demon, because I wanted to visit a graveyard in Portland. And we got kidnapped."

"I'm not going to play this game with you, Mory," Liam growled. "The who's-made-the-worse-bad-choices game."

"But you want to play it with Ben?" I whispered.

"I can be angry about it! I can be protective of Bitsy."

"Of course you can," Benjamin said smoothly. "You should."

Tension ran through Liam's jaw. He rolled his shoulders as if trying to shrug it off.

I took that as a sign that the conversation was over. For now. I pulled out my candle, setting it on the corner of the copper grave marker, respectfully not covering the military crest or the name stamped into the metal. Then I lit it.

"Paul Reid?" I asked, glancing at the name.

"Third case," Liam said. "November 1965. The girl found in the playground."

"Right. No footprints in the sand." I spread my slightly damp towel at the foot of the grave, kneeling on it.

Liam glanced at his phone. "Tony hasn't tracked down the first detective, McKinnon. And the second, Johansen, retired in Kamloops and is buried there. So Reid it is. If you still insist."

"I do still insist."

Benjamin crouched beside me. "Hey, Mory?"

"Yes?"

"You'll tell me, right? About the werewolf and the greater demon? Sometime?"

Liam swore under his breath.

I met Benjamin's intense gaze, not allowing the magic that backed his interest to pull me in, ensnare me. That was becoming easier. Maybe exposure therapy would eventually work. "Someday."

He nodded, straightening and stepping back.

After anchoring my focus within the flickering candle, I let my magic slip into the gravesite, immediately picking up random details about the corpse interred within. Paul Reid had died at seventy-two. Of lung cancer. I fed another tendril of magic into the ground, double-checking that my power was securely anchored, rooted. Various facts about Reid's life filtered through that connection to me. He'd smoked two packs of cigarettes a day since his early twenties, tried to quit multiple times. Estranged from his first wife and daughter. Married twice more. Predeceased all his wives and children.

"Good enough," I whispered. Then I coaxed the shade of Paul Reid forward and up.

He appeared standing before me, hazy and almost transparent. I didn't bolster the shade though, wary that I'd inadvertently added too much magic to the coroner's shade so that he would appear more substantial for Liam and Benjamin. Paul Reid was barrel chested, heavyset. Large hands. His dark hair was grayed at the temples. He wore jeans and what I assumed was a garish Christmas sweater, though it was presented in shades of gray. Bare feet. An idealized image of himself, perhaps, from a time he'd been the most content and settled in his life.

"Hi, Paul. I'm Mory."

The former police detective keyed in on me, crouching down to my level. His expression was blank of emotion, eyes boring into mine as if he could see my soul more than my outer shell. Or, more accurately, as if he could see my magic. The magic that drew him forth.

I offered my hands to Liam and Benjamin. They wrapped their hands around mine. Once more, Liam's touch was warm, Benjamin's cool.

"Five questions, Mory," Liam said grimly. He didn't sound as awed to be looking at a shade as he had before.

"I assume you have them worked out," I asked icily.

"Does he remember the girl found in the playground in November 1965?"

I repeated the question to the shade of the police detective.

"Yes," the shade replied tonelessly.

Liam voiced his second question. "Before the death was ruled to be from natural causes, did he have any suspects?"

Again, I repeated the question.

The shade of Paul Reid shook his head. "None. Misty had wandered off, but her parents insisted that she'd barely been gone an hour before they went looking for her. A neighbor found her, woman by the name of Biddy Thomas. Red hair, early twenties, good looking. If I hadn't been standing over the corpse of a child, I might have asked her out."

"Any signs of a struggle or foul play?" I asked.

"None," he answered as tonelessly as before. "The girl's skin was unblemished, clothing clean. Not even sand on her shoes, though she'd been found in the playground." The shade paused, but before I could ask another question, he spoke again. "I canvased the neighborhood, asking questions about the parents' background, and about who Misty usually played with. But no one had seen her that afternoon."

Liam hunkered down beside me, his grip on my hand steady. "How long did he investigate? After the death was deemed natural causes?"

"Two years," the shade of the police detective said when I asked. "Kept it on my desk for two years. Never got any further than I had on that first afternoon. Not one step further."

"What bothered you?" I asked. "About the case? You didn't agree with the coroner's findings?"

"I didn't disagree exactly." He fell silent, and I thought he might not answer. But then he spoke up. "No footprints, except from the woman who found her. Not one footprint from the child herself. And…the rose."

"The rose?"

"A glass rose. The next day. And over the next weeks, when I visited the site. There was always that rose set there at the swing set. Blown glass, I think. I'd never seen anything like it."

I tightened my grip on Liam's hand.

I had seen a glass figurine on Tanya's gravesite. A sea turtle, though. Not a rose. So it could totally be a coincidence, or a mourning custom I knew nothing about. I opened my mouth.

"That's more than five questions, Mory," Liam said.

"One more." Then to the shade, I said, "The child, Misty. Do you know if she was…" I actually wasn't completely certain how to phrase the question "Was something done to her remains before or after she was buried? Some sort of…ritual or experiment?" Okay, that sounded seriously lame. Thankfully, a shade wouldn't care.

The shade of Paul Reid shook its head once, suddenly looking bereaved. "They cremated her. I attended the memorial service myself. Broke the parents, broke the marriage. I had to stop asking questions. I kept…making it worse."

"Mory…" Liam growled.

Yeah, that was a lot of volunteered information. And emotion. "I didn't even firm the connection this time," I muttered. Then speaking louder, I said, "Thank you, Paul. You can rest now."

"Rest?"

"Yes, please."

The shade faded. Its energy slipped back through the tendrils of my magic anchored into its remains. Benjamin released my hand, immediately bowing his head over his notebook.

Liam crouched next to me, my hand nestled warmly in his. I tried to not shiver, feeling colder inside than the air around me. Touching the grave usually chilled me, but I could also still feel where the coroner's shade had dug its incorporeal fingers into my upper arms. The flesh there felt scarred, though if I'd looked, I was fairly certain that my skin would be unblemished. Unbruised.

I frowned. "Just like the children are unblemished."

"Mory?" Liam asked.

"Nothing. Just a weird connection between how my magic animates a shade, gives that shade strength…"

A shade…or a ghost.

My brother's ghost had almost drained me, feeding from me in order to manifest more fully in my plane of existence. "The succubus," I said, "assuming that is what we're tracking, does the same thing, leaving no mark."

"It's the opposite, actually," Liam said. "You feed your energy into a shade. The succubus steals."

I smiled, the expression tight on my face. It was a little odd that he was still holding my hand, but nice. "I should blow out my candle."

He nodded, then cupped my hand in both of his and blew on it. His hot breath prickled across my skin, warm, soothing. "You're so cold, Mory."

Benjamin stepped over to retrieve my candle, hunkering down on my other side and holding it near my face.

I blew it out.

"It's from raising the shades, right?" Benjamin asked. "That chills you? Using your magic?"

I nodded, suddenly very aware of being wedged between the two of them.

"I'll drop you home," Liam said. But his gaze was on Benjamin, who—as always—was writing in his notebook.

"Actually, I need to pick up pizza for games night," I said. "You want to join us, Ben?"

"No, thank you. I'll type up a report for Jasmine."

"After that."

He nodded. "I'll text to see if you're still there."

Liam shifted his grip down my arm, and then hauled me up onto my feet.

I disengaged myself from the sorcerer, retrieving my towel. Ed had burrowed into my satchel at some point during the summoning, so my knitting had probably been transformed into a nest. Again. I held onto the candle because the wax hadn't cooled.

We headed toward where Liam had parked. Benjamin trailed a couple of steps behind.

"Glass ornaments," I murmured. "That's two now. Tanya and Misty."

"Yeah," Liam said, sighing. "Not much of clue, and possibly just a coincidence. But it's something."

"Maybe…she visits the graves," I said. "The succubus. Maybe…Tony could rig up a camera? It's a long shot, but—"

"No," Liam interrupted. "It's perfect. At least it would be a solid first step." He brushed his fingers across mine. "Thank you."

"It's a dirty job," I quipped, "but someone has to do it."

He laughed quietly.

"The human investigators knew," Benjamin said, shutting his notebook and stepping up on my other side. "They all knew that something was wrong, off, about the deaths. But they couldn't put it together."

"It helps if you know there are creatures who can steal the souls of their victims," I said.

"Yeah," Liam said. "And that was news to me."

"To all of us," I said, bumping my shoulder against the sorcerer's. "Even Kett had to think about it."

I tried to not gasp as we entered the cul-de-sac on East Thirty-Seventh, crossing from grass to concrete—and feeling all the magic that had been buoying me ripped away. I drew Liam's gaze despite my efforts to suffer silently. He picked up his pace, swiftly traversing the half a block to where his car was parked at the curb. Reaching the vehicle before me, he opened the passenger door, holding it until I slid past him and climbed inside, shivering.

Liam crossed around the car, sliding into the driver's seat as I realized that Benjamin had disappeared. I scanned the immediate area but felt no trace of his magic. The vampire was long gone.

Liam started the car, cranking the heat. I raised my palms to the upper vents.

"Are you always this cold after summoning?" the sorcerer asked quietly.

"Not always." I thought about explaining what being grabbed by the shade of Charles Wells had felt like, but then clamped down on the impulse to share. Technically, Liam was my client, not my friend.

"How long do we wait on him?" Liam's gaze flicked to his rearview mirror and then his side mirror. He was looking for Benjamin.

"We don't." I grabbed my seat belt, clicking it closed.

"No goodbye?" Liam asked mockingly.

I didn't answer. Benjamin was more distant than he had been before…before he'd almost died a second time and had been revived by Kett's blood. I only knew that extra tidbit because Bitsy had mentioned it. Which meant that Liam knew as well.

Kett's blood had changed Benjamin. If I understood it correctly, that infusion would continue to change the younger vampire, continue to mold him.

And none of that was any of my business.

Liam pulled the car away from the curb, rounding the cul-de-sac. Then he headed vaguely west, slowly traversing the residential streets. Both of his hands were firmly set on the wheel. "I'm taking you home."

I opened my mouth to protest, but he interrupted. "You can order pizzas, get them delivered to the house, and have a hot bath before you need to make an appearance at games night."

I shut my mouth, trying not to shiver. "Okay." I muttered my agreement into my shawl, heating it nicely with my breath.

We drove in silence. The car warmed up enough that Liam must have been sweltering. I turned down the heat and lowered the fan. The lights of the surrounding city blurred by outside. I closed my eyes, settling my head back against the headrest.

"It's going to rain soon," I murmured.

"Yeah." Silence fell again. Then Liam added, "I don't mind it. The rain. People mentioned it a lot when we were moving here. But it doesn't bother me."

Not opening my eyes, I continued the conversation, feeling warmer now and a little lazy. Not napping, but weirdly okay. Content, even. "Do you miss the snow? It snows in Boston doesn't it?"

"It does. But we were only there for a few years."

I waited for him to elaborate.

He didn't.

"I like the rain," I said. "But I don't like getting my feet wet."

The car slid to a stop. And when we didn't start driving again, I opened my eyes. We were parked alongside looming hedges topped by a Georgian manor, car idling. Home again...home again...

Liam was looking at me, but I couldn't read his expression in the dark. The dashboard lights were too dim.

"Are you okay?" I asked.

He nodded. "Yeah..." He trailed off, then shook his head. "Just not sure where to go with the investigation..."

"I can try to question some family members. We have the glass-ornaments clue."

"Yeah." He sounded doubtful.

I unlatched my seatbelt, leaning sideways on impulse to rest my hand on his forearm. "This isn't much consolation, but the succubus appears to kill on a ten-year cycle. Tanya was killed in 2017. We have time to investigate."

He nodded. "We're guessing at the ten-year cycle, though. Maybe she only kills in Vancouver every ten years, to avoid the notice of the witches. It's also more than possible that not all her victims are buried at Mountain View."

"But it could be a pattern."

"It could be."

"But you think she might move, like from city to city? To stay under the radar of the police?"

"Of the witches," he said. "Or the pack."

I didn't like the forlorn note edging his words. I reached deeply for some resolve, firming my own tone. "We know more now."

A smile ghosted over Liam's lips, then he angled his head, looking up at the house. "Still dark."

I followed his gaze. "Yeah…necromancers." The repeat of the joke felt lame, my humor thin.

"Does your mom know you're back from the Academy?"

"Maybe not."

He made a quiet, agreeable noise in the back of his throat. A hum, really. But he didn't push the topic.

I reached for the door handle.

"Mory?"

"Yeah?"

He stared at me. Again, I couldn't discern his full expression in the near dark, but he seemed more thoughtful than tense.

Licks of warmth that had nothing to do with the heat softly blowing from the vents filtered through me, settling in my lower belly. I was tired, chilly, and suddenly fighting the urge to ask Liam Talbot to join me in a hot steamy shower. To hell with the pizza and games night.

Liam Talbot.

A sorcerer.

And me.

The shower in my en suite had a narrow seat tiled into the corner, perfect when shaving my legs…and possibly perfect for other reasons to prop up a leg or two…

And now I was visualizing it.

Us.

Hot and soapy.

Wet, slick skin. Rubbing against each other…

Liam shook his head. Again. "Want me to walk you to the door?"

"I'm okay. Thanks."

He nodded.

I exited the car, instantly chilled again the moment I hit the sidewalk. Well, that took care of any of the desire that had pooled…everywhere. Shivering, I closed the car door, crossed to open the gate, and jogged up the front walk. Liam waited until I was inside the manor before pulling away from the curb.

In my bedroom, I tucked Ed into his aquarium. I ordered and paid for pizza delivery while heating the shower and stripping off my clothing.

Then I sat on the tiled floor, letting the steaming water run over me until I had seriously drained the hot water tank, all the while continually running over the conversation with Kett, the idea of a succubus, and the summonings in my head.

I kept coming back to that moment in the darkened interior of the car—Liam staring at me. He'd wanted to ask me something. Probably something about the case or the shades.

But some part of me really wanted it to be something else.

And not because I was crushing on him. I didn't feel any urge to giggle about him with my girlfriends—possibly because two of the three were his sisters. I didn't want to write about him in my journal or stalk him on social media.

No. This feeling was something else.

Something…protective.

I GOT MY SECOND WIND—OR MAYBE IT WAS MY THIRD—ON THE way over to the Talbots'. The taxi dropped me off a moment before the pizza-delivery guy pulled up. So I took the stack of boxes from him, crossing around the side path to the back door of the Craftsman.

My hair was still a little wet, but the pizza boxes were toasty warm.

The basement windows were all lit up, as were the windows of the kitchen and the living room, indicating that the senior Talbots were probably home. I would go up and say hello later. Stephan Talbot had recently rejoined the sorcerers League, so he was more than just my friends' dad now. He was a potential work contact.

And apparently, I worked now. Like a real adult. Speaking of which, I needed to check my email for the requests Pearl had said she was going to forward. And I probably needed to email my mother. Though that was maybe taking the adulting a step too far.

A tall, shadowy figure was waiting for me in the dark hall just inside the back door. I squeaked unbecomingly when she lunged past the washer and dryer, arms outstretched. This display of bravery garnered me a throaty laugh, a harsh kiss on the cheek, and the loss of the pizza boxes.

"You're seriously late!" Bitsy snarled, stalking off through the darkened laundry area toward Tony's lair, which had been converted back into the recreation room for games night. Wearing wide-legged yoga pants and a long-sleeved tight T-shirt, Rebecca Talbot stood six feet tall in bare feet, though her wild halo of dark curls added about two inches to her height. Bitsy was a month shy of twenty-four, and halfway through her degree in sports medicine. Or at least into the second half of her degree, as best I understood it.

"I brought the pizza!" I cried out. But my protest fell on deaf ears as Bitsy disappeared through the well-lit doorway to the rec room. She—or rather, the pizza—was greeted from within by a chorus of exuberant cheering.

I tugged off my boots, adding them to the pile at the side of the exterior door, then followed the eldest Talbot sister down the hall. Unlike her adoptive parents and brothers, Bitsy wasn't a sorcerer. She was a werewolf. And while Peggy and Gabby—though mostly Peggy—were somewhat open about their past, Bitsy was as close-mouthed as I tended to be. Still, I had gathered through the rumor mill—aka Benjamin Garrick—that her parents had been real assholes when her shapeshifting abilities hadn't manifested at a young age. And then hadn't manifested at all, at least not reliably.

Bitsy was training with Kandy now, though. Kandy was an enforcer for the West Coast North American Pack, as well as for the Godfrey coven—and therefore a total hard-ass.

I seriously wouldn't want to be the one training with Kandy. Thankfully, my talents lay elsewhere.

Blinking against the abrupt change in lighting, I wandered into the rec room. The pizza boxes were already strewn open across the broad square coffee table, though Bitsy appeared to have commandeered the *Hot Licks* all to herself—spicy pepperoni, mushrooms, green peppers, and hot banana peppers, plus lots of perfectly melted cheddar and mozzarella.

Tony grinned at me, perched on the back of the sectional that bordered his workstation area with his sock feet on the couch cushion and a piece of pizza already in hand. "You remembered the pineapple."

I grinned back, skirting the opposite side of the sectional. "I did."

"Sit with me, Mory," Peggy said, patting the cushion beside her. The telepath was wearing a light-blue sweater over a navy skirt, and her light-blond, uber-straight hair was falling down her back in a glorious sheet.

Like Gabby, who had her legs folded up on the couch next to her twin, I'd opted for dark-wash jeans. Gabby's blond hair was coiled up in a loose bun, and she was swathed in an absolutely perfect, charcoal cashmere boyfriend sweater. I knew it was perfect because I'd selected it for the amplifier myself the last time we'd gone secondhand-clothing shopping. The overly large sweater had been slightly felted, so I couldn't have harvested the yarn even if I'd wanted to.

Gabby mumbled something around her mouthful of *Veggie Wedgie*—mushrooms, green peppers, zucchini, tomatoes, and a mix of cheddar and mozzarella. I had asked the pizza place to add their marinated artichokes as well.

"Nobody can understand you," Tony sneered. "Chew. Swallow. Speak."

"Screw you, asshole," Gabby said.

Bitsy chuckled. "Well, that was totally clear."

I set my satchel down, curling my legs underneath me as I settled beside Peggy.

The telepath brushed her fingers over the arch of my left foot, admiring my socks. "Rainbows on your feet! I want!"

"I'll make you some. It's self-striping yarn."

Peggy began nodding exuberantly even before I could explain any further. Presumably, the telepath was plucking the thoughts out of my head before I spoke. "Send me a link to the dyer, please. I'll buy the yarn."

"You could just learn to knit yourself," Gabby griped.

"The dyer has a goth-rainbow colorway as well," I said, tugging Ed out of my satchel and setting him between Peggy and me.

"I'm in." The normally grumpier twin grinned at me behind her sister's back. "Send me the link as well."

Peggy brushed her fingers over Ed's carapace as he made a break for the edge of the cushion. Her brow furrowed, as it did every time she tried to read the undead turtle's thoughts. "Still nothing," she muttered mournfully.

"Grab him!" Tony shouted.

Ed tried to leap off the couch—but he didn't get even a smidgen of air, simply tumbling over the edge. I lunged, nearly cracking my head into Peggy's as she did the same.

Ed thumped to the ground.

On his back.

I sighed, flipping him over. Then he scrambled off under the coffee table without even pausing to re-orient himself. "He keeps doing that."

Gabby blinked at Ed, pondering thoughtfully. "Maybe he thinks he can fly."

Under the weight of our regard, Ed turned invisible.

The Talbots cheered this development, then started passing pizza boxes around. I took a napkin and a piece of the *BBQ Chicken*—marinated chicken, onions, roasted red peppers, garlic, and a blend of cheddar and mozzarella. And for some reason, I couldn't wipe my smile off my face.

I'd never had a family. Not like this. Rusty had been older than me. And my mother traveled—a lot—after my dad had died.

"What are we playing?" I asked, savoring bite after bite of the still delightfully hot and saucy pizza.

"In honor of Mory's return…" Tony pulled a box out from under the coffee table with a flourish. "Harry Potter Trivial Pursuit!"

Bitsy snorted. "Little mainstream for you, ain't it?"

Tony pointed his finger at her. "Prepare to get your ass kicked."

"Oh, you're on, dude. I've read the books three times."

Tony snorted. "Whatever. I got it for Mory. She likes Harry Potter, don't you, Mory?"

"Sure," I said amicably, though it was doubtful that I had any chance of winning any game when competing with the Talbots.

"Though there's no necromancers in Harry Potter…" Tony frowned at the box in his hand. "But hey! If there was, I bet they'd be considered totally evil. So, bonus, eh?" He wagged his eyebrows at me.

"Please," Gabby sneered playfully. "No one wins anything having to do with Harry Potter against Peggy."

Tony shrugged. "Cheaters going to cheat."

"Hey!" the telepath exclaimed, feigning hurt.

Bitsy reached over, pressing her hand against Tony's forehead. "Did you just quote Taylor Swift?"

"What?" he cried, batting her hand away and darting a glance at me. "No way."

"Are you blushing?" Gabby asked.

Before her younger brother could gather his defenses, Peggy twisted around in her seat. "Oh!"

The rec room door opened, and Liam wandered in. His hair was still damp, and he was wearing a loose, cream-colored Aran knit sweater and worn light-blue jeans. The police detective in repose.

"Liam!" every other Talbot in the room cheered.

"Hey," he said, grinning. "I heard there was going to be pizza." He looked at me. His grin morphed, as if we had just shared some private joke. Then he crossed around, settling on the floor with his back to the couch. His shoulder brushed my knee as he reached for the nearest box of pizza.

"All right!" Tony started piling the pizza boxes to clear space on the coffee table. "Six of us. Even better."

"Oh," I said. "Benjamin might drop by. Can we add him later?"

Tony grinned. "Nope! The bloodsucker will have to wait until someone wins and we start a second round."

"Tony!" Peggy frowned.

Her younger brother snorted, then spoke with great exaggeration. "Fine. Benjamin."

"He can team up with Gabby," Peggy said enthusiastically. "She's never even read the books. She's going to lose so bad."

"Hey," her twin protested. "I watched the movies!"

"Two," Bitsy scoffed. "Maybe three. Weren't you terrified of that snake?"

"It was a really big snake," Gabby muttered under her breath.

"Doesn't matter anyway. Ben isn't going to show," Tony said, opening the box. "He's already messaged me twice. He's digging into some info about the succubus that Liam and Mory are hunting."

"What!?" the three Talbot sisters exclaimed as if on cue, pinning their eldest brother and me with incredulous looks.

"Investigating," I said. "Not hunting. Kett will do the hunting."

Tony smirked at Liam. "That right, big bro?"

Liam kept eating his pizza without comment. I couldn't see his full expression, just the line of his jaw. He didn't seem tense.

"Okay," Bitsy said. "Dish. We want to know all. And, Mory, you have to tell us about the Academy." She flashed me a toothy grin. "Gabby said you made some…friends." She wagged her eyebrows at me.

Tony frowned, though most of his attention was on sorting through the pieces of the game. "Friends?"

Gabby laughed. "Don't be heartbroken, baby bro. A gorgeous babe like Mory can't possibly go away for over a year without, you know, making friends."

Peggy giggled. Bitsy guffawed.

I snorted, leaning forward to take another piece of pizza. Ed had reappeared and was sitting on Liam's foot. Surprised, I paused as I straightened, a piece of pizza dangling from my hand. My hair brushed against the sorcerer's temple. I hadn't realized I was so close.

Or maybe Liam had leaned into me.

Tony started explaining the rules of the game in a rattle of rapid-fire sentence fragments. I settled back into the comfy couch, taking a bite of my slice and only half ignoring the way my knee brushed against Liam's shoulder every time he shifted.

It was a good thing I was tired. Otherwise, I would have been salivating over the twisted-cable-and-diamond pattern of the sorcerer's sweater, even though it was obviously store bought. Not making a complete fool of myself on my very first official case was the idea, after all.

WHEN GAMES NIGHT WAS DONE, LIAM DROVE ME HOME. AGAIN. THIS time, though, he walked me up the path, actually taking my keys from me to unlock and open the front door.

"I see you finally left a light on," he murmured, peering through the entranceway toward the library.

"Oh," I said, following his gaze. "That must be Benjamin. He forgets I know when he's in the house. And he likes a bit of light to read by."

"I see." Liam dropped my keys back in my satchel and took a step away. I hadn't realized he'd been standing so close, and I involuntarily swayed toward him when he moved.

He tucked his hand under my elbow. "You're dead on your feet, Mory."

"Yeah, sleep would be good."

He grinned, though it looked oddly forced. "Do you need help upstairs?"

I laughed. "I'll make it. Though I might have to crawl."

He frowned playfully. "Maybe I should stick around. Watch. Make sure you don't fall asleep halfway up."

"Hilarious."

He ran his hand through his hair, causing it to stick up in a bunch of adorable directions. Then he looked past me, toward the library. "Right," he said, exhaling heavily. "Right." He took another step back. "Tomorrow. We'll all compare notes. Jasmine and Tony will probably have compiled everything we know on a spreadsheet by then."

That was good, because personally I had no idea what else I could do to help the investigation. Except…"I'll ask Tony if any immediate family members of the victims are interred in town. Or other coroners or police officers. Maybe summon a few more shades and compare stories?"

"Yeah." Liam spoke as though he wasn't totally listening. "I have the case files for the more recent cases. Every one tells the same story."

"Okay."

"Okay."

He just stared at me, still two steps away. With the light of the house emanating only from the depths of the library, I couldn't really see his expression until he glanced toward the open door again.

"Might have to resort to talking to the living," I said, calling him back. Feeling some odd need to continue the conversation, even though I was really tired.

He laughed quietly. "Yeah. I'm meeting the Atkinsons for lunch."

"To ask about the glass ornament?"

He nodded, his expression downcast. Grim. "And anyone unusual hanging around. Though I already asked."

"They say that…um…some serial killers like to involve themselves in the investigation."

"They do say that."

"And if the ornaments are a clue…"

"Yeah. Then maybe the succubus visits the graves of her victims. I texted Tony your remote-camera idea as well."

"Might call for a stakeout," I said, trying to be as playful as I could be when discussing dead children.

"Oh, yeah? I'm guessing you know just the right place from which to keep tabs on the entire cemetery."

"I do. But I, uh, might get lonely."

There it was. That was as close as I could get to flirting.

A slow grin spread across Liam's face. He stepped up closer. "Lonely, hey?"

Magic shifted behind me—tiny, beguiling pulses of energy. Liam's gaze flicked past me. Benjamin had appeared, backlit by the dim light from the library.

"Mory," the dark-haired vampire said. "Just checking you were okay."

"We've been standing here talking for ten minutes, vampire," Liam said. "Took you a while to notice."

Benjamin tilted his head, possibly frowning—but I still couldn't quite see his face. "I knew you were here, sorcerer. I know your heartbeat."

Was there something dangerous in Benjamin's normally smooth, even tone?

"Is that a threat?" Liam's hand shifted to his side. To his concealed gun.

"A fact." Benjamin's tone was perfectly level. It was possible I'd imagined the previous edge. "Will I bother you in the library, Mory?"

"No."

The vampire stepped back, keeping his gaze level on Liam. Then he crossed abruptly through the entranceway and beyond the base of the grand staircase, moving so quickly he was just a blur.

I blinked.

"In the library?" Liam asked caustically.

"Yeah," I said, rubbing my face. "He sneaks in when my mother isn't home. He's reading his way through the library." I waved my hand. "For his chronicle."

"For his chronicle," Liam echoed.

I couldn't quite read his tone. Disbelief, maybe? But what part of our conversation had inspired that tone, I didn't know. "Uh, yes. Actually, I'm supposed to be proofreading the necromancy section and I haven't even started."

"Sleep first."

"Yes, sleep." I stepped into the house, glancing back at Liam. "Thanks for the ride. Again."

"You're very welcome."

"You'll check in with me? If there's anything else I can help with?"

"I will." He shoved his hands into the front pockets of his jeans and sauntered up the path, passing through the overgrown shrubbery, then carefully latching the gate behind him.

I might have watched him go a little longer than was necessary to be considered polite. The jeans fit him rather well, and the cabled sweater stretched across his broad shoulders. Thankfully, the light from the house was just enough to highlight those particular features.

I closed the door, leaning against it for a moment while I debated with myself about heading into the library to speak with Benjamin. I hadn't really put my role in all of this—as a necromancer-for-hire in Adept society—together yet. But something about hitting what felt like a dead end in my part of the investigation, along with my own crack about speaking to actual people, put it in perspective for me.

I wouldn't be getting to solve the crimes I got contracted to investigate. I would do what I was asked, and gather what info I could. But I didn't know the first thing about investigating beyond that. That wasn't my role. And neither was hunting down a succubus.

Dealing with hauntings was much more satisfying. From a short-term perspective at least.

I pushed off the door and headed for the stairs, relying heavily on the banister to climb up to my bedroom. It was Liam's frustration, edging on despair, that was upsetting me.

But the sorcerer had a lot of backup now—me, Benjamin, Jasmine, and Kett, plus Tony. He would find the succubus.

SIX

NO TEXT MESSAGES AWAITED ME WHEN I WOKE. AS I'D EXPECTED—because it wasn't my case to solve or my Adept to hunt. But still, it was disappointing. It was seriously early, not even eight o'clock, and the sun was still rising. And unfortunately, I was wide awake.

I swiped my thumb across my phone screen, calling up my 'feeling dark yet?' time-tracking app. As I did every morning. It blinked:

6 YEARS, 3 MONTHS, 4 DAYS

I waited, staring at my phone, internally critiquing the two-year-old selfie I'd used for the background. I hated taking selfies, even if I was just trying to take a shot of knitting for my Ravelry project page. I should replace the stupid picture. I could totally see my dark roots.

I waited a bit longer. But just as on every other morning since I'd downloaded and set up the timer, I didn't feel particularly homicidal.

Daily check-in complete, I set the phone on the side table, climbed out of bed, and gave Ed a pet on the way to the bathroom.

I showered, throwing on leggings and an oversized cashmere tunic that I'd pieced together—borrowing Pearl's sewing machine—from various thrift-store sweaters that I'd deliberately felted ahead of time. It had been my first attempt at sewing and looked more slovenly than chic, but I loved it.

Reminding myself that I hadn't eaten anything even vaguely resembling fruit in the last few days, I headed into the kitchen and started a shopping list while I sliced a peach that appeared still edible onto a bowl of Rice Krispies. Preemptively fortified, I headed into the library with Benjamin's notebooks and my new laptop.

There was no sign that a vampire had been working in the library into the small hours of the night. I had to drag one of the oak tables closer to the window seat in order to sit at it with the laptop plugged in. Yes, apparently I'd already drained the battery. I'd have to start remembering to plug it in overnight.

I perched in the window seat with the first of Benjamin's neatly transcribed notebooks in one hand and my bowl of cereal in the other. The day was wet and gray outside, but the rain that must have started up after I returned home had already stopped. I'd found a pad of sticky notes and a purple gel pen, so I was perfectly poised to make notes.

The first book covered necromancy in general, with a biography page for me, my mother, and Teresa Garrick. It was weird reading about myself, especially from Benjamin's perspective. And the vampire had sketched multiple pictures of me, Ed, and my necklace.

My mother's section was missing a lot of info, so I placed a sticky note and jotted down the things I needed to double-check—great-grandparents' names, objects of power, and the name of the cemetery where my mother's uncle had been slaughtered by a vampire. Well, according to him.

The section on Teresa—Benjamin's mother—was so fascinating that my cereal went all mushy while I was caught up in reading it.

It was also where I got the idea for how I could help Liam's investigation. And quickly.

A mass summoning.

According to Benjamin's notes, a necromancer of the Garrick family—all of whom had been well-known vampire hunters—had once held a half-dozen rogue vampires at bay so that the younger, less-experienced members of the family could take their heads, one by one. The notes—or maybe Teresa's recollections—weren't totally clear. But I got the gist of how the Garrick necromancer had set multiple anchor points, tying each back to herself. She'd buried silver rings in the ground, then had used herself as bait. In the case of the vampires, all she'd wanted to do was hold them. Still, it was an impressive display from an obviously massively powerful wielder of death magic.

To be fair, the tale was a little murky. There was no way that six vampires each conveniently stepped within a separate hidden trap. But I extrapolated that the necromancer of power was able to hold them for just long enough that she was able to drive them into the silver rings.

I wasn't trying to trap shades in the same way. Not long term, anyway. But with the remembrance still exceedingly fresh in my mind of how the icy fingers of the coroner had gripped me the previous night, the idea of being able to hold a shade while questioning it in a similar way was intriguing. And in theory, the silver rings would also negate the possibility of me pumping too much power into a casting.

Of course, I didn't have silver rings. But I was fairly certain I knew where I could find silver chain. I doubted it was solid silver, but silver plated should work.

I just needed names. And remains, of course.

I checked my phone.

Again.

Still no messages.

If the glass ornaments on Tanya's and Misty's graves had been left by the succubus, then she must have been seen by the family members of her victims, or even the investigating police officers. Possibly without them understanding the significance of her presence at the gravesites. Unless the succubus could completely dampen her magic or turn invisible. In that event, we were all screwed.

Except Jade, of course. The dowser could pick up even the thinnest traces of magic. But given the weird time lags Jade seemed to be experiencing during the elf peace negotiations, the succubus might well slaughter us all and dispose of our bodies before the dowser next returned. Jade would be left wondering why her bakery was suddenly turning a profit due to lack of pilfering.

Anyway. Since I was seemingly hell-bent on being useful even though my part of the investigation had fizzled out, I could try questioning multiple shades at once. Assuming I could figure out how to employ the silver rings to hold them. By asking the right questions, I might be able to form a profile of the succubus by cobbling together enough similarities—age, skin and hair color, and so forth.

Kett had said something about the succubus being known for vanity, though. So hopefully that meant she didn't constantly change her appearance by mundane means—like dyeing her hair, or colored contact lenses, or plastic surgery. And, yeah, I wasn't certain what that said about my own proclivity for changing my hair color every couple of months.

I shook off my doubts, clinging to the idea of a mass summoning now that I'd figured out a way to be of use again. Of use to the case, not just to Liam. Or at least not just to garner some praise from my elders. I wasn't that self-involved.

I hoped.

With a ten-year span between cases, none of the investigators would have been looking for a person of interest based on minor similarities between the cases. The succubus could have posed as a neighbor interjecting themselves into the investigation. Or if the local baker, or even the family's accountant, was seen placing a token at a gravesite, it wouldn't have seemed all that odd.

But I was capable of asking a series of questions regarding victims whose deaths spanned the decades.

I started the laptop, navigating to my inbox to see that I had actually been cc'd on a series of emails between Jasmine, Tony, Benjamin, and Liam. And Kett, actually. Lo and behold, the twelve-hundred-year-old executioner of the Conclave had an email address.

Not bothering to do more than scan what looked like a transcript of everything I'd either seen or discussed with one person or another about the cases, I emailed Tony, cc'ing everyone else.

Oh tech sorcerer extraordinaire. I have an idea about how to build a profile of the succubus through a mass summoning. Can you get me the names of any family members or police officers, etc., for each possible victim interred at Mountain View Cemetery? And the locations of their interments? Thanks, Mory.

P.S. For those of you cc'ed. I'm not waiting until dark to cast. I promise I'll bring a buddy along to watch my back. I'm stopping by the bakery first.

I hoped that mentioning the bakery would stop the executioner from getting all huffy about my safety. And Liam, for that matter. Even though I was at my strongest when on the cemetery grounds, and I wasn't the sort of idiot who went looking for trouble. Not anymore, at least. The same couldn't be said for any of the so-called warriors.

Plus…creeping through the darkness, having lured my wily prey onto the grounds of my seat of power was much more effective. Though I probably shouldn't wear my beaded poncho.

Not that I would mention that particular scenario to anyone bigger, badder, and way stronger than me. They didn't find my sense of humor particularly amusing. It probably didn't help that I carried an undead turtle with me everywhere.

I texted Jade about the silver chain I needed. But by the time I'd added another layer of knitwear to my ensemble, pulled on old jeans instead of leggings, packed a second satchel full of extra supplies, and reserved a car share, I hadn't heard back from her. So the dowser was probably still out of town. Out of our dimensional realm. Wherever.

Apparently, I was going to add breaking and entering to my professional resume. Though since I was keyed to the wards on the bakery and Jade's apartment, I wouldn't need to be doing much breaking. Just good old-fashioned thievery.

I comforted myself with the knowledge that Jade would have given me the silver chain if she were around. Hell, Jade would give me just about anything I asked for. The priceless protection that constantly hung around my neck was evidence of that fact. In fact, according to the rumor mill—aka Benjamin Garrick—some assholes—aka the executioner—thought I was unworthy of possessing my necklace. Or maybe Kett just thought I was incapable of protecting the artifact as well as it protected me.

Anyway, I understood that the necklace watched over me in a way that the dowser hadn't figured out how to do herself. Not without just locking me in her kitchen and keeping me a chubby, happy prisoner for the rest of my life.

With thoughts of cupcakes lingering in my head, I spun back at the top of the stairs, hightailing it back into my bedroom. There, I dug the ancient gold coin Jade had given me out of the pocket of the second-dirtiest pair of jeans currently decorating my floor.

I had no idea why I would need the coin, but I'd learned that the magic wielded by the powerful beings that called Vancouver home wasn't to be questioned. Maybe giving me the coin had just been a casual gesture, just a simple declaration from Jade that she'd been thinking of me. But maybe it was more. I wasn't stupid enough to question magic I didn't understand.

Because yeah, I believed. I believed there was a reason for everything. Even a reason that I had summoned my brother's shade without any training, to have him subsequently leech my life force and somehow trigger my latent soul-magic abilities over my death magic.

Because fate, or destiny, or however magic wanted to be personified, needed me to wield soul magic. Perhaps even so that I could be the one to close the elves' dimensional portal—me, above all the epically powerful people who had come together to wage war.

I believed.

So I tucked what was probably a perfectly benign gold coin into the pocket of my only clean pair of jeans, then hustled out of the house to grab the car share I'd reserved.

I was going to have to do laundry.

Or buy clothing.

And I loathed shopping for anything other than yarn, knitting patterns, and thrift-store cashmere sweaters.

So, laundry.

Right.

Just as soon as I finally did something useful. Like put together a profile of a serial killer so the bigger and badder Adepts could hunt her down. That was my role, after all, newly minted by the Academy or not.

And I was perfectly content with letting the others deal with the bloody fallout, just as long as I contributed. Being useful, being productive, made me happy. And maybe, just maybe, all of that was helping to keep the 'feeling dark yet' timer on my phone from becoming relevant.

AN IVORY BUDDHA WAS PERCHED AT THE TOP OF THE INTERIOR stairs leading to Jade's apartment from the bakery kitchen. I had managed to steal an unfrosted cupcake—mocha fudge cake, yum—as I snuck past Gabby. She was helping Todd, one of only two non-magical bakery employees, in the storefront. But now my passage was blocked by the three-foot-tall, round-bellied, smiling Buddha.

A statue that had been situated on the far side of the living room the last time I'd been in the apartment.

I slid around the Buddha, patting it on the head and ignoring the fact that it felt as though the statue might have been greeting me—like maybe it was bored because Jade was gone. But inanimate objects, magical or not, couldn't have feelings. Or move as they willed.

Or at least they shouldn't have been able to do so. But honestly, when Jade was involved, I wouldn't—couldn't—be surprised at any magical development.

The apartment was quiet, dark. Though epically clean. The Godfreys were blessed with a brownie, Blossom. I was completely jealous, but had no idea how to woo a magical being who liked to clean into wandering over my way. It didn't help that the only time I'd actually laid eyes on the elusive Blossom had been at Jade's wedding ceremony. The brownie hadn't even stuck around for the reception.

Maybe if I left a pair of knitted socks for Blossom with a note promising more knitting…Oh! Maybe the brownie liked to grocery shop as well. The cereal was seriously stale, and no matter how much I ignored the questionable milk, it was eventually going to make me sick.

See? I wasn't an idiot at all.

The door to the second bedroom was partially open to my far right. Perfect. Though there was a bed with the most glorious silk bedding tucked within, the room was mostly for Jade's crafts. And by 'crafts,' I meant the making of powerful magical objects such as the one I wore around my neck. Alchemy, that was called. Another of the rare talents that the dowser wielded.

Pushing the door all the way open, I stepped into the bedroom. The drawn curtains snuffed out the bulk of the daylight, what with the morning being still fairly cloudy.

A figure sprang up from the bed to my right, snarling. Teeth snapped against my neck, hands gripping me bruisingly exactly where the coroner's shade had held me the evening before.

I froze.

The magic from my coin-laden necklace coiled around my neck and collarbone, lying in wait, preparing to strike.

"What the hell, Mory?!" Hot breath battered my exposed skin. "Why are you sneaking up on me?"

The harsh grip on my arms eased—but I remained pinned by the dark-brown-eyed gaze of a pissed-off werewolf. Her normally spiked fluorescent-pink hair was mussed. Her lithe frame was barely clothed in a black sports bra and matching boy shorts. I was fairly certain she was in her early thirties, but just woken and without makeup, she looked around my age.

Kandy.

I found my voice. It had been buried underneath my hammering heart. "Why aren't you at your place?" I squeaked. Kandy, aka the enforcer of the West Coast North American Pack, aka the wielder's wolf, normally resided in the neighboring apartment.

"No bed." The pissy werewolf snarled her displeasure in my face, then spun and did a literal face plant on Jade's guest bed, effortlessly leaping five feet across the room in order to accomplish the task.

I refused to ask her about her missing bed. There were just some things I didn't need to know.

The werewolf's snarls turned into words muffled by the puffy silk duvet. I just stayed in place—worried that any sudden movement would set her off again—and waited for the rant to end.

Kandy rolled onto her side, eyeing me. "I said, 'If you aren't joining me, then go away.' "

"You said a lot more than that."

With the werewolf appearing somewhat calm, I hustled over to the shelves set on either side of the window as well as over the desk, scanning the bits and bobs collected there—sea glass, broken shards of china, tiny jade figurines, coins, and so on.

Setting my cupcake down on the desk, I opened the drawers one by one. Most of them were empty, but the top one held wire cutters of various sizes. Good to know.

"This poking around is not conducive to my sleep, necromancer," the werewolf growled from the bed. "What are you looking for?"

"The silver chain that Jade uses to make her trinkets."

Kandy groaned. "She doesn't make those anymore…"

A sudden silence fell between us—presumably because Kandy had just remembered exactly why Jade didn't casually make trinkets anymore. Other than the ones currently decorating the windows of the bakery. Years before, my brother Rusty and Jade's sister, Sienna, had used Jade's creations to steal magic from werewolves. Werewolves they had then murdered.

That was the reason Kandy had come to Vancouver in the first place, investigating my brother and Jade's foster sister.

"In the closet," Kandy finally said, sighing heavily.

I crossed to the closet, opening the bifold doors to find cones wrapped in silver chain of various thicknesses on the top shelf. I strained upward but managed to only ineffectually brush my outstretched fingers against the nearest cone. Before I could even look around to find something to stand on, though, Kandy was behind me, grabbing the thickest of the chains and handing the cone to me. It was heavy.

The werewolf then wrapped her arms around my shoulders and pressed her nose into my hair. It was like being encased in a steel cage that emanated warmth. She held me like that for a moment, breathing in my scent. And I let her. I wasn't as close to the werewolf as I was with Jade, but we had both nearly died together on a rooftop in London, then again on a beach in Tofino. And then again in the stadium, vanquishing the elf invasion.

Those sorts of bonds, you carried with you throughout life. We were magically entwined now, whether we wanted to be or not.

Kandy let me go without a word.

By the time I turned around, she was burrowed back under all the blankets. And my cupcake was gone. Only the empty wrapper remained. Seriously, there wasn't a single crumb.

"Really?" I asked, carrying the heavy cone of silver chain over to the desk.

"Toll." Kandy's reply was muffled by the blankets. "Next time, bring one with icing."

"I only barely managed to steal that one."

Kandy flipped back the duvet with both arms, glaring at me. "Be sneakier next time. Why the hell else would you need a familiar who can turn invisible?"

"The invisible part wasn't my doing," I grumbled, though I felt slightly stupid. I had never even thought about using Ed in a cupcake heist.

I unwound the chain, pulling it out to the length of the desk, about one meter. I figured that would make a circle just big enough to stand within, not that the shades I planned on calling really needed physical space for their feet. Then I selected the largest of the wire cutters and attempted to cut through a link—which went about as well as expected for a scrawny necromancer who never exercised if she could help it. I managed to make two dents. Two tiny dents.

"What are you doing?"

"Trying to cut the chain."

"Why?"

I contemplated lying, but then remembered that shapeshifters could smell lies. Or so they liked everyone to believe. "I'm making summoning circles."

Kandy was standing beside me before I felt her move. I managed to not flinch, but only from years of hanging out with people far stronger, faster, and more invincible than me. "How many lengths?"

"As many as we can get?"

Kandy quickly cut six lengths of chain without any effort, leaving about an arm's length on the spool. As a werewolf, she was naturally strong—and the golden cuffs on her wrists made her immeasurably more so. Benjamin had dubbed the rune-scribed and gem-crusted cuffs 'the wolf's bracers,' though I wasn't certain Kandy had agreed to that. So the title might not make it into the official, edited version of the chronicler's first edition.

"I texted Jade that I needed the chain."

"Okay." Kandy returned to the bed without asking me a single question.

Which, of course, made me itchy to explain. "It's for a case of Liam's. We think there's a succubus in town…or that she was in town in 2017."

"Yeah," Kandy said. "I'm in the loop. But I need a couple of more hours of sleep before I can join the hunt."

Huh, okay. That made sense. I wasn't sure where the werewolf had been, but she'd apparently returned to help out. And that suddenly made me feel a whole lot better.

"Old toothy doesn't like to hunt during the day anyway."

'Old toothy' had to be Kett. I seriously doubted that Benjamin would be making note of that nickname in the executioner's biography. "Cool. I'm going to try to put together a profile to help you."

"Yes, go be Creepy McCreeperson without me. I know where you'll be. And take Gabby. She's about to go off shift, I think."

"She might need to sleep."

"Take my SUV. Keys are in my jeans. She can sleep in the back seat."

I coiled all the silver chain in my second satchel, then found Kandy's keys in the pile of clothing slung over an antique chair in the corner of the room. The satchel was way heavy now.

I crossed out of the room.

"Hey, baby necromancer," Kandy murmured. "I'm glad you're back."

"Me too."

Lugging my heavy bag along with my regular satchel, I grinned all the way down the interior stairs as I returned to the bakery. I also smoothed my hand over the ivory Buddha's head as I passed. That seemed only right, since the statue was apparently keeping watch over the exhausted werewolf.

I HAD BARELY SET FOOT IN THE KITCHEN WHEN TEXT MESSAGES started buzzing through on my phone.

Tony.

>*You know I haven't slept yet, right?*

I texted back.

You love it.

>*I do love sleep. A lot.*

You love screen time better.

>*Give me ten minutes. I'll start sending you what I have.*

Gabby pushed through the swing doors that led into the bakery storefront. Her light-blond hair was braided tightly against her head today, likely Peggy's work. She was dressed in charcoal gray from head to toe, excepting a pink ruffled apron emblazoned with the Cake in a Cup logo. Nary a hand-knit in sight. "Mory!"

"Hey." I dangled the keys to Kandy's SUV from my free hand. "The enforcer doesn't want me mucking around alone, and she thought you might be interested in watching my back after your shift."

"Hell yeah. It's quiet. I can leave a bit early." She untied the ruffled apron. "Just let me flip the laundry into the dryer, let Todd know I'm going, and get him to brew a quadruple-shot pumpkin-spice latte. Then I'm all yours. Cemetery?"

"Yeah. I'm going to try a mass summoning. But it could take me a while to set up."

"Is this for Liam's case?"

I nodded. "Hopefully I can do something to help. Tony is looking for names and locations."

"For corpses."

"Remains. But, yeah, talking to dead people is my gig."

Gabby snorted, heading for the stairs I'd just descended. "Meet me out front."

I crossed toward the swing doors obligingly.

"Hey, Mory," Gabby called after me softly.

I turned back. She'd paused about a third of the way up the stairs, pivoting and ducking her head to talk to me.

"You know you've already helped, right?"

"Sure."

She smirked, shaking her head. "The succubus has been hunting in Vancouver for decades—"

"Maybe."

She waved her hand dismissively. "And no one would know if you hadn't put the pieces together."

"If. If it's a succubus. And even then, it's Kett who actually put that together."

She took a couple of steps down so she didn't have to crank her head to look at me, resting her hip against the railing and crossing her arms. "You know I get it, right?"

I didn't answer, though I was fairly certain where she was about to take the conversation. The elf invasion.

Gabby had amplified me continually throughout the assault so that I could close the dimensional portal while a bloody battle raged around us. I'd lost track of how many elves we'd killed together. Easily a dozen. With Gabby pumping magic into me, I'd taken control of their corpses and wielded their weapons—totally clumsily but still somewhat effectively. Slaughtering numerous sentient beings, even though we both understood those same beings would have slaughtered us without a second thought.

She huffed at my silence. "I get it. The wanting-to-do-more feeling. The reason you left, got more training." She looked away for a moment, toward the fridge but not actually focused on it. "It took months for my magic to come back, but it's like…I know now what it feels like to save the world." She laughed harshly. "At least to be part of saving the world. And now, I…bake cupcakes and take night classes to learn how to do the books, the accounting…" She trailed off.

"I never really thanked you—"

She shook her head sharply. "That's not why we were there, was it? With all the uber-powerful people.

You and me, completely outclassed…even that damn shadow leech, Freddie, is more powerful than me."

I laughed. "More powerful than us." Freddie was a demon-hybrid of sorts. She mostly hung around Jade and ate magic. Yeah, I wasn't the only magical creature in Vancouver that everyone watched closely. But Freddie was born out of darkness, whereas I'd only been dragged through it a few times.

"We didn't do it for thanks," Gabby said.

"No. We didn't." I set down my second satchel. The combined weight of the extra supplies and the silver chains was too much to hold under the onslaught of the conversation.

"We never talked about it," Gabby muttered, still not looking at me. "You and me." She snorted again. "Though Peggy dissected every moment, over and over."

"I'd do it again. In a second."

When Gabby finally looked at me, her eyes were shining with unshed tears. "Same." Then she shrugged as if negating her own emotional reaction. "Which is why, yes, I'll be your backup. Any time."

I nodded.

"Plus," she said, her tone far too bright given her normal reserve, "I've been training as well. With knives."

Um…knives. That sounded like a terrible idea.

She laughed, tugging up the right-hand leg of her jeans to reveal an ankle sheath. "Dad and Liam are a bit pissed because Talbots are normally gunslingers.

But Scarlett insisted that all of us…Peggy, me, Burgundy, Bitsy…get weekly self-defense training. Now that you're back in town, you aren't going to be able to dodge it either."

"Who trains you?"

"Whoever's in town that week. Warner, Jade, Kandy…Kett. The master vampire has only trained us twice, using Jasmine to demo. Man, she was pissed. He kept tossing her around. Even Drake's helped out, but Peggy goes all gooey eyed and useless around him, so that's boring. Bitsy trains separately with Kandy. And Tony outright refused."

Drake was the apprentice to Chi Wen, one of the guardian dragons. He was dark haired and tall. Totally swoon worthy, but not at all interested in anything other than doing his duty. And possibly sword fighting.

Oh, and cupcakes. But who wasn't gaga about baking around here?

At least that was what I remembered. I hadn't actually seen Drake in almost two years. He was the first full-blood dragon I'd ever met. Technically, he was around the same age as Gabby and me, but he was part of an epically powerful crew.

"How did Tony get out of it?" I asked, hoping that whatever technique the tech sorcerer had used could be duplicated. I really wasn't interested in getting all sweaty and tripping over my own feet for however many hours every week.

Gabby sneered. "Sprained his ankle on the edge of the mat. During warm-up. First session."

I laughed.

"Kandy refuses to communicate with Tony directly now, unless she deems it an emergency. Just so he understands how disgusted she is by his ineptitude."

My phone buzzed. I glanced at the screen. A series of names and the location of their remains appeared. "Speak of the devil. And, damn, he's fast."

"He's probably just been waiting for you to ask."

"Really?"

"Yeah. His magic works like that sometimes, making lists and stuff. Pattern recognition, and…you know."

I didn't actually know. "Huh, cool."

"Yeah. Just don't, like, expect anything you do online or on your phone to be private."

I narrowed my eyes at her.

She shrugged. "Like I said, it's a side effect of his magic. He collects all of our data, all the time, and looks for patterns. And actually, he's stopped some shitty things from happening by doing that. Before we moved here."

"Wow. Okay."

"Yeah." Gabby paused, thoughtful. "Maybe don't mention it to him. Let him tell you himself?"

"Sure."

She spun, jogging up the stairs without another word.

I dragged my heavy second satchel over to the back door, leaving it tucked to the side, then stepping out into the alley. I didn't actually like crossing into the bakery through the inner swing doors when it was open. It seemed rude. So I headed around to come in the front doors, then ordered a regular mocha for myself, along with Gabby's quadruple-shot pumpkin-spice latte. I scored another free cupcake from Todd, who was working the counter.

It took a couple of bites of the cupcake—*Rapture in a Cup*, chocolate and lemon cake swirled together and smothered in chocolate-cream-cheese icing—to shake off the heaviness of the conversation with Gabby. As I ate and waited for our drinks, I looked over the names that Tony had texted me and mapped out a plan for the mass summoning.

And now, if I needed a boost, I had an amplifier. Total score.

EVEN USING TONY'S LIST, IT TOOK MUCH STUMBLING AROUND TO try to locate the correct interments. But when it was done, I had set up a summoning that included five people connected to the child victims killed in 1976 and 1987. Tony had found the remains of a neighbor, an aunt, and a police officer connected to Anna Campbell, the nine-year old who'd died in October 1976. He'd also found a funeral-home director and the mother of Danny Pim, who had died in January 1987 at the age of five.

The late morning had brightened, the clouds clearing away, but it was chilly. Mountain View Cemetery was quiet, with no funerals going on and only a scattering of visitors, joggers, and dog walkers. Thankfully and as usual, no one seemed to notice me as I curled the lengths of silver chain into circles at each of the interment sites. No one except Gabby, that is.

The amplifier had, in fact, napped in the back seat of Kandy's SUV, waking only when I parked it near the East Thirty-Seventh Avenue entrance. I had told her to sleep a while longer, but she insisted on groggily following me as I moved carefully from gravesite to gravesite. It was the nature of my magic and my claiming of the cemetery that kept me masked from casual view. But I'd learned at the Academy that bright sunlight had a way of cutting through that sort of magic—and that some nonmagicals were more perceptive than others.

I didn't know any runes, and I couldn't imbue my magic into physical items, such as the chains. But I had scored the first link of each length with my initials, just in case that simple act of claiming the chain might help anchor the summoning. Magic was more often about intention, rather than a perfect technique. Then I carefully scraped a tiny palmful of moist dirt and grass from the edges of each gravestone or marker. In the past, I had used scrapings from the headstone or marker. That was more destructive than I liked to be, though. And also, I was worried that if I tied a silver chain that tightly to a specific gravesite, it might mean that I would get only one summoning out of each length.

And that was just wasteful.

At each site, I sprinkled the grave dirt over my initials, then pressed my fingers to the dirt-spattered chain and sent a lick of my power into the remains housed beneath it. Then I moved to the next grave.

I'd eliminated two of the names Tony had sourced for me, based on the fact that they were interred above ground in two separate white stone columbaria, and I wasn't sure how or where to set the silver chain so that it wouldn't be discovered after I stepped away. The grass was long enough at the other sites that it offered some camouflage.

I picked a central point for the actual casting, as best I could triangulate it. I laid out my towel there, let Ed out of my satchel to wander, then kneeled. I placed my candle in front of my knees, but didn't light it. I could feel the energy contained within the cemetery shifting and churning under me, tracing back to the five silver circles along the path I'd taken to and from each point. I'd brought extra candles, thinking I might need secondary focal points, but it didn't feel as though that was going to be necessary.

I focused, feeling the slight give in the damp grass under my knees, eyes open and aware of my surroundings. Listening to the power of the cemetery, I allowed myself to acknowledge the anxiety churning in my belly. I was about to call five shades at once, and if they all turned against me—if my theory about the circles of silver chain helping to hold them was garbage—then pushing all of them back at the same time was going to be way worse than the incident with the coroner's shade.

But the cemetery was my territory. All of the magic—and therefore, all of the shades—housed within Mountain View belonged to me. It was a reciprocal relationship, of course. I tended the power and it fed me, neither of us causing harm to the other.

I knew what I was doing. And I was capable of doing it.

Gabby leaned against a tall, rough-hewn headstone on my left, just at the edge of my peripheral vision. Her arms were crossed as she surveyed the site, side to side. "Need a boost?" she asked.

"I'll try casting first. Thanks." I closed my eyes, taking a few deep breaths. I allowed my awareness to first focus inward, then shifted that focus to the sensation of kneeling on the towel, on the grass, and on the magic embedded into the ground that was always eager for my attention.

Feeling well grounded, I reached my senses toward the nearest silver circle, immediately picking up impressions of Danny Pim's mother, Julie—a petite, dark-haired woman who had died only a few years after her son. Of breast cancer. That must have been devastating for their family—

I shoved the thought and the emotion that backed it away, focusing on my task. Pumping too much of anything into the casting would unbalance it. Untrained necromancers could become too attached to shades and ghosts, wasting away while trying to appease the shadow of a person who'd already moved on. That way led to insanity.

My own brother, Rusty, had tried to leech my life force to avenge his murder, almost killing me in the process. Though he hadn't been an ordinary ghost. The ghost of my mother's uncle remained with her perpetually, but they'd found a balance somehow. Possibly because she'd only been a toddler when he died—literally a baby necromancer. So she wouldn't have wielded much power, if any. In death, her uncle had latched on to what little bit of that magic he could, and hadn't left my mother's side since.

I anchored a thread of my magic at Julie Pim's gravesite, as if I was pinning the shade but not pulling it forth yet. Then I shifted my awareness to the next nearest silver circle, a neighbor of Anna Campbell's, Beverly Willis. Ms. Willis had died in her seventies, and took pride in her wild halo of curly white hair and the fact that she'd kept her own teeth right up to the moment she fell asleep and didn't wake up again. I pinned a thread of my magic to Ms. Willis's grave and moved on.

I placed two more anchor points at the gravesites of the police officer, Matt Dern, who had investigated Anna Campbell's death; and Edward Dray, the funeral director who had overseen Danny's interment. Lastly, I found and anchored a long strand of power within the ashes of Christina Campbell, Anna Campbell's aunt.

I was feeling a little thin as I set the fifth point—but a gossamer web of magic now stretched all around me. One strand was anchored to me, with five other threads stretched between and connecting the silver circles. I reached out a second time, drawing power from the pool of energy under me to place five more strands, so that each circle was anchored to me individually as well as tied to the gravesites on either side of it.

"Still good?" Gabby murmured quietly, trying to not disturb me. To her it probably looked as though I was just kneeling, meditating. As an amplifier, she couldn't feel the magic I'd just laced around the cemetery.

"Fine," I said. Wary of keeping focused, I kept my eyes closed and the bulk of my attention on the magic as I'd woven it together. Now I had to cinch the knots—just not too tightly.

"I'm going to call the shades forward now. Can you make notes for me? I'm going to ask questions, posing them to multiple shades at once."

"Gotcha."

I reached my senses along the strands tying me directly to the interments, sending a light pulse of my magic down each. "Speak to me," I murmured, gently coaxing the shades forward.

They came, rising within the silver rings. Hovering, insubstantial.

A thrill ran through me. Five shades at once. Hell, I'd just managed to impress myself.

"What are you grinning about?" Gabby asked, her tone on the edge of sharp. I could practically feel her glancing around frantically.

"No zombies," I said. "Don't worry. And it feels like the silver circles are doing their job too, containing the shades. But I don't want to hold them too long…"

"Sorry. Go ahead. I won't interrupt again."

I focused on the five shades I'd pulled forth, feeling them in my mind—a necessity, since three of them were too far away to actually focus on with my eyes. I confirmed that I held each one easily in place. "Ms. Willis, Christina, Officer Dern, Julie, and Edward," I whispered, visualizing sending the names down each of the individual strands of energy tying the shades to me. My naming drew a spark of what might generously have been called recognition from each. More of a focus. On me. "Thank you for answering my call. I would like to ask you five questions."

A slight breeze stirred my hair, adding to the chill that was creeping across my exposed skin. I ignored it. But holding five shades was going to cost me a lot of warmth—as well as a lot of my magic.

I had tried to make the questions as specific as I could without leading the answers too much. "Around the time of Anna Campbell's and Danny Pim's death, did you notice a female stranger leaving a token of some kind at their gravesite?"

"Yes," the shades of Julie Pim and Christina Campbell answered.

"No," the shades of Ms. Willis, Officer Dern, and Edward Dray responded.

"Yes from Julie and Christina," I said to Gabby. The amplifier didn't respond, so I pushed forward. "Julie and Christina." I allowed a tickle of magic to back my naming of the two shades. "Was the token some sort of ornament made of glass?"

"Yes." Once more, they responded as if in stereo.

I gave Gabby a thumbs up.

"Julie, can you describe the woman?"

The shade of Julie Pim, Danny's mother, paused for a moment as if thinking. Then she intoned in a flat voice. "Reddish hair, pale skin, around twenty. Tall, slim. Navy blue raincoat, unbelted. High heels."

I repeated Julie's description to Gabby, then asked a follow-up question. "Did you speak to her?"

"No." Magic pulsed back through the thread tying me to Danny Pim's mother, thickening it. I was fairly certain the silver circle was containing the shade, but I needed to move on.

I focused on the shade of Anna Campbell's aunt. "Christina, was the token you saw the stranger place on Anna's gravesite a glass rose or a sea turtle?"

"No," Christina's shade said.

Disappointed, I backed up. "Did you see the token the woman set on Anna's gravesite?"

"Yes."

"What was it?"

"A glass dolphin."

I frowned.

"What did she say?" Gabby asked.

"A dolphin."

Gabby grunted. "Maybe she uses different ornaments for each?"

"Christina, can you describe the stranger?"

"Twenty-five to thirty, Caucasian, tall, slim. She was wearing a belted cream raincoat, knee-high boots, and a scarf over her head, in shades of cream and blue."

"Did you see the color of her hair? Or eyes?"

"No."

I related the description to Gabby.

"Could still be the same person, Mory," the amplifier said, apparently noticing my growing disappointment. "Just using magic to change her apparent age. Move on to the police officer and the funeral-home guy."

I focused on the shades of Matt Dern, Edward Dray, and Anna Campbell's neighbor, Ms. Willis, starting my second thread of questions. "Matt, Edward, and Beverly. Did you notice any strangers asking questions or insinuating themselves in the investigation or funeral of Anna Campbell or Danny Pim?"

They answered in unison. "Yes."

"Was that woman in her…" I trailed off.

"Early to late twenties," Gabby murmured.

I repeated the age range to the shades, then added, "Pale skinned, tall, slim?"

"Yes." Again, all three.

"Did she have red hair?"

"Yes," the funeral-home director said.

"No," the shade of Officer Dern answered.

Ms. Willis remained silent.

I repeated the responses to Gabby and moved on. Magical masking or not, the longer I sat in the middle of the cemetery, the more likely I was to be noticed. Or, more accurately, Gabby was going to be noticed, and marked as loitering.

"Edward." I channeled a touch more of my power down the thread connecting me to the shade of the funeral-home director. "Did you speak to the woman with the red hair?"

"Yes."

"Did you ask her name?"

"Brigid Toohill."

I laughed quietly.

I had a name.

I relayed it to Gabby.

"I'll text Tony right away," she said. "With the description. And the date."

The connection between me and the Edward Dray shade was thickening, but I had a few more questions for him specifically. I held it steady but tried not to feed any more power through it. "What did the woman want?"

"She asked questions about the funeral arrangements, and expressed her condolences for the parents. But I pride myself in my confidentiality, so I directed her toward attending the service."

"Did she attend?"

He hesitated for a moment. "Yes."

I wasn't sure what the hesitation might have meant, but I took it as a sign that I needed to move on. I relayed his answers to Gabby, then focused on the shade of Matt Dern, adding a touch of power to my connection with him. Then I couldn't remember where I'd left off questioning him. "Damn it," I muttered. "The police officer?"

Gabby grunted. Then after a moment of presumably reading through her notes, she said, "Female stranger, yes, pale skinned, tall, yes, but no token, and not with red hair."

"Officer Dern, the stranger you met while investigating the death of Anna Campbell. Can you describe her?"

"Yes," he said in a monotone. "In her twenties, brown hair, slim, about five feet eight inches. Chatty. She asked me out for drinks, then made a joke about me being married."

Huh, okay. Flirting with the police officer investigating the child she possibly murdered seemed particularly heinous. "The hair color is wrong," I said, relaying the details. "Red hair is kind of hard to miss."

Gabby didn't answer, so I pushed forward with my questions anyway.

"Did you get her name?"

"Delia Thomas."

Damn it. I related the info to Gabby, ready to move back to Ms. Willis for the last round of questions before I let the shades rest.

"Wait," Gabby muttered.

"What?"

"Wait, I'm looking it up...red hair to brown hair."

"Sure, she could have dyed it, but the name doesn't match either."

"Well, yeah. If you were a succubus hunting in Vancouver, witch territory, every ten years, you'd use different names too."

Right. And that right there was why I was a certified necromancer, rather than a certified investigator.

Gabby whooped, quietly but triumphantly. "He's color-blind."

"What?"

"Officer Matt Dern was color blind. Red hair comes up as a shade of brown for him. Ask him. Ask him, Mory."

"Okay, all right. Calm down."

She laughed. I turned my attention to the shade of Officer Dern, adding a touch of my magic to the question. "Matt. Are you color-blind? Do you see reds as shades of brown?"

He hesitated. And for the first time ever, I felt some sort of resistance against my hold, as if the police officer was trying to not answer my question. That was unusual with a shade. But then, death magic often acted a little oddly for me. And if the previous night was any indication, casting in a cemetery I had claimed added an extrapowerful dimension to my summons. Hence my idea to use the silver rings.

Still, I wanted the answer. So I pushed, repeating the question with another press of power.

"Yes," the shade of Matt Dern said. "But the department doesn't know. I'm a good police officer."

Ah. There was the source of the resistance. He had somehow kept his condition a secret. I wasn't certain I'd ever tried to pry secrets from a shade before, so maybe that hesitation was standard. I would have to look into it.

Wait…

Ms. Willis had been silent when I asked her the last question as well.

I focused on the shade of the elderly neighbor of Anna Campbell. She had hesitated when I'd asked about a stranger with red hair. So did Ms. Willis have something to hide as well? Anna Campbell had been killed in 1976…and if I put together the inappropriate flirting with Officer Dern, and that Officer Paul Reid had mentioned thinking about asking out the neighbor tied to his investigation…

Wait…

I needed to check my notes, but I was fairly certain I remembered that the neighbor in the Reid case had red hair as well—

"You okay, Mory?" Gabby whispered, worried.

I nodded. "Just thinking outside the box a little. Well, outside my box. Being gay in 1976…a lesbian, I mean. That was probably a big deal, right?"

Gabby snorted, not disagreeing.

"Beverly," I asked, strengthening my connection to the shade of Ms. Willis as much as I could without calling her all the way over. Ghosts were unpredictable, often resistant to answering questions—and occasionally hard to put back after they'd been pulled forth. "Did you meet a woman in her twenties around the death of Anna Campbell in 1976?"

"Yes," she said without hesitation.

"Did she ask questions about Anna's death?"

A slight pause. "Yes."

"Did she visit you at your home?"

I felt that resistance again. But it dispersed the moment I pressed my magic against it.

"Yes," Ms. Willis said.

"Do you know her name?"

"Brigid Thomas."

That was a combination of the first two names. And the shade of Paul Reid had mentioned the name of the good-looking neighbor. Biddy Thomas!

Bingo. B. I. N. G. O. Bingo.

Gabby was right. The succubus changed names, but apparently rather lazily. Possibly. Assuming I was even on the right track at all.

I forged ahead, ignoring my own doubts. Being a realist was annoying, especially when dealing with magic. "Did Brigid Thomas flirt with you?"

"Yes."

"Did you talk about Anna or her parents?"

"Yes."

Grinning, I asked one final question. "Did she have red hair?"

The shade of Ms. Willis sighed. "Yes."

Feeling a little smug, I filled Gabby in on the extra confirmation I'd collected. "Did you send the names to Tony?"

"You betcha."

I allowed the magic I was holding between me and the five shades to ease, whispering, "Thank you. Sleep now."

The shades slowly dispersed, as did the gossamer tendrils of my magic, as if that power had all been consumed. Finally, only Gabby, Ed, and I remained in the cemetery. Plus the ever-present cyclists and dog walkers, of course. A chill had sunk deep into my skin, digging into my bones. I opened my eyes, swaying slightly in place.

"You okay, Mory?" Gabby asked again.

"Yeah. Just give me a minute and I'll collect the silver chains."

"Are they, like, active?"

"No."

"I'll collect them. You sit for a little longer."

I almost declined the offer. But then, not wanting to force Gabby to wait for me to recover, I thought better of it. "Thank you."

She tucked her phone in her back pocket and took off toward Julie Pim's gravesite. I wiggled my fingers at Ed, and he sauntered over to stare up at me, just out of reach so I couldn't scoop him up easily. I had no idea how he'd learned to judge such things, to make decisions for himself, but I tried to not question it too much. Magic, clearly. The magic I had originally claimed him with, perpetually tying him to me, to my life force. And which had then combined with Jade bleeding all over him, inadvertently making Ed resistant to magic and able to turn himself invisible.

Granted, the dowser had been really hurt herself at the time—hence the bleeding—and possibly not in her right mind.

Actually, I'd totally missed the opportunity to tease Jade about superpowering Ed up. She really didn't like having her magic compared to radiation exposure gone wrong.

Smiling to myself, I let Ed explore for a few minutes more. The grass was fairly dry, so I wasn't terribly worried about him getting too wet. Closing my eyes, I raised my face to the sun and internally begged the bright-but-distant orb to lend me some heat. I was really glad I was wearing hand-knits—and in multiple layers.

SEVEN

I WAS AT HOME, BURIED UNDER A MOUND OF BLANKETS AND DEEP IN the grips of a nap, when my phone buzzed with a text message from Tony. I managed to knock the cell off my side table, then had to hang off the bed to grab it because I wasn't sure my legs wanted to wake up enough to actually climb out from under the toasty covers.

>*Biddy Thomas is listed as the neighbor who found Misty Dean, as expected. But no matches for Brigid Toohill or Delia or Brigid Thomas. And no official mention of those names in any of the reports I've cobbled together.*

I groaned, texting back.

Seriously?

>*Did I stutter?*

Ugh. Don't be an asshole.

>*It was a joke, Mory. But it's too far back for a ton of digitized records or online data. 1976 and even 1987. I'll keep looking. But if we're going to track down*

the succubus in the present, we need whatever name she's using now.

Did you send the description to Liam?

>Yeah...but...

What does that mean?

>He doesn't want to harass Tanya's parents asking about a red-haired woman. Not any more than he already has.

But it's okay for me to harass the dead?

>Is that rhetorical?

I snarled, set my phone down so both of us could have a timeout, and went to take a shower.

BY THE TIME I'D BLOW-DRIED MY HAIR, A WHOLE SLEW OF MESSAGES from Tony were waiting for me. The tech sorcerer had continued texting—nagging me to answer him—while I'd showered. Over and over.

And then, gloriously, he dropped an address at the bottom of his thread.

For Tanya's parents.

I hadn't even known that was what I wanted.

So all I had to do was stake out their home, waiting until they showed up, and then pepper them with questions about a red-haired woman who might somehow be connected to their daughter's death.

And how did I know about that?

I was a necromancer.

I sighed.

That conversation was over before it even started.

But apparently, that indisputable fact didn't stop me from getting dressed, booking a car share, and mapping a route to the Atkinsons' house.

Because sure, maybe the succubus would just be hanging out? Stalking the parents of her latest victim? Which would be seriously creepy and completely screwed up, yes. But stranger things happened to me every day. Then I could text the hunters a current picture of the succubus, along with her location, and I wouldn't need to bother the Atkinsons at all.

Okay, I wasn't managing to even kid myself. This was way over the line. I knew it. Even as I pulled on my poncho and tucked Ed into my bag.

I knew. Even I couldn't pretend that I was just going for a drive.

It was the soulless graves. Of children.

I just…

Stealing flowers like I had when I was a child, to set on another child's final resting place. Whispering to shades. It just wasn't enough anymore. Not if I could do something about it.

If Liam wasn't going to ask about a red-haired woman, then someone had to. Because the other cases were too old, like Tony had said. We needed current info.

Instead of informing Tony of my intentions—because I was still having a hard time smothering the clamoring of every instinct I had—I texted back a simple *Thank you.*

He didn't respond.

The tech sorcerer had known what he was doing when he gave me the address. He would have my back. At least remotely, via the map he was constantly monitoring even when it wasn't his shift.

And it wasn't as though I would actually attempt to hunt down a succubus on my own. Needing to feel productive wasn't the same as being an idiot.

I just wasn't quite sure that anyone else—namely Liam—would see it that way. So I would keep my next plan of action to myself. For the present.

Anything less, and I wasn't certain I could live with myself. Because, yeah, once again, I believed.

I believed there was a reason that Liam had brought me the case. A reason that the sorcerer had been obsessed with Tanya Atkinson's death in the first place, when that sort of thing seemed so out of character for him.

I believed that magic wanted me involved. That magic wanted the children to be…I don't know, avenged maybe? Though that wasn't my part or my duty.

I was fine being just a cog on the wheel of fate or destiny.

Just so long as I was an active participant. Otherwise, if I had to wander Mountain View, continually feeling the blank spots—well, my own soul might wither and degrade.

Because now that I'd found them, I didn't think I could ignore the soul- empty graves of children.

Dramatic much? Hell yeah.

But I was signed on.

I believed.

Still, I intended to be really quiet about the plan, especially if it turned out that my need to do something more was just me being all arrogant and foolhardy. And possibly still jet-lagged.

TEN MINUTES AFTER PICKING THE CAR UP, I PULLED UP ACROSS THE street from the Atkinsons' yellow-sided triplex on West Fifteenth Avenue. I hadn't expected anyone to be home. But apparently, I'd forgotten that people occasionally had jobs that allowed them to schedule their shifts and time off around each other. Meaning I had somehow randomly decided to stalk the Atkinsons on a joint afternoon off.

Thankfully, even after I parked, I found I couldn't actually force myself out of the car. So I sat there, paying the car share by the minute like a moron, trying to formulate a way to approach grieving parents, to ask them all the same questions I'd asked the shades.

But I just…I couldn't do it.

Not only was it outside the scope of the contract I'd entered into with Liam—by which my actions were supposed to be guided—but I just couldn't imagine being on the other side of having that conversation forced upon me. I couldn't imagine being Tanya's parents, grieving, and having some random person question me out of nowhere. The inquest into

Rusty's death and the murders he and Sienna committed had been bad enough, and everyone—even my mother—had sheltered me from it. Though, it had broken my mother completely.

My heart ached for the dead kids that I had no ability to help, not in any meaningful way. And as I sat there gripping the steering wheel, I realized that I was scared too. Scared about the missing souls. Terrified that I'd seemingly uncovered evidence that the soul, the life force, could be removed from the body it had once inhabited. Maybe even consumed.

That wasn't how it was supposed to be. I had always thought, had always felt deeply within my own being, that death was just another dimension. That energy couldn't be destroyed.

So if that wasn't true, then…I wasn't certain what to believe. About anything.

I exhaled harshly, hot tears edging my eyes and snot filling my nose. I was spiraling. And I had no idea why, no clue as to why I was so heavily invested.

I had stood before the open maw of the end of the world and not faltered. So why was I falling apart now?

I dug through my satchel for Kleenex. I was being ridiculous.

I settled Ed in my lap, allowing myself that comfort while I got my shit together. Which is to say, I blew my nose and wiped my eyes. I had jobs lined up. I had Benjamin's journals to finish reading. I was supposed to be a damn adult.

I started the car, intending to drive away, to maybe drown my self-doubt in a tasty cupcake before heading home, when Maria and Dwayne Atkinson exited their front door.

They walked side-by-side down the front path, shoulders and fingers brushing, with their dark-haired heads canted in quiet conversation as they crossed to a green sedan on the street. Dwayne held the passenger side door open for Maria, then crossed around to climb into the driver's seat.

My heart rate had ramped up at their appearance, with only a guess and the house number letting me know I was watching—stalking, really—Tanya's parents. Catching them in what had appeared to be an intimate moment, just like the creepy voyeur I had suddenly become.

The car pulled away.

I waited a moment before I followed. I was facing the same direction that they had driven, and turning around on the tight street would have drawn too much attention, even in a tiny Smart car.

Not really knowing that I intended to do so, I also turned left onto Cypress Street after they did.

Technically, I was still heading toward the bakery for that cupcake I'd promised myself.

Then, as if I couldn't stop myself from doing so, I followed them all the way down to First Avenue.

They parked and got out.

I circled the block, trying to convince myself that I was still a step away from taking the creepy stalker fixation too far. Liam would be incensed. Not to mention that Adepts simply couldn't have casual conversations with nonmagicals about the possibility that their child had been murdered by a magically enhanced predator.

Despite the earlier tears and the self-doubt, I was apparently still contemplating digging a hole that even I, with my legion of protectors, wouldn't be able to easily get out of.

But I knew—I was absolutely certain—that their child had been murdered. The Atkinsons knew it too, in their hearts. Which was why they'd approached Liam to keep looking into Tanya's death. I felt a completely overwhelming responsibility to somehow fix the situation, to somehow fill the blank spots at Mountain View…

My chest tightened, constricting my lungs.

I understood what was going on.

The magic of Mountain View Cemetery was driving me. Magic I had taken on as my own.

The sanctity of the cemetery had been breached by a series of unnatural murders, for decades. And now that I had recognized that wound for what it was, it was my responsibility to somehow heal it.

Kett was right. The training at the Academy had been definitely inadequate. Of course, they hadn't had a soul seer specialist in a quarter of a century.

My edge of desperation eased—the edge that had been driving me since I'd woken to the realization that my part in the investigation was over. Passing the Atkinsons' parked car a second time, I caught sight of Maria and Dwayne climbing the front stairs of a heritage house that had been converted into office space. The building was in the center of a row of homes that had all been renovated into commercial suites. One of the secondhand stores that the twins really liked was on the ground floor two buildings over. I found the clothing they stocked too expensive, especially with my predilection for only buying cashmere sweaters so I could reclaim the yarn. The upper suites of all the converted homes were mostly filled with various doctors' offices, plus a dentist. A day spa occupied the lower level of the building the Atkinsons had entered.

I pulled into a parking spot designated for the car share about a half block away. I logged out of the app and locked up. Still sorting out my thoughts about having magically bonded with a cemetery and getting more than I'd expected from it, I slowly wandered up the street. I glanced at the sign posted at the base of the stairs for the house I'd seen the Atkinsons enter. Along with the spa on the ground floor, a number of different therapists maintained offices on the other levels, as well as a clothing designer.

I was fairly certain Maria and Dwayne weren't getting pedicures or being fitted for evening wear. Nope. They were seeing their therapist.

Ah, hell. Now I felt like a complete heel.

But did I do the right thing and leave? The bakery was only a ten- or fifteen-minute walk away. I could have still drowned my feelings of ineptitude in cupcakes.

Double nope.

I glanced both ways. Then, jaywalking between parked cars, I grabbed a window table at the sushi place directly across the street.

I ORDERED A CALIFORNIA ROLL, THEN SLOWLY DRANK AN ENTIRE pot of green tea. The last cups were bitter, which felt like fitting punishment for completely ignoring my better judgement and staking out grieving parents at their therapist's office.

I knew I really couldn't blame magic for my behavior. I might have been feeling some sort of compulsion because Mountain View Cemetery was my claimed territory and it had been sullied by the succubus—and even that was still all conjecture. But I was a rational being.

A believer could still be a realist. A believer still knew the difference between right and wrong. So while I might have currently been skirting along an edge, I definitely wasn't going to cross it.

I would just keep telling myself that.

The restaurant was empty, but the solo staffer didn't appear to have any problem with me hanging out and not ordering much. I read through all my emails, texted Tony a nothing update, and tried to not track the time. Unsuccessfully.

Exactly one hour and one minute after they'd entered, the Atkinsons exited the building across the street and slowly made their way down the stairs. Dwayne hovered his hand under Maria's elbow. She clung to the railing, wiping her eyes with a crumpled tissue.

A terrible, aching chasm opened in my chest.

Why the hell was I doing this?

Why was I even there?

I was a necromancer. I had no ability to help grieving parents. And absolutely no right to inflict any more pain on them.

I looked away, digging blindly in my satchel for my wallet and pulling out a ten-dollar bill. I tucked the money under my empty teacup, rose, and shouldered my satchel. I called out, "Thank you," as I hustled to the front door.

I paused, my hand on the steel handle, glancing through the inset glass in time to see Dwayne help Maria into their parked sedan about a half a block up the street. He glanced behind him as he carefully shut the car door behind his wife, as if someone had called out to him.

I followed his gaze back to the building they had just exited, to their therapist's office. A woman in her midthirties, dressed in navy wool slacks and a blazer, with a large silk scarf wrapped around her neck and shoulders, stood on the stoop. Her hair fell forward across her face as she leaned over the railing to address Dwayne. He nodded in response. I couldn't hear their conversation from the interior of the sushi place.

She had red hair. Practically orange. A totally natural shade that wasn't at all common in Vancouver, British Columbia, Canada.

I gripped the steel handle of the door, momentarily frozen in place as thoughts and recollections banged around in my head.

She wasn't wearing the sunglasses or the knit beret. But the woman—the Atkinsons' therapist, or maybe a receptionist—was the same woman who'd been watching Liam during our lunch the previous day.

I was completely, utterly certain.

She had red hair.

That bore repeating, even if only to convince myself of the fact.

Was it possible the Atkinsons were in therapy with the succubus? A succubus that had murdered their daughter? That was...that thought was...chilling, completely impossible, entirely implausible...

The red-haired woman stepped back into the office, shutting the door behind her.

Dwayne crossed around the sedan and climbed into the driver's seat. After a moment, the car pulled away from the curb.

Still frozen in place with my mind running on overdrive, I stared at the therapist's office door. It could have been a coincidence. It had to be a coincidence. Sure, the therapist or whoever she was might have red hair. And I might have seen her seemingly stalking Liam. But her age was wrong. She was at least a decade older than the shades I'd questioned had indicated.

Granted, I had no idea how—or even if—a succubus aged. The shades had all identified the red-haired stranger as being in her twenties. But the cases were decades apart. I knew vampires didn't age the same as humans, and dragons didn't either. Even witches and shapeshifters aged slowly.

And Kett had called the succubus a different sort of vampire.

I exited the restaurant, jogging between the cars parked at the curbside meters and crossing the street before I'd even made the decision to do so. I was lucky I didn't get hit, because I wasn't paying attention to anything around me.

I had promised to stay out of it.

I'd promised to not hunt the succubus on my own.

But I had also said I would help gather clues.

I tugged my phone from my satchel. Intending to pause only briefly, I took a picture of the sign hanging at the base of the stairs for the therapist's office. It listed the practitioners. I quickly scanned the names—three women and two men. No Delia Thomas or Brigid Toohill, though.

I glanced up at the main floor of the building, scanning the windows. The converted house jutted out on the right side—a bay window, I thought, though I wasn't sure that was the correct term. A series of indistinct items were arranged on the interior windowsill. I raised my phone, using the camera to zoom in, but it still took a moment to figure out what I was looking at.

Clear shapes…

Tiny glass ornaments…

Before I could try to assess the forms of the ornaments, something large moved in the background. I snapped a picture that was probably going to turn out to be just a blur, then quickly lowered my phone.

The red-haired woman was standing in the bay window.

Looking down at me.

My heart rate went wild. Somehow, I managed a weak smile, then made a halfhearted gesture toward the sign, trying to suggest I intended to call for an appointment.

The woman frowned.

I turned away, hustling down the sidewalk with no destination in mind. I scrolled through the contacts that Tony had transferred to my new phone, dialing it and pressing it against my ear.

It took four rings and a half a block before the tech sorcerer picked up.

"Are you actually calling me?" he asked, incredulous. His voice sounded hollow, like he was talking over his own phone's speaker.

"Yes," I hissed. "I've just done something seriously stupid."

Voices, clicking noises, and then something shifting in the background filtered through from the other end of the conversation. I turned the corner blindly, intending to zigzag uphill toward the bakery.

"What did you do?" Tony's voice was much more present. He'd taken me off speaker.

More questions sounded in the background, but I couldn't distinguish words or identify actual voices.

"I'm fine," I said, addressing the concern I could hear in Tony's voice rather than his question. "I have a couple of pictures to send you. I think I might have just…"

The red-haired woman was standing on the sidewalk at the corner, directly in my way. She had to have cut through the back alley in order to get in front of me.

"Oh, shit…" I muttered.

"Oh, shit?" Tony echoed in my ear. "Oh, shit what?"

The woman frowned deeply, then with her hands fisted at her sides, she strode toward me. "You!" she snarled like a pissed-off cat. "I know you!"

I gaped at her.

If she was a succubus, I couldn't feel it. But then, I likely wouldn't feel it—not even if she was a regular Adept of any kind other than a vampire or necromancer. My own magic didn't work that way.

"Mory?" Tony said through the phone still pressed to my ear.

"Just listen," I murmured, forcing myself to stay in place. Then, keeping my tone as icy as possible, I spoke to the red-haired therapist. Or whoever, whatever, she was. "I don't know you, lady."

She couldn't attack me, couldn't hurt me. Not only were there people everywhere around us—cars, pedestrians, shoppers—but if she tried to use magic against me, it wouldn't go well for her. Not only would my necklace repel any magical assault, but she would light up the boundary ward that the Godfrey coven maintained around the entire city. If she was the succubus in hiding, her magical signature would set off all sorts of warnings. The same hadn't been true in 2017 when she'd killed Tanya, because the boundary hadn't been in place then.

A thought occurred to me. If I could get her to attack me—

"Mory?" Tony asked. "You still there? I'm sending Bitsy. I can see you on the grid. She can be there in two minutes."

"Wait," I said into the phone.

The therapist halted a few steps away, her hands on her hips. She scanned me up and down, then sneered. "Oh yes, it was you. With that police officer at—"

"Detective," I said smoothly.

"Whatever," she sniffed. "I know you're harassing my clients. You and the so-called detective, filling their heads with nonsense. Why else would you be stalking them?"

I didn't say anything, aware that if I remained quiet, it would be easier for Tony to pick up every word on his end of the conversation.

"Well?"

"Well, what?" I asked, starting to get pissed off myself. I couldn't hold on to fear for terribly long. That was a bit of a shortcoming, actually. Especially when factored in with my already-limited sense of self-preservation.

"You're a terrible person," she spat. "Their child is dead! And you're giving them false hope."

"Keep moving," Tony murmured in my ear.

As if pushed forward by his suggestion, I side-stepped the peeved redhead, deliberately walking around her close enough that she could make a grab for me. If the necklace reacted, I'd know if she was an Adept.

She didn't grab for me.

I kept walking.

"I'm making an official complaint," she called after me.

I made it to the corner, looked both ways, and crossed the street, still holding the phone to my ear. I glanced back from the safety of the opposite side-walk. The red-haired woman had marched off in the other direction, back toward her office at best guess.

I kept moving, intent on making it to the bakery and behind the wards. "Tell me you saw her on the grid too," I said into the phone.

"Nope, sorry." Tony's voice in my ear was com-forting, grounding. "Want to tell me what that was all about?"

"I think she might be the succubus. She has red hair, like the shades I questioned had mentioned, but she's the wrong age. She might also be stalking Liam. I saw her when we had lunch yesterday."

Tony snorted. "Women are like that around him. No guys though, which is odd. Maybe he gives off a really straight vibe."

"Like he'd tell you," I said, momentarily distracted. Then I shook my head. "I've got pictures to send to you."

"Send them," he said. "Just don't hang up the phone."

I sighed. "I'm fine. I'm probably wrong." I lowered the phone and texted the two pictures I'd taken to Tony—one of the sign listing the names of the therapists, and one of the glass ornaments. Then I put the phone back to my ear. "Sent."

There was a pause from his end of the conversation as I approached the corner, then kept hoofing it up the hill. I was a block away from Fourth Avenue now. I planned to head west along the street, rather than up the alley, even though it seemed unlikely I was being tracked or watched.

Yeah, despite being stupid about stalking the Atkinsons, I usually wasn't an idiot.

Not anymore, at least.

I knew which battles I could fight and win. An unknown Adept of unknown power was big trouble. Hence my getting to the bakery as fast as I could.

Speaking of which…

"Hey," I said. "I know that the grid wasn't in place when the succubus killed Tanya in 2017. But if there is a succubus in Vancouver now, wouldn't she show on the grid? Like, at all times, like I do?"

Tony grunted. I could hear his fingers racing across his keyboards. "No. Only magical events and certain objects of power show on the grid. At least now. Remember when the witches had to replace Jade with Burgundy at the anchor point across from our house? That lessened the grid's sensitivity. Which is good, because none of us would have any privacy. Warded buildings show up, and objects of extreme power."

Objects of extreme power. "Like my necklace?"

"Yep. And I can see you when you cast at the cemetery."

"What about an object like Benjamin's pen or Liam's badge?"

"Nope. Only when they use them. We tested the badge, like, a year ago. Which you'd know if you'd been in town."

I ignored that last jab. "So the succubus could be living in plain sight as long as she doesn't use her magic. Or run into Jade, I suppose." When the dowser had been tied to the grid, her sensitivity to magic had practically driven her mad. Well, as mad as Jade was capable of getting.

"Or the grid isn't calibrated to pick up a succubus's magic." I could almost hear Tony's shrug, then he grunted. "Why am I looking at a blurred picture of…" He trailed off.

I gave him a moment. His fingers tapped on his keyboard, slowly now.

"Are those…"

"Glass ornaments, like the ones on the children's graves. But I couldn't make out the shapes."

"Fuck."

"Yeah."

"I'm running a search on the names of the therapists now. I'll send everything to Liam, including the recording of your conversation with the supposed succubus. But, ah…you better be prepared."

Yeah, Liam was going to be pissed. Seriously pissed, on multiple fronts. I veered right onto West Fourth. The sidewalks were suddenly full of pedestrians laden with shopping bags, carrying to-go mugs, or pushing strollers. Halfway down the block, the bakery sign came into view.

"I'm almost at the bakery. Maybe I'll just hang out there while the rest of you find the succubus, then everyone will forget I kind of stumbled into her. Assuming I didn't just piss off a regular therapist. Though clearly a really overly protective one."

"I see you," Tony said. Then he hung up without saying goodbye.

Well, that was oddly ominous.

EIGHT

I HUNG OUT AT THE BAKERY LONG ENOUGH THAT I HAD CONSUMED an entire cupcake—*Envy in a Cup*, cocoa spice cake with spiced-cocoa buttercream—downed another mocha, and almost finished knitting the marled hat before I heard from Tony. By text this time. I was actually surprised the tech sorcerer had bothered to answer his phone when I'd called.

>*You don't need to hide out any longer.*

>*The therapist is Brit Thompson.*

>*She doesn't match the profile Jasmine and I put together.*

I actually set aside my knitting to check my email, wanting to see if I'd missed an update about the case. I hadn't.

I texted back. *Profile? What profile?*

He ignored the question.

>*The hunting party will check her out when they hit the streets tonight.*

Tonight was All Hallows' Eve, aka Halloween. Though I hadn't actually realized that until I'd entered the bakery. Peggy had been liberal with the decorations, including spiderwebs strung through the window trinkets, a large, toothy jack-o'-lantern by the cash register, and little ghost and tombstone toppers for the cupcakes. I thought they might have been marzipan. Mine had been sweet, and a little crunchy.

And yeah, I was totally letting down my necromancer brethren with my disinterest in Halloween. Tomorrow—All Souls' Day—was more my sort of thing.

Admittedly, though, Halloween was a perfect cover for a succubus hunt. At least for anyone sensitive to magic, whether by taste, sight, or smell. Namely, not me. It would probably take Kandy and Kett no more than a few hours to scour the city.

I sighed, considering a second cupcake as I completed the last of the decreases, snipped the yarn, and threaded the end through the final stitches of the hat. I cinched the top closed with a couple of sharp tugs, then started weaving in the ends.

Just as my phone blew up with text messages.

Jasmine pounced first.

>*That was a stupid stunt. Don't make me regret backing you, Mory. Tony will be keeping a closer eye on you. You're allowed to hang out at the bakery until closing, then go home. End of discussion.*

Allowed? Ouch.

Then Liam.

>*We will be talking about this.*

>*All of it.*

>*I'm seriously pissed, Mory.*

> *Just not tonight. Tonight you stay home. Stay out of it.*

Well, I'd seen that coming from miles away. Though the separated texts indicated an unusual level of ire. Normally, Liam wasn't that easily agitated, and it wasn't as though I'd gotten hurt…or gotten anyone killed. Compared to the sort of shit that usually went down in Vancouver, sort-of-stumbling across a succubus wasn't even a minor infraction.

Except I knew that if everyone else had ruled the therapist out as a suspect, it was my stalking of the nonmagicals that had them all so pissed.

With just enough of a pause that I'd thought the worst of the tongue-lashings were over, I then heard from the executioner himself.

>*Benjamin will meet you at your home, thirty minutes after sunset.*

Okay, first? I was seriously surprised Kett had my phone number. And that he texted in the first place. But second? My face flushed with indignation. Benjamin Garrick had been assigned to me. As my babysitter. That was completely ridiculous.

Channeling all my adultness, I ordered a second cupcake—*Heaven in a Cup*, all fluffy white cake with coconut buttercream—continued weaving in the loose ends on the marled hat, and refrained from losing my mind via text message.

In fact, I didn't bother replying at all.

To any of them.

I had barely stepped across a line. And even then, so what? I was maybe one toe over, and all the wildly protective zealots who had claimed dominion over my well-being got to go into overdrive?

Though yeah, I was seriously surprised that Kett had bothered to text at all.

So what if I'd gotten kidnapped and nearly killed a few years ago?

Twice.

And then there was that time they'd all sat around watching the life being slowly sucked from me by the instruments of assassination when I already had my arm and both legs in casts. After being patched up, they'd all come through the final battle with the elves relatively unscathed. Except for Jade. Jade and I had nearly died together…

Damn it.

All right, then. I could see where they were coming from.

Though Liam was pushing it, tonally at least.

Still, I understood my role. I didn't need it rammed down my throat. I would step back. I'd let the big guns take over—literally, in Liam's case—so that I could happily spend the evening looking over the job offers Pearl had emailed and reading through more of Benjamin's chronicles.

But I wasn't at all interested in waiting like a good little girl until the bakery closed. So I carefully threaded my needle through a few stitches of the hat so I didn't lose it, then shoved it in my satchel. Struggling within the confines of the bag, Ed climbed over a candle and a hairbrush I had no idea why I carried everywhere, making a beeline for the hat. I paused, satchel slung across my lap to pet him as he managed to wedge his upper body within the knitting. At least there wasn't any yarn for him to tangle.

Kandy shoved her way through the swing doors that led to the kitchen, instantly finding me perched at my table by the windows and pinning me in place with a dark-eyed gaze.

Oh, shit.

Dressed head to toe in black, with her golden cuffs glinting on each of her wrists, she slowed her pace as she prowled toward me.

Slinging the satchel over my shoulder, I stood up.

"Sit," Kandy growled.

I sat.

Damn it.

She slid onto the stool opposite me. She'd done that alpha-werewolf thing on me, and I'd responded on an instinctual level. I seriously hated that.

"I'm going home," I said, refusing to look at the pink-haired enforcer.

"I've ordered Chinese. You'll join me for dinner."

"It's too early to eat."

"Mory." My name came out as a low growl. "I'll drive you home."

"I want the walk."

"Act like a baby and you'll get treated like one."

Completely pissed now, I met Kandy's steady gaze. "Actually, it's acting like a thinking, breathing individual with well-honed skills and evidence-based opinions that has me under house arrest."

Kandy bared her teeth. It wasn't a smile. "You scare us, Mory."

"Yeah," I snarled back, keeping my voice low to avoid drawing notice from the other customers. "I get it. You're all sitting around waiting for me to go dark. Because I'm damaged and…weak."

Kandy blinked. "What?"

But I just barreled on, pressing my finger to the table for emphasis. "I've stood on the same battlefields as you…four times now! I don't need some glorified babysitter to drive me home through a goddamn city in which everything I do, every move I make is tracked!"

Kandy leaned back, suddenly relaxed. Deceptively so, I thought. "Fine."

"Fine?"

"Yeah, I'm not a glorified babysitter."

I narrowed my eyes at her.

She looked at me, a curl of a smile softening her expression.

"I'm leaving," I said.

She shrugged. "Go for it. Since you're a thinking, breathing individual."

Well, it sounded stupid when she said it, but it had made sense in my head. "I'll head straight home."

"I know."

Sensing a trap, I slid off the stool and crossed toward the exterior door. Kandy snagged my wrist as I passed, holding me lightly.

So close that her breath stirred my hair, she whispered to me, "I know what it's like to believe that people think there's something wrong with you, deep down inside."

I flicked my gaze to hers, emotion suddenly tightening my throat.

She twisted her lips. "But I don't smell darkness in you, Morana Novak. I trust you."

My chest loosened, just enough so I could breathe, could speak again. "I…trust you."

She nodded, releasing my wrist. "Don't pull that shit with the mundanes again."

I huffed. "Fine."

"And go straight home." She pulled a cellphone from her back pocket, waving it at me. "I'll be tracking you."

Kandy had the grid point map on her phone. "I already said I would."

"Then why are you still here?"

I shook my head. The werewolf had serious intimacy issues. She deliberately ruined every potentially nice moment. "Enjoy your dinner."

"I won't be inviting you again," she snarled. Turning her attention to her phone, she touched the screen, sliding her fingers to zoom in. The block that represented the bakery enlarged, glowing light blue.

The werewolf enforcer was literally going to watch me walk home, because my necklace was powerful enough to show on the grid map even when not in use. Just like Tony had said.

I sighed—and only then realized that I'd left the last half of my *Heaven in a Cup* on the table. I stepped back and—

Kandy swiped the cupcake, cramming it in her mouth.

The theft actually pained me.

The werewolf moaned quietly, then smacked her lips.

I pressed close enough to speak against her ear, then articulated my threat far too loudly for her sensitive hearing. "Just remember who wields the death magic, werewolf, next time you tuck yourself into bed."

Kandy flinched away, pressing her hand over her assaulted ear while chortling madly.

I lifted my chin and exited the bakery with a sense of dignity and payback. Then I remembered the map, and the tracking that kicked in the moment I cleared the bakery wards.

Yeah, that little tidbit courtesy of Tony about my necklace perpetually lighting up the grid map was an uncomfortable nugget of knowledge. I carried that weight on my shoulders all the way home. Or maybe it felt like more of a noose?

THE WALK HOME TOOK ME FORTY-FIVE MINUTES. AS THE SUN SET and the evening cooled further, people started setting pumpkins out on their front stoops and the smaller kids took to the streets in costume. Pirates, witches, Harry Potter, and superhero characters abounded.

The Georgian manor I called home was dark. As I'd presumed it would be.

But I hadn't anticipated the sorcerer waiting for me on the doorstep.

Liam Talbot. Outwardly seething. Still dressed in one of his work suits, but without the tie. Badge clipped to his belt. He was pacing, but paused once he laid eyes on me standing on the sidewalk.

I stepped through the wrought-iron gate, letting it fall shut behind me, then walked up the overgrown front path. I wasn't going to be bullied in my own home. Honestly, my mother did enough of that already. When she actually bothered to acknowledge me. Or be in town.

Liam ran his hand through his hair, mussing it adorably as he made a half-hearted attempt to rein in his obvious ire.

I quashed an inappropriate smile, not certain why I had the impulse to grin at him in the first place.

"Really, Mory?" the dark-haired sorcerer snapped as my foot hit the bottom front step.

"Really, Liam," I said calmly, traversing the stairs and stepping around him to unlock the door. He'd already informed me, not terribly politely via his texts, that we wouldn't be having this conversation tonight. I struggled to not throw that tidbit back in his face, figuring it would backfire on me. Obviously, something else had happened since he'd texted. And I wasn't looking forward to the reveal.

The sorcerer stepped up behind me so tightly that I swore I could feel him breathing down my neck.

I opened the door, entering the house and flicking on the entranceway lights. Liam remained tight to my tail. He shut the door behind him.

I unlaced and shucked off my boots, placing them in the closet. Then I tugged Ed out of my satchel and set him on the marble floor to wander. I pulled my poncho off. The beads knotted to the thick fringe clacked together. Now that I was inside, I was too warm. Just from the walk, though. Not from the stifling anger I could feel rolling off the sorcerer.

Unable to avoid it any longer, I turned to address Liam. "A glass of water?"

"No," he said, gazing toward the open doors to the library.

"I need one." I wandered deeper into the house, past the sweeping marble stairs toward the kitchen.

After a moment of hesitation, Liam followed. I could feel his eagle-eyed gaze roving across the grand staircase with its thick banisters, the marble floors, the carved cornices, and the massive crystal chandelier dangling over our heads.

In the kitchen, I pulled two tall water glasses from an upper cupboard and crossed to the fridge, filling each with filtered water. Twenty years ago, the kitchen had probably been as high-end as Kett's was now. Gratuitously spacious, marble countertops, ornate crown moldings, custom-built cabinets. Lots of curlicues and shiny surfaces. All pristine. But only because no one cooked. Not since my father died. It was his witch magic that had maintained the manor, and it had long grown dingy around the edges. My mother did as little as possible, hiring cleaners and gardeners just often enough to maintain the house and property.

I slid a glass across the wide, gray-veined, white-marble-topped kitchen island toward Liam. After glancing around like he was a little shell-shocked, he took it, even though he'd said he wasn't interested.

I sipped my water, leaning back next to the stove that barely got used. Honestly, I wasn't sure I even knew how to operate any appliance other than the dishwasher. Gabby had baked here for us misfits a few times, but we mostly hung out at the Talbots' house.

And that was what was behind Liam's current state of quiet shock.

As far as I'd bothered to figure out, the Talbots didn't come from money. They hadn't married into a witch family that stretched back generations, as my orphaned mother had. And though Danica Novak might have been the last of the Novak necromancers at the time of her birth, her family's personal estate had been vast as well.

Liam had seen the interior of the house at least twice. But apparently, he'd missed the silver spoon figuratively hanging around my neck.

Hating what I could only imagine was going through his head, I opened my mouth to counter it with something belligerent and snarky. But then I shut up before I spoke. Technically, I was the one currently on the wrong side of whatever argument he'd come here to have.

Liam set his half-full glass down on the island. Lines of tension had returned to his face, edging his jaw. He narrowed his eyes at me.

And damn if my stomach didn't do a little thrilled flip in response.

Again, completely inappropriately. I was about to be totally chewed out. I shouldn't have been anticipating it gleefully.

"Guess where I'm about to go?" Liam asked snarkily.

"Succubus hunting?"

"No." He smiled grimly. "I've been bumped from the hunting party tonight. Care to guess why?"

"So…one guess isn't enough?"

"Mory!"

I fought another smile. God, he was so riled up. And apparently, that appealed to me. An hour ago, I'd been so pissed at him for demanding I stay in tonight, babysat by Benjamin Garrick, that I'd walked all the way home in a huff. And now? Now I was getting all keyed up myself.

"Liam…" I tried to turn his name into a snarl, as he'd done with mine, but it came out differently than I'd intended. Sort of…intimate.

He blinked.

I took a sip of my water, covering.

He shook his head once, then picked up the thread of his rant. "I have to go take an official statement from a Brit Thompson, who claims that her clients are being harassed by a twenty-one-year-old with purple-and-pink hair."

"There's no way she actually knew how old I was. And she missed the blue streaks. It's completely possible that she meant someone else."

"This is my livelihood, Mory!" Liam started pacing angrily. "Do you know what I had to do to make sure the complaint made its way to my desk?"

"Use your badge?"

"Fuck, yes. I had to use my badge! To cover your ass! Which breaks the deal I made with the dowser when she crafted it for me."

"It doesn't really," I said, trying to be reasonable. "The point of making you the badge in the first place was so you could thread the fine line between the nonmagical and magical world—"

"That's not the point! Do you know how many things could have gone wrong because you wanted to…what? What the hell did you think you were doing?"

"Putting together a profile." Thankfully, my tone was still mild, because I was definitely feeling defensive.

"Which you did," he snapped. "You'd already done your part. Which was brilliant, by the way. Very helpful."

"Shouting compliments isn't very nice."

"I am not shouting."

He wasn't.

Yet.

Close, though.

I grinned at him. I really shouldn't have, but I couldn't help it. I wasn't certain that I'd ever thought of anyone as sexy before, but an irate Liam Talbot was sexy as all hell.

"What are you smiling about?" He growled the words through gritted teeth.

I shook my head, taking a sip of water to compose myself.

"Mory. I'm really fucking mad at you."

"I get it."

"You don't get it."

"I'm standing here letting you yell at me, aren't I?"

He threw his hands out to the sides, enunciating in a measured tone. "I. Am. Not. Yelling."

"Well, that was dramatic."

He dropped his hands, then rubbed his face. Apparently that wasn't enough, because then he scrubbed a hand through his hair.

I hid another inappropriate smile behind a sip of water. Unsuccessfully, apparently, because Liam narrowed his eyes at me.

Ed chose that moment to wander into the kitchen, drawing the sorcerer's attention. The undead turtle had circled through the dining room.

"And then there's that whole thing!" Liam exclaimed, gesturing toward Ed. "And you…" He trailed off.

I waited. He didn't elaborate. "Ed?"

"Yes!' He shook his head. "No. I mean…" He hooked his thumbs in his belt, the fingers of his right hand splayed across his badge, closing his eyes briefly.

Possibly praying for patience.

The conversation had gone somewhere I wasn't quite following. So I stayed quiet. And tried to not stare at the sorcerer. It was possible I was making the situation even more awkward with whatever weird crush or attraction I had going on.

"I'm angry," Liam finally said, as if trying to get himself back on point. "For the stunt, following the Atkinsons."

"I got that."

"You put me in a shitty position at work."

"I got that too."

"Yet you haven't apologized."

No, I hadn't. "You want me to lie to you, Liam?"

He grimaced. "Of course not."

I shrugged.

"A shrug is not appropriate."

"It's better than smiling though, right?"

"Is it better than smiling…" He trailed off, staring at me incredulously. Then, without any warning, he turned on his heel and strode out of the kitchen.

Anger flashed through me, momentarily freezing me in place. What a fucking asshole. He comes into my house and…

Unable to fully articulate that thought even in my own head, I scooped up Ed, hustling after Liam.

I caught up to the sorcerer in the entranceway. His hand was already turning the front door handle.

"What about Ed?" I shouted, holding the undead red-eared slider before me.

Liam spun to face me. "What?"

"You got angry when you saw Ed," I said, stopping a few steps away from the sorcerer. "You were a little pissed about me staking out the Atkinsons' therapy session and perhaps brilliantly uncovering the succubus, but—"

"She's not the succubus."

"How do you know?" I was shouting again, not completely sure why.

Liam stepped closer, towering over me. "I know because I checked. Over a year ago. I followed up on everyone connected to the Atkinsons. Even their goddamn therapist. How inept do you think I am, Mory?"

"So you know? Like, you can…sense magic?"

"Of course I can sense magic! I'm a sorcerer."

I jutted my chin out. "What if she's wearing a charm? To mask her magic?"

"Then I'd have felt the charm," he growled. "I made sure I was close enough."

I stared up at him, holding Ed between us, refusing to back down. "I didn't do anything wrong. I followed up on a lead. I found a clue. I immediately contacted Tony, and left."

"After chatting with the therapist."

"She," I said, grinding my teeth, "confronted me."

"And now I have to go smooth everything over."

"You do that, then!" I spun away, heading for the stairs, clutching Ed.

"Mory…wait."

I paused on the first stair, turning back to Liam reluctantly. "I did my job, Liam. Like you asked me."

He paced toward me slowly, as if he was afraid I'd stomp away if he moved too quickly. "You did. But you messed up."

"Fine."

"And you put yourself in danger."

"According to you, I merely had a chat with an overprotective therapist." And suddenly, I remembered that it had been Liam who the therapist had accused of harassing her clients. And even if it had been over a year since he approached her, he hadn't even recognized her at the sushi place. So much for his ability to follow up.

I opened my mouth to shove those little facts in the sorcerer's face.

But suddenly he was standing too close.

Like, close enough that all I could really see was his eyes. Dark-hazel orbs shot through with blue and green. Eyes that were currently fixed on me.

He was close enough to kiss.

Any closer, and we might crush Ed between us.

How had that happened?

And why wasn't I moving away?

"I'm angry at you," he murmured.

"I heard. I'm angry back."

He laughed quietly, not sounding at all angry. His gaze flicked to my mouth, then back up to my eyes.

As inexplicable as it was, Liam Talbot was thinking about kissing me. And the feeling curling its way through my belly wasn't anger either. Not even remotely.

"And not just about this stunt…" he murmured.

"What else are you angry about?" I was whispering now as well, exchanging breath with him.

"A subject matter for later," he said. "When I'm not so fixated on this case."

"Okay." I had no idea what I was agreeing to. I was suddenly fixated myself, wondering what he would do if I closed the space between us. We were almost the same height, with me in sock feet standing on the first stair and him in dress shoes on the marble floor.

I swayed forward, then stiffened my back.

A smile ghosted Liam's lips.

"For an angry person, you're standing awfully close to me," I said.

Wait. Was I…flirting with him?

His grin solidified. "I am."

"So…what's up with that?"

His expression became serious. "Can we set aside the being professional stuff for a moment?"

"We haven't been being very professional."

He huffed, leaning back to allow a bit more space between us. "Right. Well, I'll try to not mix it up next time."

"Next time? You'll be hiring me again?" Okay, that sounded lascivious as well. What was wrong with me? No matter that I was apparently physically attracted to Liam, I still didn't like sorcerers in general.

So I would just keep reminding myself.

I cleared my throat, interrupting whatever Liam was going to say. "Yes, we can set aside the professional dispute for a moment."

"Good." He swallowed, then nodded as if encouraging himself. "Are you dating Benjamin Garrick?"

My mind blanked. I blinked.

"I mean, it's cool if you are," Liam said. "It's none of my business, but…and I obviously date people…" He frowned. But more like he was judging what he was saying, rather than being angry. "You're free to date whoever you want. It's not like I'm asking you to marry me…at the moment…"

Wait…. what?

"I'm not dating Ben," I blurted.

"Oh…" Liam stared at me for a moment, then he smiled. "Good, then."

"That's good? Why? Because you're afraid for my immortal soul?"

His grin widened. "Yeah, Mory, I'm worried about the immortal soul of a necromancer."

I narrowed my eyes at him belligerently. "I'm angry at you, Liam Talbot. You're pushy and demanding—"

He was standing too close again, a smile crinkling the edges of his eyes. "Sorry." His breath whispered across my lips. "I didn't mean to interrupt you. You're just damn adorable when you get mad."

My insides went to mush. "I'm not adorable. Puppies are adorable."

He made a face. "Really? Puppies?"

Holding Ed in my left hand, I placed my other hand on Liam's shoulder. I curled my fingertips around the edge of his stiff shirt collar, brushing lightly against the warm skin of his neck.

His expression relaxed, then instantly sharpened. His gaze flicked to my lips again. But he didn't otherwise move.

What the hell was I doing?

I trailed my fingertips along the back of his collar, sliding up until I teased the short-cropped hair at the back of his neck. He was so warm. And with a day's worth of growth softening all his normally perfectly pressed edges, he was almost painfully attractive.

Too attractive to be attracted to someone like me. But he was.

Even I wasn't blind enough to not see it, to not understand what was happening in the moment. The fact that Ed being between us was the only thing stopping us from pressing against each other made that pretty clear.

"Hey, Liam?" My whisper sounded slightly disembodied.

"Yeah?" His voice was a low rumble.

"Are you going to ask me out?"

He nodded. "Yeah, I've been thinking about it…a lot. For a while. And, uh, I actually thought I had, but then you thought sushi was…work related…" He trailed off, his gaze settling on my lips again.

My mushy insides warmed. "Okay."

"Okay."

We stood like that, centimeters apart, just looking at each other. Finally, Liam dipped his head toward me. I raised my chin just a little bit, lips parting—

Benjamin Garrick was standing in the doorway to the library, just on the edge of my peripheral vision.

I flinched. I'd been so focused on Liam that I hadn't felt the vampire enter the house.

Liam stilled, confused. Then he turned his head, following my gaze.

"Sorry." Smoothing a frown, Benjamin stepped back into the depths of the library.

"My babysitter is here," I muttered.

Liam nodded stiffly. "I'm late."

My hand was still resting on the back of his neck. And when he tried to pull away, I tightened my grip almost instinctively. He stepped forward swiftly, determinedly, briefly crushing Ed between our chests. He brushed his lips across mine.

I sucked in a breath, eager to close the kiss. But the sorcerer simply offered me a tight smile, then spun away and strode toward the front door.

My hand fell to my side, already missing his warmth. I watched him go, seriously disappointed. "Be careful tonight."

Liam opened the door, pausing to look back at me. "I doubt I'll have any trouble with a therapist."

I didn't want him to go, completely selfishly. And it wasn't the first time I'd thought about inviting him to stay. "Maybe we could go trick-or-treating later."

He grinned. "Or I can just bring you candy. All the candy you want."

I grinned back at him.

He sobered, pointing a finger at me. "I'm still mad at you."

I nodded. "And not just about this one thing."

"Right."

"I do listen."

He shook his head. "When it suits you."

"It's not your place to decide what I do or when I do it."

"Fine." He stepped out, maintaining eye contact with me as he swiftly closed the door behind him.

I thought about running after him, like the moronic heroine always did in some silly romance movie. Instead, I settled on yelling at the closed door. "Fine!"

While grinning.

Like the silly, totally-crushing-on-the-sorcerer idiot that I so obviously was.

Liam Talbot liked me.

Well, that was a weirdly delightful twist.

NINE

INSTEAD OF STOMPING UPSTAIRS IN A HUFF, I RETRIEVED MY satchel and joined Benjamin in the library. The vampire was situated at his usual table, but facing the back windows this time. He was surrounded by so many spellbooks that I could see wide gaps on the nearby shelves.

He didn't look up as I set Ed down on the polished hardwood floor and unpacked my laptop and phone, taking up the only clear section of his workstation. Then I checked to make sure I hadn't missed any text messages while fighting with Liam.

If we actually had been fighting. I wasn't completely clear on all the nuances of what had just occurred between the sorcerer and me. Except for the kiss.

I was really certain that I needed to experience a much longer and much more intense lip lock with Liam Talbot. Soon.

Benjamin remained silent on the subject of whatever he'd overheard between the sorcerer and me. Stupidly, I couldn't tell if I was relieved because I actually didn't want to discuss the sorcerer with the vampire—or if I was disappointed because…well…because…he was Benjamin. But if he wasn't bringing it up, then he didn't care enough to do so.

I had already known Benjamin didn't see me like that. But I really didn't need it confirmed.

"The succubus hunt has started?" I asked, redirecting my own thoughts to a more neutral subject as I retrieved the vampire's handwritten notebooks from the table I'd dragged closer to the window that morning. I settled down in the chair across from him.

Benjamin nodded without looking up from the thick, brown leather-bound tome he was reading. The edges of the pages were gilded. "They've split up to cover more ground. Jasmine with Kett. Kandy with Bitsy. Tony is in the map room. Though they're going to be pressing the boundary pretty quickly, I think."

"Because no one thinks the therapist is the succubus?"

Benjamin peered at me over the edge of his book, smiling slightly. "Kandy went by the office. She couldn't smell any residual magic."

"Fine," I huffed, dragging the first notebook toward me and flipping it open at the bookmark I'd used to note my progress. I uncapped my purple pen.

Benjamin watched me for a moment longer, then returned his attention to his study of witch magic.

I worked my way through a section detailing necromancy workings, scanning the section about Benjamin's bone bracelet with a great deal of discomfort. Even though the topic was covered in the vampire's typical dispassionate manner, I was hyperaware that he was sitting across from me with the bones of birds embedded in his skin. Meant to quell his hunger for hunting and for feasting on blood. His mother's ongoing working seethed with darkly tinted magic, ebbing and waning but never completely disappearing. To my senses, at least.

I opened my mouth twice to question Benjamin about why he was still wearing the bone bracelet. Both Kandy and Jade thought he'd be better off without it, especially now that he'd sipped of the executioner's powerful blood. Benjamin might not have been able to walk in the sun like Kett and Jasmine, but as long as he fed himself well, he should have been able to control his predatory urges.

Perhaps it was his mother's influence. Maybe Teresa Garrick preferred to keep her vampire son leashed. She was a vampire hunter by birth, after all.

"Just ask, Mory." Benjamin didn't look up from the notes he was taking. Black ink flowed from his fountain pen across the delicately lined page of his current notebook.

I shook my head, turning the page of the chronicle and focusing on a less-detailed section about vessels created by necromancers. "Where did you find this info?" I asked. "About the vessels?"

Benjamin glanced up. "The ones created to hold ghosts?"

I flipped a page, still reading, then flipped back. "To imprison ghosts, more like."

"It was in one of the oldest books in my mother's collection. With an inference that it could be made to work on more than just ghosts."

"From the Garricks?" I asked a little redundantly, even as I worked out what Benjamin was implying. "And the inference was what? That a vessel could be created to hold a vampire? Like how? In perpetual thrall?"

Benjamin nodded but didn't offer further clarification. Likely because he didn't have any substantial evidence that such a vessel could be created, or even another reference text to back up the claim.

"What does Kett say?"

"I haven't asked him yet. Keep reading. I think you'll find the section on warding with bones interesting."

"The bones of an enemy?" I said teasingly.

Benjamin didn't pick up my levity. "The bones from a family member seem more potent, actually."

"You've found accountings of necromancers collecting the bones of their ancestors to create wards?"

Benjamin laughed almost inaudibly. "Among your mother's books, actually."

"Holy hell. And I thought ripping a zombie horde out of the grave was as dark as it got."

Benjamin peered at me, then went back to his notes. I continued reading, finishing the section on necromancy vessels before the vampire picked up the conversation again.

"Does it feel dark? When you wield that sort of magic?" His tone was casual, but he didn't look up from his notebook. "When you used the dead elves as a shield?"

I stiffened.

"I asked Gabby about it," Benjamin said gently, settling his dark-eyed gaze on me. "She wasn't terribly forthcoming."

"Is she ever?"

"Around Peggy. A little more."

"It never feels dark," I said stiffly. "Using my magic. It feels…right. It feels like who I'm meant to be. It feels the same for you, doesn't it?"

His brow creased thoughtfully. "I don't use magic like you do. Or like a witch or an amplifier. Like Gabby does."

I gestured toward the pen in his hand, still poised over the half-filled page. "That's magic. You're using your magic when you write the chronicle."

His frown deepened. "You think so?"

"Yeah. And when you move quickly, or lift something too heavy for a human, or beguile someone." I didn't add 'Or drink blood,' because that went without saying.

"I don't beguile."

I snorted. "You beguile all the time. You just haven't tried it with anyone who's less powerful than you, so you haven't noticed."

Benjamin went still. Like, not-breathing, not-blinking still. Which shouldn't have been all that unusual, since a vampire only really needed to breathe in order to speak. But Benjamin still breathed regularly. Out of habit, presumably.

I went back to reading the chronicle to fill the uncomfortable silence, correcting a spelling error—the first I'd spotted—then making a note on my phone about researching bone wards further.

"I was unaware," Benjamin said quietly. "I would never hurt you, Mory."

"I know, Ben."

He went back to writing, lightly scratching his pen across the page.

"I'll find you more info about the creation of vessels and bone wards," I said, keeping my tone even. "If I can. From the Academy database."

"Jasmine hasn't started on the digitization of the necromancy collection yet."

"Hasn't started on overseeing it, you mean." My correction came out brittle, as it always did when Jasmine entered the conversation. I hated that. I really liked the golden-blond vampire. And...

Wait...

"These vessels..."

Benjamin looked up when I didn't articulate my thought. "Yes?"

"Well, I used that circle-of-silver idea you wrote about in the section for the Garrick necromancers. I used it to hold shades today."

Benjamin grabbed and flipped open a completely different notebook. I caught sight of what I thought might be a copy of the oracle sketch that featured me—the same sketch Tony had on his desktop—but the vampire flipped past it too quickly for me to be certain. He paused with his pen poised over a blank page.

Wait…had Benjamin devoted an entire notebook just to…well…me?

The vampire settled his dark-brown eyes on me, gazing at me as though I was the only thing of interest in the entire library. "Tell me."

His magic shifted, licking out toward me enticingly.

"There you go," I muttered. "Beguiling."

"What?"

"Never mind. Just tell me that notebook isn't a transcription of my entire life."

Benjamin slowly blinked.

I sighed, then went ahead and recounted my afternoon activities. As I did so, I made notes in my computer myself, since technically, I was supposed to write an official report. Benjamin's black ink flowed across three pages of his notebook before I'd finished. He didn't interrupt me with a single question.

Drawing the conversation back to where I'd tried to begin it, I tapped the section that I'd just been reading about necromancer-wrought vessels. "So my point is, if a necromancer can hold ghosts in a vessel, then what if the succubus does the same thing with souls?"

"And that would be why the imprints are missing from the gravesites?"

I shrugged, not certain. But the idea felt right to me. "It's just a guess. But yeah, what if the souls aren't missing or even destroyed, if that's even possible. What if they're simply misappropriated?"

"Misplaced," Benjamin mused, rapidly writing in his notebook. "Like Kett said."

"Still..." I sighed, pausing to assess the hasty conclusions I was eager to make. The idea of a creature being able to completely consume souls had terrified me. I had always believed—had always known without a doubt—that there was...something after death. So I understood that I might have been reaching now for straws that didn't even exist.

Benjamin was waiting for me to continue. But discussing the idea of an immortal soul with a vampire who believed himself to be soulless felt overwhelming. Intimate.

I pivoted around the subject. "Still...I can't feel magic like Liam can, or like Kandy can smell it. But if the therapist was the succubus, and if she was somehow storing souls in a vessel she carried—because it would be insane to let something like that out of your sight—I should have felt it. Which means she isn't the succubus."

Benjamin nodded but said nothing.

I groaned and stretched. "I should have bought candy."

"For the trick-or-treaters?"

"Yeah," I said, blithely lying. "For the kids."

My phone buzzed. I picked it up, tapping on a text message from Tony so I could read it.

>*Have you heard from Liam?*

I texted back.

He was here a while ago.

I glanced at the time on my phone. Ugh. Less than two hours had passed with no news. It was going to be a long night.

"Tony?" Benjamin asked. "With an update?"

I shook my head. Another text appeared on my phone.

>*He's been dodging me all day b/c he's pissed I gave you the Atkinsons' address.*

How does he know?

>*Who else could you have gotten it from?*

I never asked you for it!

>*You gave me the silent treatment until I gave you something you wanted.*

I was in the shower, asshole.

"What's wrong?" Benjamin frowned at me. "You're making all sorts of faces."

I grimaced but didn't explain. Another text from Tony appeared on my screen.

>*More details.*

About what? Seeing Liam?

>*First start with the smell of your soap… vanilla, right? And how hot do you like the water?*

"Ugh!" I tossed the phone onto the table and went back to filling out a proper report on my laptop. I would have to submit it to the Convocation in order to get paid for the work. Even if Liam had technically hired me, the Godfreys would insist on paying the bill. The succubus was hunting in witch territory.

Multiple messages flashed on the screen of my phone. I ignored them.

In the end, Benjamin sighed heavily, picking up the offending phone. He flipped the screen so it would read my face and unlock, then scanned the series of text messages.

"Tony wants one of us to text Liam and ask him to check in," the vampire said. "The hunting party has a lead, but it's taking them east. They want to know if it…"—he air quoted—"…twigs anything for Liam before they head in that direction." Benjamin lifted his amused gaze to meet my disgruntled one. "Kett would not have used the word 'twigs.'"

I snorted. "Jasmine. Kett is not texting with Tony."

A slow smile spread over Benjamin's face. "Oh, yes. Jasmine."

My heart hollowed. I looked away.

What the hell was wrong with me? Flirting with Liam while I was still all messed up about Benjamin?

I knew it was the younger vampire's magic that was beguiling, and that wasn't the same as actually being in love with him or anything. But as a necromancer, I should have been more immune. I wanted to be immune.

I waved my hand for my phone. "I'll text Liam."

Benjamin handed me the cell, carefully not making skin contact as he let it slide into my hand. Ignoring the texts from Tony, I opened the message thread with Liam instead, scanning through the last messages—all about the therapist and him demanding I stay in for the evening. Then I typed and sent:

Hey. Tony wants you to check in with Jasmine.

Hopefully, even if Liam was dodging Tony's texts, he wouldn't dodge mine. Then I texted Tony.

Just sent a text to Liam. Will text you when he gets back to me.

>K

I went back to work, but a thought occurred to me. I paused to sort through everything I knew about Liam Talbot, and about how obsessed he'd been with Tanya's death.

"What is it?" Benjamin asked, not looking up from the spellbook he was back to reading.

"It doesn't seem like Liam," I mused. "To be out of touch when he wanted to be part of the hunting party, does it?"

"No," he said carefully. "But there are plenty of places in the city where text messages don't get through."

Sure. Even a city as large as Vancouver had weird blank spots, often depending on mobile carriers and tower placements. Plus underground parking or super-large buildings not covered in a blanket of Wi-Fi.

I flipped my new phone over and over in my hand while I thought, looking at it intently. "Except," I said, "we don't carry out-of-the-box phones. We all have devices rebuilt and reprogramed by Tony, with Jasmine's input. Have you ever noticed being out of range or out of service?"

Benjamin shrugged. "I haven't tested it."

"No," I murmured. "Why would you…?"

My phone buzzed. I flipped it over, expecting a message from Tony and finding one from Liam instead. So the sorcerer was dodging his brother.

>*I'll check in with Jasmine.*

>*Can you meet me?*

I frowned. First I was supposed to stay in, but now the sorcerer wanted me to meet him? I texted back.

For what? Candy? I thought you were going to deliver?

I scrolled back through the previous messages I had exchanged with the sorcerer while I waited for his reply. Text messages in which he'd pretty much yelled at me about how 'seriously pissed' he was. Then the set of messages before those, in which I'd sent him a brief report about the profile of the succubus that I'd pieced together with Gabby's help at the cemetery.

I sighed. That entire afternoon had probably been a waste. My instructors would have told me that I'd subconsciously latched onto the red-haired thing because I'd seen the therapist at the sushi place watching Liam through the window…

Wait…

"I never told Liam…"

"Never told Liam what?" Benjamin asked.

"I never told Liam that I saw the therapist when we went for sushi yesterday, before I asked to speak to Kett. I never told him that when she confronted me this afternoon, she'd been pissed about 'the so-called detective' riling up her clients. She had seen Liam and me together at lunch."

The dark-haired vampire narrowed his eyes. "You think she was following him?"

"It's a logical leap, isn't it?"

He sighed, though not unkindly. "She's not an Adept, Mory."

I flipped back a few pages of the chronicle, pointing to a sketch Benjamin had made of an urn. "What if she can completely cloak her magic? Like the guardian dragons can?"

"Where did you hear that?"

I shrugged. "You know Jade talks."

He grimaced. "I think it has something to do with the feeding of cupcakes. The dowser never talks as much around me as she does around you."

"Because she can't fatten you up."

He waved his pen toward the sketch I was still resting my finger on. "You were suggesting that she can, what? Store her magic until she uses it?"

"I'm suggesting, like before, that she can store the souls she steals. And that she likes to interject herself in the investigations of her victims. What if she somehow passively feeds off more than souls? The way I can read gravesites or remains without actively engaging? Like how you can move quickly or lift heavy objects without exerting enough magic to register on the witches' boundary map."

"In lore, succubi feed off emotions…" Benjamin mused.

"Succubi?" I teased. "Are you sure it isn't succubuses?"

He frowned, reaching for one of his notebooks. "Very…I confirmed it with…" He narrowed his eyes at me, finally noting my smirk. "You're teasing."

I snorted. "Yeah, dummy. I'm teasing."

"Hilarious," he said, not terribly convinced of my comedic prowess. Though a hint of a smile lingered on his lips as he returned his attention to the notebook he'd grabbed. Flipping a page back and forth, he reread his notes.

"Emotions…" I murmured. "And…who would see more emotion than a therapist trained to work with grief-stricken parents?"

Benjamin nodded. "That's dark, Mory. Even for us."

My phone buzzed before I could answer. The text was from Liam.

>I've identified another victim.

I frowned, but another text came through before I could show the first to Benjamin.

>The therapist, Brit, had two more clients with similar deaths in the family. I'd like you to speak with their shades, if possible.

"Huh," I said, speaking and texting at the same time. "That's odd."

At the cemetery? You think I missed a blank spot?

"What?" Benjamin asked.

"Two more clients of the therapist had children die in the same way as Tanya. I guess she was chatty."

"Or Liam used his badge."

I laughed quietly. Of course the sorcerer had used his badge. He was cleaning up my mess, after all.

"That would break the ten-year cycle," Benjamin said.

"Yeah," I said grimly. "It would. It would also mean I missed blank spots. Or that I was wrong. Like, from the beginning."

Another text flashed up on the screen.

>Yes. The cemetery.

I sighed. There was something off about the cadence of Liam's texts. He was always straightforward, but this conversation had been seriously stilted. He was apparently still pissed at me, even though he'd made nice with the therapist.

37th Avenue entrance? 20 minutes.

>I'll be waiting.

"That's not ominous at all," I muttered.

"The sorcerer is angry." Benjamin peered at me as though he was reading the text messages I was sending and receiving through my facial expressions. "Still?"

"Apparently. You would be too, if I'd just run you around on a wild goose chase for two days."

A grin softened the vampire's sharp features. "I don't mind running around with you, Mory."

I blinked, not quite certain if he was teasing or serious. Or...

"You get into interesting messes," he added matter-of-factly. "I'll text an update to Jasmine. I'm sure Kandy or Kett will meet us there if they think it's warranted. If you can't get a read on the new grave-sites, then we were only wrong about there being a pattern."

It was kind of him to use the word 'we.'

Glumly, I stood and collected Ed, who appeared to be trying to figure out how to climb up onto the lowest shelf of my mother's bone collection. I made sure I still had a candle in my satchel as I wandered out to grab my extra-large Cowichan-inspired sweater. It was warmer than my poncho, and the skull-and-crossbones design would be far more appropriate for wandering through a graveyard on All Hallows' Eve.

Benjamin followed me out of the library, tucking his current notebook in the pocket of his jacket while texting back and forth with Jasmine.

Damn it.

If I had missed blank spots, I might have really messed up. Not only in identifying the now-ever-so-helpful therapist as the succubus, but also in getting all the badass hunters involved. Kandy had come back into town especially for this.

Yeah, the toothy warriors currently combing the city for a bad guy weren't going to be happy.

MOUNTAIN VIEW CEMETERY LOCKED THEIR GATES AT 7:30 P.M. IT would have been easy to hop the fence, but the joggers and dog walkers who populated the pathways by day generally didn't trespass.

The power embedded into every centimeter of ground within the graveyard simmered just out of my reach as Benjamin and I waited for Liam at the apex of the cul-de-sac. We had grabbed a cab from my place.

At one point, Thirty-Seventh Avenue must have cut right through Mountain View, but it had been converted and gated some time ago. The adjacent residential streets had been lightly populated with children in costume, towing their parents from house to house, as we'd driven through and had the taxi drop us off.

Fifteen minutes passed, with no sign of Liam.

The trick-or-treaters thinned to a trickle I could only see now as they crossed the street a block ahead. The houses nearest to us were dark.

"Hey, Benjamin," I asked tentatively. "Can you sense if Liam is near? Or anyone, really?"

The dark-haired vampire stood quietly at my side, his hands stuffed in the pockets of the jacket he wore because I'd bought it for him, not because he needed it for the cold.

"No," he murmured after a moment or two of thoughtful silence. He hesitated a second time, then said, "But the bracelet inhibits my range."

"Really? Why would that…" Then I put two and two together and shut my mouth. The bird-bone bracelet was designed to keep Benjamin's blood-lust at bay. And apparently, the ability to sense if people—aka potential food sources—were nearby was directly related to the vampire's ability to hear keenly.

"No one outside of a house for about a two-block radius." Benjamin nodded toward a small grouping of older kids crossing the street at the intersection. "Other than the witch, the zombie nurse, and death over there." He flashed a grin at me.

His eyesight was better than mine, even with the bracelet. I could only make out the nurse costume by color.

I checked my phone. No new messages. I texted the sorcerer.

Where are you?

A thought occurred to me. It seemed ridiculous, but what if dragging us out of the house, then standing us up, was some sort of payback or punishment? Liam Talbot didn't seem like the petty type. But he also didn't seem like the type to stop responding to his brother's texts.

"Liam was really mad at me," I said quietly. It actually pained me a little to broach the topic with the vampire. "Do you think he's playing games?"

"When was this?" Benjamin's tone was mildly amused. "Before or after he offered to bring you all the candy you wanted?"

Right. Despite the bracelet impeding that ability, the vampire's magically enhanced hearing apparently still worked within the perpetually quiet, wide-open rooms of the manor. "He was angry throughout the offer of treats. And he wasn't offering to bring me all the candy."

"Wasn't he?"

Yeah, that was amusement all right. "You know Liam is a health nut."

"But you aren't."

I sighed. Then I snapped at him, "Ben."

A smile ghosted over the vampire's pale face. "No, I don't think the sorcerer is screwing with us. Even if he was angry at you, which I would debate given the moment I inadvertently witnessed in the entrance hall, he wouldn't put you in harm's way by luring you out of the house when everyone else is off hunting the succubus."

I opened my mouth to counter his argument, but Benjamin raised a hand to quell me. "The sorcerer also wouldn't involve me. Not unless it was important. And he knows that I go where you go."

Something uncomfortable but visceral shifted through me at the vampire's pronouncement. I glanced at my phone, hoping once more that I'd missed a text. I hadn't. Huffing a disgruntled breath to cover the curl of fear that the sight of a blank screen induced, I dialed Liam's number. It rang.

"I didn't know you and the sorcerer were so close." Benjamin cast his gaze around slowly, monitoring the area around us instead of looking at me.

The phone rang again.

I shrugged in response to the vampire's nonquestion.

A third ring.

Liam's voicemail kicked in. I hung up.

"Mory?"

"We all got close," I said stiffly. "While trying to free the warriors from the elves, didn't we?" That came out way too pointed, but I couldn't take it back now that it hung between us. Specifically, the notion of who Benjamin had gotten close to in the two weeks we'd thought the aforementioned warriors were dying. Or dead. Warriors that had included Jade. And Kett.

The vampire glanced at me, then went back to gazing out at the dark neighborhood. I had no idea what he saw in my expression, but his shoulders softened a little.

Benjamin Garrick was slowly forgetting what it was to be human, to act human. Which made sense, since he hadn't been a human for some time. But watching the transition was painful. It was one of the reasons I'd left.

"Yes," he finally said. "A number of us…misfits got close while the others were held captive."

"Like you and Jasmine."

His lips slowly curled into a soft smile, as they always did when Jasmine entered the conversation. "Like…you and Jasmine as well."

I almost snarked back that I wasn't having sex with the golden-blond vampire. Instead, I decided to act like an adult and text Tony.

Can you get a location on Liam for me?

"Are you sleeping with the sorcerer?" Benjamin asked. Apparently, for once, we were actually having the same conversation as the one going on in my head. "Or…were you sleeping with him, and that's why you left?"

I looked at him steadily. "No."

"No to both questions?"

"Why? Does my bio need fleshing out?"

He frowned as if mildly affronted. "If you made your relationship official, I would note it, of course. But I don't—"

My phone buzzed in my hand. A text from Tony appeared on screen.

>Why?

He asked me to meet him at Mountain View fifteen minutes ago and hasn't shown.

>You left the house?

Obviously.

>Where is Ben?

With me. You can see that on your damn map, can't you?

>*I have been a little occupied coordinating a succubus hunt, you know.*

I waited, the three dots on my screen telling me that Tony was still texting. "Didn't you text Tony that we were leaving the house?"

"Jasmine." Benjamin shoved his hands in his pockets, still monitoring the neighborhood.

>*Okay, yeah. I've got you and Benjamin by your phones. And your necklace shows up on the grid map as well. That's cool, huh? Because it's currently inactive, right? Benjamin must have his pen, but it doesn't show. Maybe get him to use it? And then text me? We can do a test.*

I practically snarled at my phone as I responded. *Liam!!!???*

Benjamin glanced over my shoulder, reading my screen and laughing quietly.

>*Right. His phone is two blocks to your west. Heading my way?*

>*No...that's odd.*

>*Wait...as in stay where you are...I've got Kandy checking in.*

I waited, shifting on my feet. Tony took long enough to get back to me that I started running over the conversation Benjamin and I had been in the middle of.

"Why would you assume that I would leave town because something didn't work between Liam and me?" I asked. "Getting training for my magic, becoming properly accredited, isn't enough of a motivation? I have to have been spurned by a guy? Because that's who I am to you?"

Benjamin's mouth dropped open slightly. But a new text appeared on my screen before he could speak.

>*Kandy says to get your ass back home. Kett is heading for you, but he's twenty minutes away.*

"Screw that," I muttered. "Something feels off with Liam. From the first text message he sent tonight."

Benjamin shifted his focus to the ever-darkening neighborhood. Stars not completely washed out by the city lights were starting to appear overhead.

That was as much agreement as I needed. I wasn't supposed to put myself at risk? Fine. I wouldn't. I had a vampire at my side. I was as armed and dangerous as I was ever going to get. And I wasn't going to ignore my instincts, especially not with Kett twenty minutes away. A lot could happen in twenty minutes.

I started up the sidewalk. Benjamin kept pace with me without question.

My phone buzzed.

>*You're going home right? I've gotten in enough shit about you today already.*

Sure. Right after I check on Liam.

>*Mory. Liam can take care of himself. He probably left his phone somewhere.*

He was just texting with me. Plus when was the last time your brother misplaced anything?

I jogged across the perpendicular street, glancing both ways. Sporadic houses were illuminated with the soft glow of decorations and lit pumpkins. But the deep dark of the night was encroaching, and the youngest trick-or-treaters were probably already being tucked into bed.

>*How come when you give me the silent treatment I always break, but you never do when I reverse the roles?*

I snorted. *I'm not ignoring you. How close am I now?*

>*Close. His phone is near the far corner of the next cross street.*

I slowed at the curb, glancing both ways down another parallel street. I couldn't feel the power emanating from the cemetery now. Apparently, two blocks was too far away for my senses. I felt a little empty without it simmering at my back. And alone. Even with the vampire at my side.

"Liam's car," Benjamin murmured, indicating with his chin.

I could see cars parked end to end on both sides of the street, but couldn't distinguish them from each other. My night vision wasn't as good as it was when I was on the cemetery grounds.

I jogged across the street. Most of the houses there were lit, but the curtains were drawn on the first two to my left. The front stoops were also bare of carved pumpkins, indicating to alert trick-or-treaters the lack of candy on the premises. Benjamin stepped off the sidewalk into the deep shadows between the nearest house and the bushes that filled the front yard, all but disappearing from sight. I had no idea why he'd want to hide from Liam, but I could still feel the steady beacon of his magic.

I slowed, recognizing the dark navy sedan parked just ahead on my right. No sign of the sorcerer, though. I paused near the bumper of the car, glancing around. I was raising my phone to text an update to Tony, double-checking that we were at the same location as Liam's phone, when I spotted the sorcerer. He was sprawled across the lowered front passenger seat of the sedan, seemingly asleep.

Liam. Sleeping?

I stepped closer, right next to the window, holding my phone so it would cast light across the sorcerer's face.

His eyes were closed, dark-brown eyelashes practically brushing his cheekbones. I wasn't certain I'd noticed that his lashes were quite so long before. His head had settled to one side, in repose. He was still wearing his suit, but it was rumpled.

I had never seen Liam Talbot rumpled. Or looking so peaceful.

Assuming he was actually sleeping, and not—

The light of my phone winked out. I flinched like an idiot. Liam's face was shadowed, but I could still mostly see him from the low light cast by the nearby streetlamp. I raised my hand to tap on the window glass, then paused, relieved, as the sorcerer took a shallow breath.

Still alive, then.

Of course he was still alive.

Holy hell. Sometimes I was a complete moron. A dead sorcerer would have tweaked my senses from blocks away. I was a damn necromancer, after all.

"Pretty, isn't he?" a lyrical voice said behind me. "Not so much when he's angry, but his fear was absolutely delicious."

I turned, already knowing who was standing behind me. She spoke now with an accent bleeding through her words. Irish, I thought, though I didn't have an ear for it.

A woman in her late twenties stood behind me. Her build was slight enough that in the black-cat costume she was wearing, she could have been mistaken for a teenager. She still looked like Brit Thompson the therapist, though—despite the fact that she'd lost half a decade or so.

She bared her teeth in a nasty smile, though her tone remained unaffected. "It's been a long time since I drank deeply of so much magic."

"A cat?" I asked, sneering at her costume. "Really?"

She smoothed a hand down her svelte, black-leather-clad body. "A panther. What are you supposed to be? A goth clown?"

I hummed thoughtfully. "Not a bad idea for a self-striping colorway, actually."

"What?"

"Yarn. I'm talking about yarn."

Tension flitted across the succubus's face. Finally. "I'm going to suck the life out of you, necromancer. Then the sorcerer."

"Oh, good. We're onto the threatening part of your little game. I was getting bored."

She frowned, then shook it off. "Then I'm going to drag you into your precious graveyard and bury you for all eternity."

"Nope."

Her eye twitched. "No? What could you possibly do about it?"

I shrugged belligerently. "Not me."

"The sorcerer won't rescue you."

"That's okay. I'm in the process of rescuing him."

She laughed harshly. "No one can resist my kiss. Especially a child who whispers to ghosts."

"I don't really need to whisper."

She stepped forward, then checked herself, smoothing a hand through her vibrant red hair. She'd been about to lunge for me, maybe even wrap her hands around my uncooperative neck. But that would have cut short her own frighten-the-unarmed-necromancer game.

"I see," I said. "Am I ruining the hunt for you? What did you say? You like to feed off fear?" My tone hardened. "And grief. Right? That's what you're doing with Tanya's parents. That's why you get involved in the investigations of the children you murder."

She sniffed, composed again. "What are you going to do about it?"

"Absolutely nothing. But the witches are going to chew you up."

She laughed, bragging. "I've been hunting in Vancouver since the first luxury hotel was built here. The witches have no idea."

I folded my arms, slumping belligerently as though I wasn't actually moments away from losing my shit. Though that wasn't because the succubus scared me.

Oddly, I was having a difficult time not trying to tear her apart with my bare hands.

She murdered kids.

She had done something to Liam that apparently involved kissing.

I had wanted that damn kiss. At least one.

Hell yeah, I was angry.

"Well, you're out of the closet now," I said. "Normally, exposing you would be seriously rude of me. But since you're killing kids, the polite rules don't apply."

The succubus curled her lip, sneering. Then she slowly stepped forward, prowling through the darkness that edged the sidewalk as if she was actually emulating a panther.

I laughed quietly. "Right. I forgot you were hunting me."

"I lured you here, didn't I?"

"Ah! It was you who was texting as Liam."

"Obviously."

She got within arm's reach. I didn't react. She was only slightly taller than me, even in spike-heeled boots. I would have bet that those heels sank deeply into damp ground. And the ground was always damp in Vancouver this time of year.

I laughed again. "For someone so old, you really are woefully unprepared. What happens if I run? Are you going to chase me in that getup?"

She grabbed my upper arms, yanking me toward her with a snarl. Her grip was punishing.

Instead of pulling away, I closed the space between us, whispering harshly, "I've been intimidated by bigger bad guys than you, succubus."

"Well, I'm going to be the one to kill you." She dipped her head toward me, lining up to kiss me.

The magic of my necklace stirred. Becoming aware, alert.

"There's a vampire right behind you," I said.

Brit Thompson, the succubus, went completely still.

The protective magic embedded into my necklace reached out and caressed her hands. Her grip on my shoulders tightened, questioningly.

Benjamin appeared behind her.

The necklace decided it didn't like the succubus touching me, even though I wasn't reacting with fear. Its magic slashed out, biting into her flesh.

She snarled, shaking her hands and stumbling back from me—and plowing into Benjamin as though she'd just hit a brick wall.

He closed his hands over her narrow shoulders, but his dark gaze was on me. "Okay, Mory?"

I nodded. "We were just having a chat."

"Unhand me, creature," Brit spat, twisting her shoulders. The leather of her panther costume squeaked in Benjamin's grasp. She barely managed to move.

The vampire looked affronted.

I smirked. "Not very strong. Not very fast either, in those stupid shoes. But you shouldn't let her kiss you, Ben."

"Not a worry," he said smoothly. "I have no life force for her to steal, do I?"

I opened my mouth to tell him otherwise. But the succubus moved before I could.

She raised both hands, reaching behind her own head to plaster them to Benjamin's face, and then did…something…

Benjamin stumbled sideways, dragging Brit with him.

They grappled, him grabbing her hands and her attacking him somehow with a magical assault I couldn't see or feel. Just by touching him, skin-to-skin. He moaned. She panted, then hissed. They tumbled into the nearby bushes.

I lunged forward, worried I would lose sight of them in the shadows. With them both wearing dark colors, all I could really see was their paler skin.

My phone buzzed in my hand. I glanced down.

>*What the hell is going on? The map is spiking at your location!!*

Tony.

I really didn't have time to text. But I also wasn't sure it was a good idea to get between Benjamin and the succubus. The vampire was way stronger than I was. They were fighting in the deep shadows, almost silently. Though maybe some sort of magic I also couldn't feel was muffling the sound of their wrestling match, perhaps even visually obscuring them as well. I still had no idea how succubus magic worked, and the Academy training on vampires had been rife with inaccuracies.

But I could grab Brit and hope my necklace shocked her again.

The duo rolled into a lit section of the front lawn before I could make a decision. The destroyed bushes were going to need a witch's touch, but so far, the curtains of the house had remained drawn. Thankfully, the street was still empty of trick-or-treaters.

I was well versed at staying back and letting the more powerful people take the lead in physical confrontations. But we were seriously exposed, and—

The succubus came up on top, straddling Benjamin. Then, her wavy red hair cascading around both their faces, she leaned down to kiss the vampire, cradling his head in her hands.

"No!" I shouted, lunging forward.

Air boxed my ears. Once. Twice. Three times.

No.

Not air.

Magic.

The succubus arched back in pain, then tumbled to the side, half on the lawn, half on the vampire. Benjamin pushed her all the way off him, sitting up and panting in what appeared to be intense pain. I had thought vampires were impervious to most magical assaults.

I whirled around, spotting Liam propped up against his car, behind the open passenger door. His gun was raised, though as soon as he made eye contact with me, he lowered it slightly.

He'd shot the succubus.

Three times.

Dead center in her back, if her reaction was anything to judge by.

Liam tried to straighten away from the car. Then suddenly, his gun snapped back up, pointing past me again. The sorcerer swayed on his feet, but his expression was dark, focused.

I followed the direction of his gaze, expecting to see that the succubus had moved. She hadn't. I could hear her breathing, though—a quiet, rattling wheeze that spoke of lungs filled with blood.

But despite the evidence that a succubus could take three bullets from Liam's gun and survive, it was

Benjamin who'd provoked the sorcerer's renewed concern.

The vampire was still sitting on the front lawn next to the succubus, arms wrapped around his torso, hunched inward. A red tint glistened in the depths of the vampire's dark-brown eyes. Eyes that were currently trained on Liam.

Benjamin's magic coiled around him, pulsing, mimicking a steady, slow heartbeat. A heartbeat that the vampire didn't actually possess. A grimace was etched across his face.

No fangs, though.

So that was a good sign.

"All right, Ben?" I whispered.

"I'd be better if the sorcerer stopped pointing the gun at me." His tone was edged in darkness, rife with violence.

Liam's shoulders stiffened. I could sense, more than actually see, his grip on the trigger tightening. "To me, Mory."

"Benjamin isn't going to hurt me," I snapped.

"Come to me," Liam repeated without taking his gaze from Ben. "One step to your right, off the sidewalk. Walk along the grass edge. Don't get between me and the vampire."

I let out a long-suffering sigh, opening my mouth to offer up some snark.

Benjamin interrupted me. "It's hilarious that you think you could pull the trigger before I could take the gun from you, sorcerer."

I had never heard Ben sound so deadly, so taunting before. I stared at him, mouth hanging open.

Liam raised the gun slightly. His tone was perfectly reasonable. "I don't miss. I was going to take you in the gut. Despite the energy the succubus has drained from you, that's a wound I believe you could heal. You won't heal from a head shot so quickly."

The red of Benjamin's magic deepened, solidifying in his eyes. Ironically, the fear that the succubus hadn't been at all successful at rousing uncurled in my belly.

"Don't be ridiculous," I snapped, trying to smother the feeling in pissiness. "Kett is on his way. I'm texting an update to Tony." Keeping my gaze on the sorcerer, the vampire, and the succubus still prone on the grass at the same time was pretty much impossible, but I tried even while texting the tech sorcerer.

Succubus is down. Both Ben and Liam are hurt but functioning.

"Mory…" Benjamin murmured. My name started out as a command but ended in a quiet moan. The vampire hardened his tone. "Step closer to the sorcerer." He'd wrapped his hand over his left wrist.

I could suddenly feel the magic of the bone bracelet that kept him tethered to his mother's will roiling, seeping a dark miasma of power.

I shivered.

Benjamin's red eyes flicked to me. He took a slow, long breath that he didn't need, touching his tongue to his teeth.

My heart started hammering. My phone buzzed in my hand, but I didn't dare glance away from Benjamin.

"Mory," Liam growled. "Move slowly, but step to me. Now."

"Benjamin?" I asked. "Won't it be worse for you if I run?"

"Not running." He gasped, sounding again as though he was fighting an urge that had nothing to do with pain and everything to do with desire. He twisted his hand around his wrist, knuckles turning white with the effort. "Not prey. I know you, Mory."

I took a step toward Liam.

Benjamin didn't react.

I took another step, then another. Liam reached for me one-handed, still training his huge gun on the vampire. The sorcerer shoved me behind him. I grumbled, making a fuss in the hopes of defusing the situation.

"We need to move," Liam said, lowering his gun slightly. He swayed on his feet.

I pressed my shoulder to his back. Not hard, but enough that he could lean on me a little if he wanted.

"Ben?" the sorcerer continued. "Can you check on the succubus? I'll open the trunk of my car if you can carry her."

I glanced past Liam.

Benjamin rolled to his feet, gingerly. Then he turned to crouch beside the succubus.

Liam holstered his gun, keeping his gaze on the vampire as he settled his hand and a hunk of his weight on my shoulder.

"Holy hell," I muttered playfully. "What have you been eating, sorcerer?"

Liam offered me a slight smile, then gave me a gentle shove backward.

Right. Trunk.

I dutifully crossed around the sedan, letting the drained sorcerer use me as a crutch. I glanced back to see Benjamin lifting the succubus in his arms, then stepping into the deep shadow of the laurel hedge that separated the front lawn from the neighboring house.

Liam popped the trunk, opening it. It was pristinely clean inside, of course.

"What?" I asked mockingly. "No jumper cables? Or spare tire?"

Liam snorted. "Underneath."

I shook my head, finally glancing down at my phone to see that Tony had sent me a series of red-faced, foul-mouthed emoticons in response to my last text.

"Where should we take her?" I asked Liam. "Pearl's?"

"No," he said. "I don't want her anywhere near the map. Or Tony."

"The bakery. You can park in the alley while Benjamin carries her."

"Yeah. Cool."

I texted Tony again.

Alert everyone. Bringing the big bad to the bakery. Will trade for cupcakes.

Benjamin appeared on the far side of Liam, carrying the succubus slung limply across his arms. Liam had released my shoulder, but only because he was now holding himself upright on the edge of the trunk. He shifted, reaching to help Benjamin lower Brit's body inside.

The succubus didn't appear to be bleeding. I wasn't certain how many Adepts could have taken three magical bullets to the back and survived, let alone shown no injuries. "Is the trunk going to hold her?" I asked. "If she wakes up?"

Liam grunted. "I have special cuffs in the glove box. Ones she won't be able to break."

Not at all surprised that Liam apparently had a magically imbued set of cuffs alongside his police-issue pair, I turned away to grab them. Then I realized that I was also going to have to drive. The sorcerer was going to love that.

I stepped back, holding my hand out. "Keys."

"See if they're in the car," Liam said. "I didn't drive here myself."

"Maybe the succubus has them?" Benjamin leaned into the trunk, running his hand over the unconscious Brit's hips. She was half curled on her side, facing the back bumper.

I snorted. "Pockets? In that outfit? I doubt it."

I crossed to the driver's-side door of the sedan, pulling up my phone to text Tony again. I'd forgotten to tell the tech sorcerer that he would need to send a witch to fix the trampled bushes and—

Something thumped at the back of the car. I looked up from my phone, unable to see beyond the raised trunk.

Then Liam fell back, his shoulder smashing into the bumper. His arms splayed out, not even trying to break his fall. No gun in sight.

My chest constricted painfully. My mind was momentarily wiped of all concrete thought. But as though my limbs were operating of their own volition, I moved forward slowly.

I might not have been the sort of Adept who stepped in when a vampire and a gun-toting sorcerer were compromised. I had no weapons, no strength. I wasn't anywhere near immortal. But I understood the power of forward momentum, moving toward the light even as the darkness encroached.

Standing around, frozen in terror, waiting for the bad guy to slaughter everyone—or even for the good guys to show up to save the day—wasn't ever the right choice. Not for me, anyway.

I reached the back of the sedan, standing slightly in the street so I didn't accidentally step on Liam.

The succubus was wrapped around Benjamin. She had him bent backward, half lying in the trunk.

Kissing him.

Magically sucking the life force from him.

Lips still pressed to Ben's, she looked up to meet my gaze. And for a moment, I could see the energy shifting between her and him. The soul that the vampire didn't believe he possessed. She was going to kill him. Then she'd finish off Liam.

And there was nothing I could do about it.

I couldn't actively wield the magic held in the necklace. The succubus would have to attack me first.

Brit straightened, dropping Ben. His head hit the bottom of the trunk with a dull, harsh thud.

Something clattered to the ground by the succubus. Then something else.

I took another step to the right, clearing my sight line.

A third object hit the ground between the succubus's spike-heeled boots.

Bullets. Silver, judging by the way they caught the light. And presumably glinting even more with magic that I couldn't see or feel.

The three bullets Liam had shot into her back.

She was using Benjamin's and Liam's life force to heal herself.

Creepy. But not unforeseen. The succubus had already used the life force she'd taken to incapacitate the sorcerer the first time to revert to her late twenties.

Liam took a deep, shuddering breath, drawing Brit's attention. I stuffed my phone deeply within the pocket of my jeans and fisted the straps of my satchel in my hand, so I wouldn't jostle Ed too much.

"Your turn, necromancer." The succubus smiled at me. Magic writhed under her pale skin. Dark blue with streaks of red.

So I could see her magic when it wasn't masked, as it must have been when Liam and Kandy had scouted her. Or at least I could see it when the succubus had siphoned that magic from my friends.

And magic I could see, I could grab.

I smiled.

Brit frowned.

"Come catch me," I whispered, already spinning away.

Running.

Abandoning Liam and Benjamin.

Leaving the scene of a magical crime for the nonmagical neighborhood to stumble upon.

Breaking cardinal rules because those rules didn't help me, didn't apply to the sort of magic I wielded.

I ran.

God help me.

Despite being clumsy and slow, I sprinted back toward the cemetery. Because I had no offensive magic. I had no ability to fight another Adept of any power level. I had no way to help Liam and Ben.

Not while in the middle of a residential street.

So I ran, my heart already pounding, my face already flushed with unspent tears.

I ran.

And the succubus followed.

TEN

I RAN, REACHING FORWARD WITH EVERY SENSE TOWARD THE POWER
I knew lay eagerly awaiting me, only two blocks away.
In theory, all I had to do was keep the succubus distracted until someone else arrived. Because Tony
knew something was up, even after my text telling
him we were heading for the bakery. He would have
seen it all on the map. And Kett was already coming.
So help was on its way.

But I wasn't really a runner. Hell, I was barely
a walker. Still, I pumped my weak legs for all they
could give me. Sprinting, ignoring the tightness in
my chest even though I knew the succubus was feeling fear coming off me in waves now.

I had never actually run from a foe before. I'd
never had the chance to. And, somehow, even if it
gave me the ultimate advantage, fleeing made it hard
to not completely lose my shit in a completely different way.

Such as allowing myself to acknowledge how much easier it would be to just stop running, knowing my necklace would protect me.

Because I knew the necklace couldn't protect Liam and Benjamin.

I flew past the lit houses that bordered the cemetery property, praying that if anyone was looking out the window, they'd mistake my brightly colored hair and the skull design on my Cowichan-inspired sweater for some sort of costume. I was also slight enough to be mistaken for a teenager. And kids ran around randomly all the time, didn't they?

Without warning, the succubus was on me, grabbing my hair, then yanking me stumbling to one side.

Damn it. She was way quicker than I'd thought she would be in her spiky heels. I was still more than a block away from the cemetery boundary. Pain streaked through my skull. The magic of my necklace clamped onto Brit's hand. She hissed, releasing my hair.

I fell, landing awkwardly on my right hand and knee, trying to hold my satchel aloft with my left hand. I didn't want to squash Ed. Pain jolted up my arm and through my leg, both of which had been broken by a far more powerful adversary almost two years ago.

Oddly, that thought galvanized me. I'd been almost crushed by the roof of a fucking stadium. A goddamn roof pulled down by a goddamned demigod. Never mind the fact that the demigod—Haoxin of the guardian nine—hadn't actually been directing her primary assault at me specifically. I'd just been caught in the crossfire.

I practically threw myself back onto my feet, still midstride, by sheer, anger-induced will.

I wasn't some weakling.

I was running toward power, not away from it. I glanced back.

The succubus was alternating between hissing and sucking in breath, holding her hand as if it were on fire. And maybe it had been burned. Set aflame by the magic of my necklace.

The point was, Brit Thompson was simply a speck of evil in the wide world of the magically Adept.

I could deal with that speck on my own.

The back of my head hurt, though, along with my arm and leg. The succubus had probably pulled out a hunk of my hair. That so wasn't cool.

I kept running.

The succubus caught up with me again, even in her stupidly spiked heels. She was right behind me, three steps from the boundary, when the magic of the cemetery reached out with long wisps of power, wrapping around my arms and shoulders as if trying to help me, trying to pull me the last few steps onto the grounds.

I had no idea it was possible for death magic to cross the edge of the property like that. As if it were responding to my fear.

The succubus stumbled, slowing.

I plowed forward, racing through the cul-de-sac that capped East Thirty-Seventh, then stepping off the sidewalk the moment the option became available. My soles hit the edge of the grass, and then I was running directly along the boundary line. The power of the cemetery roiled underfoot, infusing each step with a bump of energy. Thankfully, because I seriously needed it.

I skirted the chain-link fence, barreling toward the locked gates. There, where the paved path was wide enough for a vehicle to enter the cemetery property, I spun around to face the succubus.

My heart pounded, chest constricting. I would have preferred to climb the fence and deepen my connection to the graveyard, but I was worried that Brit had figured out I was luring her away from Liam and Ben, not fleeing for my life. I was worried she wouldn't follow without more motivation.

The succubus was still walking toward me, slowly. As if not quite sure what she'd felt when Mountain View reached out to greet me, welcome me.

I haltingly stepped backward, closing the space between me and the gates. Hoping that the hesitant movement, the display of retreat, would entice her. The cemetery spread out on either side of the former roadway. The gravesites to the right were mostly flat mounted in the ground, uniformly spaced. But a mixture of tombstones stood to my left, including some familial monuments. And that was where I wanted to be. On the grass, near the largest rough-hewn cross.

I knew that section of the cemetery well.

I knew the family who had chosen that burial site and made use of it for over four generations. The MacDonalds. I knew that in life, they had once been pioneers, immigrants to the west. That they'd helped build huge sections of Vancouver. That they'd fought in two world wars, protecting the rights and freedoms of the ever-growing branches of their family.

I knew that they'd protect me too, if called upon.

"What are you going to do, little necromancer?" The succubus sneered, stepping across the boundary line without a hint of hesitation. "Overwhelm me with your ghosts?"

She had no idea what a necromancer could do when properly trained, when properly motivated. As old as she was. And necromancers weren't anywhere near as rare as succubi. That was just arrogant. Vain, just as Kett had said.

The feel of her magic filtered through the ground toward me, picked up and translated by the death magic I wielded passively while on the grounds of any burial site—and amplified by my claiming of Mountain View.

It creeped up my legs, prickling my skin. Blinking, I finally saw what lay under Brit Thompson's ever-youthful facade. I could feel it beckoning to me in a completely different way than Benjamin's magic called to me.

It practically begged to be released.

No.

Not it.

Them.

Souls.

The succubus was animated by the souls of her victims. By the children she'd murdered.

My heart began beating wildly, feeling out of sync and completely overwhelmed. The souls of the children. Trapped, not misplaced. The succubus was the vessel Benjamin and I had pontificated about not even an hour previously.

Souls trapped. Forever? Would their energy fade if and when Kett showed up to kill the succubus? And if the executioner chose to not kill her, then what? What would happen to the souls of her victims?

A bleak, sudden desperation threatened to overtake me, muddying my mind, my plan. The same feeling that had seized me in the car when I'd been stalking the Atkinsons.

My back brushed the gate. It was solid, substantial. I reached behind me, grasping the cool steel.

The children's souls weren't lost. They hadn't been consumed or destroyed.

Yet.

I knew what to do. At least I knew what the right thing to do was. And I wasn't going to wait for the executioner to make the decision for me.

I climbed over the gate awkwardly, trying to keep an eye on the succubus as I went.

"Luring me somewhere?" she asked mockingly, pausing with one hand on her hip. Posed. Though she still held her other hand away from herself. It must have still hurt from the bite of my necklace.

Good to know. Though I wouldn't have expected anything less from the magic contained in the layers of protection hanging around my neck.

Brit glanced back the way we'd come. I risked a look in that direction as well, seeing nothing moving in the sporadically lit darkness. Benjamin and Liam were still down. Still no sign of anyone else arriving yet.

So I had to distract the bad guy for a little longer.

I was good at that.

All I needed to do was to lure her a few more steps.

"Scared of me?" I asked conversationally. "Afraid of all the ghosts who know who you really are? Souls you condemned to this site?"

She sniffed offishly. "I already read the sorcerer's texts and emails. I know you can't call forth the ghosts of my darling ones." She gave me a slight smile. "A pity, really. I'd never thought of using a necromancer to visit them beyond death. That would have been lovely."

The succubus thought it would be delightful to torture her victims from beyond the grave.

Something tore open inside me. A well of violence and vitriol sprang forth, practically suffocating me. That utter wrath drowned any lingering doubts about the plan I was hastily cobbling together.

I struggled to keep myself in check. I just needed to distract her for a little while longer. I just needed her to follow me over the gate and a few steps farther onto the grass.

She glanced away again. She was going to leave. To finish off Liam and Benjamin. I wasn't enough of a threat to keep her attention. And she knew that someone was on the way—maybe even multiple someones. Hell, I'd been the one to tell her that.

Damn it.

I tugged my necklace free from the collar of my sweater, allowing it to settle over top, draped across my collarbone.

That snagged the succubus's attention. So apparently she could sense magic.

I brushed my fingers across the stamped gold coins, all of various sizes and shapes, attached to a thin gold chain that had been woven through the thicker links of a white-gold chain. All the coins had once teemed with enough residual magic that they'd drawn the dowser's attention. Jade had then molded the individual pieces with her alchemy into a new whole, adding to and directing the magic to obey her will. Her iron-hard unwavering will, protecting the wearer of the necklace from any and all magical assault.

It was a priceless piece, teeming with power. Beguiling. And I was just a weak baby necromancer. Even Kett didn't think I was strong enough to hold an artifact of such power.

On a different Adept, an older and more powerful magic user, such a necklace might well render them impervious to harm. Invulnerable.

Brit's eyes narrowed. She took a step toward me, trying to get a better look at the artifact strung around my skinny neck.

"Do you know what this is?" I asked casually.

"I've felt its power." The succubus wrapped her hands over the top rail of the gate.

"One coin for every soul I've ferried across the great divide," I said, bluffing like mad.

Brit snorted derisively.

But I had her attention. I could practically see her calculating how to get the necklace from me. She'd felt what it did. She was probably visualizing wearing it. With the power of the necklace, she knew she could stand against the witches.

Good thing I hadn't mentioned that it was the executioner of the Conclave who was coming for her.

I dug my hand into the pocket of my jeans, snagging the gold coin that Jade had given me two days before. I flipped it in the air. "I've already got your coin right here."

She sneered at me.

"So come and get it," I whispered. Then I turned and ran.

Just like prey ran.

Because a predator, especially one as arrogant as the succubus, couldn't help but give chase.

I knew. She wasn't my first bad guy. Just the first I'd had to deal with all on my own.

I cut across the grass, zigzagging through the flush-mounted headstones that I couldn't bring myself to simply trod over. My arm and leg hurt, jolts of pain radiating through each limb with every footfall.

The succubus was right behind me. She'd effortlessly vaulted the gate, highlighting her superior strength and speed. I could feel the nearness of her magic, of the souls she'd trapped within herself, and that spurred me forward.

I made a beeline toward the large granite cross that had been my goal all along. It stood out even in the darkness, because I could see in greater detail now that I was fueled by, buoyed by, the magic of Mountain View.

Something slammed into my back, throwing me forward. I fell badly, still trying to protect Ed in my satchel.

Even though her heels had to be sinking into the grass, the succubus was still faster than me. And she had learned—far too quickly—that if she didn't keep her hands on me, the necklace didn't have time to hurt her in return.

Tumbling, I slammed up against a huge, rough-hewn granite cross, ending up sitting upright with my back against it. My head rang. I lost the ability to see clearly for a moment.

But all of that was okay. Because I had landed exactly where I needed to be.

I let my magic loose, sinking it deeply into the ground, then spreading it out in a wide but tightly held circle.

The succubus crouched at the edge of the family plot, sneering as I blinked her into focus. Four of the eight additional stone plaques that encircled the monument were arrayed before her. And I didn't have to be able to read the block letters carved into the flecked granite to know whose remains lay beneath each one.

"Where are your jibes now, necromancer?" she practically purred. Shadows writhed and roiled under her skin—the souls she'd consumed. It probably felt like her personal magic to her, as she prepared to siphon my life force from me. After she relieved me of my necklace, of course. Because she was older and wiser than a baby necromancer.

I sneered. I knew what I was seeing, and it wasn't her power. It wasn't her life force.

Stolen souls. And I was the first soul seer to have been certified in the last twenty-five years.

"Scared to touch me, succubus?"

She laughed sharply. Then, too fast for me to track—helped, no doubt, by the fact that I felt slightly concussed—she grabbed my foot.

I grabbed her back.

Just not with my own hand.

No. William MacDonald rose to the occasion at my bidding.

Literally.

The vast ocean of death magic contained within the cemetery responded to my push. Wood cracked beneath us, then the earth erupted around us, pushing thick splinters and sod to the surface. A hand that was little more than decomposing tendons and skin tearing loose from whitening bone tore through the dirt, skeletal fingers grasping the succubus's wrists.

Brit blinked down at the hand holding her. "Oh…you're one of those."

"Yeah," I said, holding my aching arm across my chest. "I'm one of those, asshole."

I pushed again, sinking more and more of my magic into the earth. The energy of the graveyard responded, freeing three more corpses from their eternal resting places. The ground spewed forth broken coffin lids, rotted silk linings—and the third generation of MacDonalds.

I'd called upon the third generation rather than the more recently dead or the fully decomposed. It was tidier that way.

Mary MacDonald's floral dress was still hanging from her as she wrapped her arms fully around the succubus from the left. Henry's suit was still mostly intact as he pinned the succubus's left leg.

William kept hold of her wrist, pulling himself partly from his grave, wedging himself firmly between me and Brit.

Edward, who'd been young when he died of leukemia—the same cancer that had kept Benjamin Garrick in a perpetual state of nearly dying when he'd still been alive—rose fully, climbing free of the uplifting turf and soil to loom over the succubus. Then, with only a gentle prodding from me, he crouched before her, wrapping his hand around her neck.

"You think you can kill me with zombies?" The succubus sounded far too reasonable for someone pinned by reanimated corpses. "When your sorcerer couldn't kill me with his magic bullets?" She laughed, as if we were all idiots to even bother mentioning that we didn't like her slaughtering children.

I rested my head against the huge granite cross, feeling the indentations of the family name carved into it as they cut into my skull. I could call forth more corpses if needed. With little effort. But I was winded from running. I was hurting.

I was going to be seriously pissed with the succubus if she'd broken my arm and leg a second time. Bones took far too long to heal.

"There's no such thing as an immortal being," I said, matching her calm tone.

She snorted, then pressed against the hold of the zombies.

I pressed back. Prodding Edward to tighten his chokehold.

She grimaced, pulling in a hissing breath. "So you thought," she finally said.

"So I know." I reached for my satchel, tugging it against my hip and feeling Ed moving around within. He was okay. "But even if there is anyone who's near immortal, it isn't you."

"Do tell," she scoffed, testing the zombies' grips again, twisting and turning.

I had the corpses of the MacDonalds twist back, wrenching a short mew of pain from the succubus. "The Adepts who are about to come for you are as near to immortal as it gets." I tugged my phone free of my pocket, checking it for updates. Kett had to be nearby. "They don't need magic bullets. They'll simply remove your head from your shoulders."

There were too many text messages on my phone to read, with more appearing so quickly that they were just flashes of words on the screen. Getting more than just the gist would require taking my attention off the succubus—and off the MacDonalds, for that matter. I'd reanimated four corpses without a focus, without a silver circle. I couldn't lose hold of them.

I would never hear the end of it.

But yeah, the gist of the text messages was that everyone was freaking out. And Kett was definitely on his way.

So if I was going to do what I knew needed to be done, I had to move quickly. All this chatting, plus what was now clearly a concussion—ask me how I knew—was slowing me down. I needed to do something about the trapped souls of the children before the executioner showed up. If I waited, Kett wouldn't give me a chance to even ask permission.

I pulled Ed out of my satchel, petting him lightly, finding reassurance in the touch of his magic. I set him in the grass, but he snuggled up against my thigh instead of trundling off. I could use him as an anchor point if needed. But only as a last resort.

Next, with the succubus watching my every move even as she continually tested the strength of my zombies, I tugged a set of straight knitting needles free from the depths of my satchel. I had never knitted a single stitch of yarn with those needles. They weren't for making hats or scarves.

What they were was an extrapolation of my ability to knit soul magic. Or to untangle what should have never been knitted together in the first place.

And there were souls that needed untangling from the succubus.

I had never tried to pull a soul from a living person. I had no idea if such a despicable act was even possible. But I wasn't interested in the succubus's soul. She could rot in hell for all I cared. Or purgatory. Just as long as she was perpetually separated from all the energy that was released after her death. No matter where it was collected before being remade or reborn.

Because I believed in that. That much I knew. That much I'd seen with my own eyes.

There was a beyond.

I had seen people reborn.

"Knitting?" Brit asked. Her tone was mocking, but she had begun to struggle against the zombies in earnest. It was an easy guess that she could feel the power residing in the knitting needles. Power siphoned from me, then directed and cemented into the needles by the dowser.

Magic was ultimately about intention. My intention, my focus.

Unable to stand, I kneeled beside William MacDonald. Ed shifted with me, the magic embedded into him a comforting hum against my calf. The reanimated corpses all trained their eyeless gazes on me.

That disconcerted the succubus. But I understood. I was the brightest thing imaginable to the perception of the shades who had returned to animate the corpses at my unvoiced request.

"It's more like unknitting," I said, holding my needles before me and letting my eyes go out of focus. "But I've never done it on a living person before, so it might sting."

I reached for the energy writhing within the succubus, trying to see where each section began and another ended. I needed a loose tail. I tried to capture one and…

There!

"What are you doing?" the succubus snarled.

"Retrieving what you've stolen." I coaxed the loose tail forward. It came sluggishly.

The succubus growled. "Mine."

The tail of energy snapped back to her.

I lost sight of it.

I brought my needles forward again, focused solely on the energy roiling inside Brit, pulling at that trapped energy again and again—only to have the succubus snatch it back from me each time.

As I tried to free the souls trapped within the succubus's body, she fought me. Fought against the hold of the MacDonalds.

Sweat beaded on my forehead, despite the chill threading through me. All the warmth I'd shared with the corpses in order to wake them. For the first time ever, I regretted wearing a thickly knit sweater.

I had to stop. I wasn't making any progress. I had to come at it from a different angle.

Panting, I lowered the needles and settled back on my heels, almost tipping over in pained exhaustion.

Benjamin Garrick was standing behind the succubus, beyond the zombies pinning her in place. I'd been so narrowly focused, I hadn't even felt his magic as he approached.

The succubus was glaring at me with utter hatred. Her face was pale, strained. Oddly, she looked thinner and older. Fighting me had consumed a lot of her energy, and apparently that manifested physically for her.

"Everything all right, Mory?" Benjamin's tone was low, gruff. Pained.

The succubus flinched, then tried to twist to look behind her.

I still held her fast with the reanimated corpses, but I was starting to feel the strain of doing so. My own endurance was being severely tested. Maybe if I hadn't been hurt, I could have—

Benjamin lunged forward, hands on Brit's shoulder, crushing her in his grasp. She screamed as he wrenched her upright, breaking Edward's and Mary's holds on her neck and shoulders, but not William's grasp on her arm or Henry's on her ankle.

The dark-haired vampire clamped his mouth on the succubus's neck. Biting her. Then drinking from her deeply.

She thrashed wildly.

Going against every one of my screaming instincts, I used the MacDonald family to hold her in place. Coaxing Edward to grab her free arm and setting Mary at her other leg. Even as Benjamin drained her, gulp by gulp.

I watched the muscles of the vampire's neck move. He'd closed his eyes, eyelashes dark against his pale skin.

Brit stopped thrashing. She slowly stilled. Then she sank back against Benjamin, as she would have leaned back into the embrace of a lover.

She sighed softly.

Benjamin shifted his grip on her, cradling her more gently even as he reached up and shifted her head, exposing more of her neck. To get a better grip, a deeper bite, perhaps from a different artery.

My insides churned. Fear and worry were warring with a completely inappropriate, completely weird desire that heated me from within.

And then I saw the loose ends writhing just under the succubus's skin. I counted nine of them.

She'd lost her hold on the children's souls.

"Wait!" I cried. "Wait, Ben!"

The vampire didn't even acknowledge me. He'd been badly wounded. Twice. And he was in need of blood to heal. That was all he knew. That was all he cared about.

I stumbled to my feet, bringing my needles forward. As quickly as I could, I picked up a loose end, coiling the energy around the needles. Then, following some instinct I didn't have time to question, I knit the long strand of life force into a short rectangle, then bound it off one stitch at a time. I knotted the final loop, slipping it from my needle.

The soul was released from the succubus with a soft, almost pleased hum.

I didn't have time to figure out what had actually just happened, what I'd just done. I just knew it felt right. I reached for the next loose end, first knitting, then binding off the energy.

Benjamin's knees buckled. I loosened the Mac-Donalds' hold on the succubus. The vampire sank to the ground, cradling Brit, still feeding from her. She wrapped her hand around the back of his neck. Moaning, panting, with pleasure. From his venom, presumably. Or maybe Benjamin was in her head, making her feel or see things.

I found and released two more souls. "Slow, Ben. Slow down, Ben," I whispered, finding and knitting a fourth soul. Then a fifth.

The loose ends became more difficult to find. Indistinct. Fading and melting together somehow.

"Stop, Ben," I shouted. "Stop, stop!"

Somehow, he heard me through his bloodlust. He stopped feeding, though he didn't look up. His gaze remained snagged to the blood trickling down Brit's neck, over her collarbone, and between her breasts.

I released two more souls.

How many was that now? Seven? There should have been more.

Benjamin started growling. A low, keening snarl. His tongue darted past his sharpened eye teeth, lapping the blood from the succubus's neck.

I tried to ignore him. Gently stirring through the life force energy sluggishly shimmering within the succubus, I found what I thought were the last two souls—thin wisps that I carefully separated and picked up on my needles. I knit each as quickly as I could, sinking to the ground as I did so. Tapping the last of my own reserves to release the succubus's final victims.

I couldn't hold my needles aloft anymore. My arms dropped to my sides as I slumped sideways onto the grass. Ed burrowed under my outstretched hand. I'd lost hold of my needles.

Benjamin struck at the succubus's neck. Her head lolled. He snarled viciously, biting her a second and third time. He grabbed her arm, breaking it with a sharp snap, then slashing at her wrist with his teeth.

But she was dead.

I could feel it.

If I had so desired, I could have infused her corpse with the last of my energy, to pilot her. I could have added an undead succubus to my menagerie of one.

I brushed the dark thought away, pushing myself partially upright with my undamaged arm. I had Ed. I didn't need anyone else in that way.

Benjamin shoved the succubus's corpse off his knees.

I retrieved my needles, whispering a thank you to the MacDonalds, then sending them back to their rest. I had just enough energy left to do so. The re-animated corpses were drawn back into their graves, the ground shifting around them with a pulse of the magic embedded into every blade of grass, every speck of dirt, that made Mountain View. Then that magic sealed over them. I couldn't make the physical damage to the gravesite go away, but the witches could take care of that.

I half-crawled, half-slid backward, until my back rested against the huge granite cross again. I tucked my needles into my satchel and scooped up Ed, cradling him in my lap for comfort.

Benjamin began growling again, hunched over the corpse of the succubus. A low-pitched, dark-tinted sound. He wrapped his right hand over his left wrist. The bracelet's magic welled, then sputtered, abating. Then it welled again, no doubt quelling Benjamin's urges.

Other magic, other energy whispered around us. My necromancy was leaking, untethered because I was exhausted.

I risked glancing away from Benjamin to see that I was surrounded by the shades of the children I'd released from the succubus.

Nine in all, ranging from five to eleven years old. The boy I knew to be Danny Pim was wearing jeans and sneakers, carrying a soccer ball. Misty Dean was barefoot, wearing a ruffled party dress with a wide sash tied in a big, floppy bow. Anna Campbell was holding what appeared to be the glass dolphin that the succubus had left on her grave, her expression fiercely triumphant.

The attention of each and every shade was fixated on the vampire. Not me.

That didn't bode well.

Benjamin finally raised his head, pinning me with a blood-red gaze. The seething magic of the bracelet exploded, writhing over his wrist, creeping up his forearm. He grimaced, pained, cradling his arm against his chest.

Then, as he somehow managed to ignore the quelling power of the necromancy working, a slow smile curled his lips. That smile transformed his face into something more. Something otherworldly.

He had lost his fight with the bloodlust.

The vampire's beguiling magic reached out and caressed my neck, dipping under the shawl collar of my sweater. That power, that pull, slowly dripped down between my breasts, cupping me, warming me.

My nipples hardened even as my cheeks flushed.

"Mory," Benjamin whispered. His tone was deep, seductive. Alluring. "I want you."

Oh, God.

ELEVEN

I WANTED THE VAMPIRE TOO. I HAD WANTED BENJAMIN GARRICK for a long time. And in that moment, I wanted him with every fiber of my exhausted being, possible broken arm and concussion and all.

I just wanted him in a completely different way than he wanted me.

And that thought was the only thing that kept me from opening my arms and welcoming him.

Benjamin was undeterred by my lack of response. Presumably because he could hear my heart hammering in my chest. And not out of fear.

He moved toward me, practically slithering over the corpse of the succubus, his movements so smooth, so inhuman. Still pinning me with his red-eyed gaze, he wrapped his arm around the ankle of my outstretched leg. I hissed with pain as he jostled me.

He cocked his head, pausing. His voice was heavy with his beguiling magic when he spoke. "You're hurt, my necromancer."

"Yes." I was struggling to hold on to that pain actually, using it to anchor myself and keep my head clear. "My leg and my arm. Also my head."

His tongue flicked against the tips of his upper eye teeth, which had doubled their normal length. I'd never seen his fangs before. Kett's were much, much longer, as were Jasmine's.

"Bleeding…you're really hurt, Mory." The vampire frowned thoughtfully, though his head was still tilted at that odd angle, as if he was listening to things I couldn't hear.

For a moment, I thought he was going to get his bloodlust under control.

He didn't.

Instead, another slow smile replaced his frown. He gently ran his hand up my jean-clad calf as he continued to close the space between us. "I could make you feel better," he murmured seductively.

"Sure," I said, ignoring every instinct railing at me to either kick out and run from him—or to embrace the moment and let it go where I wanted it to go. "And then you'd kill me."

He blinked, obviously having a difficult time following the conversation. His control was on the edge of shredding. "I would never kill you."

"You killed the succubus. She moaned a lot beforehand, so I'm sure your venom is a hell of a high. But I'm not interested in sacrificing myself to your bloodlust, Ben."

His lip curled into a snarl. He didn't like being denied. Or at least the predator lurking within him didn't like it. Then he shook his head, sliding his hand up my thigh in a gentle caress. "Just a sip, Mory. A sip of your blood will counter the bone bracelet. So much power…running through your veins…"

I closed my eyes, though it was stupid to do so in front of a predator. God, his logic was as beguiling as his magic. The bracelet had reacted to his draining the succubus and was likely trying to exert its influence over him even now. I could feel the dark miasma of power spreading up the arm he still cradled against his chest. That same bracelet had nearly killed him when he'd been driven to bite Bitsy, but either its hold had grown weaker—or Benjamin was stronger now.

Voices whispered all around me. The shades of the children I'd freed from the succubus pressed against me. I didn't have the energy to spare to give their words the boost they needed to be fully articulated, but I could feel their concern.

Benjamin settled his hand on my hip, slipping his fingers underneath my sweater, seeking skin contact. His touch came with no warmth, and I was already cold. Terribly cold.

"Open your eyes, necromancer," he whispered.

I did, gazing deeply into the glowing red orbs pinned to me.

He smiled, his touch still gentle. His magic curled around me, teasing and licking against the skin of my neck and face.

"Ben…" I whispered, fighting the overwhelming desire that was threatening to wipe all my reason away.

"You want me," he murmured, sounding slightly surprised.

"Not like this." And that truth firmed my tone, my resolve. "I'm not a blood bag."

He frowned. Then he reached for me with his left hand—the one on which he wore the bone bracelet. He curled his cool fingers around my uninjured wrist as if he couldn't stop himself. "Of course not."

"But you're still trying to bite me."

"Just a sip," he cajoled, lifting my hand, sliding back the arm of my sweater to expose my wrist.

The magic of the necklace rose, simmering against my collarbone, as if checking on me. The ghosts pressed against me tightly, perhaps trying to place themselves between me and the vampire. But Benjamin had no idea. He had no idea at all how dangerous I was to him, and not only in that moment.

He was just…so…

And I wanted…

No.

It was his magic that was entrancing. Not that I didn't like him. I did. But Benjamin, uninjured and not driven by bloodlust, loved Jasmine. At least as much as it was possible to love for those born from death and driven to fuel themselves with the life-blood of other people.

The vampire's cool lips brushed across my wrist.

I shuddered. With desire, yes. But also with the knowledge of what I could do with all the magic pressing against me, beckoning me to submit.

Not to die under the vampire's fangs.

But to feed him.

Because in feeding him, I could own him.

Benjamin's tongue licked a sensitive spot on my inner wrist, across the veins.

I gasped involuntarily.

He took that as consent.

Sharp points bit into my flesh, and Benjamin drew a slow draught of my blood.

The voices of the ghosts became clearer. The shades of the children tried to lay hands on Benjamin, to push him away from me. He was unyielding.

The power of my necklace writhed against the skin of my lower neck and collarbone, as if it was completely aware and just waiting to be unleashed. All it needed was one concerned thought from me.

But I didn't need ghosts or the necklace to control Benjamin Garrick. I settled my free hand on his head, running my fingers through his silky dark hair. He drew another long draught of my blood. Pain streaked up my arm. I ignored it.

Benjamin had always been mine to take.

Mine to have, to hold.

To control.

But I wasn't that kind of necromancer.

Because even though I was surrounded by death, I lived in the light.

"Enough," I said, feeling the rise of my own power, hearing the magic laced through my own voice now. "Enough, Benjamin."

The vampire was either beyond listening or was ignoring me.

I sighed. I was going to have to force him. "Ben, please," I whispered. "I don't want to hurt you." Because I knew there was no going back from that. If I reached for his magic, if I controlled him—and I could feel the tie between us strengthening with every sip he took of my blood—he would know.

He would finally understand what I could do, who I really was. To him, at least.

And that would be it for us.

I wasn't even sure a friendship could survive under those circumstances. If Benjamin knew I could control him…

I squeezed my eyes shut as a different sort of pain arced through my chest. Grief. Crushed hope.

If Benjamin knew I could control him, there was no chance for us. Ever. He could never love someone capable of wielding him like a puppet.

The vampire's venom finally kicked in, making me light-headed, compliant. But I wasn't getting the hit that the succubus had so obviously gotten. It was likely that if I hadn't been already hurt, already magically drained, I would have been practically immune to the effects of his venom.

Still…

There was another way this could go…

A way that meant Benjamin would never have to know what I could do.

I could let him have me.

A ghostly hand settled on my left shoulder. I opened my eyes, finding myself meeting the gaze of a nine-year-old girl. Her hair was plaited in two perfect braids that just brushed the top of her shoulders.

Tanya Atkinson.

The ghost smiled at me, then she leaned closer to cup my face with her free hand, gazing at me with wonder as she drew energy from the contact. "Thank you," she whispered. Then, concern aging her face, she glanced down at Benjamin suckling at my wrist. She lifted her wide-eyed gaze to meet mine, squeezing my shoulder.

"Mory…that's enough."

Something cracked in my chest. Tears welled in my eyes. I was such a fucking idiot to have let any of this get so far. I had bungled around since I'd gotten back to Vancouver, as if I were out of place.

Misplaced.

But I wasn't.

I was exactly where I needed to be. Exactly where I was supposed to be.

I smiled at the young girl's ghost. Tanya. "Go now," I murmured. "I'll be okay. Take the others with you."

She nodded, releasing my shoulder and stepping back. But waiting. The other children pressed around her, vigilant.

I looked down at Benjamin, at my fingers entwined through his dark hair, lightly pressed against his head. Sighing with resolve, I reached out for the vampire's delectably pulsating magic. I gave it a push. "That's enough."

He stilled.

"Release me."

His teeth slid from my flesh.

I shuddered again, pain mixing with residual desire.

Benjamin looked up at me, confused, then horrified. He scrambled back a few feet, aghast—but at what, I didn't know. That he'd bitten me? Or that I was capable of controlling him?

I tugged the sleeve of my sweater over my still-bleeding wrist, pressing my hand over the wound.

"Mory…" He moaned with despair.

I shook my head sharply. I was too tired, too drained, to talk about what had just happened, what had almost happened.

The ghosts of the children—they really were too substantial, too engaged, to be mere shades—pressed forward, each touching me in turn. Then each slowly faded until only Tanya stood before me. She smiled. Then she turned and walked toward where I knew her gravesite lay. Her presence dissipated after a few steps.

I felt like crying. But I didn't.

I was heroic like that.

When I needed to be.

Also, I knew that acting weak might rile Benjamin up again. I really didn't want to have to do more than give him a light push.

"Where's Liam?" I asked wearily.

"In the car." Benjamin's tone was dull. He was paler than usual, hunched over his left arm and clutching his wrist again. "Still alive last I saw." He shuddered.

"Are you okay?"

He laughed, quietly but harshly. "I should be asking you that."

I transferred my attention to the corpse of the succubus. She had aged rapidly as I'd pulled the souls from her, one by one. Now she appeared to be decomposing just as rapidly. Crumbling from within.

"It won't happen again." Benjamin's eyes were still red, his cheekbones more prominent than usual. He was hurting. Or rather, the magic of the bone bracelet was hurting him. For biting the succubus, then me.

A white-blond vampire clad in dark-wash jeans and a black cashmere sweater appeared before me.

I flinched.

Damn it.

A knowing smile curled over Kett's lips, but it quickly disappeared behind narrowed eyes as he swept his silvered gaze over me. Then he glanced at Benjamin, swiveling his head to finally take in the rapidly decomposing body of the succubus.

Suddenly the elder vampire was crouched before me, his fingers under my chin, lifting my gaze to meet his. I hadn't seen him move. Again.

I hissed, jerking back and managing to slam my injured head against the massive granite cross I was leaning against. Pain exploded through my skull. I tried to blink away the black dots swimming through my field of vision. I was unsuccessful.

Kett pinned his icy gaze to Benjamin. "You put the wielder's necromancer in jeopardy. I said to grab Mory and run."

Benjamin sighed heavily. "I grabbed. Mory ran."

"Benjamin couldn't leave Liam," I said, stupidly getting involved though I knew it was a way better idea to stay silent. Especially because Kett was still propping my chin up on his fingers. Fingers that felt like frozen steel spikes.

Kett shifted his unnerving gaze to me. "If the sorcerer couldn't fend for himself, that's his problem. Not mine or Benjamin's."

"Well," I spat, "I'm not your problem either!"

"That you are, Mory. Unfortunately."

"I didn't care about the sorcerer," Benjamin said tonelessly. "The succubus was strong. I needed to give Mory time to get to the cemetery."

Kett didn't answer. He watched the younger vampire for a moment, then returned his gaze to me, disconcertedly slipping his fingers through my hair until he found the nasty bump at the back of my head.

I hissed again. Then, because I was apparently so concussed that I'd knocked all my survival instincts right out of my head, I snarled at him.

He blinked at me. Then he laughed quietly. His magic uncoiled, as if loosened by his amusement. The immense slumbering power licked against me—a terrible velvet touch that outpowered Benjamin's ability to enchant and beguile by infinity times infinity.

"You vanquished the succubus, little necromancer." Kett's cool assessment was infused with pride.

I tried to ignore the satisfaction that stoked within me. Killing any sentient being shouldn't be a thing to celebrate. "We both did."

Kett smirked knowingly.

Before I could hit him with some high-caliber snark that I didn't actually have the energy to produce, he was steps away, stirring his fingers through the remains of the succubus. The corpse was reduced almost to ashes now.

The elder vampire looked at Benjamin thoughtfully, then back down at the crumbling corpse.

The dark-haired vampire kept his head bowed, both of his arms now hanging limp over knees that were bent into his chest. Blood dripped steadily onto his jeans from his left wrist. Magic seethed from the wound. The bone bracelet was still hurting him.

"Old," Kett said. "To crumble into ash like this."

"Yes," I said. "Over a hundred years old."

Kett curled his lip. "Older than that, necromancer. Powerful. A pity that you had to kill her." He pinned his silvered eyes to me.

"She didn't give us much choice."

Kett turned his attention to Benjamin. "Look at me, fledgling."

The dark-haired vampire's head snapped up as if he were a puppet and Kett had just pulled his strings. His eyes were still blood red, but his fangs had receded. The bone bracelet's quelling was working. Or maybe my push had given Benjamin some control back.

"Did you drain the succubus?" Kett asked coolly.

Benjamin squeezed his eyes shut, clenching his fists. "She said I had no protection. No token. That I was fair game."

I frowned. I hadn't heard that exchange. And I wasn't sure what 'token' was supposed to mean in that context.

"And when you told her you were under my protection?"

Benjamin shook his head, not answering. Closing his eyes.

"Answer me. Did you drain the succubus?"

"And what if I did?"

Kett laughed coolly. "Perhaps you'll be an asset yet."

"You're such an asshole," I snarled.

"So you keep telling me." The elder vampire smirked, then tilted his head as if listening to something far away. "Our chat is about to be interrupted."

"Thank God," I grumbled, trying to gather my legs under me and straighten up. Unsuccessfully.

The executioner turned his attention back to Benjamin. "The necromancer is bleeding. From more than a head wound."

I pressed my hand over my wrist, grinding my sweater into the still-smarting puncture marks.

"Why would you let him bite you?" Kett asked, almost whispering.

I shook my head, refusing to answer. But a knowing smile spread slowly across the ancient vampire's face.

I glared back at him in response, daring him to push the topic.

He chuckled darkly, then spoke conversationally. "I imagine your blood isn't helping with healing the binding Benjamin wears. Nor the necklace, for that matter. If Benjamin could feel magic, he would have known that biting you would worsen his condition."

"What do you mean?" I asked. "My blood is making Ben sick? We thought...Benjamin thought it might quell the magic of the bone bracelet."

"His mother's blood, perhaps. But not yours." Kett curled his lip at the younger vampire. "It's polite to seal the wound, Benjamin Garrick. When you bite someone. Even with permission."

He hit the word 'permission' heavily. And suddenly I realized that Benjamin could get into a lot of trouble for biting me. 'Trouble' meaning that he might get put down.

Terminated.

His mother had secured their place in the Godfrey coven under the provision that Benjamin wouldn't, couldn't, bite anyone.

Benjamin swallowed hard. "How?"

"Your saliva will do."

"I lick my bites?"

Kett didn't clarify, meaning the younger vampire already had the information he needed.

Benjamin shifted toward me.

I flinched, though not out of fear this time. At least not from fear of Benjamin. He stilled, though, hunched over. I took a deep breath, calming myself.

Kett appeared on my other side, slipping his hand around the back of my head. I guessed that the gesture might have been meant to be comforting, but it put him in the perfect position to snap my neck.

I glared at him.

He smirked as though I'd just done exactly what he expected. "Let the fledgling finish what he started. Then I'll heal the binding."

"You'll remove the bone bracelet?"

"I'll make it so it can be removed."

I nodded, not sure what I was agreeing to—for Benjamin. I just knew I didn't like the dark-haired vampire being in perpetual pain.

Benjamin closed the space between us. Heat flushed my face again, desire warring with the embarrassment of having Kett as a witness. The younger vampire didn't look me in the eyes, reaching for my arm but hesitating the moment before he touched me. Then he looked up at me. His eyes were still dark red, stained with his magic.

"Mory?" He swallowed, clearing his throat. "I won't hurt you. Again."

I tugged my sleeve up my arm, practically thrusting my wrist in Benjamin's face. Then I met Kett's gaze defiantly as the dark-haired vampire lowered his head and licked the still seeping bite marks on my wrist.

Kett appeared amused at my defiance.

And then, without any warning, the edge of a jade stone knife slid in front of Benjamin Garrick's neck.

"No!" I shouted.

Benjamin was torn away from me, tossed aside like a candy wrapper. He crashed into three head-stones—demolishing them—before he fell onto the grass, completely insensible.

Power thundered around me, compressing my thoughts, dampening my ability to move.

I strained to lift my chin, looking up through the storm of magic.

A fierce blond was standing before me, swathed in black leather armor with her jade knife in hand. Golden curls writhed all around her face and head.

Jade Godfrey.

All the emotion that I'd been burying deeply finally broke free. I sobbed in relief, just once.

Jade flicked her blazing blue eyes toward me. "I've got you, babe."

"I know." I firmed my tone. "I'm okay."

Jade returned her gaze to the white-blond vampire standing before her. Kett's head was slightly bowed, a smile teasing his lips. He shoved his hands in the pockets of his jeans, allowing his shoulders to slump—a predator in repose.

"Why was Benjamin Garrick licking Mory?" Jade asked. Her tone was a cool, harsh lash of power.

Kett flicked his gaze toward me, arching an eyebrow.

"I...he was hurt. Like, really hurt," I said, feebly trying to find an excuse that Jade would accept.

"He's immortal," Jade growled. "He could have waited until his master arrived."

I couldn't come up with a logical counter to that on the spot, so I just jutted out my chin.

Jade sighed the sigh of the long-suffering. Which she probably was when it came to me, since it was a sound I'd heard from her before. On multiple occasions.

"The necromancer's necklace would have countered any malicious intent, Jade," Kett said coolly. "You made certain of that yourself."

"Malicious magic," she snapped.

"And what else is a vampire but dark magic incarnate, dowser?"

She eyed him. "Don't try to sweet-talk me, executioner."

I wasn't quite certain what she heard in Kett's statement that sounded sweet. But then, I also didn't quite get Jade and Kett's relationship either. I was fairly certain they loved each other, even though Jade was happily married—ecstatically, in fact—to Warner. But I was also certain that the dowser would run the elder vampire through without hesitation if he ever threatened my well-being.

That idea, paired with the vision of her standing before me, jade knife still in hand, warmed me. But I shoved that warmth away. I didn't need to be cajoled either. I'd been doing my job. I was an adult.

"Jade, we're both hurt. Benjamin and me…and Liam—"

"I've got Liam," Jade said. "That's what took me so long to get to you." She eyed Kett. "The vampire left the sorcerer's care to me."

Kett shrugged, but somehow only managed to mimic the human gesture.

She shook her head at him. "I know a distraction when I see one, vampire."

He grinned at her, unrepentant. "I needed a moment with your necromancer."

"You could have at least tempted me with magic-infused gold," she griped. "The sorcerer's family mobbed me when I dropped him home. I had to answer questions, so many freaking questions, before coming to Mory's rescue."

I grumbled under my breath at the 'rescue' crack.

Kett's smile widened, his tone becoming intimate. "Next time."

"There won't be a next time!" Unswayed by what I thought might have been the executioner's attempts to flirt or tease, Jade pointed at my wrist emphatically.

My skin was unblemished. No hint of Ben's bite remained. I tugged my sweater down, grabbing it up in my hand.

"I want this dealt with, Kett," Jade said, still pissed. "No biting allowed. As agreed."

The executioner nodded stiffly, all amusement wiped from his face. "I'll take care of it. I've simply been trying to give the fledgling some time to adjust." He turned to Benjamin. The younger vampire was still sprawled in the grass where Jade had effortlessly tossed him. "Come to me, Benjamin Garrick."

Ben made it to his knees, then stood, moving as if in great pain.

Concern etched itself across Jade's face. "Kett," she murmured. Her jade knife had disappeared, presumably returned to the invisible sheath I knew she wore.

"I'll take care of it, dowser," Kett said coolly, obviously not liking being questioned.

Jade stepped toward me, tugging me to my feet and wrapping her arm around me. Weak as I was, I didn't think I could have stood had she not been holding me. I cradled Ed against my chest. Jade retrieved my satchel and slung it over her own shoulder.

"Is Liam okay?" I asked in a whisper, watching Benjamin hobble over to Kett.

The dowser nodded. Her golden curls brushed against the side of my face. The magic of my necklace churned. Happy, I thought, that its creator was so near. Except I understood that no matter how powerful they were, inanimate objects weren't sentient. Well, they shouldn't be.

"The sorcerer is magically and physically drained," Jade said. Her gaze was also on Benjamin. "But the Talbots will have him fixed up quickly. He was pretty freaking pissy, so I took that as a good sign. Kept demanding to be taken to you."

She gave me a narrow-eyed look.

I kept my expression as blank as possible. "We've been working together."

"That's what he said." She sounded seriously doubtful.

I grinned at her unapologetically, knowing it would push her buttons.

She huffed. "You should have texted me earlier," she said. Angry, but not at me.

I didn't answer. All my attention was trained on Benjamin as he collapsed before Kett, kneeling in the ashes of the succubus.

"Benjamin Garrick," Kett said formally, "I've already accepted responsibility for your existence. Already fed you once with my blood. Would you be tied even tighter to me?"

"The token?" Benjamin asked.

"Yes. Though even with only a single exchange of blood, I would have thought our connection would be clear." Kett glanced at Jade.

She nodded in agreement.

I took that to mean that she could sense the magic that tied Benjamin to Kett—the power that was slowly transforming the younger vampire into a more perfect predator. I had noticed the consequences of that first blood exchange, but I couldn't sense any bond between the vampires.

Kett returned his attention to the dark-haired vampire kneeling before him. "The succubus might have been bluffing. She was certainly old enough to have known vampires. Traditionally, a token is a way for elder vampires to build their nonblooded shivers. Families, if you prefer. My grandsire won't have any vampire in his territory who doesn't share a blood tie with him. Or a token. For example, the blood Jasmine and I share assures that she will be known to all to be mine, under my protection. She is untouchable by any who fear the executioner of the Conclave. But…" Eyeing Jade again, the executioner smirked coolly. "Even the few who do not fear me wouldn't trespass into the territory of the dragon slayer without permission."

Jade scoffed.

"Will another exchange kill me?" Benjamin asked conversationally. "For the third time?"

Kett laughed mirthlessly. "That was a possibility when you were first turned. But I'm not as I once was."

"Because you've remade Jasmine?"

"And because you've consumed the blood of a powerful Adept and survived."

Benjamin frowned. "The succubus?"

Kett flicked his gaze to meet mine. "Yes," he said, lying.

Jade's hand tightened on my shoulder.

"Would you sip of me, Benjamin Garrick?" Kett asked. His inscrutable gaze was now riveted to Jade. "Would you become more than you are? Knowing that you have no idea what that means?"

"I'll be different tomorrow anyway, won't I?" Benjamin was still kneeling, though his head was thrown back, gazing up at the master vampire. "That's life."

"No," Kett said thoughtfully. "The immortal are often unchanging. It is always a choice."

"For better or worse," Jade murmured.

Kett nodded.

"I choose strength," Benjamin said firmly.

"Allow the dowser to remove the bracelet, then," Kett said coolly. "You will either stand with the strength of my blood, filled with the other powerful blood you have consumed. Or you will fall. The bracelet is more trouble than it is worth."

Benjamin hesitated, wrapping his right hand over his left wrist.

"Do this," Kett said. "Or I will banish you to London to suffer in the dungeon of my grandsire until you can tear yourself free of the magic that binds you."

I spoke up in spite of myself. "How long would that take?"

The elder vampire didn't bother looking at me. "Centuries."

I looked at Jade, aghast.

She shook her head, chiding me silently. It was Benjamin's decision.

The younger vampire raised his left arm toward Jade, pulling back the sleeves of his sweater and jacket to expose the seething mass of necromancy wrapped around his wrist. The bird bones embedded into his skin were edged in blood, dripping.

"If you please, dowser." Benjamin's words were stilted, pained but polite. "I would appreciate your assistance."

Jade hissed quietly, presumably responding to the feel of the necromancy working. It likely tasted as foul to her as it felt to me.

She stepped forward, bringing me with her.

Benjamin's gaze flicked to me. I tried to smile. He looked away, resolute.

Yeah, he hadn't liked me controlling him. A chasm opened up in my stomach. I promised myself that I would stuff it full of all the babying Jade was about to force upon me, if it would just let me get through the next few moments without making a complete fool of myself.

Jade placed her hand across Benjamin's wrist, covering the bird-bone bracelet. She held him like that for a moment. Whatever else was happening, I couldn't sense it.

Benjamin grimaced. Then individual bird bones began to loosen, dropping into the grass.

Jade pulled her hand away.

A seething, raw wound encircled Benjamin's wrist. "Thank you," he murmured.

"I'll speak to Teresa," the dowser said.

The dark-haired vampire shook his head. "No." He firmed his tone. "It was my decision. I'll speak to my mother." He shifted his gaze to Kett, smiling wryly. "If I survive the next few moments."

"Stand then," Kett said.

Benjamin straightened, swaying unsteadily.

Jade tugged me against her tightly, leading me away. Unable to not look, I cranked my neck, watching as Kett opened his arms to Benjamin. The dark-haired vampire was shorter than his master. He stepped forward, face turned in to the executioner's neck. Kett closed their embrace.

"Don't watch," Jade whispered. "Let Benjamin have his privacy. He's been badly hurt helping you. He won't want you to see him as weak."

"He doesn't care how I see him," I whispered. "It's not like that between us." But I looked away as the dark-haired vampire wrapped his hand around the back of Kett's head.

Jade laughed quietly. "Benjamin spent a long time slowly dying, Mory. Risking his immortal life for you wasn't something he would do flippantly."

I nodded, allowing more of my weight to fall to Jade, knowing she could carry me forever if I needed her to. "That was before."

"Before?" she asked.

I didn't answer, knowing that no one liked being controlled. And most definitely not by a friend—or someone who hoped to be more than a friend.

I was in Jade's arms before I realized that I'd stopped walking, before I realized that my knees had buckled.

"I've got you, babe." Jade said it again as she swept me up, carrying me effortlessly.

"I know." I rested my head on the dowser's shoulder, giving in to the utter weariness mugging my mind and body. I was asleep before we'd exited the cemetery.

I WOKE TWICE. ONCE WHILE ENCASED IN DARKNESS, CURLED IN A large ornate chair that I instantly recognized by feel. The gilded wood and thick cushioning were warm comfort, even though I was sleeping mostly upright.

I had spent weeks in that chair after the incident with the elves, struggling to heal three broken limbs while my own magic was completely drained. As I understood it, the chair had been constructed centuries ago by a guardian dragon who specialized in healing.

Ed was snuggled in my lap.

I knew the dowser was near, so I fell asleep again without worry.

The second time I woke, it was light outside, though the curtains across Jade's living room windows were drawn. I was still in the chair. My right hand felt heavy. I glanced down to see that I was holding a large smooth stone. I recognized the rune painted on it, but only because I knew who it belonged to. I looked up, smiling, already knowing who was in the room with me.

A witch with light-brown hair was sleeping on the worn leather couch. Her knees were tucked to her chest, her head cradled in her arms. She was wearing yoga pants, a cowl-neck sweater, and the lace socks I'd knit her for her last birthday.

Ed was perched on the coffee table, watching the witch intently.

Burgundy.

She had been away at a witches' retreat devoted to healing, taking time off from the University of British Columbia where she was also studying medicine. She'd shared her focal stone with me, to help me heal.

Ed shuffled around, opening his mouth in a wide grin when he caught me looking at him. He moved across the coffee table as if trying to build up speed, then launched himself off the edge in an attempt to jump the gap between us.

He promptly plummeted to the ground.

I lunged forward, abandoning the stone, knowing I was already too late to catch Ed. Threads of my magic shot from my outstretched fingers, twining around the undead turtle. And I held him like that, suspended just off the hardwood floor.

I blinked, disconcerted.

Then I sighed.

Apparently, I had just gained some sort of new ability.

That was what I got for draining my magic while rescuing a dozen souls, then hanging out in a dragon-wrought chair for a couple of days.

I snagged Ed with my actual hand, planning to haul him up into my lap. He wiggled madly, though, so I set him on the floor. He promptly trundled off in the direction of the second bedroom that was Jade's craft room, making me wonder if someone was sleeping there.

"Hey." A drowsy voice pulled my attention back to the witch on the couch. Burgundy rubbed her eyes.

"Hey."

Burgundy smiled at me. "You're awake."

"Yes." I found the focal stone wedged next to my thigh, holding the large smooth rock in my open palm and offering it to my friend. "Thank you."

She blushed slightly. "It's the least I could do. I'm sorry I wasn't here earlier. I didn't know you were coming home."

I wrapped my hand around the rock, settling back into the chair. The stone was warm to the touch from the magic embedded into it that I couldn't otherwise sense. "Yeah, I'm home."

She grinned, stretching. "What do you want for breakfast?"

"Cupcakes, of course."

"Of course." She laughed.

"And everyone else?" I asked. "Benjamin? Liam?"

"Not sure about Ben." She swung her legs off the couch. "But Liam kept blowing up your phone with text messages, then started calling. Jade took your phone away and read him the riot act."

Huh. Well, that was…nice. I grinned at my friend.

She gave me an assessing look. "It's like that, then?"

I laughed, then shrugged. "Not yet."

"Have you told the sorcerer that?"

I shrugged again—and couldn't seem to wipe the grin from my face.

Burgundy snorted, heaving herself from the couch and retrieving her phone from the coffee table. She glanced at the screen. "Oh, shit! I'm late. And I've already missed three days of classes."

I offered her the stone. "Rain check."

She laid her hand over it, leaning forward to crush my shoulders and neck in a one-armed hug. "Any time."

TWELVE

THREE DAYS LATER, I WAS PERCHED ON A STOOL AT A HIGH-TOPPED table in the far corner of Cake in a Cup.

Knitting, of course.

Waiting on a sorcerer.

I was early.

A steady stream of customers came and went along the glass display case and counter, ordering single treats to go with their coffees or full boxes to take home.

Jade was baking. Or she had been when I'd arrived. Todd was working the front counter, chatting amicably with his customers, unhurried but efficient. Peggy would spell him off for his afternoon break, and then she'd close the bakery. After which, I'd been guilt-tripped into going for the manicures I'd missed while hunting down the succubus.

I focused on my knitting. I was trying out a brioche-stitch shawl pattern. But no matter how many online tutorials I watched, I kept screwing up by the third row.

Next to the window and three tables over, Scarlett—Jade's mother—sat in quiet conversation with Pearl. As always, mother and daughter maintained a barrier between them. Today that consisted of steaming mugs of tea, two open laptops, and a pile of paperwork. Scarlett's strawberry-blond hair was worthy of envy, though I tended to steer clear of natural shades myself.

The witches were discussing coven business, though they exchanged as few words as possible while doing so.

I had struggled through writing my first official report as a fully certified necromancer, but had finally emailed it—along with an invoice—for services rendered to Pearl, as well as to Liam. The elder witch had shared it with the Convocation, and had already transferred the payment into my bank account. I was careful to gloss over Benjamin biting and draining the succubus. And completely failed to mention that he'd bitten me in the aftermath. The official report simply stated that he helped me hold the succubus as I freed the souls she'd consumed. And that in stripping her of that energy, we had killed her.

I hadn't spoken to Benjamin yet, but I'd felt him cross along the edge of the boundary of Mountain View Cemetery the first evening I returned to check that the MacDonald family plot was undisturbed. I had also checked each of the gravesites for the children I'd freed, including Tanya, seeing if I could pull an impression from their remains. I could, though I was careful to not rouse their shades. I included that observation in my report, along with a request for the information to be disseminated through the Convocation and the Academy, for any and all necromancers to access.

I had my doubts about the witches voluntarily sharing anything with anyone. But I also knew that between Jasmine's determination and Benjamin's chronicles, they might not have much choice anymore. The younger generation, it seemed, believed there was power to be had in accumulating knowledge and sharing it, rather than hoarding.

Though I had lingered at Mountain View and felt him watching me from afar, Benjamin hadn't said hello. His magic felt different. Just the slightest shift in the pulse of his power. A deepening of its resonance, perhaps. He was still absorbing the blood—and the magic contained within it—that had been gifted to him from Kett. Such things took time.

I knew.

I'd come back from near death myself. More than once.

The witches had fixed the broken grave markers, as well as the front lawn and bushes that Benjamin and the succubus had torn through. I'd found a medium-sized box waiting for me on my doorstep the evening I'd returned home to sleep in my own bed. It contained wax-sealed mason jars filled with ashes.

All that remained of the succubus.

That seemed fitting. For her killer to watch over her remains. It seemed likely that the ashes were powerful, steeped in magic. That in the wrong hands they might be used to do terrible things. But the Godfrey witches tended to adhere to tradition unless they had good reason not to, so the succubus's ashes became my responsibility.

Perhaps my elders weren't quite so worried about the possibility of me walking a path leading into the dark anymore.

I cleared a shelf in the library, across from my mother's bone collection, and set the jars out. The succubus wasn't the first sentient being I'd killed, but nothing remained of the elves when they died. They didn't belong in our dimension.

That I had killed Brit Thompson, I had no doubt. Benjamin wouldn't have been able to bite her, to hold her, if I hadn't helped. And it was the removal of the children's souls that robbed her of her lauded immortality.

I had traded the succubus's immortal life for the immortal souls of the children she'd murdered. And even though I'd woken up from nightmares twice now, seeing Brit disintegrate under my touch in a way she hadn't when I'd killed her, I knew I would do it again.

Liam had left a long series of text and voice messages on my phone. But I hadn't been able to return any of them when I'd finally woken, because no one had thought to charge my phone. So, of course, I'd gotten an earful about that from the uptight sorcerer as well.

Liam had asked me to meet him at Cake in a Cup to compare reports. So, not the date I'd been expecting. Maybe the all-the-candy-I-wanted idea was off the table? With Halloween done and the succubus vanquished, the sorcerer might just want to forget the almost-not-a-kiss we'd shared.

Kandy prowled through the swing doors that led to the kitchen. Bitsy trailed behind her, stopping to order drinks from Todd. The pink-haired enforcer sauntered over to claim the last empty table beside Pearl and Scarlett. She snapped her teeth at me playfully while she listened in on the witches' conversation.

I gave Kandy a belligerent smile that I was sure would set her off, but received only a wink in return.

I was losing my touch.

Liam pushed through the glass front door, setting the trinkets hanging over it chiming. He scanned the seating area before he stepped fully into the bakery, smiling when he saw me. He was dressed casually. Well, as casual as he got. A dark-brown cabled sweater fit him snugly across his broad shoulders, but slightly loosely around his waist. The ribbed cuffs hung long over the backs of his hands. Add in blue jeans and worn work boots, and I had a hard time not just staring at him, imagining running my fingers down the intricate knit cabling—

"Liam!" Bitsy beckoned to her brother from beside the cash register. She was attempting to hold two large ceramic mugs and a plate of four cupcakes.

The sorcerer crossed to her, relieving her of one of the hot drinks and the plate of cupcakes.

Kandy twisted back on her stool, eyeing the duo as they wove through the high-topped tables toward her. Bitsy slipped onto the stool across from the pink-haired werewolf, depositing the mug she carried in front of Kandy.

Looking slightly amused, Liam handed Bitsy the mug he was carrying and moved to place the plate at the center of their table.

Kandy snatched one of the cupcakes before he'd fully set the plate down. "Nice, sorcerer. Making yourself useful." She flashed her teeth at him. "You can serve me any time."

"My pleasure," Liam said evenly. Then he stepped toward my table.

"You don't want to join us?" Bitsy asked.

He shook his head, then nodded toward me. "I'm here for Mory."

Bitsy spun around on her stool, blinking at me. "Oh! Hi, Mory! Didn't see you there."

Kandy stuffed the cupcake in her mouth, muttering irately while chewing. I caught the words '…should have smelled….'

"What?" Bitsy cried, spinning back around. "I was trying to remember your crazy-complicated drink order!"

"Scarlett," Liam murmured politely in greeting as he stepped by the witches. "Pearl."

"Liam." Scarlett smiled brightly. "Lovely to see you."

Pearl nodded, barely glancing up from her laptop.

Liam slid onto the stool across from me. I tucked away my knitting. Brioche was way too complicated to do while talking. Or while thinking about anything else, really.

"You look good, Mory," the sorcerer said, casting his voice low as he swept his gaze over me. "I was worried."

"I was worried about you," I said, stopping myself from reaching across the table and placing my hand in his, just to feel the warmth of his skin. I was close enough to see the blue and green mixed within the darker brown of his irises.

All right, then. My hormones were still running rampant. Good to know.

Okay…

We were just staring at each other now.

And staring.

He shook his head slightly, then reached into the pocket of his jeans.

I took the moment to look away. Kandy was glaring at me over Liam's shoulder with narrowed eyes. Or maybe she was staring daggers at Liam's back. The angle meant I couldn't quite tell.

"You wanted to compare reports?" I asked a little too loudly, glancing back at Liam.

He blinked at me, holding something in his hand.

Kandy returned her attention to the witches' quiet conversation, occasionally adding to it. Bitsy appeared to be making notes on her phone, as if she was the enforcer's personal assistant or something. If she was, that was new.

"Sure," Liam said, resting his hand in his lap. "Did you order already? Can I grab you a cupcake? Something to go with it?"

"Oh, this is lovely," Scarlett exclaimed. She had just pulled a stack of papers from a medium-sized manila envelope. "The shapeshifters of Yukon would like us to host a wedding!"

Kandy's head jerked away from the cupcake she appeared to be trying to maul. "What?"

"And..." Scarlett continued reading from the top page of the stack she was holding, addressing Pearl across from her. "An official petition for accession to pack status."

"No," Kandy blurted.

Ignoring the pink-haired werewolf, Scarlett flipped through a few more pages, quickly scanning the contents. Pearl actually looked up from her laptop, tilting her head expectantly at her daughter.

"No. No." Kandy shook her head emphatically. "Desmond would never—"

"There's also a lovely letter from Desmond. He'd be pleased for us to host." Scarlett glanced up at Pearl, smiling. Then she quickly pivoted on her stool, including all of us in one charm-packed, massively beguiling smile. "A pack wedding! In Vancouver! Delightful."

Kandy moaned. Then she slammed her forehead down on the table.

Liam snorted, then tried to cover his amusement by clearing his throat.

"Shut it, sorcerer," Kandy muttered, speaking to the tabletop. She slammed her forehead down twice more.

"Um…" Bitsy said. "I don't get it. A wedding is bad?"

"A wedding posing as pack status negotiations when shapeshifters are involved? Yes." The enforcer groaned. "Who do you think is going to have to keep the peace?"

Bitsy glanced around, her dark curls bouncing. "You?"

"Yeah. But don't think you aren't going to be sorting out all the shit I can't stand to be anywhere near!"

"Me?!" Bitsy squeaked.

Jade pushed through the swing doors from the kitchen, predictably carrying a large round tray filled with cupcakes. She glanced at Kandy, then over at her mother, concerned. As she sauntered through the seating area, she smiled at her human customers. "What did I miss?"

Scarlett waved the sheaf of papers. "A wedding!"

"Oh!" the dowser exclaimed, pausing to offer the tray of cupcakes to her grandmother. "Fun!"

Kandy made a lunge for the tray as Jade approached, but the dowser deftly knocked her back with her hip.

Kandy snarled.

Pearl, looking awfully amused, took her time selecting a cupcake.

I glanced back at Liam, finding him watching me.

"Hey," he said.

"Yeah?"

He slid a small white box across the table toward me. I took it, tugging off the lid. Inside, three large, multicolored glass beads were nestled on cotton batting. They looked handblown. And expensive.

I glanced up at the dark-haired sorcerer.

His smile crinkled the edges of his eyes, but he looked slightly worried as well. "For your poncho."

I blinked.

"As a thank you," he added.

I looked down at the beads, suddenly grinning like an idiot. "Thank you," I murmured. I was lucky in my friends, but I wasn't certain anyone had ever bought me something that was so specific to me before.

Liam leaned closer. "I think they represent the different stages of your magnificent hair color." He gestured to the bead on my left. "You had it colored like this when we were mapping the stadium with Ed—"

Jade appeared beside our table, tray first. "Mory. Eat something."

I smirked at the dowser. "You fed me when I got here."

"That was, like, hours ago."

"Really about twenty minutes."

Jade narrowed her eyes at me.

Liam covered another laugh by clearing his throat. Unfortunately for the sorcerer, this drew Jade's undivided attention his way.

"Are you getting a cold, sorcerer?" she asked him coolly.

"No." Liam straightened his shoulders, nodding. "But thanks for your concern."

"Oh, you know me," she said airily. "I do so love keeping an eye on you." Then she turned to regard me with an intense and unrelenting blue gaze. Though what she was pissed about, I had no idea. "And Mory, of course."

"Of course," Liam said pleasantly.

The dowser tugged two napkins from the pocket of her pink ruffled apron, placing them on the table. "Take a cupcake."

I selected a cupcake, placing it obligingly on the napkin. The chocolate-blackberry cake with chocolate-blackberry buttercream—*Sass in a Cup*—was a seasonal favorite of mine.

Jade turned the tray toward Liam. He selected a cupcake without protest—*Happiness in a Cup*, a peanut butter cake with honey buttercream.

"Come see me before you leave," Jade said, stepping away before I could figure out whether she'd been addressing me or not.

But as Jade slid into the third chair at Kandy and Bitsy's table, another realization occurred to me. Something I hadn't quite put together yet.

I eyed Liam. He was toying with his cupcake.

"Jade doesn't like you," I said, pitching my voice low. Though I knew that if they'd wanted to, any of the powerful Adepts in the bakery could have listened in on our conversation.

The sorcerer grimaced. "There was an incident."

"When?"

He shook his head. "A couple of months after I arrived in town. I found Jade carrying Bitsy, unconscious, and I…" He grimaced, trailing off ruefully.

I laughed quietly. "You didn't."

"I thought Jade had hurt her!"

I started laughing. "You pointed your gun at the dowser."

"Yes."

"In her territory!"

"Well, I didn't know that at the time."

Still chuckling, I tipped the glass beads into the palm of my right hand, lifting them so they captured the light from the window, brightening their already vibrant colors.

"If we're airing truths," the sorcerer said, his gaze on the beads in my hand, "Kandy was there as well."

I snorted. "Seriously? How are you still alive?"

"Not sure." He flicked his fingers toward the cupcake he'd selected. "Apparently my magic tastes like peanut butter, and Jade was in a peanut butter mood."

I blinked at him, then nodded. "I can see that. The dowser is very logical about tasty treats." And yeah, I might have been looking right at him, steadily holding his gaze, when I used the words 'tasty' and 'treat.'

A slow grin lit his face. He leaned closer. "So…do you like the beads?"

"Very much. Thank you."

He nodded, pleased.

"Does the offer of grabbing me something to go with the cupcakes still stand?"

"Anything."

"A mocha, please. Large, but just a single shot."

Still smiling, the sorcerer straightened, crossing through the seating area.

And yeah, I might have checked out his ass the entire time it took him to reach the counter.

Kandy was watching me again.

I narrowed my eyes at her.

She narrowed her eyes at me.

I snorted, picking up my knitting.

The werewolf growled something under her breath.

I laughed. Again.
Then I dropped a stitch.
Damn it all.

SIX YEARS, THREE MONTHS, EIGHT DAYS, AND TWENTY-THREE minutes...

Still not dark yet.
Better check back tomorrow.

ACKNOWLEDGEMENTS

With thanks to:

MY STORY & LINE EDITOR
Scott Fitzgerald Gray

MY PROOFREADER
Pauline Nolet

MY BETA READERS
Anteia Consorto, Terry Daigle, Angela Flannery, Gael
Fleming, Beth Patterson, and Megan Gayeski Pirajno.

FOR THEIR CONTINUAL ENCOURAGEMENT,
FEEDBACK, & GENERAL ADVICE
SFWA
The Office
The Retreat
The Yarn Harlot – for the inspiration
Ravelry – for the knitting, and yarn, and everything else!
Ashlee Gutierrez Menke – for Harry
Potter Trivial Pursuit

ABOUT THE AUTHOR

MEGHAN CIANA DOIDGE IS AN AWARD-WINNING WRITER BASED OUT OF Salt Spring Island, British Columbia, Canada. She has a penchant for bloody love stories, superheroes, and the supernatural. She also has a thing for chocolate, potatoes, and cashmere.

For recipes, giveaways, news, and glimpses of upcoming stories, please connect with Meghan on her:

New release mailing list, http://eepurl.com/AfFzz
Personal blog, www.madebymeghan.ca
Twitter, @mcdoidge
Facebook, Meghan Ciana Doidge
Email, info@madebymeghan.ca

Please also consider leaving an honest
review at your point of sale outlet.

ALSO BY MEGHAN CIANA DOIDGE

DOWSER SERIES ● BOOK 1

CUPCAKES, TRINKETS, *and other* **DEADLY MAGIC**

MEGHAN CIANA DOIDGE

DOWSER SERIES ● BOOK 2

TRINKETS, TREASURES, *and other* **BLOODY MAGIC**

MEGHAN CIANA DOIDGE

DOWSER SERIES ● BOOK 3

TREASURES, DEMONS, *and other* **BLACK MAGIC**

MEGHAN CIANA DOIDGE

DOWSER SERIES ● BOOK 4

SHADOWS, MAPS, *and other* **ANCIENT MAGIC**

MEGHAN CIANA DOIDGE

DOWSER SERIES ● BOOK 5

MAPS, ARTIFACTS, *and other* **ARCANE MAGIC**

MEGHAN CIANA DOIDGE

DOWSER SERIES ● BOOK 6

ARTIFACTS, DRAGONS, *and other* **LETHAL MAGIC**

MEGHAN CIANA DOIDGE

ORACLE SERIES ● BOOK 1

I SEE ME

MEGHAN CIANA DOIDGE

ORACLE SERIES ● BOOK 2

I SEE YOU

MEGHAN CIANA DOIDGE

ORACLE SERIES ● BOOK 3

I SEE US

MEGHAN CIANA DOIDGE

RECONSTRUCTIONIST SERIES ■ BOOK 1

Catching Echoes

MEGHAN CIANA DOIDGE

RECONSTRUCTIONIST SERIES ■ BOOK 2

Tangled Echoes

MEGHAN CIANA DOIDGE

RECONSTRUCTIONIST SERIES ■ BOOK 3

Unleashing Echoes

MEGHAN CIANA DOIDGE